CHRISTMAS
by the
BOOK

CHRISTMAS
by the
BOOK

ANNE MARIE RYAN

G. P. PUTNAM'S SONS

NEW YORK

PUTNAM
— EST. 1838 —

G. P. PUTNAM'S SONS
Publishers Since 1838
An imprint of Penguin Random House LLC
penguinrandomhouse.com

Copyright © 2020 by Anne Marie Ryan
First published in Great Britain in 2020, as *The Six Tales of Christmas*, by Trapeze, an imprint of
The Orion Publishing Group Limited.
Published in the United States of America in 2021 by G. P. Putnam's Sons.
Published by arrangement with The Orion Publishing Group Limited.
Penguin supports copyright. Copyright fuels creativity, encourages diverse voices, promotes free
speech, and creates a vibrant culture. Thank you for buying an authorized edition of this book and
for complying with copyright laws by not reproducing, scanning, or distributing any part of it in
any form without permission. You are supporting writers and allowing Penguin to continue
to publish books for every reader.

LIBRARY OF CONGRESS CATALOGING-IN-PUBLICATION DATA

Names: Ryan, Anne Marie, author.
Title: Christmas by the book / Anne Marie Ryan.
Other titles: The six tales of Christmas.
Description: New York : G. P. Putnam's Sons, 2021.
Identifiers: LCCN 2021032025 (print) | LCCN 2021032026 (ebook) |
ISBN 9780593331248 (trade paperback) | ISBN 9780593331255 (epub)
Subjects: LCGFT: Christmas fiction. |
Novels. Classification: LCC PS3618.Y316 S59 2021 (print) |
LCC PS3618.Y316 (ebook) | DDC 813/.6—dc23
LC record available at https://lccn.loc.gov/2021032025
LC ebook record available at https://lccn.loc.gov/2021032026

Printed in the United States of America
1st Printing

Book design by Nancy Resnick

For anyone who has ever shared a great book with me—
especially my mom, Hélène Ryan, and my daughters,
Eve and Rose Williams.

And for Robert Williams,
who understands that homes need to be filled with books.

I

NORA

Nora Walden's eyes drifted from the spreadsheet in front of her to the stacks of stocking fillers on the counter—a spotter's guide to local birds, a little gift book of the world's ugliest Christmas sweaters and a reindeer-shaped board book with a squashy red nose. Any of them was more appealing than her current reading material. Despite their deceptively Christmassy color, the columns and rows of red figures on the spreadsheet were making her feel anything but festive.

Frustrated, Nora jabbed the reindeer's nose and it let out a loud squeak. A bearded man in a wool cap nearly dropped the guidebook he'd been perusing.

"Sorry!" Nora raised her hand apologetically. "Didn't mean to startle you." Tilting her head to the side, she read the guidebook's cover. "Ah, Sri Lanka. The beaches are meant to be beautiful."

Sri Lanka was on her daughter Charlotte's gap year bucket list. The travel section had always been Charlotte's favorite section of the bookshop. Apart from a few trips to Simon's parents' house in France, the Waldens' family holidays had mostly been in the UK— hiring a canal boat or a little cottage by the beach. Booksellers didn't earn enough for luxury holidays abroad, not that Nora had ever minded. She'd been lucky enough to travel the world through books, touring South America through the works of Gabriel García Márquez and Isabel Allende, visiting India through Salman Rushdie and Vikram Seth's novels. Nora had never been to the United States, but she'd camped out on Wyoming's rugged plains through Annie Proulx's short stories and soaked up the sounds and smells of Gothic New Orleans vicariously through Anne Rice's vampires. She'd climbed the hills of San Francisco with the characters from Armistead Maupin's *Tales of the City* books. She felt as if she knew these places like a native through visiting them in fiction.

But Charlotte had always wanted to see the world for herself. She'd spent hours sitting cross-legged in the travel section, charting future journeys like a tiny Phileas Fogg. Nora wondered idly if Charlotte was in Sri Lanka now, sunbathing on a beach. Or perhaps she was in Mumbai. If only she would ring . . . Charlotte usually phoned or FaceTimed on Saturday afternoons, but they hadn't heard from her today—or the previous week.

The man in the wool cap put the guidebook back on the shelf.

"Can I help you find a different travel book?" Nora offered. "I can also recommend some novels set in Sri Lanka. *Anil's Ghost* by Michael Ondaatje is—"

"No, thanks," he said, cutting her off. "I'll just use Trip-Advisor."

Nora sighed and looked down again at the Spreadsheet of Doom. No wonder the numbers looked so terrible.

The bookshop door opened with a cheerful jingle, ushering in a blast of cold air and carols from the Christmas market taking place in the square outside. Nora smiled at the woman with a dark curly bob who'd just come in. Like most of her regular customers, she knew her name. "Hi, Kath."

"It's like the North Pole out there." Kath shivered and rubbed her hands together. "I think I've lost all feeling in my fingers."

"At least the rain's holding off," Nora said, glancing out the window behind her. The Stowford Bookshop was famous for its Christmas displays, and Nora thought they'd outdone themselves this year. Bestsellers, cookbooks and local interest titles were arranged in the shape of a Christmas tree, with presents wrapped in shiny paper underneath it. But beyond the window display, ominous gray clouds hung over the bustling market.

Nora had lived in Stowford her entire life, apart from the two years she'd been away at university, so she'd seen more than her fair share of wet West Country winters. This had been the rainiest December she could remember, however. The River Coln, which meandered lazily through the village center, was so high its waters were nearly lapping over the banks.

"I'm so over this weather," Kath said, as she raked a hand through her bob. "My hair goes crazy the second I step outdoors."

Nora nodded sympathetically. "I know the feeling." Simon had always compared her wavy auburn hair to a Rossetti painting, but in this weather it tended more toward middle-aged frizz than tumbling Pre-Raphaelite waves. Even though her copper locks were now shot through with silver, Nora couldn't bring herself to chop them off into a sensible bob. She'd decided to embrace her "hair tinsel"—and in any case, it was cheaper to maintain.

But the rain wasn't just giving Nora a permanent Bad Hair Day, it was keeping customers away at what should have been one of their busiest times of the year, and making it harder and harder to ignore their leaking roof. If the weather didn't improve soon, the bookshop would finish the year in the red.

Again.

"Ooh! This is lovely," Kath cooed, warming her hands by the fireplace at the back of the shop, the flames leaping and dancing like the cast of *Hamilton* behind an iron fireguard. A squashy red velvet sofa and two old leather armchairs were arranged in a semi-circle around a coffee table with a plate of homemade ginger biscuits—the recipe passed down from Nora's mum, Penelope. A West Highland terrier was snoozing in her basket in front of the fire.

A little boy whose parents were browsing in the children's book section toddled over to the dog. "Doggie!" he cried, crouching down next to the basket.

"Careful, Joshie!" the boy's mum warned.

"That's Merry," Nora said, going over to the little boy. "Don't worry—she loves being petted."

Merry thumped her tail and licked the little boy's hand. She'd been christened Merida, after the Scottish Disney character, when they'd adopted her as a puppy eight years ago. But she'd soon been nicknamed Merry, which perfectly suited her friendly personality. Apart from the fact that her snow-white hair shed everywhere and never stayed clean for long, Merry was the ideal family dog and the bookshop's unofficial mascot.

"I see you like dinosaurs," Nora said, pointing to the T. rex on the little boy's T-shirt.

He nodded as he gave Merry a cuddle.

"Then I've got the perfect book for you," Nora said. She went over to the shelves, found a copy of *Ten Little Dinosaurs* and handed it to the boy.

Helping himself to a biscuit, Joshie climbed up into one of the slippery armchairs with the determination of a mountain climber tackling Everest. As Nora returned behind the counter, he curled up in the chair and pored over the dinosaur picture book, the biscuit going soggy in his chubby fist.

Nora had spent hours in that very same armchair with her best friends—Anne of Green Gables, Pippi Longstocking and Mary

Lennox—the heroines of her favorite children's books. As the shy only child of a single mum, Nora had learned from a young age that as long as you had a good book for company, you never needed to feel lonely. Which was for the best, as she had often had to entertain herself while her mother was working in the shop.

Penelope had come to Somerset for the first-ever Glastonbury Festival in 1970 and had had a fling with a drummer named Neil. The romance had ended before the headline act had even made it onstage, but Penelope had fallen in love with the area and stayed to raise the daughter she'd given birth to nine months later. The bookshop—the only one for miles around—had been a success, even though Penelope's bohemian ways had often raised eyebrows with the locals.

Nora glanced back down at her spreadsheet, anxiety gnawing at her belly. What would Penelope say if she knew how badly the bookshop was doing?

"What's wrong, Nora?" A small woman with a neat white bob approached the counter, her kind blue eyes filled with concern behind her glasses. "You look worried."

It was Olwyn Powell, a regular at the bookshop's monthly book club. Nora had known her for years, since she'd taught Charlotte in primary school.

"Oh, it's nothing, Olwyn," Nora said, hiding the shameful spreadsheet under a pile of wool—the start of a sweater she was knitting Simon for Christmas. "I was miles away. Can I help you find anything? I've just read a thriller you might like—there's a wonderful twist at the end."

Despite being one of the sweetest people Nora had ever met, Olwyn was hooked on crime fiction—the more gruesome the better.

"Oh, I'm just browsing," Olwyn said. "Now that I'm on a pension I'm trying to use the library more."

It never bothered Nora when people came into the shop to browse. Like her mother before her, Nora firmly believed that a bookshop was more than just a place to buy books. It was the very heart of a community. But these days, browsing didn't lead to as many purchases as it once had . . .

"How are you finding retirement? Enjoying the life of leisure?"

"I'm finding the days a bit hard to fill, to be honest," Olwyn said. "I miss the children."

"It must be quite an adjustment," Nora replied. She couldn't imagine what her life would be like if she didn't have the bookshop to run.

"I do have more time for reading," Olwyn added, with forced cheerfulness. "So that's one good thing about retirement."

Although Olwyn was putting a brave face on it, there was no mistaking her sadness. Nora hated to think that this wonderful woman, who had touched so many lives, was feeling lonely.

"Well, you're welcome to pop in here any time for a chat," Nora said.

Kath approached the counter.

"You're busy," Olwyn whispered, patting Nora's hand. "I'll let you get back to work."

"Can I help you find some poetry?" Nora asked the younger woman. "Have you read Carol Ann Duffy's new anthology of Sylvia Plath poems?" A fellow poetry enthusiast, Kath had been popping into the shop for years and Nora had introduced her to the work of Audre Lorde, Jackie Kay and Adrienne Rich.

If she'd stayed on at university instead of coming back home when Penelope got ill, Nora would have written her dissertation on Sylvia Plath. "It's a wonderful collection," she said to Kath. "I felt like I was discovering Plath for the first time."

"It sounds great," Kath replied. "But I was wondering if you could help me find some books on . . . "—she lowered her voice—"depression."

"Of course." Nora slipped out from behind the counter and headed toward the self-help section. Nonfiction was her husband's domain. From architecture to angling, there was almost no subject Simon hadn't read a book—or five—about. Every Thursday night he ran a pub quiz at the George across the road. It was notoriously tough, with teams from as far away as Cirencester turning up every week to test their wits against him. But Simon was upstairs in the flat above the shop, dealing with the leaking ceiling.

Although fiction and poetry were her main areas of expertise, Nora knew the whole shop like the back of her hand. She showed Kath the books on depression—weighty scientific studies, inspirational "I overcame depression—so can you" books, and practical guides to boosting your mood—and Kath helped herself to several.

"Matt Haig writes beautifully on mental health as well," Nora said, and Kath added *Reasons to Stay Alive* to her pile.

Nora didn't know the young woman very well, and she didn't want to pry, but she couldn't help feeling concerned for her. "Is everything OK, Kath?"

"They're not for me," Kath said quickly. "They're for my dad."

Nora had no idea if that was the truth, or if Kath was just too embarrassed to talk about her mental health. "Well, I'm here," she said, "if you ever need to talk."

"Thanks," Kath said, flushing.

They headed over to the counter and Kath paid for her purchases quickly, glancing over her shoulder as if worried someone would see what she was buying.

Nora shook her head as she watched Kath hurry out of the

shop. It was so sad that people still felt that mental illness was something to be ashamed about. Or maybe Kath just didn't want to talk about something so personal with someone she didn't know very well. As an introvert, Nora could definitely understand that.

A howl of protest came from across the shop. "No!" Joshie wailed, as his parents clipped him into his buggy. His dad wheeled the stroller over to the till, and his mum placed a guide to potty training on the counter, along with *Ten Little Dinosaurs*. "He didn't want to let go of this," she said, laughing.

Nora rang up the picture book, then reached down to hand it back to the little boy in the stroller, who hugged it to his chest. *I love my job*, she thought happily. And the very best thing about it was finding the perfect book for someone—no matter what their age.

As she held the door open for the family, Nora said, "We do a toddler story time here every Monday morning. We're reading *The Grinch* this week—you should come."

"Sounds fun." The dad tousled his son's hair affectionately as he pulled the rain cover down over the stroller.

Nora shut the door behind them just as a tall man with a thick mane of wavy salt-and-pepper hair came down the stairs from the flat above the shop. "I've mopped up the drips," Simon announced, heading across the bookshop toward Nora, "and put down buckets to catch the leaks, but—" He smacked his head against one of the low oak beams running across the ceiling and shouted, "Goddamnit!"

"Oh, honey," Nora said, shaking her head affectionately. "Still?"

Twenty-five years ago, the very first time Simon strode into the bookshop, he'd immediately bumped his head on that same beam. Clad in a leather jacket and boots, he'd looked more like an indie rock star than an advertising executive. But then at twenty-three, wearing Doc Martens and ripped Levi's, Nora didn't resemble a typical bookshop owner, either.

Nora had fetched Simon an ice pack, and he'd explained that he was in the village scouting locations for a television advertisement. They'd talked so long—about their favorite books and authors—that Simon had missed the last train and ended up checking in to the George. They'd spent nearly every moment of that weekend together, with Simon helping out at the shop on Saturday and taking her for a long walk along the river on Sunday, followed by a roast dinner at the pub. Apart from Penelope, Nora had never met anyone who loved books as much as she did. Before reluctantly boarding a train back to London, Simon had kissed her—and promised to return.

The biscuit ad ended up being filmed in Stowford and the bookshop was in some of the shots, as actors in ye olde peasant costumes filled the market square. Simon spent every spare moment of the shoot with Nora. It wasn't until they'd been dating for weeks that Nora had learned Simon was the son of the agency's founder, Charles Walden, and was expected to take over the business one day. But Simon had given it all up to marry her.

The biscuit brand—Golden Oaties—never caught on, but Simon and Nora were still going strong.

Nora went over to her husband. Going up on her tiptoes, she planted a kiss on his forehead. "Do you sometimes regret that you didn't run a mile after that first time?" she asked him, gently stroking her fingers over the angry red mark from the beam. If he had, he'd be running a successful advertising agency now, instead of a failing rural bookshop.

"Are you kidding?" he said. "It was love at first sight." Then he rubbed his forehead and grinned, his blue eyes twinkling. "Either that or a mild concussion."

Nora had long given up her Levi's for more forgiving vintage-style dresses and cardigans, though she still sometimes paired them with her ancient Doc Martens. And Simon's leather jacket and biker boots had been replaced with a corduroy blazer and brogues. The years had changed them both, but they'd never run out of things to talk about. How could they, with over ten thousand titles in stock?

"I've got to nip across the road to the George," Simon said. "It's my turn to chair the Stowford Community Association meeting. Unless you want to go in my place?"

"No, I'll stay here." Nora was more than happy to let Simon run the meeting of local business owners. He was much better at that sort of thing than she was. Back in his advertising days, he'd had to pitch to clients, so he was a confident presenter, whereas Nora always felt awkward with any sort of public speaking.

"Right, then, I'll head off now," Simon said. "I'll pop by the market when the meeting's over and pick something up for dinner."

"Great," Nora replied.

When Simon was nearly at the door, she suddenly remembered something. "Don't forget to go to the chemist and collect your prescription," she called after him. "Oh! And a packet of paracetamol!" She could feel a tension headache forming behind her temples.

Simon nodded, then headed out the door and into the drizzle.

She watched him stride across the street to the pub, which dominated the market square, its honey-colored walls strewn with twinkling white fairy lights. On the day they'd met, Simon had told Nora that, even though they were miles from the coast, the golden local stone was formed from fossilized sea urchins. Nora had never forgotten that fact, enchanted by the notion that millions of years ago the area had been under the sea. *Might be again, and soon, if this rain doesn't let up*, she thought wryly.

As there were no customers in the shop, she perched on the stool behind the counter and set to work on Simon's Christmas sweater. As her knitting needles clicked, Nora wished that the sweater could do more than just keep Simon warm. If only wrapping him up in wool could keep him safe as well . . .

In the spring, Simon had had such bad chest pains they thought he was having a heart attack. Nora had called an ambulance and held his hand the whole way to the hospital, making silent bargains with the universe for his survival. In the end, it hadn't been a heart attack, just angina, but Nora had been terrified that she would lose him.

Simon was slim and played soccer regularly, so his having a heart condition had come as a shock, but Ani Dhar, their local GP, had explained that it wasn't uncommon in men in their fifties. When the doctor had mentioned that stress could be a trigger, Nora had insisted that Simon let her manage the shop, which they'd always run together. He'd protested, but Dr. Dhar had agreed it was a good idea, at least in the short term while they monitored his condition. Which was why Simon had no idea quite how bad their finances were, and how close they were to losing the shop.

Nora felt terrible about keeping secrets from him, but she couldn't risk alarming him and bringing on another attack. They might not be so lucky next time.

She sighed and knitted another row. Too bad she couldn't knit a sweater big enough to wrap the whole shop up in . . .

2

SIMON

Simon pushed through the doors of the George and breathed in the familiar malty fug of spilled ale, dried hops and fried food. After the bookshop, the pub was Simon's favorite place in Stowford. And unlike the bookshop, it was doing a roaring trade, as Christmas shoppers and vendors from the market had popped in to shelter from the rain.

Stopping to greet several regulars he knew from his weekly pub quiz, Simon finally made his way to the bar. A stocky man in his thirties, with thinning brown hair and wearing a red-and-white Swindon Town soccer shirt, was talking to Sue, the pub landlady. Two fair-haired children, who looked to be around six or seven, stood by his side.

"Hi," the guy said. "My name's Will. I was wondering if you're looking for help at the moment. I used to be a supervisor at the Jamison's plant, but I'm willing to turn my hand to anything."

Sue shook her head. "Sorry, my lover," she said in her raspy smoker's voice. " 'Fraid I'm not hiring."

The man's shoulders slumped in defeat.

"Daddy," the little boy said, "can me and Julia have crisps?"

"And lemonade," pleaded the little girl. "*Pleeease.*"

"Sorry, kiddos," Will said, looking down at the children. "Not today. We've got to go visit Grandma at the home."

As the children whined in protest, the man took them each by the hand and led them out of the pub.

Noticing Simon, Sue said, "Shit! We've got our meeting now, haven't we?" She whipped off her apron and ran a tattooed hand through her close-cropped bleached-blond hair. "Be there in a sec," she told him, hurrying off into the kitchen.

"Pint of bitter?" asked the handsome lad behind the bar in an American accent. He was about the same height as Simon, but his abundant Afro curls made him appear even taller.

"Just a half, Mateo," Simon replied, winking. "I'm here on business." Plus, he knew Nora worried about his diet these days. And not just his diet, either. Simon felt like she was constantly watching him anxiously, as if she was worried that he was going to keel over and drop dead at any moment.

It was ridiculous; he felt absolutely fine. But every time he offered to do more at the shop, Nora flatly refused.

"You need to avoid stress," she repeated like a mantra.

Simon felt guilty that in order to spare him, Nora was having to deal with all the stress of running the bookshop herself. She never complained, but he could tell she was feeling the strain. Judging from her tossing and turning at night, she was having trouble sleeping. And she was popping paracetamol at a rate she usually reserved for chocolate buttons. Apart from helping to serve customers, updating their social media accounts and overseeing the shop's online business, which had always been his baby, Simon felt like he was barely contributing.

As Mateo poured Simon's drink, he said, "I keep meaning to go into your shop and buy some books to send my folks for Christmas."

"Home's California, isn't it?" Simon asked.

Mateo nodded, his curls bobbing. "That's right. I grew up in Santa Barbara."

"What brought you over to the UK?" Simon inquired, paying for his drink.

"I came for drama school." Mateo smiled wryly as he wiped the bar with a towel. "Guess how that's working out for me."

"Oi, Bookworm," called a portly man in a stained green sweater. He had greasy gray hair and his cheeks and rather bulbous nose were covered in broken red veins. "Fancy a game of darts?"

Simon glanced over and saw that a photo of their local MP, David Langdon, had been pinned onto the dartboard. The handsome politician had dark, slicked-back hair, a smarmy grin and a smug, well-fed look about him.

"Sorry, Howie," Simon said. "I've got a meeting now."

"Oooo!" Howie mocked. "Aren't we important." He fired a dart and hit David Langdon dead on the nose. "Bull's-eye!" He chortled, then celebrated with a long swig of his pint.

It was impressive, really, that Howie could drink so much and still have such good aim. Simon always found it hard to believe that Howie had gone to the local primary school, St. Stephen's, with Nora. Thanks to his alcohol consumption, he looked at least a decade older than her.

Sipping the froth off his own drink, Simon headed to a quiet alcove at the back of the pub, where the rest of the Stowford Community Association had begun to gather. Sebastian Fox, in his mustard-yellow corduroys, was boasting loudly about how much he'd got for a cottage on the outskirts of the village.

"They were Londoners, of course," the estate agent said with a braying laugh. "More money than sense. Paid 10k over the asking price."

Nigel Wilkinson, the butcher, snorted in disgust. "That's the last thing we need around here—more bloody second-homers."

Nora's friend Alice, who ran the Copper Kettle tearoom, shook her head sadly. "There's a rumor going around that they're going to shut St. Stephen's because pupil numbers are so low. It's such a shame ordinary families can't afford to live here any longer."

"Simon, old chap," Seb said, clapping him on the shoulder as he sat down next to Alice. "Have you and Nora given any thought to the offer I sent you? That shop of yours would fetch a pretty penny—especially since it comes with the flat above it."

"The bookshop isn't for sale," Simon said firmly. Even though the offer from the estate agent was temptingly large, there was no way Nora would ever agree to sell the shop. It was her lifeblood.

"Too right," Alice said, pounding the table emphatically. "We need to keep the high street independent."

"Well, you all know where I am if you change your minds," Seb said, pushing back his floppy blond hair.

Checking his watch, Simon called the meeting to order. After quickly taking attendance, he ran through the minutes from their last meeting.

"Nigel," he said, addressing the burly man sitting across from him, "how's the Christmas fundraising drive doing?"

"We've raised nearly a thousand pounds," the butcher answered.

Every year, the Stowford Community Association picked a local charity to support. This year they were supporting the food bank. Although the village looked like a prosperous place, with a designer kitchen shop and a deli selling imported olives and expensive wines, Simon knew that a lot of local families were struggling to get by. The food bank would ensure that none of them went hungry this Christmas.

Simon checked the next item on the agenda. "The council's

still considering a proposal for introducing metered parking on the high street," he told the group.

"Well, I hope it doesn't pass," said Maeve Philbin, who owned a flower shop, the Bloom Room, and dressed exclusively in floral-print dresses. "There's too much traffic going in and out of the village as it is."

"Bloody tourists," grumbled Nigel.

"We depend on tourists for most of our trade," said Lucy, the manager of Cotswold Couture, a fashion boutique a few doors down from the bookshop. She was wearing a chunky metal necklace and a tunic that looked to Simon like it had been stitched together from assorted burlap sacks but had probably cost a lot of money. "They need *somewhere* to park those gigantic four-wheel drives of theirs."

"They should take the train," Alice muttered.

Over the summer, a speeding tourist had killed a local girl, who'd worked for Alice at the Copper Kettle, on one of the country lanes. The driver had been jailed for reckless driving, but it hadn't done anything to improve tensions between locals and visitors.

Simon could see both sides of the situation. As annoying as it was that tourists clogged the village's narrow streets and hogged the best parking spaces, Stowford had a symbiotic relationship with its visitors. In the summer months, the tourist trade kept the bookshop afloat, with holidaymakers popping in to buy summer reading, Shakespeare plays and local interest books. And, despite Alice's anger over the girl's death, he knew that most of her customers were out-of-towners, too.

"Sorry I'm late," Sue said, hurrying over with two baskets of chips. The pub's landlady plonked herself down on a chair and set the chips on the table.

"Oooh! Lovely," Alice exclaimed, the crystal pendant she was wearing around her neck swinging in the air as she reached over to help herself to a chip.

The business owners momentarily put their differences aside as they tucked into the chips.

Simon bit into one. It was perfectly crisp on the outside, fluffy on the inside. Gorgeous. He went to take another, then pulled his hand back. *Think of your heart*, he could hear Nora saying in his head.

"Has David Langdon's office got back to us about the petition we sent opposing the retail park development?" asked Maeve.

Most of the local business owners strenuously objected to the proposed development on the outskirts of Stowford. Their petition had collected hundreds of signatures.

"I can't bear to think about the environmental impact," Alice said, toying with her pendant. The proposed site of the retail park was on meadows that were home to countless birds and wildflowers.

"Yes, but it would create a lot of jobs," Seb Fox pointed out as he grabbed the last chip without offering it to anyone else. "Which would be good for the local economy."

Simon thought about the man who'd been looking for work earlier. Unemployment was high in the Cotswolds, as there were few opportunities outside of agriculture and tourism.

"It would put me out of business." Lucy sighed.

"David Langdon still hasn't replied," Simon said, glancing over at the dartboard, where the MP's face was now peppered with holes.

"What a surprise," Alice said sarcastically.

Everyone nodded.

The one thing they could all agree on was that David Langdon was a waste of space. He seemed more interested in progressing his own political career than addressing his constituents' concerns.

"That reminds me," Simon said. "I've spoken with the council about getting the graffiti removed. They've promised me someone will scrub it off next week."

Someone had spray-painted *David Langdon is a dikhed* on the bus shelter. While Simon agreed with that opinion, the graffiti looked terrible and the spelling mistake drove Nora crazy.

"They'd better," Nigel grumbled, "considering how much we pay them in business taxes."

The council's ever-rising business taxes were another issue the local business owners griped about endlessly. Between business taxes and rent increases, it was getting harder and harder for independent shops to survive in Stowford. In the past year, the association had lost three members, as shops either sold up or went out of business.

"OK," Simon said, checking his watch. He wanted to bring the meeting to a close so he could make it to the market before it shut. "So, I'll draft another letter to the council about our concerns over business taxes, and I'll contact David Langdon's constituency office to chase for a response to our petition. Any other business?"

Once the meeting had wrapped up, and Alice was putting on her coat, she asked Simon, "How's Nora? I haven't seen her for a while."

"She's missing Charlotte, and she hasn't been sleeping too well."

He felt another stab of guilt, knowing that he was—at least in part—responsible for her worries.

"Come to the Copper Kettle with me. I'll give you some chamomile tea to take back to her," Alice said. "It's very soothing—might help with her sleep."

Leaving the pub, Simon and Alice weaved past the bustling market stalls to get to the Copper Kettle at the other end of the high street.

A spotty teenage boy with ginger hair was lurking outside the tearoom on his bike. When he saw them coming, he looked away furtively, as if up to no good. *Was this kid responsible for the graffiti on the bus shelter?* Simon wondered.

"Coming in, Harry?" Alice asked cheerfully.

The boy shook his head and pedaled off.

"Poor lad," Alice said, watching him cycle away. "It was his sister who got killed this summer."

"I'll wait outside," Simon said. The Copper Kettle had even lower ceilings than the bookshop, with Alice's collection of china teapots resting on the beams. For Simon, who was six foot two, it was like entering a minefield.

Alice ducked into the Copper Kettle and came back a moment later with a packet of tea bags. She pressed them into Simon's hand. "Tell Nora I said hi, and to pop in for a scone soon."

After thanking Alice, Simon went into the chemist's. A short woman in a white coat and glasses was bagging up a prescription behind the counter. Her long black hair was tied back in a neat bun, and there was a red bindi on her forehead.

"Hi, Lakshmi," Simon said. "We missed you at the meeting."

"Sorry I couldn't make it," she replied. "Dinesh has the flu, so I'm on my own in the shop today."

The Patels were relative newcomers to the village, having only opened their pharmacy about ten years ago. They had two grown-up daughters—the eldest was Dr. Dhar, the local GP, and the youngest was some sort of high-flyer in London.

"How are the girls?" Simon asked the chemist, handing her his prescription.

"Sam is back at home." Mrs. Patel sighed deeply as she began preparing his tablets. "She split up with her boyfriend a few months ago."

"Sorry to hear that," Simon replied, placing a packet of paracetamol on the counter.

"She works too hard. I keep telling her that she's going to end up an old maid if she isn't careful."

Simon chuckled. He hadn't seen the Patels' youngest daughter in years, but she had to still be in her twenties. "She probably just hasn't found the right person yet."

"I can't help worrying about her."

Simon smiled. "It's what we parents do best." Even though he was always telling Nora not to worry about Charlotte, he couldn't help feeling anxious, too, when she missed their weekly video call.

Mrs. Patel handed Simon a white paper bag with his tablets inside. "Take one in the morning, one at night."

Simon shoved the medication into his tote bag, along with the chamomile tea. He hated taking the tablets—a twice-daily reminder of his mortality. "Tell Dinesh I hope he feels better soon," he said.

Then, stepping back outside into the steadily increasing rain, he headed to the market to get something for dinner.

3

NORA

Nora looked up from her knitting as raindrops began to pelt the shop window. "Rain, rain, go away," she muttered under her breath.

Christmas shoppers at the market began diving for cover, taking shelter under awnings and heading to the pub in droves. An elderly man with a walking stick was making a beeline for the bookshop, so Nora dashed over to the door and opened it for him.

"That were good timing," he said, his voice a gentle West Country burr. Water dripped from his waxed jacket as he brushed raindrops off his head.

"Come and dry off." Nora offered him her arm and guided him over to the fire.

"Ah, that's kind of you." The man sank down into the sofa gratefully and took off his steamed-up glasses, rubbing the lenses on his moth-holed sweater and then putting them in his jacket pocket.

"Were you looking for anything in particular? Or did you just want to get out of the rain?"

"I'm looking for a book for my grandson, Noah. He's ten."

"What sort of things does he like?" Nora, perched on the arm of the sofa, pictured her daughter at that age—all long, skinny legs like a newborn foal. At ten, Charlotte had collected lip balms, loved animals and been obsessed with One Direction.

"He's soccer mad, he is," the old man said, his rheumy eyes shining with pride. "Supports Manchester United—but there's no accounting for taste."

Nora chuckled. "We have plenty of books about Man U., though it pains my husband to stock them." Three decades after leaving London, Simon was still a die-hard Arsenal fan.

The old man shook his head. "I'm looking for something to help him with his schoolwork. His class has been studying the Great War and I remember reading a book about the Christmas truce, years and years ago. You know, the soccer match between the Jerries and our boys. I want to get him a copy but it doesn't seem to be in print anymore. I've already tried three other book-shops."

Nora stared at him, hardly able to believe what she was hear-ing. She was almost positive she knew exactly which book he was describing.

Could it really be the same one? What were the odds . . . ?

"I—I think I might be able to help you," she stammered.

Lurching up from the sofa, she stumbled over to the nonfic-tion section. Heart pounding, she scanned the sport books, searching the shelves for a hardback with a green cover.

Where is it? she wondered, feeling flustered. She stared at the shelf but couldn't see the spine she was looking for anywhere.

Duh! she thought, smacking her forehead with the palm of her hand. She was in the wrong section—it would be in history, not soccer. She ran over to the history section, skipping past the Mid-dle Ages . . . the Stuarts . . . the Victorians . . . until she finally found the First World War books.

Please be here . . . please be here . . .

But it wasn't.

Her stomach clenched as a terrible thought occurred to her. *What if someone had bought it?* No, that was impossible. Simon would have told her if he'd sold it. It *had* to be here somewhere. She just had to keep looking.

As if being pulled by a magnet, Nora walked slowly down the aisle, past the natural history books and into the gardening section. She couldn't explain it, but something—instinct? some invisible force?—was guiding her.

Reaching the end of the row, her fingers began to tingle. She crouched down and a green spine with a glint of gold at the bottom caught her eye, sandwiched between two books on herbaceous borders. *Aha!* With trembling hands, Nora pulled a book off the shelf. She brushed a light coating of dust off the cover of *The True Story of the Christmas Truce.*

What the heck was it doing here? A customer had obviously looked at it and put it back in the wrong place.

Handling it as carefully as a precious artifact—well, it was, in a way—her fingers caressed the embossed gold type of the title. After all these years, was it finally going to find a home?

She remembered the day that she and Simon had ordered it, newlyweds just back from honeymoon. They'd set off for the Scottish Highlands with grand plans for visiting ruined castles and taking bracing hikes across the moors. But the weather had been foul, so they'd spent most of the two weeks holed up in a dilapidated rental cottage, making love, sipping cheap malt whiskey and reading a pile of books, set in Scotland, by the fire. It was the perfect honeymoon, they had both agreed.

Despite being well-to-do, Simon's parents hadn't contributed a penny toward the wedding—a modest do at the George. They were furious that their son had chosen to run a bookshop instead of Walden Creative, accusing him of wasting his talents and his degree from Oxford. Oh, they'd come round eventually, once Charlotte was born. Charles and Margaret Walden adored their granddaughter. But Nora knew they had never quite forgiven her for luring their son into her seductive lair of books.

They'd celebrated placing their first order as a married couple—and equal partners in the bookshop—with a bottle of champagne left over from the wedding reception, toasting their future together. Simon, keen to expand the nonfiction section, had bullishly ordered a wide range of titles, including *The True Story of the Christmas Truce.*

And while they had sold thousands of books since, the Christmas truce book had lingered on the shelf, lonely and unloved. After a while, it had become a running joke, with Nora teasing Simon that it was time to make space for a newer book. But Simon had always insisted that someday the book would find a home. Over the years, it had become as much a symbol of their commitment to the bookshop—and to each other—as their wedding rings. "As long as we're in business, it has a home here," Nora had promised Simon, squeezing his hand.

Now, over two decades later, it looked as if someone finally wanted to give it a new home. Nora stared down at the book in her hands. She felt strangely reluctant to part with it; somehow she'd always imagined that it would be with them forever.

But books *need* readers, she reminded herself.

Nora hurried back to the sofa, clutching the book. She placed it reverently in the old man's hand. "Was this what you were looking for?" she asked breathlessly.

As he leafed through the pages of sepia photographs, showing German and English soldiers tackling on the muddy fields of no-man's-land, the man's wrinkled face creased into a delighted smile. "Why, yes! That's the badger! It's exactly what I was looking for. I guess today's my lucky day!"

Nora clapped her hands in delight, rousing Merry from her nap. Looking up, the dog thumped her tail a few times, then promptly went back to sleep.

"Do you know," Nora said, shaking her head in amazement, "that's the oldest book in the whole shop. We've had it in stock for twenty-five years. I'd given up hope that it would ever get bought."

"Never give up hope, my dear," the man said, his eyes twinkling.

Nora beamed back at him. If the Christmas truce book had found a home, she thought, maybe there was hope for the bookshop, too . . .

"I promise you it will be very well looked after," the old man said.

Nora knew that already. She could tell from the careful way he was handling the book that the man was a fellow book lover.

The old man patted his chest and eventually found his glasses tucked inside his jacket's inner pocket. Putting them on to take a closer look at the book, he peered at the photographs through the half-moons. "Look at how young they were," he said, sighing. "Those poor lads must have been so lonely, that far from home at Christmastime."

Nora sat down on the sofa next to him and leaned over to take a closer look, pushing her long hair behind her ear so it didn't fall onto the page. Her heart broke as she gazed at the pictures and imagined the young soldiers, eating their rations in cold tents instead of tucking into a dinner with their families. One of the British soldiers, a cigarette dangling from his mouth, was offering his pack to a German solider with a cheeky grin. He couldn't have been a day older than eighteen—same as Charlotte.

"Yes," she agreed, "it's hard to be away from your loved ones at Christmastime." *Even when they're having the time of their life*, she added silently.

Charlotte had worked hard to fund her gap year—helping out at the shop every weekend and over the school holidays throughout her last few years of secondary school. Now she was on the long-awaited trip of her dreams, traveling across Asia. She'd danced at a Full Moon Party in Thailand, watched turtles lay their eggs on a beach in Sri Lanka and taught English at a school in Kerala. And even though Nora was happy that her daughter was having the adventure of a lifetime, she couldn't help missing her desperately.

"It's hard to be lonely at any time of year—not just Christmas," the old man said. He turned the page and looked at a picture of two officers—one German, one British—shaking hands in front of a makeshift goal, and chuckled. "Friendship two, war nil."

Nora thought of Charlotte's Instagram posts, pictures of the friends she had made on her journey, fellow travelers and locals alike. She'd set off on her adventure alone—something that had given Nora palpitations—but Charlotte had inherited Simon's outgoing nature and found it easy to make friends wherever she went. Like food and shelter, friendship was a basic human need, defying borders and language barriers.

The old man turned the page and studied a photograph of soldiers in a trench gathered around a straggly little Christmas tree. "My uncle fought in the Great War. He was a gunner in the Gloucestershire Regiment. Died in the Battle of the Somme. My grandmother saved his letters home from the front, including a Christmas card sent from the trenches. I suppose that's another reason I've always been fascinated with the truce. I'm named Arnold after him."

"Nice to meet you, Arnold," Nora said, extending her hand. "I'm Nora."

Arnold clasped her hand in his own, his grip surprisingly firm.

Nora glanced toward the door, wishing Simon were there to meet Arnold and witness this historic moment. A selfie would have to do.

"Is it OK if I take a picture," she asked Arnold, "to show my husband who bought this special book?" Posing close to the old gentleman, Nora held her phone out at arm's length to get both of them in the shot. As she scrolled through the photos on her phone, trying to find one in which she didn't have a double chin, she asked, "Are you happy for me to share this online? I can tag you, if you like."

Arnold let out a wheezy chuckle. "I don't go in for all that Internet nonsense. My son bought me an iPad last Christmas but I still haven't taken it out of its box."

"I'm a bit of a Luddite, too," Nora admitted, "but technology isn't all bad—it helps you keep in touch with people, especially when they are far away." She'd always teased Charlotte about her chronic need to document everything with a selfie—from what she was having for lunch to a new outfit. But now she was grateful for her daughter's social media posts. They were proof that she was alive and well, halfway across the world.

"You sound like my son," Arnold said. "He wants me to sign up for a Silver Surfers class at the community center."

"Well," Nora pointed out gently, "you would have found the Christmas truce book a lot quicker if you'd used a computer. All of our stock is available online."

Simon had created a website for the bookshop, to try to compete with the larger Internet retailers. It looked great, and Simon regularly posted book reviews, recommendations and interviews with local authors.

"Ah, but where's the fun in that?" Arnold said, his eyes shining. "If I'd just had to press a few buttons, it wouldn't have been nearly so exciting finding it—and I wouldn't have made a new friend."

Nora couldn't argue with that. One of the joys of browsing in a bookshop was that you never knew what sort of treasures you might find. Or the people you might meet.

The bell above the shop door jingled and Nora glanced over, hoping it would be Simon, but it was just someone escaping the rain. Customers were a bit like buses—you waited ages for one to come, and then two came along at the same time.

Arnold reached for his walking stick. "I'm so sorry, I'm keeping you from your work."

"Don't be silly," Nora said, waving away his concerns. She pushed the plate of ginger biscuits toward him. "Stay as long as you like—it's still pouring outside."

"Don't mind if I do," Arnold said, helping himself to a biscuit. "Is your grandson a bookworm, too?"

"Oh yes, Noah loves books. His teacher put him in the top reading group."

Nora heard the quiet pride in Arnold's voice as he spoke about his grandson. "What does he like reading?"

"He's mad about some books with stick figure drawings. Looks like the sort of thing I could have drawn myself, but there must be something special about them because I hear him chuckling away when he's reading them."

Wimpy Kid, Nora thought. They were some of the most popular books in the children's section. "Does Noah go to St. Stephen's here in the village?"

"No, my son and his family live just outside Swindon, so Noah goes to school there. But he hasn't been for a while now . . ."

There was a catch in Arnold's voice and when Nora looked up she saw that his eyes were brimming with tears.

"He's in hospital—the Royal Infirmary in Bristol. Leukemia, you see."

Nora reached out to lay her hand on his arm. "Oh, I'm so sorry to hear that, Arnold."

"Noah's a fighter." Arnold's voice quavered slightly, but his whiskered chin jutted out with determination. "He'll pull through—I know it in my heart. He's doing everything he can to keep up with his classmates, so he's not behind when he goes back to school. He's determined to do a First World War project, just like the other Year Fives. That's why I wanted to get him this book."

"He sounds very brave."

"Ah, that he is. The little lad's never complained once." Arnold sighed. "Sadly, I don't drive anymore—my eyesight's not what it used to be—so I don't get up to Bristol to see him very often."

"Then you *must* learn how to use your iPad. You can use it to have video calls with Noah. My daughter's off traveling at the moment, and I don't know what I'd do if I didn't see her face every once in a while."

"Do you have any other children?" Arnold asked.

Nora shook her head. "No, Charlotte's our one and only."

She and Simon would have loved to have had more, but there had been complications with Charlotte's birth and the doctors had warned Nora not to have any more children. Charlotte had been several weeks premature and Nora's eyes prickled with tears as she remembered her tiny preemie daughter lying in an incubator in the neonatal intensive care unit, a breathing tube up her nose, her spindly limbs practically translucent. Nora had been terrified that her precious daughter—who she already loved more than life itself—wouldn't make it.

Like Arnold's grandson, Charlotte was a fighter. By the time she was a year old, she'd nearly caught up with other babies her age and was so full of life and laughter you couldn't tell that she'd had such an inauspicious start to life. But Nora had never forgotten that she had almost lost her daughter before she'd even had a chance to get to know her.

Maybe that was why she still worried so much about her now.

Rationally, she knew that Charlotte was an intelligent, responsible young woman, more than capable of looking after herself. But that didn't stop Nora from fretting as she lay awake in bed at night, tormented by visions of her being eaten by a crocodile, contracting a deadly tropical disease or getting mugged by a thug on a motorbike. "She's fine," Simon would say, stroking her back, "you've just got an overactive imagination." He blamed it on all the stories she read, but Nora suspected the real reason was that Charlotte was an only child. If she and Simon had had more children, perhaps she wouldn't be quite so overprotective.

Of course, they *did* have another baby—the bookshop. Like a human child, it had been a source of both joy and worry for them over the years.

Though at the moment, the balance was heavily tipped toward the worries . . .

But Arnold was right—it was important to stay positive. To have hope. The fact that *The True Story of the Christmas Truce* had finally found a home was surely a good omen, a sign that things would improve.

Nora picked up the book and smoothed down the dust jacket. "Shall I wrap this up for you?"

Arnold nodded. "That would be grand. I wouldn't make a very good job of it myself, with my arthritis."

Nora helped Arnold up to his feet. Leaning heavily on his stick, he chuckled. "You wouldn't know it to look at me now, but

I was a soccer player back in the day. I even had a trial for Chipping Norton Town."

"What position did you play?" Nora asked, holding Arnold's book as they slowly made their way to the counter.

"I was a striker," Arnold said. "For years I held my team's record for most goals scored in a season. God, I miss it."

"My husband plays five-a-side every week. In his head, he thinks he's Cristiano Ronaldo." Nora had been nervous about Simon continuing to play soccer after his health scare, but Dr. Dhar had assured them that regular exercise would be good for him.

Arnold chuckled. "My Noah's a good little player, too. He's a midfielder for the school team."

"I hope he's back on the pitch soon."

When they eventually reached the counter, Nora lifted up the hatch and went behind. Arnold offered her his credit card, but Nora waved it away.

"I couldn't possibly charge you for this," she said. "I'm just grateful that you're finally giving it a home." Taking payment for such a special book just felt . . . wrong. She ignored the Spreadsheet of Doom, which was peeking out from under the knitting, silently chastising her for her generosity.

Nora cut a length of shiny gold paper off a roll and proceeded to wrap the book, folding the paper neatly at the corners with practiced movements learned from her mother. As a finishing touch, she added a red ribbon, curling it with the blade of her scissors.

"Ah, that's a proper job, that is." Arnold nodded approvingly as Nora handed him the gift-wrapped book. "I've got a good feeling about this book. It's going to bring luck, I'm sure of it."

"I hope so." Nora wished she could do something more to help Noah. A hospital ward was a depressing place for a child at any time of year, let alone Christmas. An idea suddenly occurred to her—there *was* something that might cheer poor little Noah up.

She rummaged around underneath the counter until she found a proof copy of a new children's book by a popular comedian. She popped it into Arnold's bag. "It's very funny—I think Noah might enjoy it."

"That's very kind of you." The creases on Arnold's face deepened into ravines as he smiled at Nora. "And you know what they say—laughter really *is* the best medicine."

Coming around the counter again, Nora walked Arnold to the door. Luckily, the rain was beginning to let up.

"Thanks for all your help, Nora," Arnold said, shaking her hand. "It was good talking to you."

"My pleasure. I hope I'll see you—and Noah—back here soon."

4

NORA

As Nora watched Arnold make his way slowly down the high street, the phone rang. *Could that be Charlotte?* Nora wondered. Maybe she was calling the shop's landline because she knew Nora would be working. She hurried behind the counter and snatched up the phone eagerly. "Good afternoon, Stowford Bookshop."

"Hello, can I please speak to Nora Walden?"

Nora froze, recognizing the man's voice. Her stomach filled with dread and she fought the urge to slam the phone down. "Who may I ask is speaking?" she said, trying to keep her voice steady.

"My name is Derek Brown. I'm calling from—"

"I'm so sorry," Nora said, cutting him off. "Mrs. Walden can't come to the phone—she's just popped out."

"Do you know when she'll be back? I've tried several times, but she never seems to be available."

"I'm afraid not. Would you like to leave a message for her?"

"No, that's fine—I'll try again later."

Nora hung up with shaking hands. But she knew he'd only

phone back again. Derek Brown was nothing if not persistent. *If I can just put him off until after Christmas* . . .

Glancing across the bookshop, Nora saw that the fire was petering out. She went over and put on another log. They needed to order more wood, as the supply in the shed behind the shop was running low. But their log supplier was Doug Jenkins, a farmer in the village who earned a bit of extra cash selling logs from his land. It was bad enough not being able to pay their utility bills and their business taxes on time, but Nora couldn't bear the thought of being in debt to another small local business. They were all having just as tough a time making ends meet as she and Simon were.

As the new log sparked and caught fire, Nora glanced at a stack of books on a table display. The author had been touted by the publisher as the Next Big Thing in literary fiction and she had placed a big order. Although it had been short-listed for an important prize, the book wasn't exactly selling like hotcakes—or even lukewarm teacakes, for that matter. Nora wasn't surprised—she'd gotten halfway through *The Oculist of Leipzig* before giving up, annoyed by the author's excessive use of historical detail, ponderous prose and morose narrator—an eye surgeon who had accidentally blinded the composer Bach. *We could always burn those if things get really bad*, Simon had joked. Not that they would actually do that, of course. No matter how questionable its literary merit, Nora would never use a book as kindling!

Nora's stomach rumbled. She hoped Simon hadn't forgotten to get something for dinner. *Where is he?* she wondered, eager to tell him about Arnold. No doubt her gregarious husband had stayed on at the George to chat with one of the pub quiz regulars.

"Finding everything you need?" she asked, going over to the customer who had come in to escape the rain.

"I'm looking for that book about the girl who witnesses a murder," he said.

Nora could think of dozens of books that fit that description.

"It's got a blue cover?" he said. "I think they might be making it into a film?"

That only narrowed it down slightly.

Taking an educated guess, Nora returned and handed him a book. "Is this the one you mean?" she asked him.

His wet anorak dripped on the book jacket as he read the blurb.

"Yeah," he said finally, handing it back to her. "But I can get it cheaper online."

Nora fumed inwardly. It was all she could do not to beat him over the head with the book, which she wouldn't be able to sell now that water had warped its cover. Did he not realize how impossible it was for a tiny local business to compete with a giant online retailer? The very customers who lamented the demise of the local high street were often the ones unwilling to pay the full cover price to support an endangered species—the Lesser Spotted Independent Bookshop.

As he left, the guy pulled out his mobile phone and Nora caught a glimpse of his screen. He was already placing his online order, not even having the grace to wait until he was out of her shop.

"Good riddance," Nora muttered to herself.

Shortly afterward, a woman in a raspberry-colored beret came in to buy the newly published autobiography of a pop star with a colorful past.

"Cor, what a stud," she said, putting the book on the counter with a satisfied grin. "That was the last Christmas present I needed to get—my sister and I saw him at Wembley in 1989."

Nora glanced down at the pile of wool she'd shoved

underneath the counter. She and Simon had agreed that they wouldn't exchange presents this year, in an attempt to save money. Nora didn't mind not getting a gift herself, but she hated the thought of not giving one, which was why she'd decided to make Simon a sweater. If he objected to her breaking their pact, she'd say the sweater was purely practical—so they didn't have to turn the thermostat up. But if she didn't crack on with it, all he'd be getting was a knitted sleeve that only reached as far as his elbow.

As she wrapped up the book, Nora thought about the pale blue sweater she'd already made for Charlotte, even though she probably wouldn't be home to open it. Charlotte's round-the-world ticket was flexible, and she'd refused to be pinned down on her Christmas plans. Why would she come back to the UK, when she could be sunning herself on a beach somewhere warm? But Nora had knitted a sweater anyway—it would keep Charlotte warm next year in a drafty hall of residence.

"Where's the best place in the village for a cup of tea?" asked the woman on her way out.

"The scones at the Copper Kettle are to die for," Nora told her, pointing her toward the tearoom at the other end of the high street. Her friend Alice would be grateful for the business in winter. Summer was the busiest time of year for most of Stowford's shops and cafés, when holidaymakers from all over thronged the Cotswolds' pretty villages.

And then Nora was alone in the shop. The only sound was the steady drip, drip, drip of rainwater plopping into a plastic bucket.

The shop desperately needed a new roof. Their flat upstairs, and the office—an addition tacked on to the back of the shop—had so many leaks you practically had to carry an umbrella indoors when it rained. The weather had been so terrible these last few weeks that their flat was like an obstacle course, with buckets and saucepans positioned on the floor to catch the drips. Simon was constantly forgetting that they were there and accidentally knocking them over. So now their rugs were knackered, too. But at least the books in the bookshop below were safe from rain damage so far. Well, apart from the one the customer had dripped on!

Fixing the roof was just one of many jobs on Nora's ever-growing to-do list. The chimney needed sweeping, the walls desperately needed a fresh coat of paint and the well-trodden floorboards needed to be re-sanded and polished. As it stood, they couldn't afford to do any of those things. Thank goodness shabby chic was still in vogue, the bookshop's rustic, lived-in feeling adding to its charm.

Her mobile phone rang, making Nora jump. *That must be Simon,* she thought. But when she fished her phone out of her pocket, it was an unknown number. Could it be Charlotte? Had she lost her phone and had to get a new one? That could explain why she'd been out of touch . . .

"Hello!" she answered eagerly.

"Mrs. Walden?" said a man's voice. "I've been trying to reach you on your landline. You haven't responded to our letters. My name is Derek Brown and I'm an enforcement officer with—"

"Sorry, wrong number," Nora said, ending the call with trembling hands.

Why wouldn't he leave her alone? First it was just letters, which—after the first one—Nora couldn't bring herself to read. Then it was daily phone calls to the shop. Now he was calling her mobile, too.

Feeling shaky, she went over to the sofa and sank down on it. Merry got out of her basket and stretched her stubby little legs out behind her on the wooden floorboards. She shook herself, metal tag on her collar jangling, then came over to Nora and rested her head on her knee, big brown eyes looking up at her mistress adoringly. "Hello, gorgeous girl," Nora said, feeling the knobbly bumps of the dog's head under the soft white fur. How was it that dogs always knew when you needed comforting?

Nora helped herself to a ginger biscuit and broke it in half, giving one piece to Merry and eating the other herself. The taste never failed to remind her of her mum. Penelope had baked with Nora every Saturday, after the shop had closed for the day. They'd pick a different recipe book from the bookshop each week, and carry it upstairs to the flat. Penelope would put a record on the record player and blast out classic rock music as they baked together, taking care not to dirty the cookbook's pages so they could put it back on the shelves downstairs. They took their taste buds on globe-trotting culinary adventures—making sticky, sweet Greek baklava one week, a dense Indian pistachio and rosewater cake the next. But Nora's favorites were the homely recipes Penelope had inherited from her own mum. Oaty flapjacks bursting with raisins. Dark, rich parkin with a splash of Guinness. Raspberry squares dusted with almond flakes. And of course, Penelope's famous ginger biscuits.

Even though her mother had died years ago, Nora still missed her every day. She desperately wished that her mother had been alive long enough to meet Simon. To know that Nora had found a partner who loved the bookshop as much as she did. But she was glad Penelope didn't have to see the bookshop struggling.

It hadn't always been like this. When her mother was alive, the weekends before Christmas were so busy they'd get in extra help to deal with all the customers. Of course, this was back in the days before the Internet, and before supermarkets sold discounted bestsellers alongside multipacks of crisps and family-sized bottles of lemonade.

As newlyweds, Nora and Simon had had ambitious plans for

the bookshop. They'd dreamed of expanding the shop, adding on a café and maybe even opening another branch.

Once Charlotte had come along, building a bookshop empire had taken a back seat to raising their daughter. Kids were expensive—and they never seemed to be able to save enough to expand. But Nora was proud of what they *had* achieved. They'd established a local writing competition, created a popular book club, set up an online business and hosted events and talks by award-winning authors. And they were still here—which was more than could be said of many other independents.

But for how much longer . . .

Merry barked and ran to the door, wagging her tail excitedly as the village postman came into the shop. "Hello, me babber," Ken said, tousling the dog's ears.

"I thought dogs were supposed to hate postmen," Nora joked.

"I know the way to her heart." Ken laughed, taking a dog treat out of his pocket and giving it to Merry, who gobbled it up eagerly.

"Got anything for me?" teased Nora, "or did you just come to see your girlfriend here?"

Ken grinned and handed her a pile of post. "Sorry I'm late today—it's a crazy time of year. I've got so many parcels to deliver. Everyone does their Christmas shopping online nowadays."

"Tell me about it," Nora muttered.

Good news first, she decided, ignoring an ominous-looking envelope with the local council's logo printed on it. She opened a parcel that contained the invitations they'd ordered for their annual Christmas Eve party. Next, she opened a few Christmas cards, propping them up on the mantelpiece. Then, unable to put it off any longer, she took a deep breath and tore open the envelope from the council. It contained a reminder—as if she could have forgotten—that their business taxes were in arrears.

The words swam in front of Nora's eyes.

Final warning . . . Missed appearance at magistrates' court . . .
Full amount to be settled immediately . . . Enforcement officers will
be in contact . . .

Feeling as if she was about to be sick, Nora threw the letter on
the fire and watched it burn, the edges darkening and then the
whole sheet crumpling and collapsing in on itself. A moment
later, it had turned to ash.

If only it was that easy to get rid of their debt.

Running the bookshop had long required a certain amount of
creative accounting, paying invoices at the last possible moment
when they had a rare boost in sales income. A few years back,
they'd taken out a bank loan, using it as a float to tide them over
in lean times. Unbeknownst to Simon, the money had run out a
few months ago. And because of his heart condition, she hadn't
told him.

Nora had been convinced that sales would pick up over the
summer. There was no need to worry him unnecessarily, she'd
thought. But the summer holidays had been slow, thanks to bad
weather, so she'd pinned her hopes on Christmas. One good December was all they needed. As long as she could stall their creditors until after Christmas, she'd reasoned, they could get the
shop back on track. At least, that was the plan.

Nora hated keeping secrets from her husband and the decep-
tion was eating away at her, but the longer it went on, the harder
it was to tell him. She was worried that the shock would bring on
a real heart attack. So she'd intercepted the post, pretended calls
from creditors were wrong numbers, and shoved their overdue
bills in a folder at the back of the filing cabinet in the office.

Nora knew that burying her head in the sand was only making
the problem worse. It was time to face the facts—they were halfway through December, and unless something radically changed,

they would finish the year with another deficit. She couldn't ignore their problems any longer. She was going to have to tell Simon about the serious trouble they were in—sooner rather than later.

Nora rubbed her eyes wearily. Visions of bailiffs knocking down the door and loading all of their books into a van had been keeping her awake at night for weeks.

Stop feeling sorry for yourself, Nora told herself sternly. There were plenty of people all around the world far worse off than she was. Her self-pitying was beginning to rival the annoying narrator in *The Oculist of Leipzig*.

Getting out a pad of paper, she decided to make a list. At the top of the sheet, she wrote:

Ideas for Saving the Bookshop

1. Take out another loan.

This, she knew, wasn't very realistic. The bank was unlikely to let them borrow more money, given that they were struggling to pay back the money they already owed, but Nora wanted to explore every possible option. She was willing to get down on her knees and beg Hugh Wright, the local branch manager, if necessary. Hugh was a nice guy. He owned a sailing boat, and often came in to buy nautical adventure novels. Surely he wouldn't want to see the bookshop close down . . .

2. Ask Simon's parents for help.

Simon's dad was enjoying a comfortable retirement of golf and cruises, funded by Walden Creative's success. He could have easily bailed them out, several times over, if Simon's pride hadn't prevented him from asking. Whenever they got together with

Simon's parents, he pretended that the bookshop was thriving. It wasn't as if they had to ask for a handout—they could sell his dad a stake in the business, or make him a silent partner. But Nora knew that, for Simon, asking Charles for help would be an admission of defeat. She couldn't do that to her husband. It would crush him. And dealing with his parents always stressed Simon out, which was the last thing she wanted, given his condition. She scribbled out *Ask Simon's parents for help* and replaced it with: *Rent out Charlotte's room.*

A lodger could bring in a bit of income to help with their cash flow. Maeve Philbin from the flower shop rented out her spare room on Airbnb to earn some extra money. But what if Charlotte came home? Where would she stay? Besides, would anyone actually *want* to rent a room where a leaking roof was likely to wake you up before your alarm clock?

3. *Use Charlotte's university savings.*

Even as she wrote it, Nora knew she could never sacrifice the money they'd been putting aside for Charlotte's education since she was a baby.

She'd been so proud of Charlotte when she'd got a place to study anthropology at Warwick, not to mention delighted that she'd chosen a university (relatively) close to home. So when Charlotte had announced that she wanted to take a gap year, Nora had been alarmed. She worried that one gap year might turn into another, and Charlotte might never make it to university. But Charlotte had argued that if she was going to study human societies, she needed to get out there in the world and experience different cultures firsthand. Simon had sided with Charlotte, saying that it would be good for her to have a break before embarking on the rigors of her degree.

Nora, who hadn't been able to finish her degree, couldn't imagine why anyone wouldn't want to be at university. There had been no question of her not coming home when her mother was diagnosed with cancer, and Nora certainly didn't regret for a second the last few years they had spent together. But a small part of her still wished she'd had the chance to finish her course and graduate.

No, they weren't going to touch Charlotte's university fund. If they did, Charlotte would have to take out large student loans— and Nora didn't want her to end up in masses of debt like her parents.

4. Sell up.

It was definitely an option. Seb Fox had approached them several times with offers from chains looking to move into the picturesque village, where new building was restricted. She and Simon had always insisted that the shop wasn't for sale. Other small business owners in the village, however, had jumped at the opportunity.

The latest to sell up had been Jane Norton, who sold her gift shop, Cotswold Crafts, for a huge amount of money. "I can't make a living selling a few tea towels a week," she'd told Nora over coffee at the Copper Kettle, "and I'm not getting any younger." Jane had moved to the south of Spain, and—if the tanned and beaming pictures she'd posted on Facebook were any indication—she was enjoying her sangria-soaked life in the sun. She even had a new boyfriend called Francisco. Nora glanced across the street to where the gift shop had been. Now it was a branch of an Italian restaurant chain, serving up pizzas and bowls of pasta identical to those being dished out on any other high street in the country. It made Nora sad to think that Stowford was losing its identity as chains moved in, swallowing up the quirky local businesses that had made it unique. In the last year, they'd lost the gift shop, a bakery and a family-run hardware store that had been in the village even longer than the bookshop.

Not that Nora blamed anyone for taking the money and running. She knew they were all facing the same challenges, trying to stay afloat in tough economic times. Business taxes had soared, hitting independent high street shops hard. As she listened to the insistent dripping from the roof, she knew that many people would think she was crazy for not even considering the offers.

Nora tried to picture herself and Simon living somewhere warm, in a villa where she wasn't likely to be woken up in the morning by raindrops plopping on her face. They'd have more time for reading. Simon could take up tennis. Maybe Nora would actually get around to reading *War and Peace*, which had been at the bottom of her to-read pile so long it had probably fused to her bedside table. She could even go back to university and finish her degree.

Nora went into the back room, stepping over a half-full bucket of water collecting drips, and rummaged around in the filing cabinet until she found the most recent offer. She felt almost giddy as she stared at the number with all its zeros. It was hard to believe that the shop Penelope had bought for a few thousand pounds with a small inheritance from a great-aunt was worth so much money now. But even though the roof had more holes than a slice of Swiss cheese, the offer still wasn't enough.

For Nora, the bookshop was priceless.

Giving up on the bookshop would be tantamount to giving up everything she valued most in life. It wasn't just she and Simon who needed the bookshop—Stowford needed it, too. Nora believed that with all her heart.

She crumpled up the offer letter and threw it in the bin. Selling the bookshop would solve their financial problems, but it would bring a whole other problem to contend with—Penelope's ghost. Because Nora was fairly certain that if she sold the bookshop, her mother would haunt her until the end of her days.

Penelope had been gone for over two decades, but here in the bookshop, her memory was alive. Everywhere she looked, Nora was reminded of the happy times she'd spent with her mum—just the two of them against the world. Doing her homework in front of the fire after school . . . dancing wildly to the Rolling Stones after hours (disapproving villagers peering in through the windows) . . . the scent of patchouli incense wafting down from the flat upstairs. Nora wasn't sure she believed in an afterlife, but in the bookshop, she always felt as if her mother's spirit was watching over her, a benign presence guiding her through life.

Severing that connection was unthinkable.

So, what options did that leave?

Nora sighed and added another item to her list.

5. A Christmas miracle.

5

SIMON

Simon pushed the bookshop door open with his bottom, his hands too full to work the handle. "Sorry I took so long!" he called out as the bell above the door cheerfully announced his return.

"Hi there, old girl," Simon said, dropping the bags to the floor to pat Merry, who had risen from her basket by the fire to sniff at the bags of shopping.

"Hey, who are you calling an old girl?" Nora joked, coming out from behind the counter to greet him.

Simon chuckled as an apple fell out and rolled across the scuffed wooden floorboards. He retrieved the runaway fruit and popped it back in the bag. "I was buying some bits and pieces for dinner from Doug Jenkins's farm stall, and he told me that the book we ordered in from America last year—the one about root vegetables—has been really helpful. Using the techniques in the book boosted their rutabaga harvest by twenty percent."

Simon made a mental note to add a question about rutabagas to the quiz he was compiling. *A rutabaga is a cross between which two vegetables?* Maybe he'd do a whole vegetable-themed round this week . . .

Compiling and hosting the pub quiz at the George every Thursday night was one of the highlights of Simon's week. The regulars had become like family, and the competition between the teams was fierce, but friendly.

"That's great. Looks like you bought up half the harvest."

"No, he gave it to us for free. As a thank-you." He picked up one of the bags, full of boulder-like vegetables, and handed it to Nora.

Nora's eyes widened as she looked inside. "Whoa! That is a lot of rutabaga." She laughed. "For once I'm almost glad Charlotte isn't here."

Simon laughed. Their daughter loathed rutabaga in any form. "Remember when we took her to my parents' house for the first time?"

Nora put her hands over her cheeks, looking aghast at the memory. "How could I forget that? I was so mortified."

Simon's mum had served up a roast with all the trimmings. Baby Charlotte had tried one mouthful of mashed rutabaga and tipped her whole plate of food off her high chair and onto the Persian carpet.

"Doug gave us a bottle of wine and a bunch of other stuff, too." He showed Nora another bag, full of sprouts, shallots, carrots and lovely-looking apples. "He wouldn't take a penny for any of it."

"That was so nice of him, but there's enough rutabaga here to feed an army. I guess we'll just have to use it in soups and stews—and freeze whatever we don't eat. I wonder if I could bake some of it . . . ?"

"Rutabaga cake?" Simon suggested.

"Rutabaga muffins?" Nora countered.

"Rutabaga . . . brownies?"

They both burst out laughing.

Nora grinned at Simon. "That sounds disgusting."

Simon was glad to hear his wife's laughter. It was his favorite sound in the whole world, but he hadn't heard enough of it recently. He suddenly felt guilty that he'd been gone longer than expected—the last thing Nora needed was something else to worry about.

"I would have been back sooner, love, but the meeting went on a bit longer than usual. I hope it hasn't been too busy in here."

"I wish," Nora said ruefully. "But I *am* glad to see you—I've been dying to tell you something."

"The new *Game of Thrones* book finally has a publication date?" guessed Simon.

"Even better." Nora was practically doing a jig on the spot. "You'll never guess what someone bought today."

"*The Oculist of Leipzig?*" Simon glanced over at the stack of novels on the table with a sign that read PRIZE-WINNING FICTION. Like Nora, he'd tried reading the dreary historical novel but hadn't got past the first chapter.

"Nope. I'll give you a hint—it isn't a *new* book . . ."

"So we're talking about a classic?"

Nora shook her head. "It's over twenty-five years old, but I don't think anyone would describe it as a classic. Except us . . ."

Simon looked at Nora, raising one eyebrow. Did she mean what he thought she meant? "No way . . . someone actually bought *The True Story of the Christmas Truce?*"

Nora nodded. Her hazel eyes sparkled, making them look more green than brown.

Simon whooped with delight, then picked her up by the waist and spun her around. "I knew it!" he crowed. "I knew it would find a home someday!"

Setting Nora down, he kissed her full on the lips.

"Oh, Simon," Nora said, stroking his stubble-covered cheek.

"I wish you could have been here. The sweetest little old man bought it for his grandson."

They sat down on the sofa together and Nora told Simon all about Arnold and his grandson in the hospital. Then she showed Simon the selfie she had taken of herself and Arnold.

Simon stared at the photo incredulously. "Can you forward that to me? I'll put it on the website and post about it on Twitter." Although 280 characters wasn't nearly enough to do justice to the book's story. It was so much more to them than bound pages covered in board—it represented everything the shop stood for.

"I hope Arnold comes in again," Nora said. "I'd love you to meet him. He's a history buff, like you, and used to play soccer, too." Her eyes welled with emotion. "He's ever so worried about his grandson."

One of the things Simon loved most about his wife was that she wasn't only interested in stories that came between the pages of a book. She genuinely cared about the people around her, and *their* stories. Quiet and thoughtful, Nora was a great listener. He'd always thought that if she hadn't been a bookseller she could have been a therapist.

A buzzing sound came from Nora's cardigan and, jumping up, she fished her phone out of the pocket.

"Charlotte!" she exclaimed as their daughter's happy face filled the screen. Her thick brown hair had a purple plait woven into it and months in the sunshine had made the freckles on her nose and cheeks multiply.

"Hi, Mum!" Charlotte said. The silver bangles she always wore on her wrist jangled as she waved. Simon liked to joke that her bracelets were like the bell on a cat—they could always hear her coming, making it impossible for her to sneak in after curfew undetected. Not that she was that kind of kid. "Is Dad there, too?"

"Hi, honey!" Simon said, putting his head next to Nora's so both of their faces could fit on the screen.

Hearing Charlotte's voice, Merry whined, so Simon picked her up and held her in front of the camera, waving her paw.

"Merry!" cried Charlotte.

Simon set the dog back down on the floor before she licked the screen.

"I hope I'm not getting you at a bad time," Charlotte said. "I'm sure the shop's really busy just before Christmas."

Simon glanced around. Worryingly, there weren't any customers in the shop at the moment.

"Don't worry," Nora assured her. "We always love hearing from you. We missed you last week . . ."

"Sorry about that, Mum. I was hiking in Dharamshala—the Wi-Fi was really patchy there." She held up her hands and showed them the intricate henna patterns on the backs of them. "Look what I had done today."

"Beautiful."

"How are you feeling, Dad?" Charlotte asked, her eyes—hazel like her mother's—filled with concern.

"I'm absolutely fine," Simon said. "Even though your mother insists on treating me like an invalid."

Nora swatted him gently on the arm.

After Simon's health scare, Charlotte had wanted to cancel her trip, but Simon wouldn't hear of it.

They chatted for a while about a temple Charlotte had just been to see, the books she'd been reading and some Scandinavian friends she'd made in the hostel.

"I don't mean to nag, sweetie," Nora said. "But have you decided whether you're going to come home for Christmas?"

Charlotte shook her head. "Sorry, guys. I'm really going to miss you, but Carsen and Mette invited me to go on a diving course in Goa with them. So, I'm going to stay here for Christmas. Is that OK with you?"

"Yes, of course," Nora said, her voice suspiciously bright. Simon could tell from the way she was gripping his hand that she was trying her hardest not to show Charlotte how disappointed she was. "That sounds fun."

Just then, the bell above the door jingled.

"I can hear someone coming in," Charlotte said. "I'll let you guys get back to work." She blew them a kiss and ended the call.

Nora released her grip on Simon's hand and let out a deep breath. "Well, now we know," she said, sounding glum.

Simon patted her knee. "I'm disappointed, too. But she's always wanted to learn how to dive."

The customer who was browsing by the bestsellers table cleared his throat.

"Do you need a minute?" Simon murmured to Nora. "I can go and see if he needs help."

She shook her head and stood up. "I'll stay down here—you take the shopping upstairs."

Simon carried his shopping bags to the flat above the shop. He set the bags down on the kitchen floor, nearly knocking over a saucepan that was collecting drips. Glancing up at the leaking ceiling, Simon grimaced.

The flat was quirky and cozy—a true family home, with pictures of the three of them everywhere—but it needed a lot of work. The roof was getting so bad they were practically camping indoors. The kitchen fittings were the height of eighties chic—and although that decade was back in fashion (according to Charlotte), Simon secretly lusted after a big American-style fridge and granite surfaces. Their pink bathroom suite, with its temperamental toilet, was like something out of a living-history museum. Tucked under the eaves, the tiny flat couldn't have been more different to the spacious London villa Simon had grown up in, with art on the walls and tastefully muted decor that was regularly updated by a team of professional decorators.

Running his hand over the chipped yellow paint on the kitchen walls, Simon remembered painting the flat with Nora when he first moved in. Wanting to put their mark on the flat she'd grown up in, they'd repainted every room—sunny yellow in the kitchen, vibrant purple in the bedroom, a warm red in the living room. Neither of them was any good at DIY, getting splashes of paint everywhere, but they'd laughed and talked and blasted out the Stone Roses and other indie bands as they worked. Now, most of the walls were covered up by bookshelves buckling under the weight of their favorite books, framed film posters, art prints and Arsenal memorabilia. The sofa was older than Charlotte and was strewn with blankets, knitted by Nora, to mask the stains left over from the toddler years. The heavy wooden dining table, where they had enjoyed countless Sunday lunches and lazy breakfasts, had a paperback shoved under one leg to stop it from wobbling.

Simon had never imagined that they would still be living like students in middle age. On his parents' rare visits to the Cotswolds, he never invited them upstairs, always meeting them at the George because he didn't want them to see how shabby the flat was. Parents instinctively wanted to give their children more than they had had themselves, and Simon was ashamed that he hadn't managed to provide a better quality of life for his family. Nora never complained, but Simon couldn't help feeling that he'd failed her and Charlotte.

This wasn't how it was supposed to be. When they were newlyweds, mapping out their future together, Simon had had bold ambitions for the shop. With Nora's knowledge of the book trade and his advertising background, he'd set his sights on turning the Stowford Bookshop into a regional—and maybe even national—chain. They'd even got as far as scouting out a few possible locations in other Cotswold villages. Simon had been determined to prove to his parents that he could be a success in his own right. But far from being at the helm of a successful chain, he couldn't even get one shop to make a profit.

The website had been his latest attempt to turn things around, and he'd poured all his energies into getting it up and running. But their online sales hadn't taken off in the way he had hoped. Things had changed a lot since his days in advertising. When it came to digital marketing, he was out of his depth. He knew he needed help, but pride—and stubbornness—prevented him from asking for it. Who would he ask, anyway? Nora was clueless when it came to technology. And he'd never give his father the satisfaction of asking him for anything.

As he bent to unpack the fruit and veg from the market, a drop of water fell on his head—as if taunting him with his inadequacy. "Damn!" he cursed, wiping the cold water off his forehead. This couldn't go on. They couldn't afford a new roof, but he might be able to find some inexpensive replacement tiles at the salvage yard. He wasn't much of a handyman but he could probably find a book—or a YouTube video—that would show him what to do . . .

At the bottom of one of the bags, he found the earrings that he'd bought for Nora at the market. Simon couldn't wait to see the delicate filigree teardrops, made by a local silversmith, sparkling on her ears. Hopefully they'd bring a smile to her face on Christmas Day.

He'd got a silver bangle for Charlotte, too, not that he'd be able to give it to her now. *Oh well*, thought Simon, hiding both pieces of jewelry in his sock drawer. He couldn't begrudge her for wanting to stay in India, even though Christmas would be strange without her.

The flat felt bigger without Charlotte's clutter everywhere. Now, he and Nora could actually eat dinner without clearing a heap of schoolbooks and half-drunk mugs of tea off the table first. Shaving no longer required jostling for space with the contents of half the beauty counter at Boots. But the flat felt too quiet without Charlotte. Simon, whose musical tastes ranged from Edward Elgar to Arcade Fire, never thought he'd miss the sound of Top 40 hits blasting out of his daughter's bedroom. But the other day he'd found himself playing Radio 1 in the car, just because the cheesy pop songs reminded him of her.

Shaking his head, Simon scolded himself for being sentimental. All children had to fly the nest eventually—that was the whole point of parenting. His daughter was spreading her wings and seeing the world; she'd return to them when she was ready.

In the kitchen, he made two cups of chamomile tea and headed back downstairs to the shop. Nora surreptitiously shoved her knitting under the counter, which Simon pretended not to notice. He knew she was knitting him something for Christmas, which was why he'd got her the earrings. Nora was one of life's givers. There was no way she'd be able to resist giving him a gift—even though they'd agreed not to exchange presents this year.

"Alice gave me some chamomile tea for you," Simon said, as he placed her favorite polka-dotted mug down on the coffee table in front of the fire.

"Oooh, lovely," Nora said gratefully. She came out from behind the counter and handed a small rectangle of card stock to Simon. "I forgot to tell you—these arrived from the printer today."

Simon looked down at the invitation to the shop's annual Christmas Eve party. It was illustrated with a picture of Santa

Claus reading a book. JOIN US FOR MULLED WINE, MINCE PIES AND BOOK CHAT, it read. "Looks great," he said, handing it back. One of the regulars at the pub quiz was a children's book illustrator. She'd done the drawing for them as a favor because they'd hosted the launch party for her latest children's book at the shop.

Nora fiddled with the invitation. "I'm not sure we should go ahead with it."

"Why not?" The bookshop's annual Christmas Eve party was a tradition started by Nora's mother. Penelope had begun hosting the party when she was new to Stowford, inviting not just her regular customers, but other "waifs and strays" like herself, with no family in the village. Nora and Simon had kept the tradition up, never missing a year—not even when Charlotte was a baby. It was always the highlight of the festive season.

"It won't be the same without Charlotte."

"Oh, honey," Simon said, giving her a hug. "You know Charlotte wouldn't want us to cancel the party."

"I know. But I just don't feel very Christmassy this year."

"Well, let's see if we can do something to change that."

He found a playlist on his phone, and a moment later Christmas carols were playing over the shop's speaker. Simon hummed along as he threw another log on the fire and gave it a poke to get it going. "What should we have for Christmas dinner?" he said, helping himself to a ginger biscuit.

Nora sighed. "I'm not sure there's much point in cooking a big dinner if it's just going to be the two of us."

Now that *was* worrying. Planning the Christmas dinner was normally Nora's favorite festive tradition. How could he get her in the mood? *Porn*, Simon thought. Well, food porn, to be precise.

He went over to the cookery section and returned with a handful of books.

Settling down on the sofa, he opened a book called *Earth to*

Table—101 Ways to Cook Root Vegetables. He held up a photograph of gleaming honey-glazed rutabagas to tempt her. "Those look delicious. I bet they'd go well with turkey."

"Mmm," Nora murmured absently.

Simon knew he'd have to try harder. He picked up a hardback called *The Art of the Roast* by a chef famous for his meat dishes. Opening it to a double-page spread of a glistening roast turkey, almost obscene in its plump, golden glory, his mouth began to water like Pavlov's dog. "Or were you thinking something different this year? Baked ham? Roast beef?"

Still Nora didn't respond to his advances.

Simon knew he had to go straight for her sweet spot. He picked up a new edition of a classic cookery book, written by a grande dame of British baking. "Maybe I'll find a recipe for rutabaga brownies," he joked, but she barely cracked a smile. He flicked past apple pies, trifles and Victoria sponges, looking for the most decadent dessert he could find. *Aha!* He held up an enticing picture of a Yule log with thick, artery-clogging cream oozing from between its dark chocolate rolls. "Now *that* is what I call a pudding . . ."

Nora leaned over the back of the sofa, her long hair tickling his face, to take a closer look. "Oh yes, that does look nice . . ."

Joining him on the sofa, she took the book out of his hands and began to leaf through it.

Yes! thought Simon, stifling a grin. His culinary seduction had succeeded. Well, you couldn't stay happily married for as long as they had without understanding your partner's appetites . . .

"This was Mum's go-to cookbook," Nora said. "She used the Christmas pudding recipe every year. She'd start making it months in advance, keeping it in the cupboard and feeding it a slug of brandy every weekend—then treating herself to one, too."

Penelope had died before Simon had met Nora, but he felt as

if he knew her because Nora spoke about her often. She sounded like an amazing woman—a feminist and free spirit who had raised an equally amazing daughter, all on her own.

"We always had a Christmas pudding, but Mum didn't like turkey so we used to do something different," Nora said. "One year, we cooked an Indian feast—with Brussels sprouts and paneer curry." She wrinkled her nose and laughed. "We couldn't get rid of the smell for days."

Simon thought about his own childhood Christmases. Shivering through a boring church service, yawning through the Queen's speech on television and then a formal dinner prepared by the family's cook. Simon and his younger brother, Daniel, had had to sit through the meal in their uncomfortable suits and ties, not allowed to speak unless spoken to. All they'd wanted to do was get down from the table and play but they'd had to politely endure the interminable dinner as the grown-ups drank too much and argued about politics and the family business. Despite an enormous Christmas tree in the corner of the room, with piles of expensive gifts underneath, it was a joyless occasion.

Simon's father, Charles, was a workaholic, who only seemed to care about growing Walden Creative into London's largest advertising agency. His mother, Margaret, hadn't exactly been hands-on, either. She rarely went out, drank to blot out her loneliness and spent days at a time lying in her darkened bedroom with a cold flannel on her forehead. With the benefit of hindsight, Simon realized that she'd probably been suffering from undiagnosed depression. He remembered creeping into her room and lying down on the bed next to her, hoping for a cuddle that was never forthcoming.

Simon and Daniel had both been packed off to boarding school at seven. His parents believed that an exclusive private education was the best possible start in life that parents could

give their children, but, as a father, Simon couldn't imagine sending Charlotte away. He remembered her as a seven-year-old, missing her two front teeth, with a tireless appetite for knock-knock
jokes. He wouldn't have wanted to miss even one day of her company.

Simon had hated boarding school, until he'd discovered the
library, which became his sanctuary. He'd found escape from his
bullying schoolmasters and boorish classmates, who'd mocked him
for preferring soccer to rugby, in biographies. He'd immersed
himself in real-life stories about people—from astronauts and
athletes to explorers and leaders—who had achieved amazing
feats. As he read their stories, he dreamed about his future, imagining that he might do great things one day, too.

Reading had been the making of Simon. His passion for
books sustained him through boarding school, and eventually led
to a degree from Oxford in modern history.

As the oldest, it was assumed that Simon would take over the
family business, and after graduating he'd duly started working
for the agency. He'd enjoyed it, too. The work was creative, he was
good at winning clients and he'd had a knack for coming up with
innovative advertising campaigns. But as soon as he met Nora he
knew he'd found what he'd been searching for all his life.

His parents had been furious when he'd announced that he
was getting married and quitting the agency. A penniless bookseller with no family of note was hardly the sort of match they
could announce in *The Times*. His father accused Simon of wasting
the education he'd worked hard to provide. His mother said un-
forgivable things about Nora, suggesting—to her face—that she
was a gold digger. Simon had cut off all contact with them, refus-
ing to invite them to the wedding.

Nora, ever the peacemaker, had encouraged Simon to reconcile
with his parents. But though a fragile *entente cordiale* with Charles and

Margaret had been established, they weren't close. And from the very beginning of his marriage, Simon had always been adamant that he didn't want to spend Christmas with his parents. He wanted to make his own traditions. Finally, he had the chance to experience the sort of family Christmas he'd read about in books—opening stockings together in their pajamas, reading out the silly jokes in crackers, playing charades in front of a roaring fire and watching films together. Now Christmas was his favorite time of year.

"I suppose I'd better put these back." Simon gathered up the cookery books. But then he caught sight of the table piled high with copies of *The Oculist of Leipzig*. "What do you say we return some of these duds and use the table to display Christmas-themed cookery books?"

Nora's face lit up. "Good idea!"

They carried armfuls of the novel into the back room. "I'll pack them up and send them back to the warehouse tomorrow," Simon said.

Nora and Simon arranged the cookbooks artfully on the table, propping them up on wooden bookstands and opening them to mouthwatering photographs. When they had finished making their display, they stepped back to admire their handiwork.

"It looks wonderful," Nora said, "but it's making me hungry— I didn't eat lunch."

"Why don't you go up and get dinner started? I can manage down here on my own."

"Are you sure?" Nora asked, looking worried.

"Of course," Simon said, rolling his eyes. "There's nobody in here—it's hardly stressful."

"Well, if you're sure, that would be great. I'll make a stew and use up some of the veg." Nora took one of the cookbooks off the display and tucked it under her arm. "And for pudding, I'll bake an apple tart from a recipe in this book."

"Sounds delicious."

Nora gathered up their empty mugs, kissed Simon on the cheek then headed upstairs to cook dinner in their leaky kitchen. As he watched her go, Simon was reminded of how fortunate he was. True, he might not have provided his family with the material comforts of his own upbringing. Nor had he achieved any deeds worthy of writing a biography about. But Simon knew that in the ways that truly mattered, he was a success. He'd married a penniless bookseller and gained the most valuable thing in the world.

Love.

6

SIMON

Simon went over to the window, his forehead pressed to the glass as he looked out at the market, which was beginning to wind down. Doug Jenkins was already packing up his fruit and veg stall. Shoppers were starting to head home for their dinners, clutching their purchases of artisan cheeses, soy wax candles and aromatherapy soaps. One man was carrying a lumpy brown ceramic vase, and Simon felt sorry for whoever was going to receive that for Christmas.

Come in here! Simon wanted to bang on the window and shout at them: *Books make the best Christmas presents of all!*

But people hurried right past the bookshop, barely glancing at the festive display in their eagerness to get out of the rain. Simon probably could have sat naked in the window wearing just a Santa hat and nobody would have taken any notice.

I'll check the online sales. Hopefully people had chosen to stay out of the rain and do their book shopping from the warmth and comfort of their own homes.

"Let me know if anyone comes in," Simon told Merry, who

looked up from her basket and thumped her tail as he walked past her into the back room.

Simon sat down at the desk and switched on the ancient desktop computer, which wheezed asthmatically as it loaded. Opening up the shop's e-mail account, he saw that there were four new orders. No, scratch that—three orders and one complaint. Simon sighed. Three orders were better than none, but Jeff Bezos wasn't exactly going to be quaking in his boots.

Thank God they still had the loan money to tide them over.

Simon packaged up the orders, noting down the stock that they needed to reorder, then he dealt with the complaint, from a customer who had ordered a copy of *The Oculist of Leipzig* and wanted a refund.

Simon typed out a polite response, explaining that while he was sorry she had found the novel a "derivative pile of excrement," a description he personally agreed with, they would only provide a refund if the book had arrived damaged. He added a list of ten other historical fiction novels that the customer might enjoy more.

As he clicked SEND, the bell above the shop door jingled and Merry yipped.

Simon came out of the back room and stifled a groan as he saw a disheveled man with a nose redder than Rudolph's. Howie obviously hadn't been able to persuade anyone in the George to play darts or buy him a drink, so he'd wandered across the street to the bookshop.

"Oi! I have a bone to pick with you, Bookworm," Howie said, assailing Simon with a blast of boozy breath. "You marked me down at the quiz last week—for saying that Israel is in Europe."

"But Israel is in *Asia*," Simon said wearily.

"So why is Israel in the Eurovision Song Contest, then?" Howie demanded. "And the UEFA Championships. Eh?"

Simon sighed and went over to the reference section. He got

out a huge atlas, found a map of the Middle East and pointed to a tiny sliver of water between Israel and Egypt. "Culturally, Israel has a lot of links with Europe. But the Suez Canal is the border of western Asia and Africa. Although if you consider the tectonic plates, one could argue that geographically speaking, Israel is technically in Afri—"

Howie interrupted Simon with a dismissive wave of his hand. "All right, all right, I get the picture." He peered around the shop. "Got any of them ginger biscuits Nora makes?"

"Over by the fire."

Simon grimaced as Howie helped himself to several biscuits, biting into one noisily and scattering crumbs all over the floor. Howie's geographical query had probably just been a ruse for accessing Nora's baked goods. To be fair, her ginger biscuits *were* out of this world.

Having gone to school together, Nora had endless patience for Howie—she'd told Simon about Howie's violent, alcoholic father. While Simon sympathized, he didn't particularly want Howie hectoring him—and any customers that came into the shop—for the rest of the evening.

Luckily, a woman passing by the shop window caught Howie's eye. "There's Dr. Dhar. When I fell over last winter and broke my toe, she told me that I'd better cut down on my drinking." He slapped his chest, his eyes, with their yellowy tint, looking wild. "But look at me—I'm fit as a fiddle."

Simon nodded toward the door. "Better hurry. She's getting away." *Sorry, Dr. Dhar,* he apologized silently.

"Later, Bookworm," called Howie. He knocked over a stack of novels on his way out to chase after the GP, calling, "Doc! Doc!"

As Simon picked up the fallen books and put them back on the table, his phone pinged. He took it out of his pocket and saw that Charlotte had played a Scrabble word.

Zati.

The little imp. She'd only gone and used a Z on a triple-letter square. But what the hell was a *zati*?

A message from Charlotte popped up, as if she'd read his mind.

It's a type of Indian monkey. xxx

Simon smiled and, as he put his phone back in his pocket and filed that fact away for use in his next quiz, he tried not to dwell on how much he'd miss playing Scrabble with her in person over Christmas. The three of them usually had a board game marathon over the holidays.

Simon got a dustpan and brush out from behind the counter to sweep up the trail of crumbs Howie had left behind him, like Hansel in the forest. Only, it wouldn't lead to a gingerbread cottage but straight to the George.

The shop door jingled and a moment later a woman's voice called out, "Hello? Anyone in there?"

Simon stood up quickly. "Shit!" he shouted, bashing his head on the beam. Twice in one day!

"Oh, sorry," said the woman, who looked to be in her late thirties. She had blond hair with dark roots, was wearing jeans and a fleece jacket, and was holding a carrier bag with an enormous box of cereal sticking out of it. "I didn't see you down there." Her eyes darted around the bookshop nervously.

Simon rubbed his smarting forehead. "Occupational hazard. My wife says I should wear a helmet to work." He emptied the dustpan into the bin and went over to the woman, who was looking as if the books might bite her. A classic case of bibliophobia.

He'd seen a statistic that less than twenty percent of the UK population ever went into a bookshop. Many people avoided them, feeling intimidated by the hushed, rarefied atmosphere. Simon and Nora had always gone out of their way to change that perception, wanting to ensure that their shop was bright, friendly and welcoming to everyone. He approached the woman, holding out his hand. "Hi, I'm Simon. Let me know if I can help you find anything."

"Liz," said the woman. "I'm actually looking for some books for my kids."

"How old are they?" Simon asked.

"Travis is ten and Jamie is eight."

Simon grinned. "You have your hands full."

Liz nodded at the jumbo box of cereal. "They're growing like weeds at the moment—eating me out of house and home."

Simon laughed. "Don't expect that to change anytime soon. What sort of thing do your boys like reading?"

"They don't," Liz said, furrows appearing between her eyebrows as she frowned. "That's the problem. They're struggling at school. Their teacher called me in for a meeting to say I need to get them to read more at home." She looked at Simon plaintively. "But how am I going to do that? All they want to do is watch TV and play games on their tablets."

Simon nodded sympathetically. It was a common refrain from customers with children.

"I can't say I blame them," Liz said. "The books the school sends them home with are dead boring."

"What sort of computer games do they like playing?"

Liz thought for a moment. "Travis likes games with lots of fighting—knights having battles, that sort of thing. But Jamie prefers *Mario Kart*. Says he wants to be a racing car driver when he grows up."

Simon chuckled. "A future boy racer, is he? Lots of those around." He'd lived in the countryside for decades, but he still couldn't get used to the speed at which locals tackled the narrow lanes. It made even a trip to the next village into a white-knuckle ride. Nora accused him of driving like an old lady when he steered their ancient, battered Golf down hedgerowed lanes. But Simon ignored angry honks from tailgaters and stuck stubbornly to the speed limit. After all, a girl had died this summer. It was better to be safe than sorry.

Simon led Liz into the children's section, which had a comfy beanbag chair, a spinner of picture books and a wooden rocking horse that had once been Charlotte's. Rubbing his chin, he scanned the bookshelves, looking for action-packed adventure stories. For Travis, he found a book about a boy who was a dyslexic Greek demigod. "This series is really popular and the vocabulary isn't too tricky."

For Jamie, he found a book about Formula One, packed with facts and photographs of sleek cars and famous drivers. "A lot of boys prefer nonfiction," Simon said. "Including me."

"They're worth a try," Liz said, taking the books from Simon.

But he wasn't done yet. Simon got out a copy of *The Hobbit.* "This would be a great book to read aloud to them—the battle scenes are epic."

Liz frowned. "Aren't they too old for bedtime stories?"

"I read to my daughter for years," Simon replied. Between them, he and Nora had read Charlotte everything from the complete works of Beatrix Potter to *The Chronicles of Narnia* and every book in the *Northern Lights* trilogy—twice. The day that Charlotte had decided—well into secondary school—that it was too embarrassing to be read to by her parents, Nora had cried. Although Simon had remained dry-eyed, he knew exactly how she felt. Those evenings with his daughter snuggled up next to him, a book on his lap, were some of the most precious moments of his life.

So Simon had suggested that he and Nora keep up the habit

of reading aloud to each other, taking turns to choose the book. They were currently halfway through *All Creatures Great and Small* (Simon's selection), and were enjoying making each other laugh with their rubbish Yorkshire accents.

"People of all ages love listening to stories," he told Liz. "That's why audiobooks are so popular."

"But isn't that cheating?"

"The main thing is to get your boys to love reading. Once they realize that it's a pleasure, they'll want to read themselves."

Holding the pile of books to her chest, Liz followed Simon out of the children's section. On the way to the till, she stopped abruptly in front of the cookbook display.

"Oh!" she exclaimed. "I need this." She began to leaf through *Foolproof Christmas Dinners* by a popular TV chef.

"Are you cooking for many this Christmas?" Simon asked as she studied a recipe for Brussels sprouts and bacon.

To his surprise, Liz burst into tears.

Simon dug into his shirt pocket and took out a clean white handkerchief. Charlotte and Nora teased him about his old-fashioned hankies, which he always carried on him—a rule enforced by his mum that he'd been unable to break. But they often came in handy. He offered the handkerchief to Liz.

"I'm so sorry," she said, dabbing her eyes on the soft cotton.

Simon sat down on the sofa and patted the seat next to him. "Now I'm guessing this isn't just because you really hate Brussels sprouts."

Liz sat, and blew her nose on the hankie. Taking a shaky breath, she said, "I'm not cooking for anyone this Christmas. My husband and I split up a few months ago. I've got the boys most of the time, but my ex has them every other weekend. We agreed to share holidays and he's got them for Christmas this year."

"That's tough," Simon murmured sympathetically. He would

have hated to spend Christmas apart from Charlotte when she was little. It was going to be hard enough spending it without her now that she had left home.

Liz's eyes welled up again. "I can't believe the boys won't be waking me up at the crack of dawn to open their presents. Christmas is going to be so lonely without them."

"Do you have any other family locally?"

Liz shook her head. "My family's scattered all over. My ex's family live in Milton Keynes, where we used to live. But when we split up we had to sell our house. I bought a cottage in Stowford for a fresh start. I thought it would be easy to get to know people in a small village, but I was dead wrong about that. I work from home, so I haven't really met anyone here at all." She gestured to her carrier bag. "Unless you count the cashier at the corner shop."

"I found it tricky to meet people when I first moved here, too." Locals had initially been suspicious of Simon and his "fancy London ways." Over the years he'd made lots of good friends, but he hadn't entirely shed his outsider status. Over twenty years on, some locals *still* considered him a newcomer.

"I've joined the Stowford Friends group on Facebook," Liz said. "I've made lots of 'friends' online, but I haven't actually met any of them. Wouldn't know them if I bumped into them on the high street."

"It's not the same, is it?" Simon said. These days, whole relationships could be carried out online. Simon knew what his brother was up to thanks to holiday pics and updates about his nephews' sporting achievements on Facebook, but he hadn't seen Daniel in person for months. Online "likes" were no substitute for real human connection.

"We hold a monthly book club here," Simon said. "Why don't you come along to our next meeting? It would be a great way to meet some people, in the flesh."

"Between work and the kids I don't have a lot of free time for reading," Liz said. "I might not get through the book in time."

"That needn't stop you from coming." Simon chuckled. "I swear half our members only come for the wine and the gossip."

"It's difficult for me to get out in the evenings, because I can't leave the boys without a sitter."

"How are they doing with all of this change?" Simon asked.

Liz twisted the handkerchief anxiously. "They've been having a hard time adjusting. They miss their dad, and their old friends."

"It's early days," Simon said. "Kids are very adaptable. I'm sure they'll settle in soon. The village school is great."

"I really hope so. My parents went through a messy divorce, and I always swore I'd never put my own kids through one. Steve and I tried to make it work—marriage counseling, the lot—but in the end we decided we were better off apart." She bit her lip and tears welled up again. "I feel so guilty."

"Hey, don't beat yourself up," Simon told her. "Try not to focus on what you've lost. It's about making the most of what you *do* have."

Liz nodded. "I've got the boys on Boxing Day and I want to make it really special for them. But Steve, my ex, used to do all the cooking. I can do fish fingers, jacket potatoes, beans on toast, easy things like that—but I've never actually cooked a Christmas dinner. That's why I need a cookbook."

Simon thought about the quirky Christmas dinners Nora had shared with her mother. "I'm sure Travis and Jamie will be happy with whatever you serve. The important thing is that you'll be together."

"I know," agreed Liz. "But still, I'd like to get better at cooking. It will give me something to do on Christmas Day, to distract me from missing them."

"Well then, this is the one I'd recommend," Simon said, going over to the table and picking up a classic cookbook. "My wife swears by it—especially the Christmas pudding."

Liz sniffed the air. "If her cooking tastes as good as it smells, that's quite an endorsement."

Simon leaned over and pushed the plate of biscuits toward Liz. There were still a few left. "See for yourself—these are her famous ginger biscuits."

"No, thanks," Liz said. "I should probably get going—I've got loads of chores to get on with while the boys are at their dad's." She looked down at the bunched-up hankie in her hand. "I'll wash this and bring it back soon."

"You don't need an excuse to pop in. I'm nearly always here, so come in anytime you need some company. I know Nora will want to meet you, too."

Simon carried the children's books and the cookbook over to the till. After ringing up Liz's purchases, he slipped an invitation into her bag. "I hope you'll come to our Christmas party," he said. "It's always a great evening."

"But I won't know anyone," Liz said.

"You'll know me," Simon said, smiling.

"That's true," Liz replied, waving goodbye as she left the shop with one more friend than she'd had when she came in.

Talking about Stowford Friends had reminded Simon that he hadn't updated the bookshop's social media accounts yet today. He went back to the office, sat down in front of the computer and signed into the shop's Twitter account. It had nearly two thousand followers, and Simon's tweets—book recommendations and humorous observations about the day-to-day life of a rural bookseller—garnered lots of "likes." But the social media account didn't seem to translate into book sales in the way he'd hoped it would. Or maybe people *were* buying the books he tweeted about, just not from the Stowford Bookshop.

He posted the picture of Nora and Arnold with the message: *Sold after twenty-five years on the shelves in @StowfordBookshop! Never give up hope #happyending.*

Simon scrolled through his Twitter feed idly, trying to think about what else he could post that might drive people to the bookshop's website. *Maybe a competition*, he thought. Those had always worked well back in his advertising days. They could give away some of those copies of *The Oculist of Leipzig* that they didn't seem to be able to shift . . .

As he scrolled through tweets from people he'd never met, he realized how lucky he and Nora were to have so many good friends in the village—Alice and the other shopkeepers, all his mates from the pub quiz, and even Howie. He thought about Liz, and how lonely she had seemed. There were probably lots of other people in the village feeling just as lonely as she was. If only there was something he could do to reach out to them. To give them hope. He looked at the picture of Nora and the old man again and, inspired, began to type.

> Do you know anyone in Stowford who could use a random act of kindness? We are giving away six books to anyone who needs a bit of hope this festive season. Send us a private message with the name and address of your nominee by midnight tonight. Happy Christmas from the Stowford Bookshop!

Simon clicked SEND, and the message went whooshing off into cyberspace.

7

SIMON

The tantalizing smells wafting down from the flat were making Simon's stomach rumble. He checked his watch and saw that it was past six o'clock. Time to close up shop.

He emptied the till and counted up their takings for the day. A grand total of 1,200 pounds. Not good at all. Simon sighed deeply. A few years back, the shop would have easily turned over close to 4,000 pounds on a Saturday before Christmas. He knew their balance sheet couldn't be looking very healthy . . . But after getting the blow about Charlotte not coming home for Christmas, this probably wasn't the best time to ask Nora about it. He was determined to be cheerful for her sake.

Stowing their cash in the safe in the back room (an unnecessary precaution, given Stowford's almost nonexistent crime rate), Simon took Merry outside for a wee, then locked the front door, switched off the lights and headed upstairs, the terrier's nails skittering on the wooden stairs.

"Honey, I'm home!" he called out, in a parody of a fifties sitcom husband.

"Perfect timing," Nora said, her cheeks flushed pink from the heat of the kitchen. She'd tied her hair up in a messy bun, but a few curly tendrils at the front were making a bid for freedom. Nora slid a blue casserole dish from the oven. "I decided to make lamb hotpot."

"Smells absolutely delicious." Simon went over to the cupboard to get out two plates and noticed the apple tart cooling on the counter. "I was just bragging about your baking to a woman called Liz who recently moved into the village. She's finding it a bit hard to get to know people."

"Did you tell her about the book club?" Nora asked, setting the steaming hotpot down on the table.

"Of course. Gave her an invitation to the Christmas party, too." Simon rummaged in the cutlery drawer for matching cutlery, but gave up and settled for a random selection. Periodically, he tidied the drawer, putting every utensil into its proper place. But somehow dessert spoons always gravitated to the fork section, and the knives decided to hang out with the teaspoons. Some just vanished into thin air. The Case of the Disappearing Teaspoons was one of the great unsolved mysteries of life. Perhaps the nursery rhyme was right and they'd run away with the dish . . .

"Talking to Liz got me thinking about how many lonely people are out there," Simon said. "I decided to run a competition. People can nominate someone they know who's lonely this Christmas and we'll give away six books."

"That's nice," Nora said.

She didn't seem quite as excited about it as he'd hoped she would be. No doubt because she was thinking of who she'd be missing this Christmas.

Returning to the cupboard, he got out two wineglasses and opened the bottle of red Doug Jenkins had given him at the market.

He was half expecting her to object, because of his heart, but she just raised her eyebrow and said, "What's the occasion?"

Simon sniffed the wine—a decent merlot. "We're celebrating *The True Story of the Christmas Truce* finally finding a home."

Nora held out her glass for Simon to fill.

"To happy endings," Simon toasted.

"Hear, hear." Nora clinked her glass against his.

Simon tasted the wine and nodded approvingly. "That's not half bad."

The hotpot tasted even better than it smelled. The lamb was meltingly tender, and Nora had chucked in a medley of root vegetables. As they ate their dinner—Merry sitting under the table, hoping for scraps—Nora said, "I still can't believe we actually sold that book."

"Just goes to show," Simon said, taking a big swig of wine, "you should never give up hope."

"That's exactly what Arnold said to me."

"It's true," Simon said. Patting his belly, he grinned at Nora. "And right now, I'm hoping that there's something delicious for dessert."

"Well then, you're in luck."

As Simon cleared away the hotpot and dirty plates—scraping the leftovers into Merry's bowl—Nora brought out the apple tart and cut two generous pieces. "Apple pie counts as one of your five a day, right?"

"Absolutely," Simon agreed wholeheartedly.

"How's your forehead?" Nora asked, touching the bump on his head lightly.

"I bashed it again. Got to be some sort of record."

"Poor baby." Nora leaned down to give him a kiss, and Simon could taste the wine on her breath. Maybe there was even more than dessert to look forward to tonight . . .

Simon chuckled and put his arms around his wife's waist. "Good thing Charlotte isn't here—rutabaga for dinner, and her parents canoodling in plain sight."

Nora pulled away and sat down again, the playful light in her eyes extinguished as quickly as it had appeared. Simon could have kicked himself. *Idiot! Why did you go and mention Charlotte?* He needed to salvage the situation—fast.

Simon tipped the wine bottle over Nora's glass, but only the dregs were left. "Let's open another bottle."

"I don't think we've got anything else," Nora said. "Unless you count the cooking sherry."

"There's one bottle of the Châteauneuf-du-Pape in the loft." Every year for Christmas, Simon's parents gave them a case of wine from a vineyard in France they'd invested in, near their holiday home in Provence. It rankled Simon to admit it, but it was seriously good stuff—fruity and full-bodied. They usually saved it for a special occasion, rationing the bottles over the course of the year, but there was still one left and no doubt they'd get another crate in a few weeks' time.

Nora frowned. "I'm not sure—"

Not wanting her to mention his heart, Simon cut her off. "You only live once."

He pulled the hatch down from the ceiling, climbed up the ladder to the loft and switched on the light. The ceiling, too low to allow anyone to stand up, let alone someone over six foot tall, was crisscrossed with ancient wooden beams. Taking care not to bump his head again, Simon crawled along the rough floorboards. His hand landed in a puddle and he let out a yelp.

"Everything OK up there?" Nora called anxiously.

Looking up, he saw water dripping through a gap in the roof tiles.

"Just a spider," Simon fibbed. *I'll go to the salvage yard tomorrow,* he told himself. It would be a bodge job, but he had to do something to try to stop the leaks.

Breathing in the loft's musty, dusty smells, Simon shuffled along to the crate of wine. "Aha!" he called down to Nora. "Got it!"

As he shuffled back, he spotted a box of Christmas decorations tucked under the eaves. Popping the bottle of wine in the box, he pushed it along the floor to the hatch, then carried it down the ladder.

"What's all this?" Nora asked.

"I found a box of Christmas decorations up there—thought I'd get it down and save myself from making another trip up to the loft."

Nora opened the box and took out a lumpy angel made from of salt dough, with garish bright yellow hair. "Charlotte made this in nursery." She set the angel back in the box gently and sighed sadly. "I don't know how I'm going to get through Christmas without her."

"Hey," Simon said, taking her hands. "We've got to count our blessings. Charlotte might not be here this Christmas, but we have each other."

"You're right," she said, nodding. "We're so lucky compared to lots of other people—like Arnold and his family. His grandson will be spending Christmas in the hospital." She shook her head. "I can't even begin to imagine what they're going through."

"Even if we miss her, at least we know Charlotte's happy," Simon said. Their daughter had practically glowed with contentment on the video call. "And that's something to be grateful for." Blowing dust off the top of the bottle, he twisted in the corkscrew and pulled out the stopper with a satisfying pop. He poured the wine, so dark it was almost purple, into each of their glasses.

"To Charlotte," he proposed.

"To Charlotte," Nora echoed, touching her glass against his.

They sipped the wine. Cherries and blackberries, warmed by the Mediterranean sun, danced on Simon's tongue. The wine slipped down his throat like silk and had a peppery finish, giving it a rich, luxurious depth.

"Mmm." Nora sighed happily. "That's gorgeous. Your parents might have their faults, but they definitely know their wine."

They ate the apple tart and sipped their wine in companionable silence. When they'd finished the dessert, Simon fetched the copy of *All Creatures Great and Small* they'd been reading aloud to each other. "Ey up, lass," he said, in his best attempt at a Yorkshire accent. "Shall we read for a bit?"

Nora laughed. "Yes, but maybe we should read something Christmassy tonight. That might help me get in the mood." Grabbing the bottle of wine and their glasses, she said, "Let's see what we can find downstairs."

"We can put up some decorations while we're down there," Simon said.

After settling Merry onto her bed—a frayed tartan beanbag—Simon picked up the box of decorations and they went downstairs. He lit the fire, then put on some Christmas music. Mariah Carey's festive classic "All I Want for Christmas Is You" blasted out of the speaker.

"Charlotte loves this one," Nora said, holding her wineglass in one hand and dancing around the bookshop in her socks. She twirled, sipping her wine. "This reminds me of when I was a kid. Mum and I used to dance around the shop all the time, after shutting up for the night."

As "Baby, It's Cold Outside" began to play, Simon bowed gallantly and held out his hand. "May I have this dance, madam?"

"Oh, Mr. Walden, to what, pray, do I owe this honor?" Nora replied in an equally plummy voice.

Simon pulled Nora close and she rested her head on his

shoulder as they swayed to the music together. A movement caught his eye and he saw a group of young men peering in through the window at them, laughing and wolf-whistling. They were obviously on their way to the George for a night on the town.

"We're making a spectacle of ourselves," Nora said.

"Ah, they're just jealous," Simon replied, grinning. "I've already pulled the most beautiful woman in Stowford."

Nora danced over to the Christmas decorations box and pulled out a length of silver tinsel. She wrapped it around her neck like a feather boa, then stood on her tiptoes and gave Simon a kiss. "Come on—let's get decorating."

The wine and music certainly seemed to be doing the trick . . .

In between sips of Châteauneuf-du-Pape, Simon and Nora draped garlands of tinsel along the bookshelves and hung stockings from the mantel. As Simon placed a string of fairy lights around the counter, Nora set up an artificial Christmas tree that had belonged to her mum. Together, they hung ornaments from its branches—delicate glass baubles, little handmade snowmen and elves knitted by Nora, and Charlotte's creations from primary school.

"Too much?" Simon asked, hanging up the salt dough angel. It was so heavy the branch drooped under its weight.

Nora put a gold star on the top of the tree and stepped back. "Just right."

"So, what should we read?"

He threw another log on the fire as Nora browsed through the fiction section. Soon her arms were full of books—from *Little Women* to *A Christmas Carol*.

"I guess we're going to be reading all night," Simon joked.

"I can't decide," Nora said, setting the stack of books down on the coffee table. "There are so many good books about Christmas."

"What's this?" Simon asked, picking up a collection of short stories by O. Henry from the top of the pile.

"There's a Christmas story I love in this collection—I'll read it to you."

They settled down on the sofa, and Simon rubbed Nora's feet as she read "The Gift of the Magi" aloud. It was about a young couple determined to find each other the perfect Christmas present. The young woman sells her long hair, her crowning glory, to a hairdresser on Christmas Eve in order to buy a fancy fob for her husband's pocket watch. But on Christmas Day, she discovers that he has sold his watch in order to buy her a set of jeweled combs for the long hair she no longer has. The couple's love for each other was so deep that they had both willingly sacrificed their most prized possession.

Finishing the story, Nora shut the book.

"That's quite a twist." Simon sighed.

"They didn't call O. Henry the master of the surprise ending for nothing."

Simon reached over and gave a gentle tug on a lock of Nora's hair. "Don't get any ideas."

"I can't imagine anyone would pay much for my hair these days," Nora said, frowning as she examined a strand of silver in the firelight.

Still thinking about the story, Simon glanced down at his own watch. The chunky Swiss timepiece was a family heirloom—a gift from his grandfather on his graduation from Oxford—but he'd part with it in a heartbeat for Nora. Maybe if he pawned the watch, they could afford to repair the roof? Simon couldn't believe he hadn't thought of that before. He had no idea how much he would get for it, but it was an antique, so probably worth a few bob . . .

A stack of books on the prizewinners' table caught his eye. "Oh, by the way—I thought we could give away copies of *The Oculist of Leipzig* for the competition as we have so many of them."

Nora frowned. "Please tell me you're joking. That book is likely to make people feel even more depressed."

"Then what do you suggest?"

Nora thought for a moment, then she jumped up so quickly she almost knocked over her wineglass. "Christmas books!" she said, her eyes flashing with excitement. "We should give away Christmas books!"

8

NORA

Nora wasn't sure if it was the O. Henry story, or because the shop looked so festive, with the fairy lights twinkling away and the garland glittering on the bookshelves, or maybe it was just the effect of the wine, but she was finally feeling Christmassy!

When Simon had first mentioned the book giveaway she hadn't been very enthused. They were hardly in a position to be giving away books. But rereading "The Gift of the Magi" had made her realize that, even though the shop was on its last legs and Charlotte wasn't coming home for Christmas, they were still so much better off than many others. They had each other.

Besides, they might as well give away books before the bailiffs came to take them away.

Nora knocked back the last of her wine. "There's nothing more joyful than a good Christmas story, so that's definitely what we should give away if we're meant to be cheering people up."

Hopefully, by sending out some uplifting books, they would give people hope—or at least provide an entertaining distraction. Nora knew well how comforting a good book could be. When Penelope had been diagnosed with cancer, Nora had returned home from university. As she kept her mother company at her weekly chemotherapy treatments, she'd worked her way through Georgette Heyer's historical romances. To this day, Nora couldn't see one without smelling hospital antiseptic. But the Regency romances had been exactly the escape she'd needed to get through a difficult time.

Stop, Nora told herself. She wasn't going to dwell on the past. She was going to focus on the present—and how they could help people who were struggling *this* Christmas.

She held out her hands to Simon. "Come on, get up," she said, tugging him to his feet.

He let out a little whimper of protest. "Don't make me. The sofa's so comfortable . . ."

"We need to choose the six best Christmas books of all time. Shouldn't be too hard, right?" She rubbed her hands together in giddy anticipation.

"You've already made a start." Simon picked up *A Christmas Carol* from the pile of books on the coffee table. "This has got to be in there, obviously."

"That's a no-brainer," Nora agreed. "I cry every time Tiny Tim says 'God bless us, every one!'"

Simon chuckled, but his eyes were full of affection. "You are such a softie." He poured them each another glass of wine, draining the bottle. "First we need to fortify ourselves for the important work ahead."

Nora took a sip, the wine warming her belly and lifting the cloud of worry she'd been carrying around with her for months. "If I didn't know better, I'd think you were trying to get into my pants."

"The night is still young," Simon said, waggling his eyebrows suggestively.

Nora giggled. Taking Simon's hand, she led him into the children's section. "Let's start here. There's lots to choose from."

They stood in front of a table displaying Christmas stories and stocking fillers. There was Raymond Briggs's *The Snowman*, Dr. Seuss's *How the Grinch Stole Christmas!*, a gorgeously illustrated edition of *The Night Before Christmas* and a pop-up retelling of the nativity story.

"Aw . . . I love this one," Simon said, picking up *The Snowman*.

"Remember when we took Charlotte to London to see the ballet?"

Simon chuckled. "The thing she liked best was the light-up wand we bought her at the interval."

"And the chocolate ice cream, which she got all over her dress."

Nora picked up an illustrated collection of fairy tales and leafed through the pages. "Why are so many fairy tales set at Christmastime?" she wondered out loud. "There's 'The Little Match Girl'. . ."

"The Little Fir Tree," Simon countered.

"Isn't Oscar Wilde's 'The Happy Prince' set at Christmas, too?"

Simon nodded. "I think you're right."

"I suppose it's because it's the most magical time of year," Nora said. "At Christmastime, anything is possible." She flipped through the story of "The Elves and the Shoemaker," admiring the illustrations of the tiny elves sewing shoes from the pieces of leather the destitute shoemaker had left out on his workbench on Christmas Eve.

I wish elves would visit us, she thought, taking a swig of wine. Maybe they could work some magic and rescue the shop. Hell, she'd even settle for a new pair of shoes. It had been ages since she'd bought herself anything to wear.

Nora set the fairy tale collection back down on the table. This was real life, not a fairy tale. She could make all the wishes she wanted, but unless she had a fairy godmother she didn't know about, it wasn't going to get them anywhere.

"I think *The Lion, the Witch and the Wardrobe* is my favorite kids' book set at Christmas," Simon said.

"Oh, me too. I used to climb into the wardrobe and try to get through to Narnia." Nora remembered the silky feel of her mother's flowing, hippie-style dresses brushing against her cheeks, the musky patchouli perfume that Penelope always wore clinging to the fabric. After Penelope's death, Nora had squeezed into the wardrobe again, sobbing as she inhaled her mother's signature scent. Nora shut her eyes tight and took a deep, steadying breath as a wave of sadness hit her.

Another book by C. S. Lewis had helped her through the dark, lonely days after her mother's death. Nora's friends from university and various distant relations had come for the funeral at St. Stephen's, but once all that was over she'd found herself alone and overwhelmed by grief. *A Grief Observed*, which Lewis had written about the loss of his wife, had broken through Nora's isolation and pain. Lewis had described her suffering, and the ever-changing nature of grief, exactly. He understood that grief wasn't a linear process, for all the talk about its different stages. Despair can hit you out of the blue, Nora knew, months—even years—after losing someone you love. Just when you thought you'd accepted your loss, you suddenly wanted to rage at the universe. And he understood the fear of forgetting. *A Grief Observed* had helped Nora realize that moving on with her life wasn't a betrayal of her mother, but the best way to honor her.

She was never far from Penelope's memory in the shop. But right now, she was determined to focus on the happy ones. "Mum read me *The Lion, the Witch and the Wardrobe* when I was about seven, and I used to reread it every December. We should definitely send it to someone."

"We should probably chuck in a box of Turkish delight, too," Simon said. "I always used to crave it when the White Witch tempted Edmund." He smacked his lips. "Actually, I could murder a piece of Turkish delight right now . . ."

Nora suddenly found herself craving something sweet, too. "Hang on a second," she told Simon. Going into the back room she got the first aid box out of the desk drawer.

When she came back, Simon chuckled. "I don't think a craving for Turkish delight constitutes a medical emergency."

"Then I guess you don't want any of these." Opening the box, Nora took out a bag of chocolate buttons from among the bandages, rolls of gauze and an ancient tube of antiseptic.

Simon laughed. "You keep a secret stash of sweets in the first aid box?"

Nora thought guiltily about the other secrets she was hiding at the back of the drawer in an unmarked folder—the unpaid invoices and the final notices. But she pushed those thoughts away. "I guess it isn't a secret anymore." She tore open the bag and offered it to Simon. "I'll have to find a new hiding place." Grinning, she popped a button in her mouth.

Taking a copy of *The Lion, the Witch and the Wardrobe* with them, they headed out of the children's section, munching chocolate buttons.

"God, red wine and chocolate might be the best taste combination in the whole world," Nora said happily, letting a chocolate button melt on her tongue.

She stopped at the romance section. The shelves were heaving with festive love stories—couples meeting when the heroine tumbles on the ski slopes and finds herself spending Christmas at the chalet of the Prince of Snowdovia, or when the brooding boss draws the sassy new assistant's name in the office Secret Santa and discovers that he *does* have a heart after all. Their covers sparkled with foil, and they looked as sweet and inviting as a tub of Quality Street.

"I think we'd better give these a miss."

"I agree," Simon said. "They're revolting."

"Hey, don't be like that," Nora replied, nudging him. "I love a Christmas romance." But anyone spending Christmas on their own might not take much comfort from reading about a couple getting together underneath the mistletoe. They moved into the general fiction section.

"How about this?" suggested Simon, holding up a copy of *The Turn of the Screw.*

"You are joking, aren't you?" Nora said. "We're trying to help people—not give them nightmares."

"I'm totally serious," Simon insisted. "It's set on Christmas Eve. Ghost stories are a Christmas tradition. After all, what's *A Christmas Carol*, if not a ghost story?"

Nora shook her head. "We've already got one, so we don't need another. But we *could* include a mystery . . ."

"Which one?"

"Elementary, my dear Walden," Nora said, finding a copy of *The Adventure of the Blue Carbuncle* by Arthur Conan Doyle. "Spoiler alert—the jewel was hidden in the Christmas goose's crop."

"That's ridiculous. A goose doesn't have a crop," Simon said. "Chickens and turkeys do, but not geese."

Nora rolled her eyes. Trust her husband to know all about the digestive systems of poultry. He'd probably written a pub quiz question about it. "Only you would know something like that."

"Me and any good butcher," Simon said. "Speaking of which, we should probably place our Christmas order with Nigel soon. Should we have goose this year for a change?"

"The two of us can't possibly get through a whole goose."

"Speak for yourself. I'm sure we can find recipes to use up the leftovers. Goose pie . . . goose sandwiches . . . goose risotto . . ."

"Fine," Nora said, holding up her hands in defeat. "I'll order a goose from Nigel." She ignored the nagging voice in her head telling her that beans on toast would be more appropriate, given the perilous state of their bank balance. But Simon loved Christmas. If this was going to be their last Christmas in the shop, they'd better make it special. She went over to the window and gazed out at the butcher's shop across the quiet high street. Maybe Nigel Wilkinson would accept payment in books. She knew he was a fan of Tom Clancy novels.

Simon joined her at the window, putting his arm around her shoulders. " 'Twas the night before Christmas, and all through the house, not a creature was stirring, not even a mouse.' "

Nora smiled at him. "Oh, come on. We can do better than that." She tugged him over to the poetry section, which was possibly her favorite section in the whole shop. "There are so many good poems about Christmas. Auden's 'For the Time Being' . . . Milton's 'On the Morning of Christ's Nativity' . . . and I've always loved Christina Rossetti's 'Love Came Down at Christmas.' "

"Ah, but *this* is the ultimate Christmas poem," Simon said, pulling out a copy of *A Child's Christmas in Wales.* "Dylan Thomas is basically describing the sort of Christmas I dreamed about as a kid and never got—full of snow and fun and roaring fires."

"My mum had a recording of him reading it on vinyl," Nora replied, looking through the book, which had gorgeous illustrations by Edward Ardizzone. "I used to close my eyes and pretend he was my dad."

"Not sure you would have wanted Dylan Thomas as your father," Simon said. "He was quite the hell-raiser."

Nora rarely thought of the father she'd never met. For all she knew, he was dead. As a child, though, she used to pump her mum for information about him. But Penelope hadn't even known his surname—only that he was a drummer. She couldn't even remember the name of the band he'd been in. Nora would scour the sleeve notes on any album she bought, wondering if any of the drummers listed on it were called Neil. She'd fantasize about him turning up at the bookshop, explaining his long absence with amnesia or a shipwreck, like something out of a Shakespeare play—

"Shakespeare!" Nora cried, snapping her fingers.

"What about him?"

"We should include a Shakespeare play. This *is* Shakespeare country, after all."

Stratford-upon-Avon was less than an hour away from Stowford, and they went to see a show by the Royal Shakespeare Company a few times a year. Simon loved the history plays, of course, but Nora preferred the comedies. They always kept the plays in stock, because a lot of tourists who visited the Cotswolds were on the Shakespeare trail.

"How about *A Winter's Tale?*" Simon suggested. "It's not exactly Christmassy, but at least it's got a wintry title."

"Bit weird, that one," Nora said. "How about *Twelfth Night* instead? It's so funny, and Shakespeare wrote it as entertainment for the close of the Christmas season."

"'Some are born great, some achieve greatness, and some have greatness thrust upon them,'" Simon quoted.

Nora found a copy of *Twelfth Night* and added it to the pile of books in his arms.

"And others just have books thrust upon them," Simon said, sighing. He glanced down at the pile. "That's five—we just need one more."

"Hang on a sec," Nora said, before delving back into the fiction shelves. Would it be under *V* . . . or *D*? Running her finger along the spines, she finally found what she was looking for and pulled out a slim volume by Philip Van Doren Stern.

"*The Greatest Gift*," Simon said, frowning at it. "I don't know that one."

"Oh, it's so lovely!" Nora gushed. "It's about a man contemplating suicide on Christmas Eve. He meets a stranger and tells him he wishes he'd never been born. The stranger grants his wish, and then the man goes back to town and realizes that the people he loves would be a lot worse off without him in their lives—"

"This is sounding oddly familiar," Simon said.

Nora grinned. "That's because *It's a Wonderful Life* was based on it!"

One of their festive traditions was to make popcorn and watch movies together every night between Christmas and New Year's Eve. Simon's favorite was *Die Hard*, while Charlotte could quote whole chunks of *Elf* verbatim. Nora's go-to festive flick was *Meet Me in St. Louis* (even though some would—and did—argue that, strictly speaking, it wasn't a Christmas film). But they all loved *It's a Wonderful Life*. That one made *everyone* cry.

"It's a bit like the story we read tonight," Nora said. "The Jimmy Stewart character—he's called George Pratt in the book—has sacrificed his own dreams for the people he loves."

"And the gift in the title?" Simon asked.

"Life, of course," Nora said.

Simon checked his watch. "I set a deadline of midnight for the nominations. Think you can stay up a bit longer?"

Nora nodded. She'd passed beyond exhaustion and was getting her second wind. "Of course. Do you think we'll get many responses?"

"I guess we'll find out soon enough. I put it on all our social media accounts—and on Stowford Friends. What should we do in the meantime?"

"Let's wrap up the books."

They went behind the counter and Nora tore off six sheets of wrapping paper from the roll under the till, which was running low. *That's another thing I need to order,* she thought, adding wrapping paper to her mental list, alongside firewood and the Christmas goose. It would all have to go on her credit card.

"I'll fold, you tape," she told Simon.

Working together, they soon fell into a comfortable rhythm, with Simon supplying pieces of sticky tape before Nora even needed to ask for them. Soon, the books looked festive in their gold wrapping. There was just one problem—they all looked identical.

"Now we don't know which one is which," Nora said, hands on her hips.

"Well, we did say that these were *random* acts of kindness."

"True." All six books that they'd selected were uplifting and entertaining, so it didn't really matter who got what, did it?

Just then, the bells from St. Stephen's began to chime.

"It's midnight!" Nora exclaimed, clutching Simon's arm excitedly. "Let's see if we've got any messages!"

9

NORA

They hurried into the back room and Nora sat down at the desk. As she jiggled the mouse to wake the computer up, Simon opened the desk drawers and rummaged through them.

"What are you looking for?" Nora asked, trying to keep the alarm out of her voice. What if he found the bills she'd hidden?

"Just checking to see if you have any other sweets hidden in here."

"Nope," Nora said, distracting him with the last few chocolate buttons.

Simon pulled another chair over to the desk and quickly logged on to the shop's Twitter account.

Nora gasped and pointed at the envelope icon. "Look at all those notifications!" Heart pounding with excitement, Nora clicked on the first message, from an account she didn't recognize:

One of my students lost someone close to him and is having a very hard time.

Simon read the next message out loud:

My mate's a single dad who lost his job recently and seems
really down.

"Poor guy," Nora said sympathetically.

Despite the late hour, they read every single message they'd
received. Many were so heartbreaking, tears sprang to Nora's eyes.

My daughter just split up with her partner. She's convinced
she's going to be alone forever.

My neighbor suffers from anxiety and is finding it hard to
leave the house.

My colleague is far from home and really homesick.

Their in-box was filled with nominations from teachers concerned about their students, children worried about their parents
(and vice versa), spouses worried about their partners, colleagues
worried about their friends. Nora didn't think it was just because
they were giving away free books, though of course everyone liked
a freebie.

I've been feeling a bit down in the dumps, and a free copy
of the new Stephen King novel would really cheer me up.

"Nice try, cheeky." Simon chuckled.

But apart from a few chancers, most of the other messages
were sincere, and some were deeply worrying.

I think my dad might be having suicidal thoughts but he
won't talk about how he's feeling.

"I had no idea there were so many lonely and unhappy people right here in Stowford," Simon admitted.

"Well, you wouldn't, would you?" Nora said. "It's not the sort of thing people feel comfortable talking about." She thought about Kath, who'd looked so embarrassed when she came in to buy books on depression.

Although a few brave celebrities had spoken openly about their struggles with anxiety, or their battle with depression, Nora knew it was still quite hard for ordinary people—especially older people—to talk about their problems, especially when it came to mental health. Some people just didn't have anyone they *could* talk to. So people soldiered on, keeping a stiff upper lip, even when they were barely coping.

Nora was just as guilty of this as anyone else. When people asked her how she was, she didn't tell them the truth—*I'm missing Charlotte so much it hurts and the bookshop is in serious financial trouble.* No, she would be her usual cheerful self, pretending that everything was absolutely fine. *The bookshop's keeping us busy. Charlotte's having the time of her life traveling.*

Not lies as such. Rather a rose-tinted version of the truth, like the filters Charlotte put on her Instagram photos.

"I wish we could send books to all of these people," Nora said. "They *all* need a boost. How on earth can we choose only six of them?"

"It will just have to be random," Simon replied.

After they'd checked all their social media accounts for messages, Simon took a block of notepaper from the desk and wrote the name and address of each person who had been nominated on a separate piece. Nora fetched her knitted wool hat from a hook by the back door, then they folded up all the pieces of paper and put them inside the hat.

As Simon shook the hat to shuffle up the names, Nora sighed. "I can't help feeling bad for all the people who won't be getting books."

"At least someone cared enough to nominate them. That means that none of these people is totally alone."

Simon was right, but still Nora felt concerned. Stowford looked idyllic on the outside, but the golden cottages hid more secret sadness than she had ever realized. She'd always tried to make the bookshop a welcoming place for anyone who needed a chat, but if it went out of business, that support would be gone. She *had* to find a way to save it, even if it seemed like an impossible feat.

Arnold had said not to give up hope, so she resolved to cling on to her last tiny sliver of hope with all her might.

"Ladies first," Simon said, offering Nora the hat.

Her fingertips tingled with anticipation as she reached in, fished around, pulled out a piece of paper and unfolded it to reveal a name: *Mateo Ajose.*

"He doesn't sound very English," Nora said, showing Simon the slip of paper.

"He's American," Simon replied. "You'd recognize him—he's the young guy who works at the George."

Ah yes, Nora thought. She knew who he meant—a tall guy with a mop of curly brown hair and a smile that had clearly benefited from braces. His good looks and American accent made him hard to miss, though she'd never spoken to him properly.

Taking it in turns, they each drew out three names from the hat. When it was Nora's turn to pick the final name, she hesitated. "I'm going to cheat," she told Simon. "I know this is supposed to be random, but I really want to send a book to Olwyn Powell. She popped into the shop today and seemed down. She said she's really missing the children. Someone who touched so many lives as a teacher shouldn't be feeling lonely."

"Let's put an invitation to the Christmas party in with each book, too," Simon said. "A book can be a great companion—but I'm sure they could all benefit from some human company, too."

They put a book and an invitation into six padded envelopes, then set to work addressing them.

Nora scrawled Olwyn's name on the first envelope. She didn't bother with the address—she knew where the retired schoolteacher lived. Then she started on the next one—*Sampriti Patel.* Was that the chemist's daughter? She couldn't remember what the youngest one was called. She misspelled the name, so she had to scribble it out and start again. "This looks like it was written by a drunken sailor," she said, laughing.

"Well, I hate to point out the obvious, but—"

"Hey!" Nora protested, bumping her husband with her hip. "I'm not drunk. Just . . . tipsy."

"You keep telling yourself that," Simon said, grinning.

When they had finished addressing all the envelopes, he announced, "Time for bed."

"I'm not sleepy," Nora said. She was wired from all the messages they had received. She couldn't wait to give people their books. If it wasn't pitch-black outside, she'd deliver them right now!

"Who said anything about going to sleep . . ." Simon said, raising his eyebrow. Then he took Nora's hand and led her upstairs.

Nora woke to someone licking her face. Either Simon had the worst morning breath in the world or Merry wanted her to get up.

"No!" she protested, pulling her pillow over her face to shield herself from the dog's slobbery good-morning kisses.

Merry tugged the pillow off Nora's face and yapped, hitting Nora with another blast of dog breath.

"OK, OK, I'm getting up," Nora said. She fumbled for her phone on the bedside table and automatically checked her messages. Her stomach twisted with anxiety as she saw several voice messages on her phone from the unknown number that had rung her yesterday. She didn't need to listen to them to know what they were about. She scrolled down.

Nothing from Charlotte.

Sighing with disappointment, Nora sat up and dragged herself out of bed. She shoved her feet into her slippers and shuffled over to the window, drawing back the curtains.

"Whoa!" She squinted and shielded her eyes like a vampire whose coffin had just been pried open. After days of rain, the sun had returned with a vengeance, and the thick white hoarfrost covering the rooftops and the distant fields sparkled in its dazzling light.

Nora's head was pounding and there was a terrible taste in her mouth. She had a sneaky feeling that her breath was even worse than Merry's. Cupping her hand over her mouth, she breathed into it and confirmed her suspicions.

Pulling on her dressing gown, she shuffled into the bathroom. As she brushed her teeth she blinked at her reflection in the mirror. Her eyes were puffy and bloodshot, her hair Medusa-like and her complexion pallid.

Not a good look.

At least she didn't have to work today. The bookshop was shut on Sundays, as it always had been. Nora had been brought up with a pick-and-mix approach to world religions. Penelope had dabbled with different forms of spirituality, trying out Buddhism (long before anyone had heard of mindful meditation), taking Nora to a Quaker service (which went on so long she fell asleep), and briefly adopting Kabbalah (before Madonna made it trendy). But they had always attended the Christmas carol service at St. Stephen's. They both loved the pomp of the organ music, the bright, boiled-sweet colors of the stained-glass windows and the spicy scent of the incense. The only other Christian tradition Penelope had embraced enthusiastically was the idea of Sunday as the "day of rest."

Some of the shops on the high street opened on a Sunday, but Nora and Simon had always dedicated their day off to spending time with Charlotte, going on country walks, playing board games or just slobbing out in front of a film. *Maybe we should have opened on Sundays . . .*

No, even that wouldn't have made enough difference to their bottom line. Besides, by the time Sunday rolled around, they were both exhausted from working six long days in the shop. Even God had needed a break on the seventh day, after all.

Nora entered the kitchen just as Simon came bounding up the stairs, whistling the theme tune to *Match of the Day* and carrying the Sunday papers.

"No whistling," she grumbled.

"Looks like someone's hungover," Simon said, dropping the newspapers on the kitchen table and giving her a kiss.

"Coffee?"

Nora grunted in reply, trying not to wince as Simon clattered around the kitchen. The throaty gurgle of the kettle, the clunk of mugs hitting the countertop, the metallic clank of teaspoons seemed painfully noisy as Simon made their drinks; it was as if the percussion section of an orchestra had set up their instruments in her kitchen.

"Thanks," she muttered, as Simon put a steaming mug of coffee in front of her.

"And a chaser of paracetamol," he said, handing her two tablets.

After a few sips, her head started to clear. "Why aren't you suffering, too?"

"Years of practice," he replied, grinning.

In truth, neither of them were big drinkers. Simon usually limited himself to a pint or two at the George on quiz nights, and though Nora had overindulged as a student—boozy nights out in the student union dancing to indie rock—these days she didn't often have more than a glass of wine with dinner. Her pounding head reminded her why that was.

"I know what you need," Simon said, cutting her a thick wedge of leftover apple tart. "Stodge."

Nora's stomach churned. "Not sure I can face food this morning."

"Go on—take a bite," Simon coaxed. "You'll feel better for it."

Nora reluctantly took a bite of the tart. "Breakfast of champions," she said wryly, taking another bite.

"Hair of the dog a bit later?" Simon suggested. "We could go to the George and read the papers."

"I think I'd better focus on this dog," Nora said, patting Merry, who was sitting by her chair in case she decided to share her breakfast. "Merry needs a walk—and I could use the exercise."

Simon opened *The Sunday Times* and divvied up their favorite sections—Culture, Food and Travel for Nora, Opinion and Sports for himself. Neither of them bothered with the Business and Finance sections, apart from using the pages as tinder in the fireplace.

As Nora sipped her coffee, Simon made loud harrumphing noises as he read the Opinion section.

"What is it?" Nora asked eventually.

"Oh, just David Langdon's column," Simon said, lowering the newspaper. Nora glanced over and saw their local MP's byline photo smirking out at her. If gossip column rumors were to be believed, that smile was devastatingly effective at seducing interns and political aides—like the one he'd left his wife for.

"What's he on about this week?"

"Bragging about the government's new trade deal with China." Simon shook his head. "Says it will stimulate economic growth. Pity he doesn't care as much about economic growth in his own constituency."

Although David Langdon was a mainstay on television, oozing charm and confidence on current affairs shows, Nora had only seen him in person once, several years ago, when he'd opened the St. Stephen's school fete. He'd cut the ribbon, shaken a few hands and scarpered, disappointing the mums hoping the handsome politician would judge the cake competition. Langdon had been tipped as a future party leader but he'd been passed over in the recent leadership contest. Come to think of it, Nora hadn't seen him on television much recently—he was probably off canoodling with his latest conquest.

As Simon perused the Sports section, Nora opened up the main News section with a sense of trepidation. Since Charlotte had gone traveling, the world news was scarier to read than a horror novel. She scanned the headlines for reports from Asia. A political protest quashed in Taiwan . . . a terrorist attack in Cambodia . . . a typhoon in the Philippines . . .

"Oh no," she said. "There was an earthquake in Bangladesh. I hope Charlotte's OK."

"I'm sure she's fine. She was nowhere near Bangladesh when we last spoke."

Nora tried to push images of Charlotte buried under a heap of rubble out of her mind. She needed something else to occupy her thoughts—something more cheerful. "I'll deliver the Christmas books while I'm walking Merry."

"All right, Mrs. Claus," Simon said. "But be careful—the roads will be slippery."

"I will, *Dad*," Nora teased. "What are you going to do?"

"I'm going to pop down to the salvage yard and see if I can find some replacement roof tiles. I thought I'd try and fix the roof myself."

"Are you sure that's a good idea?" Nora asked doubtfully. When he'd helped her paint the flat when they were newlyweds, he'd somehow managed to get as much paint on himself as on the walls, which was why Nora had never suggested repainting them. The last time Simon had attempted DIY was when he'd put up a bookshelf in Charlotte's room. It had come crashing down in the night, narrowly avoiding crushing their sleeping daughter.

Simon kicked the plastic bucket next to the sofa lightly. "I've got to try something, unless this is a deliberate design statement?"

After Simon left for the salvage yard, Nora took a quick shower and got dressed, bundling up in a woolly sweater—her own creation, of course.

"Walkies!" she said, holding up Merry's lead.

Wagging her tail, Merry bounded over to Nora and danced around her legs excitedly.

"Steady on," Nora said, laughing. Merry was getting on a bit, but she moved surprisingly quickly when treats or walks were on offer.

Heading downstairs to the shop, with Merry following at her heels, Nora carefully placed the six mystery packages in a tote bag that read BOOKS ARE MY BAG. Then, pulling on her wellies and her wool hat, she slung the tote bag over her shoulder and stepped outside, inhaling deeply. The cold, crisp winter air cleared her fuzzy head the way the coffee and paracetamol hadn't quite managed.

Her breath coming out in puffs, Nora crossed the road to deliver the first package, for Mateo, at the pub. The George wasn't open yet, so she wandered down an alleyway to the rear entrance.

Merry whined hopefully as the aroma of roasting meat drifted from the pub's kitchen. Nora pushed the parcel through the letter box, then headed on her way down the high street.

Today the market square was empty, apart from the Christmas tree, and the only other people about were fellow dog walkers. Nora resisted the urge to pop into the newsagent's for some chocolate to replenish the "emergency" stash they'd depleted last night. *Must be healthy today*, she resolved. Although apple tart for breakfast wasn't a great start . . .

Nora and Merry progressed down the high street, where the shop windows were all decked out for Christmas, with fake snow sprayed on the panes. The antiques shop—Attic Treasures—had put its toy train up in the window, the locomotive chugging around a model village enrobed in cotton-wool snow. Charlotte had been enthralled by the train as a toddler, standing for ages with her nose pressed to the glass, as Nora impatiently stamped her feet to keep warm. *If only I'd known how quickly time was going to fly by* . . . It seemed like just yesterday she'd been standing there, holding her daughter's tiny, mittened hand.

Nora passed Seb Fox's estate agency and a listing in the window with a big red SOLD stamped across it caught her eye. It was a fairly ordinary cottage, but the asking price was an eye-wateringly large amount of money. On a morning like this, it was easy to understand why people were so keen to live in Stowford. Blanketed in frost and glowing in the morning sunshine, the high street looked picture-postcard perfect in its golden glory. Nora couldn't imagine living anywhere else.

You might have to, she told herself, remembering the voicemails she'd ignored.

She glanced across the street at the bank and resolved to speak to Hugh Wright about extending their loan or taking out a new line of credit. Bleak as their finances seemed, there *had* to be some sort of solution. Surely the bank wouldn't want to see a long-time local business go under. It wouldn't be good for the village to lose its only bookshop, and there wasn't another independent one for miles.

The next address wasn't one she recognized, but a quick check of her phone told her it was in a row of cottages just over the bridge. As she approached the right one, she could hear cartoons blaring from the front room. Nora pushed the parcel through the letter box and it dropped to the floor on the other side with a thud.

"Dad!" she heard a child's voice call. "The post's come!"

"But it's Sunday," a man's voice answered back.

The curtains in the front room twitched, and Nora scurried away, not wanting to be seen.

She and Merry set off again, the tote bag a bit lighter now. The war memorial, a faded wreath of poppies resting at its base, stood on a little island that marked the end of the high street. On one side of the intersection was a small church with a square tower, a spectacular stained-glass window in the nave. St. Stephen's was the oldest building in Stowford, dating from medieval times, though Nora couldn't have said when exactly (dates were Simon's forte, not hers). Rousing organ music floated out; the ten o'clock service was just beginning. Humming along to the hymn, Nora walked past the churchyard, where her mum was buried, and the vicarage. A bit farther on, she paused by the familiar gates of the school.

From the outside, the Victorian brick building didn't seem to have changed a bit since she was a pupil there. She knew, of course, that the chalkboards had been replaced with whiteboards, but when she had attended parents' evenings and school assemblies, perched on too-small plastic chairs in the school hall, Nora just needed to close her eyes and the smell of the waxed floors, PVA glue and overcooked vegetables took her straight back to her own school days.

Gazing out at the playground, hopscotch markings painted on the squidgy rubber surface (that was another thing that had changed—knees skinned on hard asphalt had been a badge of courage), Nora thought of all the afternoons she'd waited there with Merry to greet Charlotte with a hug and a snack. Full of warm memories, Nora pictured her pinafore-clad daughter rushing out of school, socks bunched around her ankles, hair slipping out of its ponytail and her latest junk-model masterpiece clutched in her hand.

Merry whimpered mournfully. "I know, sweetie," Nora said, patting her head. "You miss her, too."

Merry was Charlotte's dog, really. When she'd started school, and realized that most of her classmates had siblings, Charlotte had been desperate for a baby brother or sister. That being impossible, they had adopted Merry instead when Charlotte was eight. From the moment she'd found Merry under the tree on Christmas morning, a red bow around her fluffy white neck, Charlotte and her dog had been inseparable. Taking out her phone, Nora snapped a picture of Merry and sent it to Charlotte with a message:

Someone's missing you. Xxx

Then, tugging gently on Merry's lead, Nora carried on to Olwyn Powell's cottage, a short distance from the school. Two cats sat in the window, glaring at them through the glass. Nora strode up to the front door, not bothering with stealth because she knew that Olwyn—a soprano in the choir—would be at church. Admiring the beautiful wreath made of holly and pine on the door, Nora posted the third parcel through the letter box.

Halfway done.

She almost wished she could hide behind the shrubs and spy through the window to see Olwyn's reaction when she came home and discovered her package. Nora had always gained as much pleasure—more, even—from giving gifts than from opening her own presents. But she didn't want to get arrested for being a Peeping Tom, and she still had three more books to deliver.

Their next stop was a quiet cul-de-sac on a modern estate on the outskirts of the village. Simon thought the modern town houses were eyesores, but Nora thought they looked quite smart. *And their roofs probably don't leak*, she thought, wondering how Simon was getting on at the salvage yard.

She approached the house the parcel was intended for. Its front garden was unkempt, and—unlike the rest of the houses on the street—there were no Christmas lights or decorations. The front door opened and a teenage boy with ginger hair came out, wearing only a hoodie despite the cold. "I'm going out!" he shouted, slamming the door behind him. He pulled up his hood, picked up the bike that had been cast aside on the unmown lawn and pedaled past Nora, scowling.

Was this Harry Swann, the recipient of the package in her hand?

Nora tiptoed up the path, dropped the parcel through the letter box and hurried away. By coincidence, the next house was on the same estate, a few streets away. This one had neatly tended shrubs and an inflatable snowman in the front garden. Merry strained on her lead, her nose twitching as she picked up a scent. Someone inside was cooking curry, and it made Nora's mouth water, too.

Maybe I'll make a vegetable curry for lunch, she thought, posting the parcel through the door.

The last package was a bit of a mystery.

There was only an address, with no name. Presumably the occupant lived alone. To get to Yew Tree Manor, Nora and Merry strolled down a country lane, enjoying the birds singing in the hedgerows that lined either side of the road. The only traffic they passed was a tractor chugging along, a woman on a horse taking a morning ride and a runner who, if Nora wasn't mistaken, was the cute American guy who worked at the pub. Mateo Ajose. She smiled to herself as he sprinted past her, thinking of the surprise that awaited him when he got back from his run.

Yew Tree Manor was one of the oldest—and grandest—houses in Stowford, but Nora had never seen it up close before. It was hidden from the road by trees and hedges. She hadn't realized anyone actually lived there. The words PRIVATE PROPERTY—NO TRESPASSING were written underneath the house name. Ignoring the warning, Nora walked up the long, winding drive, her boots noisily crunching over the gravel.

So much for stealth . . .

At the end of the drive, a new-model Mercedes with tinted windows was parked outside an elegant Georgian house, flanked by carefully sculpted yew bushes. All the curtains were drawn.

Someone likes their privacy.

The house had ivy crawling up its walls and Greek-style pillars on either side of the door. She dropped the parcel through the letter box, half expecting a burglar alarm to start screeching, then made a hasty retreat.

Deciding to take a shortcut across one of Doug Jenkins's fallow fields, Nora climbed over a stile and let Merry off her lead. Merry shot off, yapping at two chestnut-colored mares on the other side of the field. The horses looked up briefly, then went back to their grazing, unconcerned by the little dog.

As she strolled back toward the village center, guided by the church tower in the distance, Nora noticed holly bushes growing on the edge of the field. Remembering how festive Olwyn's wreath had looked, she decided to gather some branches to decorate the shop.

She picked up a bough of holly that was lying on the ground, its scarlet berries vibrant against the glossy dark green leaves. "Bloody hell!" she cursed as the prickly leaves cut her hand. Nora sucked a drop of blood off her finger and tried to remember whether a lot of berries meant it would be a cold winter or a mild winter. She'd have to ask Simon when she got home—it was the sort of thing he would know.

When she reached the end of the field, she whistled and Merry ran back to her, muddy and panting. "You need a bath," Nora said, tousling Merry's ears, "and I need a cup of tea."

As they walked back along the high street, Nora spotted a woman with hennaed hair unwinding the awning above the Copper Kettle. Alice had obviously been hard at work all morning, as the windows displayed delicious-looking cakes, scones and muffins, arranged on tiered china stands.

"Nice buns," she teased her friend.

Alice turned around and grinned. "Very funny." But when she noticed what her friend was carrying, her eyes widened. "Oh, Nora! You can't come in here with that—it's bad luck to bring holly inside before Christmas Eve."

Nora chuckled. "Don't worry, I'm not coming in. Merry's too mucky."

"Seriously—don't bring that holly inside, Nor."

Nora rolled her eyes at her friend's superstition. Alice went in big for crystals and dream catchers and other New Age stuff. "I'll just have to take my chances."

She and Merry continued along the high street to the book-

shop. As soon as she got in, she arranged the bough on the mantelpiece, admiring how its bloodred berries gleamed like rubies.

"Gorgeous," she said with a satisfied nod. Alice's warning was
just an old wives' tale. Anyhow, she was in debt up to her eyeballs
and the roof was leaking like a sieve—how much worse could
things get?

10

OLWYN

As the organ pumped out the last bars of the closing hymn, Olwyn and the rest of the choir sang, "Rejoice! Rejoice! Emmanuel / Shall come to thee, O Israel!" It was one of Olwyn's favorite Advent hymns, and she let her voice ring out joyfully. She loved to see the church decorated for Christmas, with poinsettias around the pulpit, a nativity scene in front of the altar and pine garlands around the columns. From her position at the front of the church, Olwyn gazed out at the congregation. She'd taught at St. Stephen's for so long, she'd ended up teaching the children of many of her former pupils. As she looked out at the wooden pews, she recognized several children among the congregation.

There was Jamie Griffiths, sticking his tongue out at his brother, Travis, and trying to make him laugh. His mum, Liz, whispered in his ear and Jamie stopped fidgeting, but only for a moment. The family were newcomers to the village, but Olwyn had cast Jamie as Joseph in the carol concert. The kid was a born performer.

Jessica Jenkins, sitting with her parents and her three younger siblings, was back from university for the Christmas holidays. If

Olwyn's eyes weren't mistaken, there was a silver stud glittering in her nose. Her parents, Doug and Sandra Jenkins—both of whom Olwyn had taught—ran the biggest farm in the area.

Her eyes drifted to an empty pew near the back of the church, where the Swann family used to sit every Sunday morning, the mum and two children with their eye-catching ginger hair.

Such a tragedy.

Some people took comfort in their faith after a loss, while others turned away from it, questioning why a supposedly benevolent god would allow something so terrible to happen. The Swann family had obviously fallen into the latter camp, as Olwyn hadn't seen them at church since Emma's funeral. She could hardly blame them. It was hard to believe that Emma, whom she'd taught in primary school, was gone.

After the service, Olwyn joined the rest of the congregation in the church hall for biscuits and too-weak coffee served from a big silver urn.

"Lovely sermon, Pam," she told the vicar, dipping a custard cream into her coffee.

"Thanks, Olwyn," the vicar said. "How are rehearsals coming along?"

"Very well." Olwyn organized the annual Christmas carol concert—a mixture of music, seasonal readings and a little nativity play acted out by children from the school. "I've invited David Langdon, but his office still hasn't got back to me." She invited the MP every year, but he never came.

"It really would be a Christmas miracle if he turned up." The vicar chuckled before moving on to greet another parishioner.

Seeing Liz standing on her own, nursing a cup of coffee, Olwyn approached her with a cheery greeting. "How are you finding Stowford?" She leaned in and lowered her voice. "Apart from the terrible coffee."

Liz returned her smile. "It's lovely, thanks, Miss Powell. I hope Jamie isn't giving you any trouble at rehearsals."

Olwyn glanced over at her leading man, who was trying to stuff a whole digestive in his mouth in one go. "He's certainly full of beans."

"Thanks for giving him a chance. He's struggling a bit at school, so it's nice for him to feel special."

To Olwyn, all children were special, each in their own unique way. A good teacher recognized each of her pupils' talents and gave them all a chance to shine. "He's going to be wonderful," she said. "And Travis will be a great shepherd."

"Oh, dear," Liz said, as Jamie attempted to cram a second digestive in his mouth. "I'd better go before he chokes to death."

"Miss Powell!" Jessica Jenkins exclaimed, wrapping Olwyn in a hug.

"How are you enjoying university?" She vaguely recalled that Jessica was studying somewhere up north. Olwyn and her former pupil chatted for a while about how she was enjoying her chemistry course at Durham University.

"If it wasn't for the fun science experiments you did in class," Jessica said, "I probably wouldn't be studying chemistry today."

Olywn beamed. It was always nice to hear that she'd made a difference in someone's life. Teaching was a demanding profession, and it had got tougher and tougher over the years, thanks to impossible Ofsted targets and budget cuts. But comments like Jessica's made it all worthwhile.

Olwyn mingled with other friends from the parish, and, after everyone had drifted off to pub lunches, soccer matches, homework and other Sunday pursuits, helped tidy up—cleaning out the coffee urn and washing up all the mugs and teaspoons.

"Thanks so much, Olwyn," the vicar said, as Olwyn finished drying the last mug. "I don't know what we'd do without you. I can finish up here—I'm sure you've got other things to be getting on with."

"It's no trouble," Olwyn replied, reluctantly putting on her winter coat. There was a brooch shaped like a reindeer on it with a nose that lit up and flashed when you pressed it. The children at school had adored it.

The truth was she didn't have anywhere else to be.

At her retirement party in July, everyone assumed that Olwyn would be thrilled about quitting teaching, especially as she had carried on long after the normal retirement age. She'd said it was because the school had trouble recruiting new staff, but in truth she would have happily carried on forever if she could.

"You'll be glad to be shot of this place," her colleagues said.

No more early mornings.

No more marking papers and writing reports.

No more dealing with difficult children (and their even more difficult parents).

But Olwyn missed all of it—even the bad bits.

"You can travel now," her colleagues had urged her. "Do the garden. Finally enjoy some me time."

Me time? Olwyn didn't even know who she was anymore. Teaching had been her entire life. Without it, she was . . . nobody.

She'd known she wanted to be a teacher ever since she was a little girl, forcing her younger sister and all their teddies to play school and sit through her lessons. Though she'd never married, Olwyn had never felt lonely because her job gave her so much satisfaction. She hadn't had children of her own, but she cared deeply about each and every one of her pupils—even the challenging ones, like Jamie, were precious to her. It was so rewarding when you finally got through to a child and saw that spark of intellectual curiosity ignite in their eyes. But she didn't just miss the children, she missed the sense of purpose teaching gave her.

As she trudged home from the church to her cottage, she had no idea how she was going to fill the rest of the day, let alone the rest of her life. The only thing she had waiting for her at home was a Marks & Spencer's ready meal for one. She made her way up her front path. Her hedges were perfectly trimmed, and there wasn't even a leaf out of place. Her garden had never looked better, but there was only so much pottering one could do—especially at this time of year.

She unlocked the front door, momentarily cheered by the sight of the wreath she'd made from evergreens in her garden. The moment she stepped inside, the cats started purring and rubbing their heads against her legs. "Hello, Tommy," she said to the ginger one. "Hello, Tuppence," she greeted the tortoiseshell. Having overcome her reservations about conforming to the cliché of a spinster with cats, Olwyn had adopted them from a pupil whose barn cat had had a litter of kittens. She'd named them after her favorite Agatha Christie detectives and doted on them to an embarrassing degree. Crouching down to stroke them, she noticed a parcel on the floor.

She picked it up and peered at the writing on the padded envelope. Her name was hastily scrawled. (Back in her teaching days, she would have reprimanded her pupils for such messy handwriting.) The parcel had no stamps on it, and it was Sunday, so it had clearly been hand-delivered.

Opening the door again, she noticed muddy pawprints on her path, too big to be Tommy's and Tuppence's. Whoever had delivered the mystery parcel had had a dog with them.

Hmmm . . . curiouser and curiouser.

Going back inside, Olwyn tore open the padded envelope and drew out a gift-wrapped parcel. *Oooh! It feels like a book.* She ripped off the paper eagerly and found a copy of *The Adventure of the Blue Carbuncle* inside.

There was no return address, but tucked inside the book was

an invitation to a Christmas Eve party at the Stowford Bookshop. Unless she was beginning to go doolally (and that was certainly a possibility now that she was seventy), she hadn't ordered the book herself. It must be a gift.

How kind, thought Olwyn, *whoever sent it.*

Well, she did love a mystery! It had been ages since she had read a Sherlock Holmes story, but she'd always had a soft spot for the pipe-smoking, cocaine-sniffing, violin-playing detective. She wished she could summon him now, so she could work out who to thank for the book. But, in Sherlock's absence, she settled down in her favorite armchair, with Tommy on her lap and Tuppence resting along the back of the chair, and began to read.

WILL

"DADDY!" Adam shouted over the blare of CBeebies in the living room. "Julia pinched me!"

Will groaned and rolled over in bed. Glancing at his alarm clock, he saw that it was already past ten. Not that he had been asleep. He'd woken up before dawn and couldn't fall back asleep as worries spiraled through his head, spinning round and round in endless circles. It was ironic—for the first time in his adult life he could lie in, but he was getting less sleep than ever before.

Julia barged into the bedroom and sat down on his bed cross-legged. "Daddy, there was only one portion of Coco Pops and Adam ate it, even though he knows I hate cornflakes."

Her twin came into the bedroom—his fair hair was tousled and he had chocolate stains around his mouth. "Own-brand cornflakes are gross," he said. "Besides—I'm the oldest."

"By two minutes!" Julia said, the glare in her blue eyes partly obscured by her shaggy blond fringe.

I really need to give her a haircut. The last time, he'd cut Julia's fringe too short and she'd complained that all the other girls in her class got their hair cut at a salon. But when he'd looked into booking an appointment at Shear Bliss on the high street, he was shocked to find out how much a ladies' haircut cost. Until he found a new job, Julia would either have to grow out her fringe or put up with his haircuts.

Maybe I should add hairdressing to my CV . . . He definitely needed *something* to give him an edge against candidates who weren't single parents to six-year-old twins. He'd been looking for a job for three months and had only had two interviews—both for jobs he was overqualified for. Not that it helped, as he didn't get either of them.

It wasn't that he was being too fussy, there just weren't many opportunities in this quiet corner of the Cotswolds. Some friends had suggested that he move to a bigger town—Cirencester or Gloucester—where there would be more jobs, but the twins loved their school and his mum was in a home in the village. He couldn't uproot them all and start again somewhere new.

When his boss had called him into his office a few months back, Will had naively assumed he was going to be offered the promotion to deputy manager he'd been after. He'd worked at Jamison's Pork Products, on the outskirts of Stowford, since leaving school, working his way up from the production line to quality control supervisor. He'd never intended to stay there as long as he had. As a kid he'd dreamed of being a professional soccer player. But while making sausage rolls and chipolatas wasn't quite playing for the Premier League, Will *did* feel like he was part of a team. His colleagues were friendly, Mr. Jamison was a fair employer, and Will took pride in doing a good job and staying calm, even when things got stressful on the production line. When the twins had started school, the flexible shifts and short commute had suited him. He dropped them off early and was finished with work by 3 p.m., just in time to collect them from St. Stephen's.

But instead of getting promoted to manager, Will had been made redundant.

"We brought in some management consultants and they told us to cut some of the less profitable production lines," Mr. Jamison had explained regretfully. "I'm sorry to lose you, Will, but we're struggling to stay afloat. Too many people going veggie these days . . ."

Will was one of those vegetarians now, though not by choice. Meat was expensive, so he was eating a *lot* of baked beans.

"Why don't I make you some toast." Will pushed the duvet off himself, the faintly sour smell reminding him that he needed to wash the sheets, and got out of bed. He rooted around, looking for a clean pair of jeans. *I'll do some laundry on Monday—that will kill a bit of time.* The hours while the kids were at school dragged, without the routine of work giving the day structure. There was nothing to do but surf the Internet for job ads and watch daytime TV. Will was ashamed to be seen around the village when he should have been at work, so he stayed indoors, avoiding other people and feeling like a loser.

Redundancy hadn't just cut off his salary—he felt like his balls had been chopped off, too. Not that he had much use for them these days . . .

Going into the kitchen, he stuffed bread into the toaster and made himself a cup of tea.

"Can we go somewhere fun today?" Julia asked.

"Yeah," Adam said. "Like bowling or trampolining."

"Or the cinema," Julia added.

"And waste a day like today?" Will peered out the kitchen window at the sunshine. The kids had been cooped up indoors for days because of the rain, and they could all do with some fresh

air. Of course, the weather wasn't the only reason he was reluctant
to agree to their suggestions. Cinema tickets and trampolining
cost money, and Will's redundancy payment was nearly gone.
"How about we take a walk to visit Grandma?"

The twins groaned.

"She thinks I'm her little sister," Julia complained.

"She always calls me Will," Adam said.

"It's good for her to have company," Will replied. "We'll just
stay for a bit."

Will's mum had dementia. On a bad day, she didn't even recognize her own son anymore. He'd cared for her at home for as
long as he could, but two years ago she'd left the oven on while he
was at work and nearly burned down the cottage. After that, Will
had had to accept that he needed help. He was grateful for the
staff at the care home and popped in to visit his mum regularly.

"We can have hot chocolate when we get home."

"With marshmallows?" Adam bargained.

Will nodded, hoping they still had some marshmallows in the
cupboard.

As Julia munched her toast with peanut butter—cut into tri-
angles, not squares, the way she liked—she announced, "We need
to take our costumes for the carol concert to school tomorrow."

"We're shepherds this year," Adam said.

Will groaned. He had a secret theory that primary school
teachers devised these assignments just to torment parents. The
previous weekend they'd had to fashion two Viking ships from
the contents of their recycling bin for homework. Adam's and
Julia's creations had looked as if they'd barely make it across the
bathtub without sinking, let alone the North Sea. Will dreaded
World Book Day the way other people dreaded going to the dentist. Last year Julia had insisted on going as one of the monsters

from *Where the Wild Things Are*. At times like that, Will could have used a partner—ideally one with a talent for crafts.

The twins' mother, Oksanna, had been a colleague at the factory, a pretty Ukrainian girl who'd worked on the production line. They'd been seeing each other casually—drinks with the team in the pub after work, that sort of thing. When Oksanna had announced she was pregnant, Will had been shocked—but his surprise had quickly turned to delight. He'd always loved kids, and he liked the idea of starting a family while he had the energy to enjoy them. He and Oksanna didn't know each other very well, but Will was determined to make a go of it for the baby—or rather, as they found out at their twelve-week scan—babies.

Some of his colleagues had assumed that Oksanna had got pregnant to snare herself a British husband. That couldn't have been further from the truth. When the twins were only four months old, Oksanna had traveled back home to the Ukraine, telling Will that her father was in hospital. She was supposed to return a week later, but Will had never heard from her again. He'd tried to contact her repeatedly, but she obviously hadn't wanted to be found.

"Don't take it personal, son," his mother had comforted him. "Some women just ain't cut out to be mums."

Maybe she was right—perhaps Oksanna had left because she couldn't cope. Or maybe she'd just decided she didn't like England— or him—enough. After trying everything he could to track her down, including hiring a private investigator, he'd made his peace with the fact that he'd never know why Oksanna had deserted them, and focused on being the best parent he could be to Julia and Adam.

He'd learned how to plait hair from watching YouTube videos. He could cook a decent shepherd's pie and Bolognese. He never missed the twins' soccer matches or class assemblies, cheering loud enough for two parents.

"You're amazing," the mums would tell him at the school gates, as he handed the twins their lunch boxes. "I wish my husband was involved the way you are."

It wasn't as if he had much choice in the matter. Most days, he thought he was doing an OK job of solo parenting, but it was hard not to have someone to share it with. He'd signed up for Tinder and been on a few dates, but they never amounted to anything once he mentioned the kids. But until he'd lost his job, and with it his teammates, Will hadn't appreciated quite how lonely he was.

"Daddy—costumes!" Julia said, snapping him out of his reverie.

Will stared at his children across the kitchen table—Julia still in her unicorn onesie, Adam in his dressing gown. He thought for a moment, then stood up. *You've got this*, he told himself.

Will opened a drawer and took out a tea towel. Then he found some twine in a different drawer. He placed a tea towel on Adam's head and wrapped some twine around it to keep it in place. "Boom!" he said. "You're a shepherd."

"My dressing gown has pink polka dots on it," Julia moaned. "Shepherds don't wear pink."

"You can wear my dressing gown," Will said. Anticipating her next objection, he added, "Just roll up the sleeves."

"I can't wait for Christmas," Adam exclaimed. "I'm going to write my letter to Santa this weekend. I'm going to ask him for a new console. Ben from my class said he's getting one, too, so we can play together."

"I want soccer boots," Julia said. "And a new bike."

Will sat down again and sipped his tea, unable to look at his children's faces. There was no way he could afford consoles and bikes this year. He'd found a few bargains in the charity shop— a puzzle still in its plastic wrapping, a board game that looked brand-new—and had picked up some cheap chocolates in the pound shop. He hated to think of their disappointment come Christmas morning. He'd never been extravagant, but in previous years there had always been one big present under the tree. Adam and Julia knew money was tight, but they were still firm believers in Santa Claus. The only way to manage their expectations would be to ruin the magic of Christmas.

"You haven't opened your package yet, Dad," Julia said, putting her crumb-covered plate in the sink.

"What package?"

Julia rolled her eyes. "The one that came in the post."

Adam ran to fetch it and placed the padded envelope on Will's lap. "I bet it's a Christmas present for us," he said to Julia.

Not unless Santa's real, thought Will.

The envelope was too big to be the only thing he really wanted—a job offer—and he didn't recognize the writing on the envelope.

"Open it!" Adam urged.

Will opened the envelope carefully, so he could reuse it later, and slid out an object wrapped in gold paper. *Huh*, he thought in surprise. It really *was* a gift.

"Who's it from?" Julia asked.

"Maybe it's from Granny," Adam said. "She's always muddled up—maybe she thinks it's already Christmas."

"I don't think so." His mum barely knew what month it was anymore. "Do you want to help me open it?" Will said, offering them the mystery parcel.

The twins eagerly tore off the shiny gold wrapping paper, revealing a hardback picture book.

"*A Child's Christmas in Wales*," read Julia, carefully sounding out the words. As she held the book up for her father to see, an invitation slid out.

"A party!" Adam said. "Ooh—maybe there will be cake!"

Will took the book from Julia. It was beautiful—but he had no idea why someone had sent it to him. For a second he wondered if it might be from Oksanna. *No.* She'd walked out on them six years ago; she was hardly likely to start sending the twins Christmas presents now. In any case, his address had changed since they were together—he and the twins had moved into his mum's little two-up, two-down cottage.

"I like the pictures," Adam said, peering over Will's shoulder.

"Me too," Julia agreed.

"Why don't I read it to you now?" Will asked. Sunday was stretching out ahead of them. Their walk could wait.

So, they all snuggled up on the sofa—one twin nestled on either side of him—and Will read Dylan Thomas's famous Christmas poem aloud.

11

MATEO

"L ast orders!" Sue called, ringing the bell above the bar. The clang was music to Mateo's ears as he squirted a round wooden table with cleaning spray and wiped down the sticky, scuffed surface, the varnish worn away by the bottoms of pint glasses. He'd done a double shift, serving Sunday roasts since noon, and now that it was nearly ten thirty he was exhausted.

The George was what Mateo's fellow Americans would call quaint—a roaring fire, an original flagstone floor, horse brasses, hops and toby jugs hanging from the beams, and the day's specials written on a chalkboard above the bar.

As the last few drinkers drained the dregs of their local ale, the same golden hue as the pub's exterior, Mateo gathered up the empties and brought them over to the bar.

"Oh, Mateo," Sue rasped. She reached under the bar and extracted a padded envelope. "This came for you earlier. I've been meaning to give it to you all day but I kept forgetting."

Mateo set down the tray of glasses and took the envelope from his boss, his heart rate—usually a low sixty beats per minute thanks to his daily runs—speeding up with excitement.

Howie, who was propping up the bar, peered over at the envelope and let out a wolf whistle. "Gift from a secret admirer, eh, Pretty Boy?"

Mateo blushed, even though after working at the George for the past four months he should have got used to Howie's teasing by now. "It's probably from my agent," he mumbled.

The padded envelope had been hand-delivered, rather than posted, suggesting it had been couriered. With any luck, it contained a script. Mateo was itching to tear it open and see what part Bea was putting him up for. He'd heard rumors that the Globe was casting a new production of *Romeo and Juliet* . . .

"Oh, I forgot," Howie scoffed, "you're not just a waiter, you're an *actor*." He drew out the last word mockingly and smirked at Mateo, revealing a mouthful of yellowed teeth with more gaps between them than a jack-o'-lantern. Mateo's dentist back in Santa Barbara would not have been impressed. "Well, go on then," said Howie. "Aren't you going to open it?"

No way was he going to open it in front of Howie. If he didn't get the part, he'd never hear the end of it.

"Time to go home, Howie," Sue said, swatting him lightly with a bar towel that had the HOOK NORTON BREWERY logo on it.

"Go on—another half?" Howie wheedled.

Sue pushed up her sleeves, revealing a busty mermaid tattooed on her left forearm, and leaned over the bar. "I think you've had enough, mate," she said firmly.

"All right, I'm going, I'm going." Howie slid off his bar stool obediently, raising a hand in farewell, before heading out into the cold night.

The pub's landlady looked tough, with her cropped peroxide-blond hair and an earlobe full of piercings. She had to be, to deal with punters who'd had a few too many. But Sue had been a good boss to Mateo. She gave him one free meal a day from the pub kitchen and let him take time off to attend auditions.

Not that there had been many of those lately . . .

Mateo had come to the UK after winning a scholarship to study at the prestigious London Academy of Music and Dramatic Art. After three years of intensive movement classes, speech lessons, combat training and character work, he'd won the much-coveted role of Macbeth in the final year production. His performance had been widely praised—"Mateo Ajose dominates the stage with the leonine grace of an athlete and the brooding intensity of a young Derek Jacobi." (Not that he'd memorized the whole review or anything.) Afterward he'd had offers from several different agents, eventually signing with Bea Rosenstock. If all Bea's clients' awards and trophies had been melted down, there would have been enough metal to forge a life-size Oscar. She was the best in the business.

Mateo's tutors and classmates were convinced he was destined for stardom, that the name Mateo Ajose would soon be appearing in lights. Along with commissioning a new set of headshots, Bea had tried to suggest that Mateo change his stage name to something "a bit less ethnic, darling." But with an Italian-American mum and a Nigerian-American dad, Mateo was undeniably "ethnic." Equally proud of both sides of his heritage, he had no interest in hiding who he was.

When he'd signed with Bea, Mateo had thought his acting career was about to take off. So how was it that six months after his triumphant Macbeth, the only script he was having to memorize was the list of daily specials?

While the other actors at LAMDA dreamed of making it big in Hollywood, what Mateo, the only Californian in the group, wanted more than anything was to join the Royal Shakespeare

Company. He'd been obsessed with Shakespeare ever since playing Romeo his senior year in high school—the same year he was captain of the track team. When Bea had lined up an audition with the RSC for him, Mateo had been ecstatic.

He'd spent hours rehearsing his two monologues—Macbeth for the tragedy, of course, and Lysander from *A Midsummer Night's Dream* to show his flair for comedy. When the big day had finally arrived, he'd been nervous but thought the audition had gone well. Afterward, with time to kill, he'd decided to explore a bit more of the area. Holed up in rehearsal studios and dressing rooms, he'd barely set foot outside London in the time he was at LAMDA. So, he'd hopped on a train from Stratford-upon-Avon and ended up in Stowford.

He'd got the call from Bea while nursing a pint at the George. It was a no.

"They've gone in a different direction, darling . . ."

To his embarrassment, Mateo had burst into tears. Sue had provided a sympathetic shoulder to cry on and by the end of the evening, he had a job offer.

Just not the one he'd been hoping for.

"Nightcap?" Sue offered, pouring two half pints of Hobgoblin before Mateo had a chance to reply. The last few stragglers had left the pub and Mateo and Sue were alone. She clinked her glass against his and said, "Cheers, kid."

Perching on a barstool, Mateo sipped the foam off the dark brown ale.

Sue lit a cigarette and took a drag. As she exhaled, she drummed her chipped, blue-painted fingernails on the envelope expectantly. "So, this could be the one?"

Mateo knew Sue was just as curious about what was in the envelope as Howie was. But he wanted to be on his own when he opened it, so no one would see his disappointment if it wasn't what he was hoping it was.

"Hopefully."

But Mateo was beginning to lose hope. The first part he'd got after finishing drama school was playing Prince Charming in a kids' show at a theme park. He'd spent the summer shouting his lines over a cacophony of crying babies, carousel music and the crunch of popcorn. He'd consoled himself by remembering that it had been even worse for actors in Shakespeare's time, when groundlings would throw fruit at the actors. His next gig was as understudy in a fringe production of *Peer Gynt*. He'd hoped the lead would quite literally break a leg, but the guy had an iron constitution. Mateo had spent the whole run stuck in the dressing room, doing crossword puzzles and watching Netflix on his phone. But now he looked back at his time as an understudy almost fondly—at least it had been an acting job. Since then there had been nothing.

What made it even harder was that some of his mates from LAMDA were already making it big. One girl had scored a supporting role in the latest series of *Doctor Who*. Her face had been obscured by hideous alien makeup, but even so—it was television. His friend Alex, Macduff to his Macbeth, had just got cast in a new Jez Butterworth play. The last time Mateo had gone down to London for an audition, his mate's face had been plastered on posters lining the tube escalators.

"I don't know why I keep bothering, though. It's probably not going to happen for me."

"Hey—keep your pecker up," Sue told him, exhaling smoke (something that would get a punter thrown out of the pub). "But I'd be sorry to lose you, Mat. You're a bloody good worker."

I used to think I was a bloody good actor, thought Mateo, knocking back the rest of his drink. Now he wasn't so sure.

Unless the parcel contained a lifeline—his big break. Unable to resist opening it any longer, he made his excuses.

"Night, Sue," he said to the landlady, jogging upstairs to his room under the roof gables. As he unlocked the door, the smell of mildew hit him. The room was tiny and damp, and Mateo couldn't stand up straight where the ceiling sloped, but it was free—a perk of the job. To cover up some of the faded floral wallpaper, he'd hung up a poster from his graduation production of *Macbeth*, a brooding black-and-white picture of himself holding a dagger dripping stage blood.

Mateo kicked his running shoes out of the way. That was another good thing about living here—he had the mornings off, so he could run every day, rain or shine. (Rain, more often than not.) He'd grown to love the countryside around the village—the winding lanes, the meandering River Coln, the gently undulating hills and fields, where even in the depths of winter you could find greenery and hardy flowers in bloom. It was so different from the dry, sun-drenched landscape of Southern California, but no less beautiful.

Mateo was just about to tear open his package when his phone buzzed. Glancing at the screen he saw it was a video call from his mother.

"Hey, Mom," he said, as her beaming face filled the screen.

"Hi, sweetie," she chirped. "Hope I'm not waking you up. I always forget whether we're eight hours ahead of you or behind you."

"Behind," he told her for the millionth time. "I just got home from work."

"Good rehearsal?"

"Um, yeah." When he'd told her he was living in the Cotswolds, his mother had assumed that his audition for the RSC had been successful. She'd been so proud, Mateo hadn't had the heart to correct her.

"Are you sure you can't come home for Christmas, honey?"

"I wish I could, but I've got to work." *Plus, I can't afford the flights.*

"We're all going to miss you so much. We're finally going to meet Ciara's boyfriend and Langston's bringing his new puppy. Nonna's baked so many pizzelles we could practically use them to pave a path from Santa Barbara to London."

Mateo laughed, wishing it were true. His grandmother made the thin, anise-flavored cookies every year at Christmastime. When Mateo had been little he'd always helped her to make them, using a special waffle iron.

This would be the first time Mateo hadn't been home for Christmas, and he was absolutely dreading it. The rest of the family would take their usual walk on the beach on Christmas morning. While they tucked into Nonna's lasagna and his dad's famous jollof rice, Mateo would be eating leftovers from the pub, all by himself.

"I'm worried about you all the way over there on your own, hon."

"Don't worry about me. I've got loads of Christmas parties to go to."

It was only a white lie. Mateo *was* going to lots of Christmas parties—but he would be serving turkey and mince pies to drunken office workers wearing paper hats from their Christmas crackers.

"Sounds very glamorous," his mom said. She paused. "And will you be going to these parties . . . on your own . . . ?"

Mateo laughed. "I'm not seeing anyone, if that's what you're not very subtly hinting about." The only woman in his life right now was Sue, and she was gay.

"Well, you don't want to leave it too late to settle down . . ."

"I'm only twenty-six, Mom!"

Mateo had split up with Zoe, his university girlfriend, a few months after graduation, when she started law school on the East Coast. He'd hooked up with a few people (OK, lots of people) in drama school, but there hadn't been anyone serious since Zoe.

"That's not so young—I had your sister when I was twenty-six . . ."

"I'm focusing on my career right now, Mom."

"I'm just teasing you," his mother said. "I'm glad the acting's going so well. You're going to be a big star."

Some of his friends at LAMDA had faced disapproval from their parents over their career choice, but Mateo's family had always been totally supportive of his dreams. He was desperate to make them proud, but it was getting harder and harder to believe that it was going to happen.

His last audition had been three weeks ago—for a serial rapist in a gritty police procedural. Bea had broken the news to him over the phone. "Darling, I'm afraid they said you were just too handsome."

Rapists can't be good-looking?

It wasn't as if Mateo had particularly *wanted* to play a serial rapist, but it was so frustrating to be judged on his appearance rather than his performance. His classmate Zeke was a great actor but had acne-scarred skin and a prematurely receding hairline. He'd been told by their tutors with brutal honesty that his only future was as a "character actor." At the time, Mateo had felt grateful for being genetically blessed with leading man looks. And yet, while Mateo was channel surfing the other night, who had popped up on-screen, playing a anesthetist trainee on a popular medical drama?

Zeke.

Mateo definitely didn't feel like the lucky one anymore.

As his mom chattered on, about her work, his dad's attempts

to grow avocados in the garden and how the LA Lakers were doing this season, Mateo let his mind drift.

His tutors at LAMDA had warned Mateo and his classmates that the vast majority of them wouldn't succeed. "In a decade's time, only two or three of you will be making a living from acting," one of them had predicted. "This is a tough profession."

It was beginning to look as if Mateo wasn't going to be among the ones who made it.

He'd meant what he said to Sue—maybe it was time to give up. He could put the flight home on his credit card and move back in with his parents. Maybe get a job as a high school drama teacher . . . It didn't sound very appealing, but he wasn't exactly living the dream here, serving roast dinners and beer-battered fish and chips. At what point did a resting actor stop being an actor?

"I've got to go, honey," his mom said. "It's time for my yoga class. But before I go—is there anything you want for Christmas?"

Yeah, a decent part. He glanced down at his worn, muddy sneakers on the floor. "Maybe some new running shoes?"

After saying goodbye, Mateo picked up the package again. It was a bit strange that Bea hadn't rung him to let him know a script was coming. Then again, his agent was a very busy lady. She always seemed to be in a meeting when Mateo rang (or that's what her assistant claimed, to fob him off).

He opened the parcel and saw not a script, but a gift. But then, weirdly, when he opened the present, it *was* a script, or rather a play—*Twelfth Night*.

He looked inside the envelope for a note and found an invitation to a party at the bookshop across the road. So, it wasn't from his agent. He turned the invitation over in his hand, confused. Had Simon from the bookshop sent him the play because he'd mentioned he was an actor a few days ago? If so, that was kind of a weird thing to do—he barely knew the guy.

Mateo had been meaning to pop into the bookshop to buy gifts for his parents, but he'd missed the Christmas posting date for the US so he'd ordered them a gift basket online instead.

Mateo eyed the book warily. *Twelfth Night* was one of his favorite comedies. He'd always wanted to play the hopelessly romantic Duke Orsino. But he hadn't read a word of Shakespeare since getting rejected by the RSC.

He glanced up and caught sight of the *Macbeth* poster. His own eyes seemed to be challenging him: *Don't be a pussy.*

Picking up the book, he opened it to a random page, alighting on a scene between Sir Toby Belch and Feste. He laughed out loud at one of Feste's bawdy ripostes. Then, flopping down on his single bed, he turned back to Act I, Scene I, and started reading from the beginning, letting Shakespeare's words weave their magic spell.

"If music be the food of love, play on . . ."

NORA

On Monday morning, the bookshop was crammed full of so many buggies a passerby might have mistaken it for a nursery. Toddlers and their carers—a mixture of mums and dads, grandparents and childminders—were squeezed onto the sofas, armchairs and cushions on the floor, their little ones on their laps. Of all the events the bookshop ran, toddler story time was Nora's favorite. She loved to watch the children's faces light up with delight as they listened to a story.

"Today I thought we'd read a Christmas story," Nora announced to the children, standing in front of the fireplace. It was unlit, of course; the last thing they needed now was a lawsuit. "Because who is coming down the chimney soon?"

"Santa!" cried Joshie, the dinosaur-mad boy who'd come into the shop with his parents on Saturday.

Nora beamed at him. "That's right—Santa! Are all of you excited about Santa coming?"

The children nodded. One little girl, who looked around three, lisped shyly, "Thanta is going to bwing me a baby doll that weally goes wee-wee."

"I'm getting a train set," boasted a little boy in a THOMAS THE TANK ENGINE T-shirt.

"If you're good," his gran said.

"Well, I'm excited about Christmas, too," Nora replied. "But I'm going to read you a story about someone who *wasn't* very excited about Santa Claus coming. In fact, he hated Christmas so much, he decided to spoil it for everyone!"

Nora opened *How the Grinch Stole Christmas!* and began to read, holding up the pages so the children could see the pictures. She'd read the book so many times, she barely needed to look at the words. There was a fair amount of wriggling and squirming to begin with, but Dr. Seuss's rhymes soon had the children listening attentively. There were gasps of horror as Nora described the people of Whoville waking up on Christmas morning to find all their presents and decorations had gone.

When she'd finished reading the story and they'd all sung a few carols (like the Whos of Whoville), Nora served a plate of biscuits and rang up a few purchases, including three copies of *How the Grinch Stole Christmas!*

By eleven o'clock, the bookshop was empty again, the toddler brigade having headed home for lunch and naps. As usual after story time, the shop looked like a bomb had hit it. Nora tidied up, wiping the coffee table down with a paper towel, then yawned. She had only managed a few hours of sleep the night before.

Brushing biscuit crumbs off the sofa, Nora fought the urge to curl up on it and take a power nap. Simon had found some roof tiles at the salvage yard yesterday, and he'd gone to the DIY shop this morning to buy some other materials, so she was alone in the shop. Nora felt more than a bit nervous about the idea of him scrabbling about on the roof—especially with his bad heart—but he'd assured her that he knew what he was doing.

I need caffeine.

Nora popped up to the flat to make herself a cup of tea. As she came back into the shop, holding a steaming mug of Earl Grey and thinking she might get a bit of knitting done if the shop was quiet, the bell above the door jingled. Nora looked over, expecting it to be Simon, or a parent looking for a lost mitten or a favorite pacifier that had been left behind after story time. But to her surprise, two men stepped into the shop—an older, bearded one wearing a gray suit and holding a briefcase, and a well-built younger guy with a shaved head and a leather jacket.

Merry, who had been happily licking up biscuit crumbs from the floor, began to growl.

"I'm so sorry," Nora apologized to the men. "She's usually very friendly. I don't know what's got into her. Shh!" she scolded Merry. "It's OK."

Merry stopped growling, but her teeth were bared, white fur bristling.

That's odd. Merry normally greeted customers with curious sniffs and friendly licks, her tail wagging. Now, her whole body was tensed as if ready to attack, not that a little Highland terrier would be much threat to a man-mountain like Leather Jacket over there.

"Can I help you find something, gentlemen?" Nora asked

cheerfully, not wanting Merry's unfriendly reception to scare off the customers. "Are you looking for Christmas gifts?"

"We're not here to shop," Leather Jacket said, his face serious.

"We've tried to get in touch with you, Mrs. Walden," Briefcase said.

Nora froze, feeling like all the blood was draining out of her. She recognized that voice.

"But you haven't returned our letters. Or our phone calls." The older man stepped toward her, handing her an identification badge. With trembling hands, Nora fumbled for her reading glasses, even though she had already worked out who he was. She stared at the badge and it confirmed her suspicions: DEREK BROWN, SENIOR ENFORCEMENT OFFICER.

"We were appointed on account of you not paying your business taxes," Leather Jacket said. He handed her a letter from the local council, with FINAL WARNING marked on the top.

The words swam in front of her eyes, then Nora dropped the mug she was holding. It smashed on the floor, splashing Nora and Leather Jacket with hot tea.

"Shit!" Leather Jacket howled, but Nora was too numb to feel anything.

"Let's sit you down here, madam," Derek said. The man Nora had been avoiding for weeks took her by the elbow and guided her to the sofa.

Merry whined softly, nudging Nora with her damp nose.

Picking up the roll of paper towels Nora had been using earlier, Briefcase—or rather, Derek—began to clean up the spill. "I'm sorry," he said sympathetically. "I know this must be hard on you and your husband."

Simon!

Nora took out her phone and rang Simon.

Pick up, pick up, she pleaded silently, but the call went through to voicemail. *Please let him be driving home.* This wasn't how she had wanted Simon to find out what was going on, but Nora had never needed him more than she did at this moment.

When Derek had finished mopping up the tea, he set the broken bits of Nora's polka-dotted mug on the coffee table. "I think it's beyond fixing," he said apologetically.

Like the shop.

"You're bailiffs," she said shakily, her worst nightmare finally coming true.

"We're called enforcement officers these days," Derek explained. "But yes, it's basically the same thing."

"Are you here to take all of our things away?"

"Hopefully it won't come to that," Derek said. "If you pay off your debt, we'll leave you in peace."

Nora took a deep breath, trying to sound more composed than she felt. "I'm afraid I can't pay you now, but I'm working on it. We just need a bit more time."

"That's what they all say," Leather Jacket sneered.

"It's true," Nora said. "December is a busy trading month— we should have the money after Christmas." If she could stall them a bit longer, maybe she and Simon could work out a plan between them.

"If you can't pay off the full amount," Derek said gently, "we can always put together a repayment plan, so you can pay off your debt in installments. That's why we were trying to talk to you— we want to help. Debt isn't something you can just ignore."

Derek seemed like a nice guy, even if his henchman was clearly a jerk. But Nora couldn't see how a repayment plan would solve their problems, as the bookshop was operating at a loss.

Derek opened his briefcase and handed his partner a clipboard. Leather Jacket started walking around the shop, taking notes.

Nora felt panic rising again. "I thought you said you weren't taking anything away—"

"We're just doing an inventory of your possessions today," Derek said.

"But you said—"

Derek cut her off. "I'm sure it won't come to that, but I'm afraid we have a legal obligation to carry out an inventory."

Nora's skin crawled as Leather Jacket poked around the shop, picking books up and roughly casting them aside. Then he wandered into the back room, without even asking for permission.

Returning with a scowl on his face, he muttered, "Only thing of value in here is a clapped-out computer."

"Don't forget all the books," Derek said. "How many would you say are in stock?" he asked Nora.

"Just over ten thousand."

Leather Jacket wrote the figure down. "I've got to do up there now," he said, jerking his thumb toward the stairs.

"Is it OK if my colleague takes a look at the flat?" Derek asked. "You can accompany him if you like."

"It's fine," Nora said.

It wasn't fine at all. But the only thing worse than Leather Jacket snooping through her home was having to watch him do it. She scooped Merry up onto her lap and stroked the dog's soft fur, trying to stay calm and willing Simon to come back.

"As you probably gathered, my colleague's not much of a reader," Derek told Nora as the other bailiff went up to the flat, his boots thudding on the stairs. "But I've always loved this shop."

"Really?" Nora looked at him in surprise. She didn't recognize Derek as a regular customer.

"I live in Cheltenham now," Derek explained, "but I grew up in Stowford. I was a science-fiction nerd and your mother introduced me to all my favorite writers—Isaac Asimov, Ray Bradbury, Philip K. Dick . . ."

"She tried to get me into those writers, too." Aliens and alternate universes always left Nora cold. Who needed dystopia when there were enough problems in the real world?

She could hear Leather Jacket's heavy footsteps on the floorboards as he moved around the flat above them. She tried not to picture him snooping in her wardrobe and poking around in her underwear drawer.

"Is she still alive?" Derek asked.

"Oh no, Mum passed away years ago."

"I'm sorry to hear that. She was a very nice lady."

Nora buried her face in Merry's fur, not trusting herself to speak. She could feel tears prickling her eyes. It was funny how, even now, grief could catch her by surprise. But a part of her was glad Penelope wasn't there, to see bailiffs in the bookshop she'd founded.

"I follow the shop on social media," Derek said. "I saw your post about that old man buying the First World War book."

Nora nodded, remembering what Arnold had said about never giving up hope. "It's moments like that that make me want to keep this shop going."

"Well, I really hope you can find a solution. There are some debt charities that might be able to advise you. If this place closes down it would be such a loss to the community."

"I'm done, boss," Leather Jacket said, coming back downstairs and handing Derek the clipboard. "Nowt in the flat, either—just furniture and stuff. A few paintings. TV's not even a flat screen."

Derek handed Nora the inventory for her to check, her life's worth of possessions reduced to a list. She nodded, barely taking it in.

"Just so you know," Derek said, "even if worst comes to worst, we would never take away your furniture or any necessary household items."

If that was supposed to be reassuring, it wasn't working.

"By the way," Leather Jacket said. "Your roof has a leak."

"Gosh," Nora said sarcastically. "I hadn't noticed."

"Right," Derek said, snapping his briefcase shut and standing up. "I think we've finished. We'll be on our way now."

Nora rose to see them out.

"You have until the second of January to either pay the amount in full or agree to a payment plan," Derek said. "But if the matter isn't settled by then, I'm afraid we'll have to come back and confiscate your possessions."

"We'll have it sorted by the new year," Nora promised.

From the disdainful way Leather Jacket was looking at her, she could tell he thought that was as likely as him reading a book.

"Good luck, Nora," Derek said, as the two bailiffs left the shop.

Nora gripped the mantelpiece, worried that if she let go her knees would buckle. She stared at the holly, feeling hollow. It *had* brought her bad luck, after all. She chucked it in the fireplace.

But she couldn't blame her problems on a plant. The situation was entirely of her own making. If only she hadn't ignored the letters . . . If only she had told Simon what was going on . . . If only . . .

The bell above the door rang again and Simon came in holding a bag. Merry ran over to greet him, her tail wagging wildly. "Sorry that took so long, love," he said, bending to pat Merry. "I got talking to a chap at the DIY shop—he had lots of good tips about roofing. I'm pretty sure I know what I'm doing now."

When Nora didn't respond, Simon looked over at her. "What's wrong?" he asked.

Nora took a deep breath. "We need to talk . . ."

12

SIMON

Is it Charlotte?" he asked, dread twisting his gut.

Had she been caught up in an earthquake or a terrorist attack or a freak bungee-jumping accident? A million and one disasters—all things he'd told Nora not to worry about—flashed through his mind.

Nora shook her head. "No, this isn't anything to do with Charlotte."

Exhaling deeply, Simon's shoulders relaxed. Their daughter was safe; anything else he could handle.

And then Nora began to cry.

"Oh no!" Simon said, rushing over to hold her. He stroked her back and rested his chin on the top of her head. "Please don't cry, sweetheart. Whatever it is, it can't be as bad as you think it is."

"Oh, but it is," she sobbed. "It's so much worse."

"Has someone died?"

Nora shook her head. She tried to speak, but she was crying too hard to get any words out, her breath coming in juddering gasps. Simon pulled a handkerchief out of his shirt pocket and handed it to her.

He noticed pieces of her polka-dotted mug lying on the coffee table. *Surely she's not crying because her favorite mug broke?*

Simon took Nora's hands. "Whatever it is, you'll feel better for getting it out in the open."

"I can't," she said. More tears spilled out. "I'm too ashamed."

"Nora, you know you can tell me anything. But for the moment, just take some deep breaths."

Simon sat patiently while Nora drew shaky breaths, her eyes closed. When her breathing was finally steady, she said, "Bailiffs came to the shop today."

"Bailiffs?"

"Well, they're not called that anymore," Nora said, dabbing her eyes with the handkerchief. "They're called enforcement officers."

"I'm sure it was just a misunderstanding."

Nora shook her head. "It wasn't a mistake. They were here to collect our business taxes—and penalty fees." She took the crumpled letter out of her pocket and handed it to him silently.

Simon scanned it quickly, trying to make sense of its contents. Court order? Arrears? Penalty fines? There had to be some mistake . . . "Bailiffs can't turn up out of the blue like that just because you've missed a payment. They need to give you notice."

"They *did* give me notice," Nora wailed, "but I ignored it. I didn't think they would actually come. I thought they were just trying to scare me and that I could sort things out before it came to this." She buried her face in her hands and said in a muffled voice, "I've been such an idiot. I've made a mess of everything."

"But I don't understand . . ." Simon said, still trying to process what was going on. "Why didn't you use the money from the loan to cover the business taxes?" They'd dipped into the bank loan from time to time, using it as a float to cover bills when the shop's income was particularly lean.

There was a long pause. "The loan money's all gone, Simon."

What? How could it be gone?

Simon sucked in his breath. It felt like he'd just been punched in the gut.

"How?" he demanded. "How could you not tell me something so important?"

"I didn't want to cause you any stress," Nora said, tears streaming down her face. "I was worried about your heart."

Simon stared at his wife in disbelief, his anger building. They were partners—not just in life, but in the business. Why hadn't she told him that the bookshop was running on fumes? That their loan was gone? He looked down at the letter from the council. It listed the dates of their previous correspondence. Nora had been keeping things from him for months.

"So, you just kept it a secret?" he exploded, screwing the letter up in a ball and throwing it on the ground. "Instead of giving me the chance to try and find a solution?"

"Simon, please calm down," Nora pleaded. "Think of your heart."

"I am not a fucking invalid!" he shouted. "And I wish you would stop treating me like one!"

His chest felt tight. He needed air. "I've got to get out of here."

"Simon, wait—" Nora cried, reaching out for him.

Brushing her off, Simon stormed out of the bookshop, slamming the door behind him.

As if on autopilot, he went into the George and ordered a pint from Sue. Looking around, he was relieved to see that the pub was almost empty. For once in his life, he wasn't in the mood to chat.

"Anything else?" the landlady asked him.

Fuck it, Simon thought. He was done with being mollycoddled. "And a basket of chips."

Fuming, he carried his pint to a dark corner of the pub and flicked through the pages of a two-day-old *West Country Gazette*, barely taking in an article about a proposed bypass on the A429.

Why didn't you know this was going on? said a guilty voice in his head. *How could you be so oblivious?*

Nora may not have told him about the unpaid bills or the loan money running out, but Simon wasn't an idiot. He knew that their book sales were low, but he'd never asked for the full picture of their financial situation.

Simon took a big swig of bitter. *Because you didn't* want *to know.*

They'd *both* buried their heads in the sand. He had seen the toll running the shop was taking on her—the evidence was right there in the dark circles under her eyes. He should have fought harder to be more involved. Should have pressed her to share her worries—then maybe things wouldn't have got out of hand.

"Oi, Bookworm," Howie said, sidling over to him. "Why the long face?"

Great, Simon thought. *Today just gets better and better.*

Howie slumped down onto the stool next to Simon. "You know, if I was lucky enough to be married to a perfect woman like Nora, you wouldn't catch me with a face like a slapped arse."

"Nobody's perfect, Howie," Simon said grumpily.

"She's pretty damn close."

Simon took another drink and didn't bother responding, hoping that Howie would take the hint and go away.

Howie regarded him for a moment, picking his teeth with a dirty fingernail. "You know, when I was a kid, nobody else in the class would sit next to me. I came from a bad lot, see. The other kiddies avoided me. But Nora don't care what anyone else thought—she shared her sandwiches with me every single day." He shook his head. "That woman of yours has an 'eart of gold."

Mateo came over and set the basket of chips on the table.

"Don't mind if I do," Howie said, helping himself to a chip.

Simon stared into his pint glass. *I've been such an ass.* Nora had only been trying to protect him. Yes, she'd made some bad choices—but she'd made them out of love.

"You can have them," Simon told Howie, pushing the basket of chips over to him; then he stood up and said abruptly, "I've got to go."

"Cheers, Bookworm," Howie said, picking up Simon's half-empty pint glass and draining the dregs.

Simon hurried out of the pub and across the road, nearly getting run over by a muddy four-wheel drive. Nora had turned the bookshop sign to CLOSED and when he came through the door he saw her curled up on the sofa in a fetal position.

Hearing him come in, she sat up. "I'm so sorry," Nora said.

When Simon saw his wife's stricken face, any residual anger evaporated.

"Oh, honey." He went over and squeezed her hands. "I'm sorry, too. I shouldn't have blown up like that. I just wish you'd told me what was going on. I hate that you've been dealing with this all on your own."

"I was in denial. I couldn't accept how bad things were. I kept thinking that if I had a bit more time, I could work out a solution that didn't mean selling the shop." She shook her head ruefully. "But now I can see that it's the only option."

"Not necessarily." Simon hugged her. "We're going to sort this out together. Two heads are better than one, after all."

He stood up and took her hand. "But first—we're going to need tea." Simon led Nora upstairs, then filled the kettle. When the water had boiled, Simon brewed two mugs of tea and brought them into the living room. Nora was cuddling Merry, who was licking her mistress's salty cheeks. Simon set the mugs down and put his arm around Nora.

"Oh, Simon," she said, burying her face against his shoulder. "I'm just so ashamed."

"You don't need to be ashamed. I'm responsible, too. I could see that something was worrying you, and I should have asked. I knew our sales were declining, and I should have realized that the loan money would be running low."

"I didn't want to admit how bad things were—to you, or myself."

"From now on, we need to be completely honest with each other. We're a team."

Nora nodded.

"And you've *got* to let me do more," Simon said. "At my last check-up, Dr. Dhar said I'm doing really well. There's nothing to worry about."

"I just can't bear the thought of losing you," Nora whispered. "Not after losing Mum."

"I promise you I'm not going anywhere."

"Well, we might both be," Nora said sadly. "I can't see any way out of this apart from selling the shop."

"Try to stay positive. There has to be another solution. First thing tomorrow, we'll go to the bank and ask them for another loan."

"But what if they turn us down?"

"We'll cross that bridge when we come to it," he told her, keeping his voice more upbeat than he felt.

As they sat on the sofa, Nora resting her head on his shoulder, Simon suddenly remembered the short story she had read him the last time they were sitting there together. "The Gift of the Magi" was about the sacrifices we make for love.

There was one other solution to their problems. It was something he'd vowed he'd never do. But if the bank wouldn't come through, he'd just have to swallow his pride.

Because nothing was more important to him than Nora.

DAVID

David Langdon stared out his dining room window at the field outside, sparkling with frost. The sunshine, after weeks of rain, felt like a personal affront. The dark, insidious cloud that had settled over his head a few months ago showed no sign of shifting, even if the weather had improved. At least when it was gray and bleak outdoors, he derived some satisfaction from the fact that the world outside reflected the way he felt inside. There was a word for that in books, when the weather matched a character's emotional state. What was it . . . ?

"Pathetic fallacy," he muttered to himself, retrieving a literary term from his distant school days.

That's about right. Pathetic, he thought, catching his reflection in the window. Still in his dressing gown. Dark circles under his eyes. Cheeks gaunt and grizzled with several days' worth of stubble. He knew he should shower, get dressed and shave, but just couldn't muster enough energy to do any of it.

"Dad, I made you some breakfast." His daughter, Kath, came in carrying a tray with a pile of mail and a bowl of porridge sprinkled with what David assumed was some antioxidant-packed berry. Kath was a thorough and tenacious researcher—that's why he'd hired her to work in his parliamentary office after she'd got her master's degree in philosophy, politics and economics. She'd quickly moved up the ranks and was his most-trusted adviser. He strongly suspected that she'd been researching links between diet and depression, as if some miracle food would suddenly snap her father out of his despair.

"I'm not hungry."

"You need to eat." Kath set the bowl down in front of him. "You're skin and bones."

His appetite had completely disappeared. Food no longer held any pleasure, so it hardly seemed worth the effort of chewing it.

But Kath was hovering expectantly, so David obediently took a bite of his breakfast.

He forced himself to swallow the mush down. "Lovely."

It tasted like a bowl of glue.

The irony was that David Langdon was famous in Westminster circles for his voracious appetites. Not just for women, though he'd had more than his fair share of those, but also for food. He'd regularly dined out at London's finest restaurants, pushing his parliamentary expenses to the absolute maximum. One of his aides had jokingly nicknamed him "Marie Antoinette" because of his fondness for foie gras and Kobe steaks, even in times of austerity.

"How are you feeling?" Kath asked.

David avoided his daughter's eyes, not wanting to see the concern in them. "Fine," he lied.

She wasn't fooled. "Have you thought about going to see the doctor?"

This again . . .

"No."

"Dad, I'm worried about you. I think you might need medication. Tablets will help you feel better. And the doctor would be able to recommend a therapist—"

"I. Said. No." He used the authoritarian voice he normally reserved for delivering speeches in Parliament.

David had always suffered from what his ex-wife called "dark spells." His affair with an aide had been the last straw, but his "dark spells" had also played a big part in the breakdown of his marriage. The depression had always shifted, eventually, without needing medical assistance. But he'd never had an episode that had lasted this long.

"Please just think about it, Dad."

He *had* thought about it. A lot. He was an elected government official. What if word of his depression got out? What if someone saw him at the surgery? Noticed his prescription at the chemist's and leaked the news? No, he couldn't risk it. Thousands of people had voted for him, trusting him to lead. What would they think if they found out that their MP was mentally unstable? He was supposed to be strong, not weak. His was among the safest seats in the UK, but that didn't mean it couldn't be lost . . .

Instead, he'd retreated to his constituency house, not wanting any of his colleagues in Parliament to know that he was ill. Nothing remained a secret long in the corridors of Westminster. Kath had moved into Yew Tree Manor with him, basing herself in the constituency office in nearby Cirencester. She'd been watching him like a hawk, nagging him constantly to seek help.

Whoever said misery loves company was a liar. All he wanted was to be left alone, to lick his wounds in peace.

Since his first run for Parliament, back in the nineties, David had had his eyes on the big prize. With an abundance of charisma and conviction, he'd been tipped for success from the very beginning of his career. He'd bided his time, building his profile with television appearances and his newspaper column, serving on a variety of committees, and eventually working his way up to a Cabinet role. Oh, he'd made plenty of enemies along the way. It was impossible not to in politics. But he'd collected an army of powerful allies, too. Six months ago, when the moment finally seemed right to grab the brass ring, David had instigated a vote of No Confidence.

His allies had promised him their support, assured him he had it in the bag. David could practically feel the keys to Number 10 jingling in his pocket.

Instead, it had been a crushing defeat. The press had had a field day, digging up all the dirt they could find on him. When push came to shove, all but his closest cronies had abandoned him. It was totally humiliating.

He'd had setbacks in his career before, but this time he just couldn't seem to bounce back. Becoming prime minister was the goal he'd spent most of his adult life working toward. He'd put it ahead of everything else—friends, family, relationships. It had all been in vain. What was the point of carrying on? There was nothing left for him anymore.

No, that wasn't true. He had Kath. His daughter had been there for him every step of the way, her loyalty unwavering and completely undeserved. He hadn't exactly been the world's best father when she was growing up. His ex-wife had raised Kath on her own, while he was busy chasing skirt and political glory.

Getting to know his daughter properly, through working together, had been one of his biggest joys of the past decade. Like him, Kath had a quick, analytical mind. But she wasn't motivated by power, and genuinely seemed to care about the people in their constituency.

He glanced over at her, her curly brown bob hiding her face as she sorted the post. "These are the most urgent ones," she said, handing him a stack of letters. "And this came for you, too." She handed him a gift wrapped in gold paper.

He glanced at it warily.

"Aren't you going to open it?"

David shrugged. "I'll open it later."

Kath seemed disappointed, but in his experience, a gift rarely came without strings attached. MPs had to declare any gifts they received from constituents, to prevent allegations of bribery. More than a few of his colleagues had fallen foul of the rules.

Kath got out her tablet and pulled up a schedule. "There are a few things I wanted to run by you: you'll need to go up to London on Wednesday for the vote on the Renewable Energy Bill . . . the Secretary for Digital, Culture, Media and Sport sent the latest draft of the bill proposing stricter age limits on social media . . . and the Rural Regeneration steering committee has rescheduled the debate on wind farms to after Christmas . . ."

David zoned out as she filled him in on various meetings and requests for interviews and speaking engagements. His head felt filled with static and it was hard to concentrate on anything these days.

"Dad?"

"Sorry, Kath." He shook his head. *Focus!* "Can you repeat that last one?"

"St. Stephen's has invited you to their annual carol concert."

David groaned. Every bloody year—why wouldn't they take the hint? He'd have to make some excuse. He couldn't muster any cheer at the moment, let alone festive cheer.

"That reminds me," Kath said. "Last time I went into the village, I got a few books I thought you might be interested in . . ."

Kath was an avid reader—she was always popping into the bookshop opposite the local pub. David had never been in there himself—he had more than enough reading material with an endless supply of government policy documents to digest.

Kath went over to the bookcase and returned holding a stack of books. She set them down on the dining table and David saw the title of the one on top—*Beat Depression Fast.*

He grimaced and waved them away. "I don't need those."

"But Dad—"

"I'm NOT depressed," David lied. "I'm just a bit run-down."

Kath sighed. "I've got to go into the office today. There's a meeting about the proposed retail park outside of Stowford. Will you come in for that?" She looked at him hopefully.

He shook his head.

"What are you going to do instead?"

"I'm going to write my newspaper column." The article was already two weeks late, and he'd received the latest in a series of increasingly frantic chasing e-mails from the editor this morning.

"OK, then . . ." Kath said, watching him anxiously. "Are you sure you'll be OK?"

"I don't need a babysitter," he snapped. He forced himself to stand up and look like he was going to be productive, otherwise she'd never leave.

Before Kath left, she tapped the gold parcel. "Don't forget to open this. It looks exciting."

As soon as he heard her car's tires crunching down the gravel drive, David went into his office and sat at his desk, the antique mahogany surface covered with a thin layer of dust, the stacks of papers on top untouched for days. He opened his laptop and stared at the screen saver of a snowcapped peak, hoping to find inspiration.

Words had always come easily to him. He could normally knock out an article in an hour or so. He used his weekly column to share witty anecdotes from the halls of government and to champion the causes he believed in. After Kath had come out to him while she was at university, he'd become a staunch advocate for gay and trans rights. The day the Marriage Act—a bill he'd argued for passionately—was passed, was among the proudest of his career. But since losing his leadership challenge, David didn't care about . . . anything.

For the first time ever, he had no idea what to write about.

As he stared at the mountain on his screen saver, his only thought was what it would be like to throw himself off the summit. Now *that* would be a fast way to kill himself. Over the past few weeks, he'd considered several different options. He was a coward, so that ruled out anything painful. And he didn't want Kath to have to deal with a mess, which precluded quite a few other options.

Too bad there are no mountains in Stowford.

It wasn't that he wanted to die. He just wanted the pain to go away.

He was so tired of feeling miserable.

Who would even truly care if he died? His parents were both dead. He hadn't spoken to his sister in years. His parliamentary rivals would swoop in like carrion, feasting on the vestiges of his power. His exes would probably dance a jig on his grave. And as for his constituents, he'd seen the rude graffiti on the bus shelter. They'd be only too happy to replace him with a newer model.

Averting his eyes from the image of the mountain, his gaze fell on a framed picture of him and Kath with matching grins. They were both wearing helmets and giving the camera a thumbs-ups. It had been taken after they'd done a charity rappel down the Shard to raise money for Stonewall.

Kath would miss him, but she was strong. Far, far stronger than he was. She'd be sad, of course, but she'd get over it.

He slammed his laptop shut. The only idea he had was that the world would be a better place without David Langdon in it. But he couldn't write a column about that, could he?

13

NORA

H ave you got the application?" Nora asked Simon outside the bank. "And the business plan?"

They'd stayed up late cobbling together an application for a new loan. It had taken even longer than expected, thanks to their computer crashing every time they fired up Excel, but Nora thought their proposal looked pretty impressive. They'd spelled out why the business was important to the local community and included some ambitious targets for growth.

"Don't worry," Simon said, patting the leather portfolio he had tucked under his arm. "I've got everything in here." They'd agreed that he would present their proposal, as Nora's voice tended to quaver when she was nervous.

Nora brushed white dog hair off her skirt. In an attempt to look businesslike, she was wearing a blazer and had coiled her hair in a bun. She felt like a candidate on *The Apprentice*. "Here goes," she said, as they went inside.

Simon took a seat in the waiting area, resting one of his lanky legs on the opposite knee. He looked calm, but Nora could tell from the way he was twisting his watch around his wrist that he was anxious, too.

Nora didn't bother to sit—she just paced up and down the lobby, running the proposal over and over in her head.

"Relax, Nor. Hugh is a nice guy. I'm sure he'll want to help us."

Nora nodded, but there was no point pretending that this meeting was anything other than what it was—a desperate visit to the Last Chance Saloon.

Finally, Hugh popped his balding head out of his office and beckoned them inside a glass-walled cubicle. "Ah, Mr. and Mrs. Walden! Come in, come in."

"Thanks for fitting us in today, Hugh," Simon said, shaking his hand.

"My pleasure," Hugh said jovially. "You've just reminded me that I need to pop into your shop and pick up a guidebook to the Caribbean. The wife and I are going away over Christmas for a spot of sailing."

"Lovely," Nora said, though she could never understand why people would want to spend Christmas surrounded by palm trees, when Stowford was so pretty at this time of year.

Hugh offered them seats across from his desk, then he leaned back in his chair and clasped his hands over the ample belly that was straining the buttons of his finely striped shirt. "What can I do for you today?"

Hugh listened respectfully as Simon ran through their presentation. Listening to her husband, Nora was proud of how confident and intelligent he sounded. How could Hugh fail to be impressed? When Simon finished speaking, Hugh studied their business plan, rubbing his chin. Nora's stomach clenched anxiously as they waited for him to reach his verdict. A frown deepened on Hugh's face as he ran a plump finger along the columns of their spreadsheet.

He looked up at them and shook his head. "I wish I could help you both, I really do, but your projections don't seem realistic."

"We're not in profit at the moment, but with additional investment, we believe we can turn the shop around," Simon said.

Hugh ran his hand over his head. "It doesn't work that way, I'm afraid. We can only extend your line of credit if we're confident that the money will be paid back. Given your current sales levels, and the scale of your debt, the bank just can't take that risk."

Nora leaned forward. "Please, Hugh," she pleaded. "If we don't get a loan, we're going to have to close down."

The banker looked at them apologetically from across his desk. "Look, you know I love your shop. It would be a real loss to the community to see it go. What about family? Do you have any rich relatives who might be able to help you out?"

Nora and Simon exchanged glances. While they'd been working on their proposal Simon had raised the subject of his parents, but Nora had told him not to get them involved. She knew how stressed Simon became when he was dealing with his father. Simon had told her not to worry about his heart, but she couldn't help being concerned. "That's not an option," she said.

Hugh sighed. "If you want my advice, I think you two should consider selling up. You'd make a tidy profit and would be set up for an early retirement. Get yourself a little place in the sun."

Nora blinked, trying to keep her tears at bay, as Hugh escorted them out of his office.

Do not cry.

It was bad enough that he'd made her beg—he wasn't going to make her cry as well.

"I'll pop in later to get that travel guide," Hugh said, shaking their hands.

"Don't leave it too long or we might not be there," Nora muttered under her breath.

When they were alone on the pavement outside the bank, Simon put his hands on her shoulders. "I know that didn't go the way we wanted it to, Nora, but we still have a bit of time. Just because this bank said no, it doesn't mean other banks will turn us down."

"Of course they will." Hugh Wright had been their best hope for a loan.

"Well, I'm still going to make a few more appointments," Simon said. "I'll go up to London if I have to."

Nora knew he'd be wasting his time.

"Want to grab a sandwich at the Copper Kettle before we go back to the shop?"

Nora shook her head. "I'm going to take a walk if that's OK with you. I need to clear my head."

"Of course." Simon gave her a kiss and headed back toward the shop, while Nora headed off in the opposite direction. At the end of the high street, she turned to go toward St. Stephen's. But instead of going into the silent church and praying for a miracle, she skirted around the nave to the churchyard at the back. The iron gate gave a protesting creak as she pushed it open and went into the graveyard.

Most of the tombstones were so old that they had half sunk into the ground, their surfaces furred with lichen. Dotted among them were a few newer graves, too. One, with wilting bouquets of flowers resting against it, was fresh enough that the surrounding grass was still sparse.

Nora wove her way through the graveyard, turning at an angel statue marking an old Victorian grave. Although she wasn't religious, Nora liked the idea of guardian angels. She hoped one was watching over Charlotte, wherever she was in the world. She'd always felt like there was one looking out for her, too. Now she wasn't so sure.

If there's anybody out there, I could really use your help right about now . . .

Heading toward a weeping willow tree, she passed rows of ivy-covered urns and crosses, memorials to Stowford's long-dead residents. She came to a stop in front of a simple headstone with tiny purple flowers blooming all around it.

"Hi, Mum," she said quietly.

A rebel through and through, Penelope had loved cyclamen because they defied winter's gloom with their bold violet petals. After the funeral, Nora had planted the purple flowers all around her mother's grave. She'd planted other bulbs, too. In the new year, delicate snowdrops would emerge, then as the weather grew warmer, daffodils and tulips would blossom. Later, once summer's blooms had come and gone, there would be autumn crocuses in vivid yellows and purples. There was never a time of year when Penelope wasn't surrounded by vibrant color and vitality, in death as she'd been in life.

Nora came to check on the flowers, pull up weeds and chat with her mother a few times a year, but she hadn't been here since the start of autumn. She brushed dried leaves off the gravestone that marked her mother's final resting place so she could read the inscription carved into the granite.

PENELOPE COOPER, 1947–1991

When I come to the end of the road,
And the sun has set for me,
I want no rites in a gloom filled room,
Why cry for a soul set free?

It was a verse from the Christina Rossetti poem Nora had read at her mother's funeral. And just as she had been unable to heed the poem's advice on the day they buried Penelope, she couldn't help herself from crying now.

"I'm so sorry, Mum. I've failed you. We're going to lose the shop." She slumped down on the damp ground. Resting her head against the cold gravestone, Nora wept tears of defeat. "I tried, Mum," she sobbed. "I tried so hard to keep the shop going."

Nora wasn't sure how long she sat there—long enough for moisture from the ground to soak through her skirt to her bottom—but at some point she heard the gate squeak again and realized she wasn't alone. She scrambled to her feet and saw a teenage boy in a school uniform enter the graveyard. He looked about fifteen or so, with messy ginger hair and pale cheeks that retained a hint of childhood softness, despite the angry blemishes of adolescence. She had a vague notion that she'd seen him before. He was probably one of the teens who loitered outside the George, hoping someone would buy them a drink.

Spotting her, he scowled and turned away.

Bunking off school, no doubt.

Nora glanced up at the clock on the top of the church tower and saw that it was nearly two o'clock. Simon would worry if she didn't get back soon. *It's all yours, mate,* she thought, hurrying through the graveyard. She slipped through the gate, leaving the boy to smoke or vape, or whatever it was teenagers got up to in graveyards when they should have been at school.

HARRY

When the lady had gone, Harry made his way to Emma's grave and crouched down in front of it. The bouquet of flowers he'd brought last time had withered and turned brown. Emma would have hated how scruffy it looked, the grass still patchy and thin.

He'd have to bring something to spruce it up—maybe one of those red Christmas plants. Or some tinsel. Better yet—some battery-operated fairy lights, like the ones she strung all over her bedroom every December.

Emma had loved Christmas decorations—the blingier the better. She'd owned a huge collection of Christmas sweaters, most of them with sequins on them. They were probably still in her wardrobe. Their parents hadn't touched a thing in her room, as if they still expected her to come home from her Saturday job as a waitress at the Copper Kettle. Sometimes, Harry went into her room and lay down on her bed, something Emma would never have allowed him to do if she'd still been alive. If he closed his eyes, he could just about smell the fruity body spray that he'd always told her smelled like dog farts, but was actually really nice, on her pillow.

"It's going to be so weird without you at Christmas," he said, shoving his hands in his blazer pockets to keep them warm. His parents hadn't bothered to put a tree up. They were doing their best to ignore the festive season, as if Emma's death meant that nothing was worth celebrating anymore: "We probably won't go to midnight mass." They hadn't set foot in St. Stephen's since the funeral. The vicar had come to visit them at home, but Harry's dad had slammed the door in her face.

Harry had always moaned about going to church on Sunday mornings, but he'd give anything to go again, if it meant that Emma would be there in the pew next to him, giggling over Miss Powell's soprano solos.

The weirdest thing was that they didn't even get on most of the time. Less than two years apart, they'd played together all the time when they were little. But when Emma started secondary school, everything had changed. Suddenly, she didn't want to play Lego or ride bikes with her little brother anymore. They fought all the time, over who got to use the TV, whose music was better and who got to take the first shower in the morning (god help him if he accidentally used her posh shampoo). The last conversation they'd ever had had been an argument—Harry had screamed at Emma because she'd borrowed his new Beats headphones without asking and had accidentally broken them.

He winced, tormented by the last words he'd ever said to her: *I hate you!*

Now that Emma was gone, Harry missed her constantly. It was a dull ache that would suddenly flare up with a stab of acute pain when something reminded him of her. Which was, like, all the time.

Harry tried to keep his defenses raised, but grief didn't play fair. It would creep up on him unexpectedly and then . . . POW!

He found himself wanting to tell her things—even just stupid things, like how Jason Kelly had started going out with Melissa from her class, or that Mr. Hanley the geography teacher had got a (very bad) hair transplant or that the cat next door had had kittens. Then he'd remember that she was gone, and sadness would snatch his breath away.

That was why he'd started coming here to talk to her. He knew it was weird. People at school would think he was an even bigger freak than they already did if they found out he was hanging out in a cemetery, talking to a dead person. He knew Emma couldn't answer him, knew it was just her body down there in the ground.

Everyone from school had turned out for the funeral. The church had been standing room only—busier than midnight mass on Christmas Eve. Everyone had been crying their eyes out, even though half the people there had barely known her. Harry hated having everyone's eyes on him, in his too-tight suit that he'd got for his cousin's wedding the year before. As he and his father carried Emma's coffin out of the church and into the hearse, he hadn't shed a tear. Everyone had said all sorts of crap about how "brave" he was. But Harry wasn't brave—just numb.

If it had been him that had been hit by a car, he'd wondered, would his funeral have attracted as big a crowd?

Probably not.

Everyone loved Emma. She was the good-looking one, ginger hair being way nicer on girls (not that Harry would have ever admitted that to her). She got good grades, but never showed off about how clever she was. She and her friends were supposed to go to Glastonbury to celebrate exams being over, but she'd never got to see Lizzo or Vampire Weekend or George Ezra (who she totally had a crush on) or any other bands at the festival. A car was driving too fast down a country lane and hit her while she was walking home from work.

She was killed instantly.

For a while, Harry was kind of a celebrity at school. The Boy Whose Sister Died. Kids who wouldn't normally give him the time of day said hi to him and asked him how he was doing. He'd hated the pity in their eyes and was relieved when they went back to ignoring him as usual after a few weeks. His actual friends, Scooter and Sanj, the guys he played computer games with and rode bikes with, never spoke to him about Emma. It was as if grief was contagious, and nobody wanted to risk catching it.

The school had tried to get him to speak to a counselor, but that was a complete waste of time. Harry hated the way Mrs. Garvey nodded her head every time he said something. Hated the box of tissues on her desk, reminding him that he was a Bad Person because he still hadn't cried. Hated how her office had smelled of lavender like his grandmother's bathroom.

He'd spent every session with his arms crossed, giving monosyllabic answers until at last his dad wrote him a note saying he didn't have to go anymore.

For the first half-term, the teachers had been understanding. They'd let it slide when he didn't hand in his homework. Now, their patience had run dry and they were doling out detentions on a daily basis. His grades had never been amazing like Emma's, but they'd always been OK. Now he was failing in every subject except English—and it wasn't just because Emma wasn't around to help him with his homework. Harry found he couldn't focus on anything the teachers said.

What was the point of any of it, when—BOOM—just like that, you could die?

The detentions weren't just for his academic work, either. Harry had picked a fight in the locker room after PE and ended up with a black eye. He'd *wanted* to be punched, had taunted the other boy until he'd managed to provoke violence. Even as his face was smarting with pain, Harry had felt happy.

Because he deserved it.

The school counselor had taken him aside afterward and said, "Look, Harry, we all know you are going through a really tough time and we want to help. You're a bright boy—and you're throwing it all away. Emma wouldn't want this for you."

Fuck you, Mrs. Garvey.

How would that old cow know what Emma would have wanted?

Glancing down at her headstone, Harry sighed. It was true. Emma definitely would have said he was acting like a total dickhead.

"I know I should be at school," he told his sister now. "But you don't understand what it's like . . ."

He hadn't planned on bunking off. This morning, he'd got dressed in his uniform, gone downstairs for breakfast. On his way out to work, his dad had handed him a parcel. "This came for you but I only just noticed it."

What a surprise. There was a stack of post on the kitchen counter, which his parents hadn't bothered opening. Somewhere, buried in the pile of condolence cards and bills, there were probably letters from school about his behavior. But his parents weren't exactly on top of things. His mum was a zombie, still taking the tranquilizers Dr. Dhar had prescribed for her after the accident, even though she was supposed to have stopped. She sat around all day in her dressing gown, making cups of tea and forgetting to drink them as she stared into space. On the surface, his dad was doing better. At least he was still going to work, but when he got home all he did was sit in front of the television drinking himself into a stupor. Harry barely registered on their radar.

He'd opened the parcel, wondering if his gran had sent the Xbox game he'd wanted for Christmas. But it wasn't a game, it was a book—*The Lion, the Witch and the Wardrobe.*

What the fuck?

Was this some kind of sick joke?

Who the hell would do something so messed up? Harry was furious and had flung the book across the kitchen, ripping its cover.

His mother had barely blinked.

He'd been way too upset to go to school. Instead, he'd spent the morning traipsing around the fields, freezing his arse off. He was desperate to warm up with a hot chocolate from the Copper Kettle, but he hadn't been inside the café since Emma's death. There were too many memories of her in her white apron, an order pad tucked into the pocket. When he and his mates had gone in there, she'd always given them free cakes. His mates all thought Emma was really cool, not that Harry had ever told her that.

Now he never could.

As he'd stomped angrily through the frost-covered fields,

Harry had had a weird thought: What if Emma had sent him the book? Maybe it was some sort of message from beyond the grave . . .

He'd known it was crazy, but somehow he couldn't stop his feet from walking toward St. Stephen's. As if she could somehow talk to him, from heaven or whatever.

"Was it from you?" he asked her now. "Did you send me that book?"

Silence.

"Well, was it?"

But the only sound was the wood pigeons cooing from their roosts under the eaves of the church.

Harry let out a howl of anguish. "Why?" he shouted, his voice echoing across the graveyard. "Why did you have to die, Emma?"

14

SIMON

The next morning, Simon slipped out of bed just before six o'clock and got dressed in the dark. He buttoned his smartest shirt—a birthday present from his brother, from a tailor on Jermyn Street. *Tie or no tie?* Nora had been tossing and turning all night. Not wanting to wake her now by rooting around in the wardrobe, he decided to give the tie a miss. He pulled on his best corduroy blazer and tiptoed out of the bedroom, avoiding the creaky floorboard. In the living room, Merry climbed out of her basket and turned circles in front of the door, whining. "Shh!" Simon whispered, holding his finger to his lips.

After taking Merry out for a wee, he came back upstairs and quickly scribbled a note for Nora: *Gone to London for a meeting.*

"Wish me luck," he said, ruffling Merry's ears. Then, grabbing his car keys, he headed back out again.

As he drove the Golf down the country lanes to the train station on the outskirts of the village, the sun was just beginning to rise, casting a rosy pink glow over the rolling hills. He parked and went into the tiny station office, with its pretty white wooden gabling, to purchase a day return to London Paddington.

"Christmas shopping, here I come," said a plump woman, waving her ticket excitedly as she stepped away from the window so Simon could buy his ticket.

Simon wished he was going Christmas shopping, too. The crowds of Oxford Street would be a doddle compared to what he was about to face. After purchasing his ticket, he crossed the little footbridge over the tracks and waited on the platform for the early train. There were only a few other people waiting there—the Christmas shopper, a girl in a school uniform holding a hockey stick and singing along to music on her headphones, an elderly Japanese couple studying a guidebook to London, and a young Indian woman in a smart suit and glasses who was typing on her smartphone as she sipped from a reusable coffee cup. At the very end of the platform, well away from the others, a dark-haired man in a black overcoat stood at the platform edge, a smart leather briefcase by his bespoke leather brogues.

"Good morning," Simon greeted the Japanese tourists. They bowed politely in reply as he passed. He sat down on a bench and took a paperback out of his jacket pocket. But Simon found himself unable to concentrate on the biography of Benjamin Disraeli he was reading. His gaze kept returning to the man in the overcoat, who was staring down at the tracks. He was standing much too close to the edge. Rising, Simon strolled down the platform to stand next to him.

"Nice morning, isn't it?" he said casually.

Startled, the man looked up. "Is it?" he mumbled. His eyes darted away from Simon's as he pulled up the collar of his overcoat, obscuring his face.

Is that who I think it is? The guy looked a lot like David Langdon. But this man was thin, grizzled and haggard-looking, with a haunted look in his eyes, whereas the MP was always clean-shaven and on the heavy side. Though to be fair, the last time Simon had seen him in person was a few years ago in the local deli, where he'd cut to the front of the queue and bought the most expensive wine in the shop.

"Off anywhere interesting?" Simon asked.

"No." The man clearly didn't want to engage in conversation, but to Simon's relief, he stepped back behind the yellow line, just as a train whistle broke through the stillness of the morning. A few moments later the 7:03 to London Paddington rounded the bend and came into view.

Without a backward glance, the man—was it David Langdon?—picked up his briefcase and hurried down the platform toward the first-class carriage.

He thinks I'm a nutter. Whoever he was, the man clearly didn't want to be stuck sitting next to Simon for the whole journey.

Simon found a window seat and set his book down on the table in front of him. As the train pulled out of the station, he looked around at his fellow passengers. Everyone was playing games on their smartphones or listening to music on their headphones. The Indian woman who'd got on at Stowford was working on her laptop. The plump woman had sat next to the Japanese tourists and was advising them on all the best places to shop in London. The man across the aisle from him was doing the crossword in the newspaper, but apart from him, he could only see one other person with a book. Nobody was reading.

No wonder the shop's going bust.

Simon opened his book and tried to read, but he found himself skimming the same paragraph again and again. Closing his book, he gazed out the window, watching the green fields zip past, with occasional flashes of bright red dogwood and spidery yellow witch hazel. Woolly Cotswold sheep munched on frost-tipped grass and round hay bales encased in black plastic gleamed in the morning sunlight. He remembered how Nora had teased him for being such a city boy when, years ago, he'd asked her about those mysterious black cylinders. Over the years, Simon had grown to love the beautiful Cotswold countryside as much as any native, finding out everything he could about the local flora and fauna.

A refreshment trolley came trundling up the carriage, but even though he hadn't had breakfast and the bacon rolls smelled good, Simon shook his head. He was too tense to eat. As they got closer to London, and the landscape grew more built up, so did the dread in the pit of his stomach.

The train pulled into Paddington station and commuters spilled out the doors, hurrying toward the tube station. As he walked through the busy concourse, Simon noticed a poster advertising *The Oculist of Leipzig* as "a perfect Christmas gift."

Only for someone you hate, Simon thought.

Leaving the station, he walked along the Grand Union Canal to Maida Vale. The towpath was moored with barges, their rooftops cluttered with potted plants, bicycles and brightly painted enamelware. Stovepipes puffed out smoke, filling the air with the scent of burning coal. The names painted on the sides of the boats conjured up adventure and romance—*Highland Lady . . . Joie de Vivre . . . Dragonfly*—and reminded Simon of the narrow-boat holidays he'd taken with Nora and Charlotte, chugging their way through the Norfolk Broads and stopping for lazy pub lunches along the way.

I could do with a pint right now. Simon glanced at his watch, which he hadn't got around to pawning. It was too early for the Warwick Castle to be open, so he'd just have to face the ordeal ahead without Dutch courage.

Turning off the towpath, he walked down a street lined with elegant Edwardian villas. He paused outside one of the houses and looked up at its pristine white walls, rising four stories high.

A gardener was busy at work, trimming the box hedges at the front with the precision of a surgeon.

It had never felt like home, even when he'd actually lived here. He'd rarely gone home for the weekend while at school, preferring empty dorms to the house's museum-like atmosphere. As an adult, he'd avoided visiting his parents' house on his own. He usually took Charlotte along, their beloved granddaughter providing a distraction from their disappointing eldest son.

Simon fought the urge to turn around and head straight back to the station. Then he remembered the heartbroken look on Nora's face when she'd come back from her walk yesterday. If the bookshop closed, a part of her would shut down, too.

Do it for Nora, he thought, forcing himself to climb the stairs and ring the bell.

Not that his wife knew anything about his plan. She'd expressly forbidden him from asking his parents for help, but Simon knew it was because she was still trying to protect him. He was sure Nora would forgive him for going behind her back if his parents agreed to a loan.

His parents' latest housekeeper—Agata? Or was it Agnieszka?—answered the door in her black uniform and led him into a sitting room with sleek mid-century modern furniture. They'd redecorated since his last visit. A Murano glass chandelier sparkled from the ceiling and there was a new painting above the fireplace. Simon would have wagered money, if he'd had any, that it was by David Hockney.

"Simon!" exclaimed his mother. "What a lovely surprise." Margaret was immaculately dressed in a cashmere sweater and camel-colored wool trousers, her thick white hair elegantly coiffed into a chignon. As she offered her cheek for a kiss, Simon caught a familiar whiff of Chanel No. 5.

"Son," his father said, putting down his copy of *The Times* and standing up. Like Simon, Charles was tall and lean, but he'd lost most of his hair. He peered at Simon through the glasses that were resting on the tip of his hawklike nose, his coolly appraising eyes the same shade of blue as his son's.

Charles crossed the room and shook his son's hand. Margaret and Charles didn't do hugs. Not even when their sons had been little and needed them most.

Simon's father, who was wearing a suit, looked at his watch and frowned. "We weren't expecting you. I have a board meeting at noon."

Nice to see you, too, Dad.

"I thought you were retired. Isn't Daniel running the company now?"

"Oh, I'm a non-executive director," his father said, returning to his chair. "But I like to stay involved." He tapped his head. "Keeps the gray matter active."

"I'll get right to the point, then," Simon said, sitting down on an uncomfortable leather armchair. He cleared his throat. *Just stay calm,* he told himself. "The bookshop is in serious trouble. We've fallen behind on some of our bills and the bank won't help us. If we can't raise some cash soon, we're going to have to sell the shop."

There was a long, awkward pause, broken only by the housekeeper carrying in a tray of coffee. "Thank you, Agatha," Margaret said, pouring the coffee and avoiding her son's eyes.

"I'm not asking for a handout," Simon plowed on. "It would be an investment in the business. Nora and I believe we can make the shop profitable again."

Simon's father snorted. "I can't say I'm surprised—it's a miracle that shop's lasted as long as it has."

"It's a tough trading climate," Simon said defensively. "We've worked hard to keep it going."

"Books are a dying industry," Charles said, shaking his head disparagingly. "I told you back when you first took up with Nora that you were throwing your future away."

"I did NOT throw my future away!" Simon snapped, clenching his fists.

So much for calm.

He had a wonderful wife, an amazing daughter and a job he loved—how dare his father act like none of that mattered?

"There's no need to get so worked up," Simon's mother said, handing him a cup of coffee. Emotional displays of any sort were not welcome in the Walden household. "Sugar?" she asked, offering him the sugar bowl.

Simon shook his head. He'd given up sugar in his tea and coffee after his heart scare—not that he'd bothered telling his parents about that. He took a sip of black coffee and scalded his tongue. *Shit!*

"Anyhow, this isn't good timing," Charles said, crossing his legs. "We've just invested quite a bit of money in another vineyard. This one's in Italy."

Simon gripped the delicate bone-china cup so hard he thought the handle might snap off. "So, you're not going to help us?" he said, hating how he sounded like a petulant teenager. Why did his father always have that effect on him?

"I didn't say that," Charles replied. "If you need a job, I'm sure your brother could pull some strings. There will always be a place for you at Walden Creative."

Simon slammed his cup on the side table, sloshing coffee onto the expensive wood. *Good.* "I don't want a job, damn it. I like the one I already have. I'm just trying to save my family's business."

As his mother darted over and started mopping up the coffee with a linen napkin, Simon's father leaned forward and glared at him. "And where was that sense of family loyalty when you walked away from *my* business, eh, Simon?"

Simon gave a humorless laugh. "You're still punishing me for choosing my own path in life?"

Charles gave him a pitying look. "I'm not punishing you, Simon. I'm a businessman, and the reason that I've been so successful is that I only invest in businesses I believe will make a healthy return."

Simon paced up and down the living room in frustration. "Do you want me to beg?" he asked. "You know I wouldn't be here if I wasn't desperate."

"Begging won't change anything." Charles took off his glasses and began to polish them on his silk tie. "Of course I'll give you money—we don't want you and Nora to be out on the streets. And we can help with Charlotte's university fees. But I'm not giving you a single penny to keep that sinking ship of yours afloat."

"You'd rather buy vineyards and art," Simon said, "than support your son's business?"

"Now *that's* an investment," his father declared, folding up his newspaper and pointing at the painting. "It's already gone up a quarter of a million in value since I bought it."

"Isn't it beautiful?" Margaret said, gazing up at the artwork. "I saw it in the Christie's catalog and just knew it would look perfect in this room."

Simon resisted the urge to yank the painting down from the wall and stamp on it.

"Now, if you'll excuse me," Charles said, checking his watch again, "I don't want to keep the board waiting." He tucked *The Times* under his arm and left the room.

Simon took a deep breath but couldn't seem to get enough air into his lungs. Being in this house made him feel like he was suffocating. Always had. He needed to get out—fast. It was a mistake to have come.

"I should be going, too," Simon said.

"Oh, what a shame," his mother said, looking crestfallen. "I thought you might stay for lunch. Agatha's made smoked salmon quiche."

"I need to get back to the shop."

To my home. To my real family.

"Don't go yet," Margaret said. "I've got something for you." She left the room and Simon went over to the painting and squinted at the signature. It *was* a Hockney.

When his mother came back, she was holding a bottle of wine. She pressed it into his hands. Simon glanced down at the label. It was a bottle of prosecco with a label that said CASA DI CARLOTTA. "We named it after Charlotte."

"Great," Simon said unenthusiastically.

"Have you heard from her? Is she coming home for Christmas?"

"No." Would she even have a home to come back to?

Simon gave his mother another peck on the cheek and hurried out of the house, greedily filling his lungs with cold air, like a diver who'd stayed underwater too long.

He'd bought an open return, but Simon couldn't face going home yet. He'd hoped he would be returning to Stowford with good news, a conquering hero, but instead he was coming back empty-handed. He was too ashamed to face Nora, knowing that he hadn't been able to save the shop for her. Before asking his father for help, at least he'd had his pride.

Now that was gone, too.

Simon sat down on a bench along the towpath and loosened the wire cage around the cork. He twisted the bottle until the cork popped and then he began to drink.

SAM

"Ladies and gentlemen, the 19:42 to Cirencester will be delayed due to signaling problems . . ."

Sampriti Patel groaned and pressed her head against the seat back in frustration. *Great . . . just great.* As if her day hadn't been long enough already. With back-to-back meetings and conference calls, she'd barely had time to go for a wee. And it wasn't over yet—she still had tons of work to do. Sam pulled her laptop out of her bag and opened a report she was drafting for a client, a mid-market restaurant chain making heavy losses. They weren't going to like her recommendations—which started with closing their least profitable branches and cutting staff by twenty percent—but as a management consultant, it wasn't her job to sugarcoat the truth. She and her colleagues were brought in to see the bigger picture and create efficiencies. Companies paid consultants like Sam big bucks to be the bad guys, to deliver the news nobody wanted to hear.

Pity South Western Railway wasn't one of her clients. After commuting between London and Stowford for the past three months, Sam could think of several improvements the rail service to the Cotswolds could make. Trains that ran on time and Wi-Fi that worked were right at the top of the list.

God, she missed her flat in Canary Wharf. She'd been able to walk to her office in fifteen minutes. But when she and James had split up, she'd been too busy to look for a new place to live, so she'd moved in with her parents. It was meant to only be for a few weeks, but somehow she was still there. True, there were some advantages—her mum prepared little tiffin boxes of samosas and leftover dal for Sam to take to work, which meant that she was actually eating lunch these days—but overall, moving back to Stowford felt like a giant step backward.

"Look for a new flat over Christmas," she said into her phone, recording a voice memo. She couldn't take this commute much longer.

The train was even more packed than usual, with Christmas shoppers jostling with commuters for the last remaining seats. A plump woman leaned over, bumping Sam's head with her bulging shopping bags as she squished them into the overhead compartment. "Sorry, love," the woman said, "I got a bit carried away on Oxford Street. But why not splash out, eh? It only comes once a year."

Thank god.

Sam hated Christmas, not that she ever dared express that unpopular opinion out loud. It was nothing to do with the fact that she was Hindu, though that's what people might have assumed. The Patel family loved a celebration. Her parents had enthusiastically embraced all British traditions, including Christmas, when they'd immigrated to the UK. They didn't seem to find it contradictory that their statue of Ganesh sat next to an equally rotund Santa Claus decoration, or that rather than a nativity scene, there was a silver mini-temple twinkling merrily in the Christmas tree's fairy lights. On December 25, they ate nut roast with vegetable biryani, and Christmas pudding with pistachio kulfi for dessert.

No, it was the wasted time and enforced merriment that bothered Sam. Christmas ate up valuable hours that she could have spent working. Tedious Christmas lunches sitting next to her loutish colleagues. Elaborate Christmas dos that inevitably had a fancy-dress theme. Christmas Sweater Day, which meant sending her assistant, Connie, out on a last-minute dash to buy an acrylic

monstrosity with a snowman on it. Secret Santa, which also required sending Connie out to buy some tat for a colleague she
didn't even know.

Which suddenly reminded Sam that she still needed to get
presents for the people she *did* know. Taking out her mobile, she
called Connie. She drummed her fingers against the table impatiently as she waited for her assistant to answer. *Come on*, she
thought.

"It's Sam," she barked into the phone when her assistant finally
picked up. It sounded from the din in the background that Connie was in the middle of eating dinner. "I need you to buy Christmas presents for my family—just get gift vouchers, as usual, and
put them on my Amex card." Hanging up, Sam ignored the slight
pang of guilt she felt about disturbing Connie at home. Everyone
at Apex Consulting was expected to work round the clock—even
the PAs.

"Up or out" was the mantra at Apex Consulting, one of the
world's leading management consultancy firms. Sam's elation at
getting onto their prestigious graduate trainee scheme was quickly
replaced by panic. Because it didn't take long to work out that
there was a very good reason she and her colleagues were paid
enormous salaries. If they didn't work all hours, they'd soon find
themselves out of a job.

That was the deal—work hard, play hard. Her parents, who
had met while studying pharmacology, had instilled their work
ethic into Sam and her sister from a young age. They'd worked
long hours to afford the best education for their daughters. It had
taken them years, but they'd eventually saved up enough to achieve
their dream of owning their own business and had moved from
Birmingham to Stowford shortly before Sam went off to university. So Sam didn't mind the work-hard bit.

But she resented the obligation to play hard, too. The work

parties, the long evenings in bars charging the most expensive bottles of wine to the company, the outings to strip clubs with clients, pretending she was cool with watching girls her own age gyrate around a pole, were supposed to be "fun," but that was where the real deals were done. Even her playtime was worktime. It was impossible to have any sort of life outside of work.

Sam caught a glimpse of her reflection in the train's window— long black hair framing a face that looked wan and exhausted. Her left eyelid had developed an annoying twitch. She took off her glasses and rubbed her eyes. Usually it went away after a day or so, but it had been twitching for the past five days and it was driving her nuts.

With a lurch, the train pulled out of Paddington. Maybe she'd have time to fit in a quick run when she got back to Stowford, after all. Running was the only thing keeping her sane. Her mum worried about her running in the dark, especially after that girl got killed by a car over the summer, but with her working hours she didn't really have much choice, and she wore enough fluorescent gear to kit out an eighties-themed disco.

Too bad that wasn't the theme for this year's Christmas party.

"Oh, that's a relief," said the woman opposite Sam. "I thought we might be spending the night on the platform."

Sam gave her a faint smile in return, not wanting to encourage conversation.

"They say we might get some snow next week. Wouldn't a white Christmas be lovely?"

"Mmm," Sam said noncommittally. She stuck her earbuds into her ears, signaling the end of the discussion. She wasn't actually listening to music, but she didn't intend to waste time chatting with a complete stranger.

As the train trundled through the outskirts of West London, Sam worked on her report, ignoring the bickering couple across the aisle and the little kid kicking the back of her seat. It was harder to ignore the drunken commuters at the other end of the carriage when they broke into a rousing chorus of "Jingle Bells." A dark-haired man holding a briefcase got up and made his way toward the first-class compartment.

Sam added another bullet point to her cost-cutting recommendations and a warning message appeared on her laptop screen—LOW BATTERY.

Shit!

She scrabbled around in her bag for a charger, but it wasn't in there. She had given a presentation to a prospective client in the conference room that afternoon, and she must have left the charger there in her rush to get to her next meeting.

Shit. Shit. Shit.

Her eyelid danced a crazy jig as she saved her document just in the nick of time. A moment later, the laptop screen went black as her battery died.

She dug her phone out of her handbag. Her computer was dead, but that didn't mean she couldn't catch up on her e-mails. There'd be at least a hundred messages waiting for her, for sure, as she hadn't had a chance to check them this afternoon. *Open*, she thought, jabbing the e-mail icon on her phone. Nothing happened. She waved her phone around, trying to pick up a signal.

"Oh, it's no use," the woman opposite her said cheerfully. "The reception on these trains is dreadful."

Shitty shit shit.

By now Sam's eyelid was twitching like a frog leg hooked up to electrodes. She pressed her fingers against her temples, trying not to freak out. Her time was billable in fifteen-minute intervals, so every second of the day counted. She couldn't just sit there on the train doing nothing.

She rummaged in her bag, looking for any paperwork she

could catch up on. The only thing in there was a copy of *A Christmas Carol*. The local bookshop had delivered it to her parents' house by mistake. She'd been meaning to get Connie to send it back but she'd forgotten to give it to her.

Sam looked at the book's cover with a picture of an old man in a cape and stovepipe hat. She hadn't read a book for pleasure in ages. She'd brought a Marian Keyes novel on the last holiday she and James had taken together, but never made it past the first chapter. She'd spent most of that week in Cuba dozing on her sun lounger, catching up on sleep, while James explored the island on his own.

She'd checked her work e-mails every day, even on holiday.

"I always come second to your work," James had complained—and not for the first time.

"It's because of my work that we get to go on holidays like this," she'd retorted. It was a low blow. James worked in IT; they'd met when he'd fixed her laptop. He worked hard, too, but earned a fraction of what Sam did. But he didn't seem to understand that her salary came at a cost.

He worked nine to five and went to the gym on his lunch break. But at Apex Consulting, if you left the office before seven, people called you a "part-timer."

At first, James had seemed proud of her success. Eventually, though, he'd grown frustrated by how often she had to cancel their plans at the last minute due to work. She'd even been late to his thirtieth-birthday party because of a work emergency.

Her job had caused plenty of arguments, but the thing that had brought their relationship to an end was kids. James had never made a secret of the fact that he wanted to be a dad. When they went to visit her older sister's family, he was great with Richa and Ash, her little niece and nephew. But after turning thirty, having children became something of an obsession for him. James had spent the whole holiday in Cuba pointing out cute babies, as if that would somehow set Sam's biological clock ticking.

"I can't wait for that to be us," he'd said, pointing out a couple dipping their squealing toddler's feet in the water. "We'd make the cutest babies."

The kid was adorable. But that didn't mean Sam was in a hurry to produce one of her own. She wasn't even thirty yet.

"I can't have kids until I make partner," she'd told him.

Sam loved her niece and nephew. And she knew that James would be a good dad. But if she took a career break now, she'd never get back on track. Apex Consulting paid lip service to parental leave and flexible working arrangements. The higher you climbed in the company, though, the fewer women there were.

Even fewer had kids.

Sam's mentor, Kasia, had been one of the company's highest flyers. That is, until she got pregnant. When Kasia had returned from maternity leave, she'd been passed over for partnership. The board told her that they had doubts about her "commitment" to the company.

No way was Sam going to let that happen to her.

Shortly after they'd returned home from Cuba, she and James had split up. Sam didn't blame him—she'd been a crap girlfriend. When it came down to it, she hadn't loved James enough to sacrifice her career for him. And she resented being forced to choose.

She didn't regret her decision, but that didn't mean she wasn't lonely. It would have been nice to have someone to cuddle up with in bed, these cold winter nights. Someone to share her worries with, to celebrate her successes.

Sam shook her head. It was no use dwelling on the past. James certainly hadn't wasted any time finding someone new. She'd seen on Facebook that he'd started going out with one of his colleagues, while her status remained resolutely single.

That was another reason she was dreading Christmas. Her family had liked James. Everyone had thought that they would be getting engaged this year. Her mother had practically picked out her wedding sari already. They hadn't concealed their disappointment when Sam had told them about the breakup. A lot of her friends were surprised, too. They couldn't believe that she'd walked away from that rarest of things—a single, straight man in his thirties who wasn't afraid of commitment.

"You don't want to end up alone," her auntie had said at Diwali.

"It's a medically proven fact that your fertility drops after thirty-five," said her sister, Ani.

"Guys like James don't grow on trees, you know," her mother said.

Her parents had even brought home a young pharmacist who worked at their shop for an excruciating dinner that was blatantly a setup. The only thing that had come out of it was Sam's realization that her parents had the World's Worst Gaydar.

Over the festive period, her parents' house would be filled with relatives. They would all know a "nice boy" they could introduce to Sam. It was impossible for her family to accept that she was OK with being single.

"I'm perfectly capable of finding a man on my own," she always told them, rejecting all offers of blind dates. But the guys at work were workaholics like her, and she didn't exactly have time to look anywhere else.

The only thing she was likely to snuggle up in bed with this Christmas was the book in her hands.

A Christmas Carol. She'd never read it. The fact that it was about Christmas didn't exactly appeal. She turned it over to read the blurb on the back cover—*Ebenezer Scrooge . . . ghosts . . . Victorian classic . . .* Nope, she wasn't loving the sound of it.

Sam looked up and the woman opposite offered Sam her bag of cheese-and-onion crisps with a smile.

Sam shook her head and quickly looked back down at the book.

It was either read or talk to the lady opposite.

Bah humbug to that.

With a resigned sigh, she opened the book and began to read.

15

NORA

Nora's phone rang as she was sitting behind the bookshop counter, putting the finishing touches on Simon's Christmas sweater.

"Nora, it's Seb Fox," said the unctuous voice on the other end. "I wanted to confirm what you discussed yesterday with my colleague. I understand that you want to put the shop on the market in the new year?"

"Yes, that's right," Nora said. While Simon was in London, she had gone into the estate agency to arrange for the sale of the shop.

"That's terrific news. Glad you came to your senses. I'm going to get you and Simon an amazing deal."

Nora didn't share the estate agent's enthusiasm, but she was resigned to her fate. There was only one viable solution now—selling the shop.

"I'll be over in the next day or so to take pictures and measure up," Seb said.

As Nora hung up, Simon came down the stairs.

"Hey," she said, turning to face him. "How did you get on?"

Simon had been up on the roof all day, replacing the broken tiles. After what he'd said about not treating him like an invalid, Nora had left him to it—even though she couldn't help worrying.

"It's a bit of a bodge job," Simon said, shrugging. "But it should hopefully stop the leaks."

"Shall I make us some tea?" she asked him. She wanted to tell him about her visit to the estate agency and hear about his trip to London. Nora suspected his meeting hadn't gone very well, because Simon had come home late and gone straight to bed, saying he was too tired to talk. She guessed another bank had turned him down for a loan, and he couldn't bring himself to tell her.

"Sorry, Nora," Simon said, avoiding her eyes. "I've got to head over to the pub to get ready for the quiz."

"OK," Nora replied, disappointed. "I'll see you there." Tonight's quiz was Christmas themed, and she'd arranged to make up a team with Alice and a few of the other local shopkeepers. As she watched her husband head over to the George, she had the distinct feeling he was avoiding her.

Shortly afterward, Ani Dhar came in with her two kids, Richa and Ash. They went into the children's section then came over to the till with *The Chamber of Secrets* and *The Prisoner of Azkaban*.

"Someone's a *Harry Potter* fan," Nora said approvingly, placing the books in a bag and handing it to Ash as his mother paid.

"He finished the first book last night," Dr. Dhar said. "I was going to wait for Christmas, but he was desperate to start the second one straightaway. I thought I'd better get the third, while we're here—I'm sure he'll finish it soon and you'll be shut over Christmas."

Soon we'll be shut permanently.

Nora couldn't bring herself to tell customers yet, so she said to Ash, "I'm a big *Harry Potter* fan, too."

"Ooh—I've just remembered something else I need to get," Dr. Dhar said. She hurried off and returned with a copy of a self-help book called *Meet Your Mate*.

"Should Vikram be concerned?" Nora teased.

"It's for my sister," Dr. Dhar said. "She's single again." As Nora rang up the book, the doctor asked, "How's Simon?"

"He's fine. He keeps telling me not to treat him like an invalid. But I worry about him."

"You don't need to," the doctor said reassuringly. "His last checkup was really good. The beta-blockers are working well."

When Dr. Dhar and her kids left the shop, Nora started getting ready to close up for the day. Before she could lock the door, her phone rang again—a video call this time.

"Hey, Mum," Charlotte said, beaming out from the screen.

"Hi, sweetheart." Nora had been so preoccupied by what was going on with the shop, she'd barely thought about Charlotte all day. "What have you been up to?"

Nora listened distractedly as Charlotte described a yoga move she'd recently learned and told her about a market she'd been to with her friends.

"How's everything with you guys?" Charlotte asked. "What have you been up to?"

"Nothing much. Just the usual." She hated lying to Charlotte, but she didn't want to burden her with the shop's problems.

"Are you sure?" Charlotte said. "You sound kind of strange."

"I'm fine. Just a bit tired—you know what it's like in the run-up to Christmas."

"Is Dad there?"

"He's over at the George. It's his Christmas quiz tonight. Actually, I should probably get going—I don't want to miss the start."

After saying goodbye to Charlotte, Nora exhaled and rubbed her temples. It was hard to pretend everything was OK when it was anything but.

The bell above the door jingled and Kath came into the shop.

"Oh, you're just in time," Nora said cheerily. "I was about to shut."

A man in a dark overcoat walked in behind Kath. "Nora, this is my dad," Kath said.

"Hi, I'm David Langdon," the man said, coming over to shake Nora's hand.

"Oh, my goodness, of course you are!" The MP looked so different to how he appeared on the news, Nora hadn't recognized him. She'd had no idea he was related to her poetry-loving customer.

"Is it OK if we come in?" Kath asked.

"Of course," Nora said, ushering them in. "It's an honor to have you."

"What a beautiful shop," David said, gazing around. "I can't believe I've never been in here before." He looked much frailer in person, but his voice was deep and silky, just as it sounded on television. "I wanted to say thank you. A few days ago you sent me a gift."

Did I? For a moment Nora was confused. As far as she knew, she hadn't sent anything to David Langdon. His name would have definitely caught her eye. Maybe he'd ordered something online and Simon had sent it out?

"You sent me a copy of *The Greatest Gift.*"

Ah . . . This *was who lived at Yew Tree Manor.* Suddenly the huge gated house and the car with the tinted windows made sense.

"I nominated Dad for your random acts of kindness," Kath explained, "because he's been having a hard time lately. I didn't include his name, because of his position."

Nora suddenly remembered the books Kath had bought the last time she had come to the shop. *I guess they weren't for her, after all.*

"Please, come and sit down." Nora gestured them over to the sofa by the fire, trying not to show how flustered she was feeling. As they sat down on the sofa, she offered them the plate of ginger biscuits. David Langdon looked as if he could use feeding up. "Can I get you a hot drink?"

"Tea would be lovely," Kath replied. "We both take it white, no sugar."

While her famous visitor and his daughter got acquainted with Merry, Nora dashed upstairs to make the drinks. She gave the milk a quick sniff, checking it hadn't gone off. *Better not give an MP food poisoning . . .*

Gathering together three unchipped mugs, Nora carried the teas downstairs on a tray. She placed them down on the coffee table, then settled into an armchair across from the sofa. "Did you like the book?" she asked David.

"It really *was* the greatest gift."

"It's a beautiful story," Nora agreed, nodding.

"No, it's more than just a nice story. It was a wake-up call. That's why I had to come in and thank you in person."

Nora's confusion must have shown on her face.

"I've been suffering from severe depression," David said. "Though I haven't wanted to admit it. I've been holed up at home so that the press wouldn't get wind of the fact that I'm unwell."

"How long have you been depressed?" Nora asked.

"I've had bouts of depression in the past, but this latest one came on after I lost out on the party leadership."

That was several months ago, Nora realized. "I'm so sorry to hear that." She wasn't just sorry that he was ill, she was sad that he'd felt compelled to keep it a secret. If it had been a physical ailment, he probably wouldn't have felt the same need to keep it hidden.

"Yesterday, I had to go to London to vote on a new bill. I was feeling so low that I considered jumping in front of the train instead of boarding it. Might have gone through with it, if someone hadn't come and stood next to me."

"I'm so glad they did," Kath said, touching his arm. Her forehead was furrowed with concern, the love she felt for her father unmistakable.

"Last night, I couldn't sleep. In the middle of the night, I finally opened the gift you sent me. I haven't read any fiction for years, but something compelled me to read the whole book in one sitting." David shook his head in astonishment. "It was as if the author was speaking directly to me. I knew *exactly* how George—the man in the book—was feeling. Like I should never have been born. Like the world would be a better place without me."

Kath gasped. "That's not true."

"It got me thinking. Although I'm not prime minister, I *have* made a difference over the years. I've worked hard on behalf of my constituents. I've voted for changes I believe in. Oh, I've made plenty of mistakes, too—Kath's mum would be the first to tell you that—but hopefully the good I've done outweighs those mistakes."

"Of course it does," Kath murmured.

The MP took a sip of his tea before continuing. "Most of all, the book reminded me that if I'd never been born, then Kath wouldn't have been, either." David reached for his daughter's hand and his voice cracked with emotion. "And *that* would be a tragedy, because she's my greatest accomplishment of all."

"Oh, Dad." Tears glistened in Kath's eyes. To her surprise, Nora felt her own eyes misting up, too. Where was Simon's hankie when she needed it? She hurried over to fetch a box of tissues from the till counter and gave David and Kath a moment to compose themselves.

"Sorry," Kath said, mopping her eyes. "You're probably regretting sending those books out now that you have two strangers blubbing in your bookshop."

"Of course not. I'm delighted that it made a difference."

"More than you know," David said. "Today I went to see the doctor and finally got a prescription for antidepressants. I should have done it weeks ago, but I was too ashamed to ask for help."

"There's no shame in illness," Nora said quietly.

Kath squeezed her father's hand. "You're going to get better, Dad. Even if it takes a bit of time."

"Dr. Dhar said it could take up to six weeks for the tablets to work . . ."

"Well, I'm not going anywhere," Kath said, giving him a hug. Then she turned to Nora. "I'm so grateful you sent Dad that book. I'd been trying to get him to go to the doctor for weeks."

They all sipped their tea, and Nora was pleased to see David Langdon help himself to one of her biscuits.

"So where did you get the idea, Nora?" the politician asked her when he had finished eating it. "I mean, to send out the books?"

Nora thought for a moment. "I suppose it all began with Arnold." She told David and Kath the story of how the elderly gentleman had come into the shop and bought the oldest book in the whole shop for his sick grandson. "It got my husband and me thinking," Nora said, "about how books bring people together, and make us stronger. How even at the loneliest and most difficult times in our lives, books give us hope and remind us that we're not alone."

"That's very true," David murmured. Then he stood up. "We should go. We've taken up enough of your time."

Nora waved his concerns away. "It's been my pleasure. Stay as long as you like." She wasn't in a rush, and she found herself liking the MP a lot more than she'd expected to.

David hesitated for a moment. "Well, if you're sure we're not imposing, maybe I *could* buy some poetry?"

"Seriously?" Kath asked, raising her eyebrow. "Now that really is a surprise."

Ignoring his daughter's teasing, David asked Nora, "Do you by any chance happen to have a book of Christmas poems?"

"We've got several." Nora led them into the poetry section and found a few different anthologies to choose from. David and Kath browsed through the poetry collections, with Kath pointing out some of her favorite poems to her father.

"I'll take this one," he said finally, selecting an attractive hardback volume.

At the counter, David tapped his credit card to pay. "I would have expected the shop to be busier, just a few days before Christmas."

Nora paused for a moment, deliberating whether or not to confide in the MP. He'd bravely opened up to her; she owed it to him to be honest in return. "We're actually shutting down in the new year. We've fallen behind on our bills and can't afford to run the shop any longer, so we have to sell it."

"Oh no," Kath exclaimed, looking upset. "That is such a shame. I love this place."

Nora smiled sadly. "So do I, but we just can't make it work anymore. Our deadline to pay off our debt is the second of January, but there's no way we'll be able to scrape the money together. We've lost so many customers to online shopping, and our business taxes have gone up astronomically," she explained. "We're luckier than many other shops, because we don't pay rent, but even so, we're struggling. If something isn't done about it, high streets like ours will die out."

The MP nodded thoughtfully. "I'm very sorry to hear that, Nora."

Nora chose to believe it was genuine concern, rather than a practiced show of empathy from a seasoned politician.

As Nora walked them to the door, Kath gave her a quick hug. "Thank you so much," she said. "I'm really sorry you're closing down."

"If you feel up to it, I hope you'll both come to our Christmas Eve party," Nora said. "It's usually a lot of fun. We're determined to go out in style."

"We'll definitely be there," Kath promised.

After they'd gone, Nora emptied the till, switched off the lights and locked up the shop. She took Merry out for a quick walk, then brought her upstairs for her dinner. Nora heated up her own dinner in the microwave—leftover cream of turnip soup, from the last of Doug Jenkins's bounty—and after eating it, she headed across the street to the pub, where Simon's quiz was already underway.

Every table was taken, with teams huddled over their answer sheets. Simon stood at the back, speaking into a microphone. *He's so good at this*, Nora thought proudly, looking on as he bantered with the different teams.

"Last question of the history round," Simon said. "What did the soldiers do during the Christmas Day truce of the First World War?"

Played soccer, Nora answered in her head. She thought about Arnold again, wishing she had a way to get in touch with him— to find out how Noah was doing, and to let him know that, without even realizing it, he had changed someone's life.

She made her way to the bar and ordered a glass of wine from the handsome American bartender, then hurried over to join her friends' team.

"Sorry I'm late," she said, slipping onto a stool next to Alice.

"You're just in time for the music round," Alice told her.

"I'm going to play you the introduction to a song," Simon announced. "You need to name the song title and artist. They're each worth one point."

Easy-peasy, Nora thought, as the opening bars of Wham's "Last Christmas" filled the pub. She leaned forward to tell her teammates the answer, but Maeve was already writing it down on their score sheet. Nora wasn't sure if she was wearing floral perfume, or if Maeve always smelled like flowers from running a florist's.

"I had a massive crush on George Michael when I was a teenager," confessed Lucy from the clothes boutique. She was wearing a sparkly top that struck Nora as a bit OTT for quiz night at the George.

"Moving on to question two," Simon said. "In which MGM musical did Judy Garland sing 'Have Yourself a Merry Little Christmas'?"

"Meet Me in St. Louis," Nora whispered to her friends. It was one of her favorite films; she'd forced Simon to watch it with her countless times.

She glanced over at her husband now. When she caught his eye, he winked and she knew he'd put that question in just for her. Grinning, Nora blew him a kiss in return.

"You two are revoltingly adorable," Alice teased.

"Question three—in the Christmas carol 'The Twelve Days of Christmas,' how many lords are leaping?" Simon asked.

The pub buzzed as the teams hunched together over their tables, humming the carol to themselves and debating the lyrics.

"I'm sure it's *nine* lords a leaping . . ." Alice said.

"No, it's nine ladies dancing, *ten* lords a leaping," Lucy insisted.

"Are you sure it's not ten drummers drumming?" Maeve asked.

As her friends counted leaping lords and dancing ladies, Nora counted her blessings. Yes, she was losing her beloved shop. But in the years she had been running it, she'd helped thousands of readers discover authors they loved. She had her health, and after speaking with David, she was reminded of what a blessing that was. Her daughter was happy and having the adventure of a lifetime.

And she and Simon still had each other. What more could she ask for?

16

SIMON

The last Saturday before Christmas the bookshop was busy with last-minute shoppers panic-buying presents. Simon and Nora were rushed off their feet serving customers. The till had hardly stopped ringing since they'd opened at ten.

Simon handed a woman the expensive cookery book she'd just purchased and wished her a Happy Christmas.

But a happy Christmas seemed unlikely to Simon, seeing as it would be their last one in the shop.

"Honey, can you top up the humor books when you get a sec?" Nora asked Simon as she headed over to the children's section to help a customer choose presents for her grandchildren.

"I'm on it." Simon knew he should be glad Nora was finally giving him more to do, but it all seemed a bit futile now. Even if today was their best trading day ever, it wouldn't be enough to save the shop.

He went into the back room and got some books to replenish the display by the till. Humorous gift books had been selling briskly all day as people searched for stocking fillers. There were spoofs of classic children's books, parodies of presidents and photo books of cats in funny costumes—and an alarming number of books about poo.

When he'd finished topping up the display, Simon picked up a copy of *The Best British Joke Book* and flicked through it.

Since his visit to London, Simon had been feeling down. He'd forced himself to host the quiz the other night, not wanting to disappoint the regulars, but it had been an effort to act lighthearted. His father's rejection still smarted badly. He'd thought about asking his brother for help, but Daniel had recently gone through an expensive divorce, and had financial problems of his own to contend with.

Come the new year, Simon and Nora were going to lose their jobs and their home. He'd failed to protect his wife from losing the thing she cherished most.

Sighing, Simon put the book back on the display. It was going to take a lot more than a joke book to make him smile.

The future looked bleak. But for now, while the shop was still open, there were customers to serve. He noticed a man in his thirties milling around uncertainly.

"Can I help you find anything?" Simon asked him.

"I need to get my wife a Christmas present."

"OK, what does she like to read?"

The man frowned and scratched his beard. " 'Er, we've got three kids, so she doesn't really have much time for reading."

Then what are you doing here? Simon thought irritably.

"I thought I'd get her a diet book," explained the man. "She's put on a stone since having our third."

Simon stared at the man. Was he for real? A diet book was about as thoughtful as a lump of coal. This guy's wife needed to lose far more than a stone. *About fourteen stone,* Simon guessed, estimating the customer's weight. If he presented his wife with a slimming guide on Christmas morning, she'd probably use it to bludgeon him to death! Simon couldn't be an accessory to murder.

"Look, mate," he told the man. "I'm going to level with you— if you buy your wife a diet book for Christmas, you'll probably find yourself single by New Year's Eve. My daughter's grown up now, but I remember how tiring little ones are. I'm guessing that with three kids on her hands, what your wife could use most is a bit of escapism."

Simon steered the man toward the fiction section and helped him choose a feel-good romance with a festive cover. *Maybe you should read it yourself and take notes*, Simon thought. Instead, he suggested, "You could offer to take the kids out for the day so she can actually read it."

"Steady on," the man said, looking at Simon as if he were nuts.

As the clueless husband left the shop, Seb Fox bounded in.

"Simon, my good man," Seb said, shaking Simon's hand vigorously. "I'm so glad you've decided to sell. I'm going to make us all a very tidy profit in the new year—just you wait and see." The estate agent looked around the shop, practically salivating with excitement. He knocked on the nearest wall approvingly. "Solid Cotswold stone, that is. They don't make them like they used to."

"Hello, Seb," Nora said, coming over to join them. Nora had told Simon over breakfast that she'd contacted the estate agents, but somehow Simon hadn't expected to be confronted with the reality of that decision quite so soon.

"Is now a good time for me to take photos?" Seb asked, holding up the camera he had around his neck.

"As good as any," Nora said, shrugging.

Seb took the cap off his camera lens and gleefully snapped a few pictures of the fireplace. "Shame about the roof—that will knock a few bob off the price—but buyers are going to go crazy for all these original features."

"Do you mind showing Seb round?" Nora murmured to Simon. "I'll see to the customers."

"Of course," Simon said, squeezing her hand.

The estate agent turned around to take a picture from a different angle. "Look at those oak beams," he enthused. "Gorgeous."

Simon touched his forehead, which still bore a slight bruise from his most recent encounter with the beam. He'd miss everything about the shop—even that bloody beam.

By the time Seb had got all the shots he needed—upstairs and down—a short queue had formed at the counter.

"So sorry for the delay," Nora said as she changed the roll of paper in the register.

"Honestly, if I'd known it was going to take this long, I would have bought it online," huffed the woman at the front of the queue impatiently, drumming her manicured fingernails on the counter. From the look of her pristine wellies and immaculate waxed jacket, Simon guessed she wasn't a local, though she was trying to dress the part. No doubt she was one of the many holiday-home owners in the village. He supposed he should be grateful for people like her—the market for second homes had driven up property values across the Cotswolds, which was about the only thing he and Nora had going for them at the moment. But it made him sad to think that he and Nora probably wouldn't be able to afford to stay in the area they both loved.

Simon slipped behind the counter and took the book off the rude woman's hands. He noted, with satisfaction, that she was buying a copy of *The Oculist of Leipzig*. "An excellent choice," he said, tapping the book's cover. He passed it to Nora with a wink and she bit her lip, trying not to laugh.

Toward the end of the afternoon—which had been so busy that they'd worked through lunch—Alice hurried into the shop, still in her apron. Her hennaed hair was in a messy bun and her cheeks were flushed from the heat of the Copper Kettle's kitchen.

"What's up?" Nora asked her.

"I need gifts for my two Saturday girls," Alice said. "I completely forgot that this is their last shift before Christmas."

"Simon, can you help Alice?" Nora called to Simon, as she was in the middle of ringing up a customer's purchases. "I've got my hands full."

Simon came round the counter. "Let's see what we can find for them."

"Thanks, Simon," Alice said, looking relieved. "I haven't a clue what seventeen-year-old girls are reading these days. I'm guessing it isn't Jilly Cooper anymore . . ."

Simon led her over to the young adult section and scanned the shelves. "Charlotte loved all of John Green's books," he said, handing her a copy of *The Fault in Our Stars*.

That morning, Charlotte had sent him a picture of a curry with the teasing caption TOO HOT FOR YOU, DAD. x. It was going to be so strange not having her with them this Christmas, reading on the sofa in her pajamas. But maybe it was a blessing in disguise. He couldn't face seeing her disappointment when she learned that they had lost the shop.

That her dad hadn't been able to save the day.

"These look perfect," Alice said, selecting two John Green books. "You're a hero."

If only, thought Simon.

Simon carried the books up to the till and Nora wrapped them up for her friend. "Good choices," she said approvingly.

"Thanks so much," Alice replied, as Nora handed her the books. "See you both at the carol concert later?"

The carol concert! Simon had completely forgotten it was tonight. Practically everyone in the village turned out for it. He wasn't sure if Nora would want to go this year. They'd see loads of people they knew, and they still hadn't told Alice and their other friends what was going on with the shop. Of course, everyone would find out soon enough, once the property details were hanging in the estate agent's window.

Nora nodded and said, "Wouldn't miss it for the world."

She seemed to be coping with it all better than Simon had expected. Better than he was, in fact. Nora had been upset after their meeting with the bank, but for the past few days, she seemed to have quietly come to terms with their fate.

Just after six o'clock, Simon flipped the OPEN sign to CLOSED, then flopped onto the sofa, exhausted. Merry scrambled up on top of him and promptly began licking his face.

"Best day of the year," Nora called from the counter. "We took nearly three grand." She laughed and shook her head. "Ironic, isn't it? Now that we're shutting down, we're finally making money."

Simon forced himself to smile, but his heart wasn't in it.

After a quick supper of beans on toast, they walked to the church holding hands. The air was bitterly cold, stinging Simon's nostrils when he inhaled. A halo around the moon gave the dull, overcast sky a fuzzy appearance.

"Feels like it might snow," Simon said. For a moment he worried about whether the roof could withstand a snowstorm. Then he remembered that it wasn't his problem much longer. The shop's new owners could deal with the roof. "We might be in for a white Christmas."

But Nora didn't want to talk about the weather. "So, are you going to tell me what happened in London? You haven't been yourself since you got back."

Simon sighed. He didn't want to tell her that his own parents had declined to help them, but he and Nora had promised not to keep secrets from each other. "I went to see my parents," he finally admitted. "I know you told me not to, but I had to try."

Nora listened quietly as he told her about the visit.

"I don't know why I ever thought my father would put family above business—he never has before. He's still bitter about me not taking over his company. The whole trip was a complete waste of time."

"That's not true," Nora said fiercely, stopping to face him. "You tried—that's the main thing. I know how hard it must have been for you to ask them, and I know you only did it for me."

Simon shook his head. "I tried—but I failed. I just couldn't convince them to help us. They don't believe in the shop—or in me. I'm so sorry, Nora. I've let you down."

Simon's wife gazed at him, the soft moonlight burnishing her copper-colored hair. "You could never let me down, Simon. I didn't think it was possible to love you any more than I already did—but turns out I was wrong." Nora reached up, pulled his head down and gave him a kiss. Her lips felt cold as they touched his, but they soon warmed up as the kiss deepened.

"Oi, Bookworm," called a voice. "Get a room."

They pulled apart and, turning around, Simon saw Howie on the other side of the road, leering at them wolfishly.

"See you at the carol concert, Howie!" Nora called, waving to him. She linked her arm through her husband's. "If we don't hurry, we won't get a seat."

Or worse, thought Simon, *we'll have to sit next to Howie.*

Simon definitely wouldn't miss him if they had to move away from Stowford!

17

SIMON

When they arrived at the church, the cast of the nativity play was assembling in the porch. Simon recognized Doug Jenkins's youngest in a shepherd's costume. *Typecasting*, he thought with a chuckle, as he watched the farmer's son clutching a cuddly toy lamb. Dr. Dhar's daughter, Richa, was an angel. She and her fellow angels twirled around, making their white dresses spin out. One king wearing a shiny gold crown wasn't looking particularly regal as he picked his nose, while the innkeeper proudly showed another king the gap where one of his front teeth was missing. A teacher wearing a camel onesie was trying to keep the children under control, to no avail. The boy playing Joseph and the third king—the doctor's son, Ash—were playing catch with a grubby-looking plastic baby doll while the girl playing Mary tried to snatch it back.

"Give me back baby Jesus!" she wailed.

Olwyn Powell stood among the children talking on her mobile phone. The worried look on her face contrasted with the reindeer brooch flashing merrily on her cardigan. "Oh dear," she said, tucking her phone back into her enormous tote bag. She pulled a pocket pack of tissues out of its depths and silently handed one to the king excavating his nasal passages.

"Everything OK?" Simon asked her.

Olwyn shook her head. "Nothing's going to plan. I've had to ask Deacon Stanley to do the final reading, but goodness knows if he'll be able to stay awake long enough."

The elderly deacon had a habit of falling asleep in the middle of services and snoring loudly.

"I'm sure it will be fine," Nora said.

"That's not all," Olwyn continued. "Mr. Greenwood, the soccer coach from the school, was supposed to play the donkey. But he's just rung to say that he slipped on some ice and hurt his leg, poor chap." She looked at Simon hopefully. "I don't suppose you would be willing to step in?"

Nora chuckled and nudged him with her elbow. "He'd love to."

Simon shot her a look, but knew there was no point trying to get out of it.

"Oh, that's grand." Olwyn produced a gray donkey costume from her apparently bottomless tote bag and handed it to Simon.

But when he tried to zip the onesie up, it didn't fit. He was much too tall.

"Oh, dear," Olwyn said. "That won't do." She checked her watch anxiously. "The performance is due to start in a few minutes."

Simon was about to suggest nipping over to the pub to see if Mateo was available—the guy was an actor, after all—but then he remembered that the young American would also be too tall for the costume. Fortunately, just at that moment, a short, stocky man sprinted into the church with a boy and a girl who were wearing bathrobes and tea towels tied precariously around their heads. "Sorry we're late!" the man panted. "We were dealing with a wardrobe malfunction."

"Julia spilled Ribena on my bathrobe."

"That's because Adam pushed me."

"Stop squabbling," their father hissed. "You're in church."

"Oh, Mr. Fitzpatrick," Olwyn said, as Simon stepped out of the donkey costume. "I don't suppose you'd be willing to be our donkey?"

"Say yes, Daddy!" the girl cried, as her brother hopped up and down chanting, "Do it! Do it!"

"Looks like I don't have much of a choice," the man said, unzipping his coat to reveal a Swindon Town soccer shirt underneath it. "Anyway, I'm good at making an ass of myself."

"Daddy said a rude word!" The girl giggled.

"I'm a Gunners man, myself," Simon said, handing the costume to the new recruit.

"Oh well," the man replied, chuckling, "there's no accounting for taste."

Simon thought the guy looked familiar, but he couldn't quite place him. Perhaps he was on a rival five-a-side team? "Do you play soccer?" Simon asked.

"Only with these two," the man said, stepping into the costume.

"Gentlemen, we don't have time to talk about soccer," Olwyn cut in impatiently.

"Sorry, Miss Powell," the man said, winking at Simon as he zipped up the onesie.

As a latecomer in a dark overcoat came up the church steps, Simon and Nora hurried down the aisle, looking for somewhere to sit. They squeezed into the end of a pew near the back. Sitting a few pews in front of them were Lucy, Maeve and Alice, and Alice turned and waved to them.

"At least it's nice and warm in here," Nora whispered.

Candles flickered in sconces around the church, making the

stained-glass windows glow. Parents chatted excitedly as they waited for their little darlings to make their theatrical debuts. Up at the front of the church, there was a wooden manger filled with hay in front of the altar.

A few moments later, the organ began to play "Silent Night" and Olwyn led her cast of angels, shepherds and wise men up the aisle, to the collective sound of "*awwww*" from the audience.

"Remember the year Charlotte played the angel Gabriel?" Nora whispered. "She loved that costume so much."

Simon nodded. It seemed like only yesterday their daughter had been standing behind the manger, holding a star on a stick in her tinsel-trimmed wings.

Olwyn approached the pulpit. "Welcome to our annual nativity play and carol concert," she said. "We'd like to dedicate tonight's performance to Emma Swann, who was once a pupil of mine at St. Stephen's and a member of the school choir. Very sadly, she passed away this summer."

Around the church, people bowed their heads solemnly, remembering the tragic accident. Simon's heart went out to the girl's family. He and Nora were missing Charlotte, but at least they knew they would see their daughter again eventually. Nora reached for Simon's hand and gave it a squeeze, and he knew she was thinking the same thing.

The somber mood soon lifted as the children playing Mary and Joseph led the donkey out and asked the innkeeper, whose grin was so wide that Simon could see the gap in his teeth from the back of the church, for shelter. When the innkeeper told them there was no room, the donkey gave a dejected "hee-haw" and the audience laughed appreciatively.

As the cast gathered around the manger, the organist began to play "O Little Town of Bethlehem."

"Too bad they didn't have Airbnb in biblical times," Simon whispered in Nora's ear as the congregation sang along.

Nora laughed and rested her head on Simon's shoulder.

As the carol faded away, a different noise filled the church—the unmistakable sound of Deacon Stanley's snoring.

When the three kings arrived at the manger, Simon chuckled as the one holding myrrh began to pick his nose as soon as he had delivered his gift.

After the children had sung a rousing rendition of "We Three Kings," Olwyn approached the pulpit once more. She beamed out at the congregation. "To close this evening's performance, we have a very special guest for our final reading . . ."

Someone better give Deacon Stanley a poke, thought Simon. ". . . Please give a warm welcome to our local MP, David Langdon!"

Simon turned in surprise and watched a thin, dark-haired man make his way down the central aisle. As the politician walked past, to a smattering of applause, Simon recognized the man from the train platform the other day. *So, it* was *him*, Simon thought.

The politician cleared his throat and read "Ring Out, Wild Bells" by Alfred, Lord Tennyson. Although he looked frail, his voice was powerful as he read the poem with the confidence of an experienced orator.

> *Ring out the old, ring in the new,*
> *Ring, happy bells, across the snow . . .*

As Simon listened to the beautiful verses, Tennyson's words resonated with him. There would be big changes ahead for him and Nora. Perhaps not all of them would be bad.

When the MP had finished reading, the organist began to play

"Hark! The Herald Angels Sing." As Simon joined in the chorus, he felt his heart swell along with the uplifting music. It was impossible to hear that carol and not feel joyful.

Afterward, the audience filed into the church hall for refreshments. The dad in the donkey costume was on his hands and knees, gamely giving little kids rides on his back.

"Just think," Nora said, grinning, "that could have been you."

Thank god it wasn't. His knees couldn't have withstood donkey rides.

Simon got himself and Nora a mince pie each. "Not bad, but not as good as yours," he said, taking a bite.

He noticed a woman taking a photograph of the boy who had played Joseph. He was pulling a face and making rabbit ears with his fingers over a shepherd's head.

"Could you please stop that, Jamie."

"Liz, isn't it?" he said, going over when she'd finally managed to get a shot of both boys smiling. "It's Simon—from the bookshop."

"Oh, of course," Liz said, looking a bit flustered.

"Great job, boys," he said, giving the kids a thumbs-up.

As the boys ran off to get hot chocolates, Simon introduced Liz to Nora. "Liz came in to buy children's books a couple of weeks ago," he told her. "To help her boys with their reading."

Nora smiled. "How are they getting on?"

"I'm reading them *The Hobbit*," Liz said. "They really like it. I've promised them they can watch the film over the Christmas holidays once we finish it."

"Have you chosen your menu for your Boxing Day dinner?" Simon asked her, remembering that she was going to be on her own on Christmas Day.

"I'm going to do gammon. I found a recipe for a honey and orange glaze that doesn't sound too tricky. I can make most of it in advance, so I can focus on spending time with the boys. Oh, and I'm making a trifle for pudding."

"Sounds delicious," Nora said. "I've got an amazing recipe for a chocolate one . . ."

As Nora and Liz discussed cooking, Simon chatted to a few customers and regulars from his quiz. He helped himself to another mince pie, then noticed the Patels from the chemist's shop standing with their grandkids and Dr. Dhar. He went over to say hello.

Dr. Dhar tutted at the mince pie in Simon's hands. "I won't tell you off because it's Christmas," she said, with mock disapproval.

"Great job, kids," Simon said to Ash and Richa. Ash barely looked up from the copy of *Harry Potter and the Chamber of Secrets* he was reading.

"What do you say, Ash?" Dr. Dhar scolded, nudging her son.

"Oh," said the boy, his crown nearly falling off as he looked up, "thank you." Then he stuck his nose back in the book.

"Don't worry," Simon said, laughing. "Far be it from me to come between a reader and a good book."

"Nani-ji, did Auntie Sam come?" Richa asked, tugging her grandmother's hand.

Mrs. Patel sighed and shook her head. "She had to work, *beta*."

"But it's Saturday," Richa said, her bottom lip jutting out with disappointment.

"I'm afraid we can't come to your Christmas Eve party this year," Mr. Patel told Simon. "We have a family party—my cousins will be visiting from Birmingham."

"How much do you want to bet my sister works through that, too?" Dr. Dhar muttered.

Simon chatted with the Patels for a few more minutes, then made his way over to Nora. "Ready to go home?" he asked her.

"Not quite. I want to congratulate Olwyn first."

They waited until a group of proud parents had finished congratulating the show's organizer, then Nora gave her a hug. "You really outdid yourself this year, Olwyn."

"Fancy David Langdon turning up," Simon said.

"I was as surprised as everyone else," Olwyn said. "We invite him every year, but he's never accepted before. He turned us down this year, too, but he arrived just before the start. Said he'd had a last-minute cancellation."

"He popped into the shop the other day," Nora said, "and bought a book of Christmas poems. I guess now I know why!"

Simon gave his wife a quizzical look, slightly surprised that she hadn't mentioned the MP's visit earlier. Then again, he *had* been avoiding her.

"Oh, speaking of books," Olwyn said. "I wanted to thank you both for the one you gave me. It was a lovely surprise. At least, I assume it was from you?"

Nora nodded. "We decided to do some random acts of literary kindness and I wanted to send you one, because you've been such a loyal supporter of the shop."

When Olwyn was still teaching at St. Stephen's, she'd often invited local authors to speak at the school, and the bookshop had supplied books for the children to buy and get signed.

"Which one did you get?" Nora asked.

"I got a Sherlock Holmes mystery," Olwyn said. "And you know how much I love detective stories. In fact—I'm thinking about writing one myself . . ."

"You should," Simon urged.

"I've taught so many children how to write stories," Olwyn said, "but I've never had the courage to do it myself. And when I was teaching, I never had the time. But now that I'm retired, I have all this time on my hands—"

"It's snowing!" the nose-picking king cried, running into the church hall. "It's snowing!"

All of the children rushed outdoors. Nora grabbed Simon's hand and dragged him outside, too. Thick flakes of snow were swirling in the air, sticking to the ground when they landed. A fluffy layer of white blanketed the churchyard, with only a few blades of grass poking through the snow. The big weeping willow in the graveyard looked like a ghost, its branches enrobed in white.

"Snowball fight!" cried the man in the donkey costume, organizing the children into two teams. Simon suddenly remembered where he'd seen the guy before—he'd come into the George looking for work a few weeks ago. He'd had the two kids with him then, too.

Soon, angels were pelting innkeepers, while kings fired snowballs at shepherds.

"Gotcha!" shouted the little girl who had played Mary, taking aim and throwing a fluffy white missile at the third king—and (appropriately enough) hitting him dead on the nose.

As the man in the donkey costume bent over to scoop up more snow, a shepherd in a too-big bathrobe darted forward, launched a snowball and hit him right on the bottom.

"I got Daddy!" she chortled, doing a triumphant jig before someone from the other team retaliated.

"They're having fun," Nora said, beaming at the snowy scene in front of them.

"Want to join in?" Simon teased, gently brushing snow off Nora's hair.

She looked up at him tenderly, snowflakes dusting her eyelashes. "Let's go home. I'm in the mood for some indoor fun."

As they walked home through the falling snow, Nora pressed up against his side, Simon listened to the church bells ringing out as the clock struck nine. The words of the poem David Langdon had read echoed in his head:

Ring, happy bells, across the snow . . .

To his surprise, he *did* feel happy. He was about to become homeless and unemployed, but tonight, Simon felt like the luckiest man on earth.

18

NORA

When Nora woke on the morning of Christmas Eve, something felt . . . different. She reached out for Simon, but his side of the bed was empty. That wasn't unusual—her husband was an early riser. No, it was the light. Dazzling sunlight was streaming into the room. Sitting up and looking out the window, Nora saw the reason why her room was so blindingly bright. Snow had continued to fall through the night and now sunlight was reflecting off the thick blanket of white that had settled over the countryside.

A white Christmas! For a moment, Nora felt like a little girl again.

From the kitchen, she could hear Simon whistling along to the radio as he made breakfast. Pulling on her dressing gown, she went to join him.

"Morning," she said, stealing a piece of his toast.

"Hands off, cheeky!" Simon said. But he smiled as he said it and put two more slices of bread in the toaster.

And now for the news, said the radio presenter's voice. *Businesses have been given a deadline of two years to comply with new regulations passed by Parliament this month. The Renewable Energy Bill, championed by MP David*

Langdon, was a victory for environmental campaigners and the result of several years of lobbying.

"No wonder he looked so rough," Simon said, pouring Nora a cup of tea. "Here I was thinking he spent all his time in Westminster trying to get into his assistants' pants."

Nora chuckled, but didn't comment. She hadn't told Simon about the MP's illness. David had told her about his depression in confidence, and she didn't think it was her place to share something so private. Not even with her husband.

Heavy snow fell over Southern England and Wales overnight, with more snowfall expected. Airports and trains are facing severe delays on one of the busiest travel days of the year . . .

"Good thing Charlotte isn't trying to get home," Nora said. "Traveling today will be a nightmare." Charlotte's last Instagram post had been a picture of herself with a monkey on a beach. No chance of snow there.

Nora frowned as a thought suddenly occurred to her. "Do you think we should cancel the party? People might not want to go out in the snow."

"I think it should go ahead. Most people aren't coming from very far away."

Nora could tell from the look on Simon's face that he was thinking the same thing she was: *It will be our last one.* Neither of them said it out loud. They didn't need to.

~~We'll just have to make it our best one ever,~~ Nora told herself, determined to stay cheerful.

"Guess I'd better shovel and grit the pavement in front of the shop," Simon said. "Wouldn't want anyone to slip and sue us for millions."

"Ha! Just let them try."

Merry began to dance around, wagging her tail expectantly, as Simon pulled on his boots and coat.

"Sorry, Merry," Nora said, scooping up the little dog so she didn't follow Simon downstairs. "You're stuck with me."

While Merry whined impatiently, Nora got dressed in a thick sweater with a snowflake pattern which her mother had knitted for her years ago. She always thought of it as her Christmas sweater, even though Christmas sweaters weren't A Thing when Penelope had made it. It was bobbled and there was a moth hole under one arm, but Nora wore it every Christmas in her mum's honor.

When she'd finished dressing herself, Nora fastened a tartan jacket around Merry's plump tummy. "Very smart. Red is definitely your color." Merry obviously agreed because she licked Nora's nose.

Once they were both bundled up well enough to survive an Arctic expedition, Nora led Merry downstairs and opened the back door. The little dog stepped outside tentatively, her paws sinking deep into the snow. Her black nose was the only thing to stop her face from blending in with the pristine white drifts.

Nora decided to steer clear of the high street. Like Simon, a lot of the shopkeepers would be sprinkling salt to melt the ice on their pavements, and Nora didn't want it to sting Merry's paws. Instead, they cut down an alleyway and headed toward the fields that backed on to the village. Once she'd got used to it, Merry was in heaven, frisking and frolicking through the powdery snow.

Nora brushed off a wooden fence and leaned against it, gazing out at the countryside around her. It looked like a winter wonderland, straight out of a fairy tale. *Little Red Riding Hood*, she thought, watching Merry's red jacket disappear and reappear as she plowed her way through the snow.

On the other side of the field, a man and two children were trudging up a slope that locals called Blackberry Hill. When they reached the top, the man handed each child a plastic tray. The kids sat on the trays and sledged down the hill, their whoops of delight ringing across the field.

Drawn by their excited squeals, Merry barked and bounded over to the children, eager to join in the fun.

"Merry! Come back!" Nora called. But the terrier ignored her, too busy befriending the children at the bottom of the slope.

Nora trudged through the calf-deep snow after her. Soon, despite the bitterly cold air, she was sweating through her layers.

"Sorry about that," Nora said breathlessly when she finally reached the family. "She's mine. Her name is Merry."

"No worries," the children's father said. She hadn't recognized him from a distance, because he was wearing a hat and scarf, but it was the man from the carol concert—the one who'd played the donkey. "My kids love dogs."

"You were great last night," she told him.

"Thanks," he said, laughing. "Maybe I missed my calling."

"Can Merry go sledging, too?" the girl asked, her cheeks rosy from the cold and exertion.

"Please?" the boy begged.

Nora laughed. "You can try, but I'm not sure she'll like it."

"Race you to the top," the girl cried, picking up her tray and charging up the hill with Merry chasing after her.

"Not fair! Julia got a head start!" her brother complained, charging after them.

When she reached the top, Julia sat on her tray. Merry jumped onto her lap and they whooshed down the hill together. When they reached the bottom, Merry jumped off, barked and rushed off up the hill again.

I guess she does like it.

The children's dad chuckled. "It's nice to see them having some good old-fashioned fun for a change."

Nora nodded in agreement. She had sledged down this very

hill, as had Charlotte. A wooden sleigh that had been Simon's was still somewhere in the shed, covered in cobwebs. It made Nora sad to think they'd probably need to leave it behind when they moved.

"How old are they?" she asked.

"Six," he said. "They're twins."

The boy ran up to his father, his breath coming out in puffs. "Daddy, is the snow going to melt today?"

"It's too cold for that. Besides, there's more on the way."

"Yay! Santa can land his sleigh on the snow and bring us lots of presents!" The boy ran back up the hill, the tea tray tucked under his arm.

Nora smiled. "I bet they'll be too excited to sleep tonight."

"I just hope they aren't disappointed," the man said, his smile fading. "Money's a bit tight this year."

Nora nodded sympathetically. The Stowford Community Association was raising money for the local food bank this year, as it was in high demand. She and Simon obviously weren't the only people in the village struggling financially.

After each child had taken Merry on another run down the slope, Nora checked her watch. It was nearly time to open the shop. Her toes were beginning to feel numb, despite the fact that she was wearing two pairs of thick socks. "Come on, Merry!" she called, clapping her hands. "Time to go home."

"Merry Christmas, Merry!" Julia giggled, giving the dog a final cuddle.

Back home, Merry flopped into her basket, worn out from her snowy walk, while Nora performed the world's least sexy striptease, peeling off layer upon layer of woolens. Then she went downstairs to light the fire and open the shop.

Moments after she'd flipped the sign to OPEN, a young man rushed in, his eyes darting around the shop wildly.

Nora quickly diagnosed his problem and calmly took the situation in hand. "Who do you need presents for?"

"Everyone."

Half an hour later, Nora had helped him find presents for his mother, girlfriend and assorted friends and relations. He'd chosen a book called *Organize Your Life* for his mum, who was a fan of the author's television show about decluttering. Nora was tempted to suggest that he get another copy for himself, so he didn't find himself in the same situation next year.

As the customer left, clutching a big bag of gift-wrapped books, Simon came in, stamping snow off his boots and holding an enormous goose by its legs. "Merry Christmas, one and all!" he said.

"Wasn't it a prize turkey Scrooge bought for the Cratchits?" Nora asked, examining the goose dubiously. What had they been thinking? It was enormous!

Simon peeled off his gloves and rubbed his hands together. "It's colder than a toilet seat in the tundra out there."

"You were gone a long time."

"After I did our pavement, I helped Alice clear the front of the Copper Kettle."

Nora smiled and shook her head. Typical of Simon to ignore the cold and help their friend. "You warm up by the fire. I'll put Big Bird here away and make you a cup of tea."

Merry gave the goose a curious sniff when Nora carried it up to the flat.

"Don't even think about it," Nora warned her.

Trying to fit the goose into the fridge was a bigger challenge than she'd expected. She had to empty the entire contents and rearrange them, stacking yogurt pots, tubs of hummus and wedges of cheese on top of each other like a game of culinary

Jenga. Eventually, once she'd chucked out several out-of-date con-
diments and a forgotten Tupperware container of moldy turnip
stew, Nora managed to squash the goose onto a shelf.

Shortly after she went back downstairs with Simon's tea, a
burly man came into the shop, holding two huge crates. "Delivery
for Simon Walden," he announced.

What could that be? Nora wondered. They definitely hadn't ordered more stock. Not when they were going to have to get rid of
the thousands of books they already had on the shelves.

The crates make a clanking noise as the man set them on the
ground. Simon signed for the delivery, then he opened the note
that had come with it. Reading it, he scowled, then screwed the
note into a ball and threw it in the fire.

Ahh . . . it must be from Charles and Margaret.

Simon was still furious at his parents. He'd ignored their invitation to get together over the Christmas holidays.

Nora opened the crates. The first one contained bottles of the
usual French red, but the second box contained Italian prosecco.
She whistled. "Two cases this year." Her in-laws were really pushing the boat out.

They must be feeling guilty. Good.

"All the better to toast our failure with," Simon said darkly. "I
should pour it all down the drain."

"Don't be ridiculous. We can serve it at the party tonight.
Speaking of which . . . I still need to get a few bits and pieces."

"The main roads should be clear by now. I can drive to the
supermarket," Simon offered.

Nora scribbled a quick list, grateful that she wasn't going to
have to brave Sainsbury's, full of last-minute shoppers panic-
buying tubs of Quality Street and Brussels sprouts.

Ooh! That was another thing they needed! She added Brussels sprouts to the list. Simon hated sprouts—they reminded him of over-cooked boarding school dinners—but Nora loved them. She'd even been known to munch them raw.

"I may be some time," Simon quipped, taking the list from her and heading back out into the snow.

There was a steady trickle of customers as morning became afternoon. In between customers, Nora added cuffs to Simon's Christmas sweater. When she was done, she took out her phone and tapped out a quick message to Charlotte.

> Hi, honey. Hope you can call us tomorrow. When would be good for you?

Nora checked Charlotte's Instagram again. She hadn't updated it since the monkey picture, over forty-eight hours ago. *She's fine*, Nora told herself. It was ironic, really. She'd nagged her teenage daughter about being on her phone too much. Now, she relied on those frequent updates.

"Hello, Nora."

Nora looked up from her phone and froze, her stomach seizing with panic. It was Derek Brown, the bailiff. *No, enforcement officer*, she corrected herself. "You're early! Our deadline is the second of January. We haven't—"

Derek held up his hand to reassure her. "Don't worry, I'm not here in a professional capacity. I'm just looking for a Christmas gift."

Nora's stomach unclenched. He wasn't here to collect the money.

Yet.

"My son's just getting into science fiction and I want to get him a copy of one of my favorite books for Christmas. I couldn't find it in any of the bookshops in Cheltenham and I'm too late to order it online. I drove all the way over here, even though the roads are a mess. You're my last hope."

"What's it called?" Nora asked, guiding him to the science fiction and fantasy section.

"*House of Stairs,* by William Sleator. It's about a group of teenagers trapped in a house with an evil red machine that turns them against each other."

Nora squatted down to check the bottom shelf—S to Z. "You're in luck," she said, producing a copy of the book. Judging by the rather dated jacket artwork, it had been on the shelves a long time—though not quite as long as *The True Story of the Christmas Truce.*

"I knew you'd have it!" Derek said, beaming. "Your mum recommended this to me when I was my son's age. It had me hooked from the very first page."

"I hope he enjoys it as much as you did." In spite of everything, Nora couldn't help liking the bailiff—he was a fellow book lover.

Not long after Derek had gone, Simon returned with the shopping, looking harried.

"Nightmare before Christmas?" Nora asked sympathetically.

"A car skidded on the A429 and the crash caused a massive bottleneck. By the time I got to the supermarket, there was a brawl going on in the aisle over the last jar of cranberry sauce. I had to fight them off with this—" He pulled out a stalk of Brussels sprouts and collapsed onto the sofa.

"My hero," Nora said, laughing. She picked up the bags of shopping and took the sprouts off Simon. "I'd better go and get started on the mince pies. If it gets too busy down here, just shout."

In the kitchen, Nora switched on the radio, preheated the oven and set out the ingredients she needed. Flour, butter, sugar, a jar of mincemeat, an orange, assorted spices . . . She knew her mother's recipe by heart.

First, she grated the orange, then she mixed the zest with the mincemeat and spices, adding a generous slug of brandy—Penelope's not-so-secret ingredient. When the filling was ready, Nora measured out the flour and sugar, then rubbed the dry ingredients into the butter, working it into a crumbly mixture with her fingertips.

Her mother's voice echoed in her head. *It should feel like damp sand.*

The kitchen smelled of Christmas spices, but Nora felt blue. The bailiff's visit had thrown her. Seeing Derek, nice as he was, had brought home how little time they had left here.

And how much she wished they could stay . . .

As she kneaded the lump of pastry, Nora was suddenly overcome with a wave of longing for one of Penelope's patchouli-scented hugs. She pounded the dough, taking her frustrations out on it.

Don't over-knead the dough, Nora. It will make the pastry tough.

"Sorry, Mum," Nora said aloud.

She rolled out the dough, then pressed out circles with a pastry cutter. She wasn't just missing her mother—she was missing Charlotte, too. When Charlotte had been little, she'd loved cutting out little stars and hearts to decorate the tops of the mince pies. As they'd baked together, they'd sung along to cheesy Christmas songs on the radio. It just wasn't the same without her. Nora felt horribly sad to think that Charlotte would miss out on spending one last Christmas in her childhood home.

Should we have told her? That question had been nagging Nora ever since their phone call.

No. They'd done the right thing. If Charlotte knew about their problems, she'd want to help, and there was nothing she could do.

As the mince pies baked in the oven, Nora filled bowls with crisps, nuts and olives, then she arranged some local cheeses on a wooden board with crackers and a chutney Simon had picked up at the market. She emptied two bottles of the red that Simon's parents had sent into her biggest saucepan, chucking in some spices and the remains of the orange she'd used to make the mince pies, and let it simmer over a low heat. It pleased her to think of how horrified Charles and Margaret would be if they knew their expensive wine was being used to make mulled wine. *Serves them right.* She'd never criticize her in-laws out loud, but Nora was angry at them. Not because they hadn't invested in the shop, but for making Simon feel unloved.

While dozens of mince pies cooled, Nora got herself ready, changing into a long red velvet skirt and a white ruffled silk blouse that always made her feel like a heroine in a Brontë novel. She twisted her hair into a bun and put on some mascara, blush and lipstick—she didn't want to take the consumptive Victorian look *too* far.

"You look gorgeous," Simon said, coming into the bathroom to shave.

When they were both in their party best, Simon and Nora carried the food downstairs. They cleared books off one of the tables and arranged napkins, plastic wineglasses, the nibbles and plates of mince pies on it. Simon put on Christmas music and threw another log on the fire, which Merry settled down in front of for a nap. The scent of mulled wine wafted down from the flat. Outside, it had begun to snow again, and flakes drifted by outside the window. The shop couldn't have felt more Christmassy unless Father Christmas himself walked through the door.

So why couldn't Nora muster up even the tiniest bit of Christmas spirit?

As they waited for their guests to arrive, she wandered around the aisles, running her fingers lovingly over the books' spines. They were like old friends. What would happen to them when they sold the shop?

Tears began to spill down Nora's cheeks. She grabbed a

napkin and dabbed at her eyes, trying to salvage her mascara. *Typical. The one time I actually put on some makeup I go and ruin it by crying.*

"Hey," Simon said, noticing her tears. "What's wrong?"

"It just sort of hit me this afternoon." Nora looked around sadly at the shop she knew and loved every inch of. "How much I'm going to miss this place."

"Oh, honey, me too." He gave her a hug and stroked her hair. "Are you sure you're up for this? I can always say you're not feeling very well and cancel."

"Don't be silly—these mince pies aren't going to eat themselves." Now that she'd had a cry Nora felt a bit better. "And it's our last chance to give something back to all the people who have supported us over the years."

Although, saying that, where was everyone? She looked at her watch and frowned. It was already ten minutes past seven, and not one guest had arrived. "Maybe nobody's going to turn up."

"I'm sure they're just fashionably late," Simon said. "It's probably taking people a bit longer to get here because of the snow."

Nora nibbled an olive nervously as she watched the minutes tick by. By quarter past, there were still no guests . . .

Just as she'd resigned herself to an evening of comfort-eating mince pies (there were worse ways to spend Christmas Eve!), the bell above the door rang. A young Indian woman burst into the shop, her black hair dusted with snowflakes. "Please tell me you're still open," she gasped. "I really need to buy some gifts!"

19

SAM

"All the other shops are shut," Sam said, clutching her side as she tried to catch her breath. "Except for the newsagent's."

She'd sprinted from the train station down the high street, desperately looking for anywhere still open to buy gifts. She'd been about to give up when she'd suddenly remembered the invitation she'd received along with the copy of *A Christmas Carol*.

It was Charles bloody Dickens's fault that she was looking for Christmas presents, anyway.

As usual, Sam had delegated her Christmas shopping to her PA, who'd bought gift vouchers for Sam's family, friends and underlings. Connie had even written messages on the cards, including the one for herself. But when Connie had popped into Sam's glass-walled office and handed the envelopes over, Sam had felt miserly, despite the generous gift cards.

She'd tried to shrug it off, telling herself a voucher was better than a present the recipient might not even like. But as she'd watched the office empty, even her most conscientious colleagues hurrying home to their families or to celebrate in the pub, Sam could no longer ignore the worry that had been nagging her ever since she'd finished reading *A Christmas Carol*: that if she didn't change her ways, she was going to end up like Ebenezer Scrooge—rich and successful, but miserable and alone.

Through the glass, she had seen Connie tapping away at her keyboard, stuck at work until her boss went home. And Sampriti Patel never knocked off early—not even on Christmas Eve.

Just like Scrooge.

Sam had come out of her office and stood by her assistant's desk. "Why don't you head home?"

Connie had been unable to conceal her shock. "Really?"

"You probably have a lot to do. I'm sure your kids will want to see you."

To her shame, Sam couldn't remember the names of the two girls in matching school uniforms in the snow globe on Connie's desk. She never bothered making small talk with her colleagues—it wasn't an efficient use of her time. She barely knew anything about the calm, no-nonsense woman who organized her diary with the precision of a Swiss watchmaker and who'd popped out to buy her tampons on more than one occasion.

Connie had needed no further encouragement. "Thank you so much, Sam," she'd said, powering down her computer and pulling on her coat. "I can beat the rush and get a head start on the cooking for tomorrow. And I still have presents to wrap . . ."

Sam had picked up the snow globe, turning it over in her hand, trying to find the right words. She could quite happily tell her clients that they needed to lay off staff or cut whole divisions. Why was this so hard?

Scrooge, the voice in her head had said again.

Slinging her bag over her shoulder, Connie had hesitated. "Did you need me to do anything else before I go?"

Sam had taken a deep breath. "No. Er . . . I just wondered if you fancied going out for lunch in the new year?"

"That would be lovely," Connie had said, smiling and then sprinting to the lift. Just before the doors shut, she'd popped her head out and called across the office, "Oh, and Sam—Happy Christmas!"

Back at her desk, Sam had stared at the client proposal on her computer screen for a few minutes, before switching off her own monitor. *Sod it—I'm going to take a half day, too.*

She had plenty of holiday left. In fact, she hadn't had a day off since her disastrous final holiday with James.

So, shoving the gift cards in her bag, she'd headed to Paddington. Her plan was to buy real Christmas gifts for her family once she got to Stowford, but the weather gods had conspired against her. It had started snowing heavily on the way from Canary Wharf to Paddington. Her train had been delayed for hours, only pulling into Stowford just before seven.

Now, Sam gazed around the Stowford Bookshop and hoped that the lady in the gorgeous red velvet skirt and the tall man in a corduroy jacket would sell her some books, even though it was long past closing time.

"I know you're having a party," Sam said. "But I have an invitation."

"Welcome," the woman said warmly. "I'm Nora. And this is my husband, Simon."

"Hi," Sam said. "I'm Sampriti—but everyone calls me Sam."

The couple exchanged an excited look.

"Sampriti Patel?" Nora asked.

"Er, yes?"

Nora clapped her hands in delight. "We sent you a book!"

"Yeah," Sam admitted, nodding.

"Which one?" Nora asked.

"Um . . . *A Christmas Carol.*" OK, this was getting weird—why didn't they know what book they'd sent her?

"Did you like it?" Nora asked.

"I guess . . . it got me thinking." What she was thinking right now was that it had been a mistake to read it. She should have just returned it, the way she'd intended. She'd been perfectly happy before Charles bloody Dickens had made her question all her life choices.

No, you weren't.

"I'm so glad you could make it to our party," Simon said, offering her a glass of mulled wine.

Sam looked around nervously. Where were all the other guests? Had this nice, normal-looking couple lured her to their shop for some sort of kinky threesome? Were they going to chop her up into pieces and feed her to the little white dog snoozing by the fire? She took a step back nervously. "Er, where's everyone else?"

"We were just wondering that ourselves," Nora said. "I expect that it's taking people a bit longer to get here because of the snow. In the meantime, shall we find you some presents?"

The only other alternative was to buy her family a Terry's Chocolate Orange and a dusty bottle of bubble bath each from the corner shop. Thinking, *Please don't murder me,* she followed Nora into the aisles of books.

"Your nephew will love this," Nora said, handing her the fourth book in the *Harry Potter* series. "He was in here a few days ago with your sister."

"Wait—you know Ani?" Sam asked, confused.

"And your parents," Nora said, "but I don't think we've met before."

Well, I guess that explains why they sent me a book, Sam thought. They were friends with her family. Probably knew her parents through the Community Association her mother was always going on about.

"I went to university shortly after they moved to Stowford,"

Sam explained. "And I've lived in London since graduating." Unlike her sister, who'd chosen to work at a surgery in Stowford to be close to her parents, Sam had always considered herself more of a city person.

The bookseller helped her choose a story collection for Richa, an art book for her sister, a biography about her dad's favorite cricket player and a jumbo Sudoku book for her mum who did puzzles every day (she'd read an article saying that it would ward off dementia).

"Oh!" Sam said. "I'm forgetting Vikram, Ani's husband. I have absolutely no idea what to get him—he's pretty dull. He likes watching history documentaries, though."

"I have just the thing for him," Nora said, adding a copy of *The Oculist of Leipzig* to the top of the pile. "What about you?" she asked Sam. "Do you have a special somebody in your life?" Then she shook her head. "Sorry—I'm being nosy."

And so it begins . . . She was going to get asked that question a lot over the next few days. "No, I'm single at the moment. I'm too busy with work to have a relationship."

If she said it enough times, maybe she'd actually believe it. Because deep down, Sam *did* want to find "a special somebody." Her brother-in-law might be dull, but Vik and Ani were really happy together. Sam secretly yearned to find a love like that.

"You probably just haven't met the right person yet," Nora said. "When you do, you'll find a way to make time for them."

But how am I going to meet anyone? thought Sam. *All I do is work.*

They carried the books over to the till.

"I think you might take the prize," Simon said, going behind the counter to help Nora wrap the books.

"Prize?"

"This takes last-minute Christmas shopping to the next level."

"I didn't mean to leave it quite this late. I was going to do my shopping this afternoon, but my train home from work got delayed because of the snow."

"I hope you're going to stay for the party," Nora said, as they wrapped the books.

Not if I can help it. Sam racked her brain for an excuse. She obviously no longer thought Nora and Simon were kinky serial killers, but it had been a long day. Then again, if she went home, she'd have to deal with all her aunties from Birmingham . . .

"You can't leave without trying one of Nora's mince pies," Simon said, offering her a plate. "They're the best."

But before Sam could reply, the bookshop door opened and a man and two little kids came in.

WILL

"Sorry we're late," Will said.

He wasn't expecting to know anyone at this party. But he actually recognized two out of the three people in the bookshop— and the only dog.

"Merry!" Adam and Julia cried, running over to the terrier dozing by the fire. She woke up and yipped excitedly as the twins greeted her with cuddles.

"I hope you don't mind that I brought my kids—it's hard to find a sitter on Christmas Eve."

"Merry is delighted to see them again, and so am I," said the woman they'd met sledging. "I'm Nora, by the way." She gestured to the pretty young woman standing by the till. "And this is Sam."

Sam nodded indifferently at Will. "Hey."

"I'm Will." He pointed over to the twins, who were sitting on the floor, feeding a mince pie to Merry. "And those two menaces are Adam and Julia."

The tall man shook Will's hand. "I'm Simon."

"The Arsenal fan," Will said, remembering their conversation on the church porch.

"That's right," Simon said, nodding. "Do you play? My five-a-side team could use a young gun like you."

Will chuckled at the expression "young gun." At thirty-seven, it didn't really apply. But it would be nice to play soccer again. "I do—or rather, I did. I played for my school team, but these days it's mostly just a kickabout in the park with the kids."

"Can I get you a drink?"

"Love one." Free booze was the main reason he'd decided to come to this party. "Cheers," he said, accepting a glass of wine and taking a sip.

Whoa! He wasn't exactly a connoisseur, but this tasted like seriously good stuff. Or maybe it was just because he hadn't had a drink in ages. He took another gulp, and felt the wine go straight to his head.

Slow down, he told himself. *At this rate you'll be dancing naked on the counter before nine o'clock.*

"Er, I wanted to thank you," Will said. "For sending me *A Child's Christmas in Wales.*"

Nora beamed. "Oh, so *you're* Will Fitzpatrick! What did you think of the book?"

"It was a really nice surprise—the kids loved it."

"Wait a minute," Sam said, looking confused. "You sent out books to other random people—not just me?"

"Only six of you," Nora explained. "We did an online appeal for nominations. The idea was to cheer up people having a tough time."

Sam looked slightly offended. "Oh."

"Well, it worked," Will said. "I'm out of work at the moment, so I've been worrying about not being able to buy the twins expensive

Christmas gifts. The book reminded me that I have a lot to be thankful for. Presents aren't the most important thing about Christmas. It's the time you spend with your family and friends."

"Well said," Simon agreed. He topped up Will's glass, then went over to greet the small group of guests who had just arrived, stamping snow off their shoes.

The snow had been a godsend. Hopefully, when the twins looked back on this Christmas, they'd remember the sledging and the snowball fights rather than the meager gifts under the Christmas tree. But that didn't mean Will wasn't lying awake in bed every night worrying about how he was going to support them when his redundancy package ran out.

"This may be a bit cheeky," Will said, "but I wondered if you had any vacancies here? This seems like a nice place to work."

"Oh, it's the best," Nora said. She gazed around the shop and gave Will a smile that seemed a bit sad.

Then she shook her head. "But I'm afraid we're not hiring at the moment."

"Nowhere seems to be."

"I'll keep my ear to the ground and let you know if I hear of anything."

"Thanks, I'd appreciate that."

"And what do you do for a living, Sam?" Nora asked, turning to the smartly dressed younger woman. "Your mum says you work in the City."

"I'm a management consultant," she said. "I work for Apex Consulting."

Apex Consulting. Will's hackles rose as he heard the name. That was the consultancy that had been appointed by Jamison's Pork Products. It was thanks to them that he'd lost his job.

As Nora and Sam chatted, Will excused himself before he said something rude. He made his way over to the food. He'd given the kids dinner at home, but hadn't eaten anything himself. Party food was going to have to be his dinner. He gobbled up a handful of peanuts (protein), olives (did they count as a veg?) and several extremely tasty mince pies (pudding).

When he had eaten his fill, he reluctantly moved away from the snacks. He was dreading having to mingle with the other guests, who were continuing to arrive in droves. Most of them looked posh and successful, like Sam. He suspected that they lived in houses with granite kitchen countertops and front doors painted expensive shades of gray with tastefully ridiculous names like Mouse Fur. The first thing they would ask him would be: *And what do you do, Will?*

Nothing killed a conversation quite like, "I'm an unemployed single dad." He might as well have been wearing a T-shirt with the slogan MASSIVE LOSER on it. Or better yet, the donkey costume from the other night. He caught snippets of their highbrow conversation—

It's a dead cert for the Booker . . .

I didn't like her latest novel at all—much too derivative . . .

The Oculist of Leipzig *is a modern masterpiece . . .*

Instead of trying to bluff his way through a conversation about books he'd never even heard of, Will headed across the shop on the pretext of checking on the kids, even though it was perfectly obvious that they were fine as they played with Merry.

As he made his way over to them, he felt a light touch on his arm. "Hi," said a female voice. "Do your kids go to St. Stephen's?"

Will turned and saw a woman about his age with blondish hair. She was clutching a glass of mulled wine for dear life and looked about as awkward as he felt. He nodded. "I'm Will. My twins are in Year One."

"I thought I recognized you from the school run. I'm Liz. My boys and I moved here at the start of the school year."

"Are they here?" Will asked, looking around the room for other children. "I'm sure the twins would love to play with them."

Liz shook her head. "They're staying with their dad until Boxing Day. Probably a good thing, as my Jamie would trash this place. No, I'm on my own over Christmas."

Will grimaced sympathetically. "That's got to be rough." He couldn't imagine waking up on Christmas morning without Julia and Adam leaping on his bed at the crack of dawn. "I'm a single parent, too—but the twins' mum is out of the picture."

"It's going to be weird." Liz lowered her voice. "This isn't really my scene, but I thought it would be good to get out of the house."

"How are you finding Stowford?"

Liz sipped her wine, considering her answer. "It's hard to meet people. I get the feeling that all the other mums at school are afraid I'm out to steal their husbands." She gave a self-deprecating laugh. "As if I'd have the energy to do that. Most nights, I'm ready for bed before the kids are."

Will laughed. "Just as well—Stowford isn't exactly famous for its nightlife."

They chatted about the school and arranged a playdate over the Christmas holidays. It was nice to talk to another single parent, who could relate to how hard it was, trying to do it all. Will was the only dad on the Year One parents' group chat, and he was willing to bet that he was the only father in the school who combed out nits, made flapjacks for the school bake sale and checked homework while also being a linesman for the twins' soccer team and an expert at *Mario Kart*. Caregiver *and* breadwinner. At least he used to be both of those things . . .

I need another drink.

"Can I get you a refill?" he asked, gesturing to Liz's empty wineglass.

"Why not?" she said, shrugging. "It's not like I need to get up early with the kids tomorrow."

Will took her glass and headed back over to the refreshments.

As he was pouring more wine, Miss Powell bustled up to him, wearing a reindeer brooch pinned to a sensible cardigan. "Ah, Mr. Fitzpatrick," she said. "I was hoping I would run into you."

She'd better not ask me to wear another costume. He definitely wasn't up for playing Father Christmas tonight, if that was what she had in mind.

"Simon tells me that you're looking for a job?"

"That's right."

"As you know, Mr. Greenwood, our soccer coach, slipped on the ice the night of the carol concert. His leg's broken and he's going to be in plaster for a good few weeks. You were wonderful with the children after the carol concert, and I know you help out with the youth soccer team. I wondered if you'd be interested in filling in for him up at the school?"

Will stared at her in disbelief. "But I don't have any coaching qualifications . . ."

Olwyn waved her hand, dismissing his concerns. "I'll need to speak to the head, but I'm sure she'll be interested—especially as you've already got a background check. What do you say?"

"That would be amazing."

"Excellent!" Olwyn said. "I'll make some calls."

"Daddy!" Julia cried, running over to them. "Merry is *soooo* cute. Can we get a dog for Christmas? Please?"

Will tousled her hair and chuckled. "It's a bit late to ask Santa for a dog. He's probably already packed up his sleigh."

But if this job worked out, who knows? Maybe next year they could get a pet. It all seemed too good to be true, but for the first time in months, Will felt a glimmer of hope.

20

OLWYN

Olwyn was relieved to hear that Will Fitzpatrick was interested in the job and was delighted that Simon had suggested him. It was hard for rural schools like St. Stephen's to attract staff. It wasn't her problem anymore, of course, but she hadn't stopped caring about the school where she'd worked for so many years. The children deserved someone patient, energetic and enthusiastic—someone like Will. After being a teacher for so long, Olwyn had a sixth sense about these things. She usually wasn't wrong.

"Hi, Miss Powell!" said Will's daughter, Julia. The twins had been in the last class she'd taught at St. Stephen's. "Can you make your reindeer's nose light up?"

Olwyn was happy to oblige. She pressed her brooch, making Rudolph's nose flash. "You and your brother were wonderful shepherds the other night," she told Julia.

Liz came over to join them, and Will handed her a glass of wine.

"And your Jamie stole the show," she told Liz. As Joseph, Jamie had made the audience laugh by sniffing baby Jesus's nappy and pretending the wise men's gifts were for him.

"Daddy—come and give Merry a cuddle," Julia said, dragging Will over to the dog.

Olwyn looked around. "Are Jamie and Travis here?" She suspected she would have noticed them by now if they were. Jamie would probably be break-dancing on the coffee table or leaping off the back of the sofa.

"No, they're with their dad."

"I thought it was a bit too quiet," Olwyn said, smiling.

"I bet you're glad you retired so you don't have to put up with kids like him anymore."

"Not at all," Olwyn replied. She'd always had a soft spot for class clowns like Jamie. "He's a cheeky monkey, but he's clearly a bright boy."

Liz shook her head. "That's good of you to say, Miss Powell, but he's really struggling with his schoolwork."

"I still volunteer at the school once a week. I've been helping your boys with their reading. They've both made a lot of progress in the last few weeks."

"Really? I've been reading to them at home," Liz said. "We've almost finished *The Hobbit*."

"That's wonderful—keep it up," Olwyn said. "If they enjoy fantasy, they might enjoy Philip Pullman's books, too."

Liz took out her phone and made a note. "I wish I could do more to help them," she said. "But it's hard as I work full time."

"I'd be happy to tutor them." Olwyn leaned forward and lowered her voice to a conspiratorial whisper. "I'll let you in on a little secret—I miss teaching. I've been rather lonely since I retired."

"If you're sure Jamie won't drive you crazy, that would be amazing."

After they'd exchanged contact details and made arrangements for the boys' first tutoring session, Olwyn chatted to some friends from book club before excusing herself and slipping off into the nonfiction section.

Ever since reading the Sherlock Holmes story Nora and Simon had sent her, she hadn't been able to get the thought of writing her own mystery out of her head. Last night, she'd woken up at 2 a.m.—thanks to Tuppence kneading the duvet before curling up next to Olwyn on the bed—and a detective character had suddenly popped into her head. She'd scribbled a note down on the only piece of paper she could find in her bedroom—a dry-cleaning receipt—and gone back to sleep.

In the morning, she was afraid that the idea that had seemed so clever in the middle of the night would just be gibberish. But as she deciphered her nocturnal scrawl, she grew even more excited about her crime story.

Her detective, Clay Thorne, would be a former Metropolitan police detective forced to retire early due to PTSD. (She was considering giving him a limp, bravely incurred in the line of duty.) The story would open with Thorne relocating to the Cotswolds— to a sleepy village, not unlike Stowford—and joining the local gardening club in order to cultivate some outside interests. But when one of the club members is poisoned with oleander from his own garden right before the annual horticultural show, Thorne has to come out of retirement and crack the case.

Olwyn had spent the whole day in a frenzy of brainstorming— writing character descriptions, dreaming up clues and sketching out a rough story line. Fueled by multiple cups of tea, she'd plotted and planned, her excitement growing as she fleshed out her curmudgeonly hero. She could practically hear his gravelly Cockney accent, see his trademark tweed cap and smell his signature Old Spice aftershave. She'd lost track of time and had been late for the party. She still hadn't decided whether to make the murderer the victim's wife—a piano teacher who's having it off with the handsome young village vet (Clay Thorne could find some telltale dog hairs on the piano teacher's clothes)—or his main rival for the horticultural prize, the snooty and fiercely competitive Lady Primrose Goodwood. Maybe she'd only decide who the culprit was once she'd started writing it.

That was why she was scanning the bookshelves now, looking for a guide to writing fiction. Because it was one thing to have planned out her story, but quite another to start writing it. Olwyn hadn't written anything longer than an end-of-year report since her own schooldays, and she was feeling rather daunted by the scale of her endeavor. Was she crazy to think she could actually write a book?

Maybe.

But she was determined to try.

As she browsed through the writing books on the shelves, Olwyn heard a commotion over the Christmas carols and party chatter. Her teacher's instincts for breaking up fights kicked in, and she rushed over to see what was going on.

A teenage boy stood in the entrance. His face was flushed, his ginger hair was a mess and despite the snow he wasn't wearing a coat. There was a wild look in his eyes. All conversation had stopped, as the party guests stared at him.

"Why did you send this me this book," he shouted, throwing the book he was holding across the shop. It hit a bowl, scattering crisps all over the floor. "I don't want it!"

"I'm so sorry," Nora said, looking stricken as she picked up the book. "We didn't mean to upset you. It was meant to be a nice surprise."

"Fuck you!" raged the boy, his fists clenched. "Fuck you and your nice surprises!"

Simon stepped in front of his wife protectively. "You need to calm down, son, or I'll have to ask you to leave."

"I'm not your son, you arsehole," the boy spat.

Olwyn caught sight of the book in Nora's hands—*The Lion, the Witch and the Wardrobe*. A vivid memory of Emma Swann dressed up as the White Witch on World Book Day flashed through her mind.

Oh, the poor lad, she thought, suddenly understanding.

Olwyn went over and placed her hand gently on his arm. "Come on, Harry," she said softly. "What do you say we go and have a cup of tea and a chat?"

HARRY

Reluctantly, Harry sat down on a faded sofa in the flat above the shop as his old primary school teacher moved around in the kitchen, boiling the kettle and muttering to herself as she peered into various canisters, searching for tea bags. He looked around the flat and saw a framed picture of a girl he recognized from school—Charlotte Walden. She'd been a prefect, so she used to sit up front for assemblies in her blazer. Sanj and Scooter (or Dumb and Dumber, as Emma used to call Harry's friends) thought she was hot.

Harry hoped she hadn't witnessed his meltdown in the bookshop. Not that he stood any chance with a pretty older girl like Charlotte. Or even girls his own age. Not when he acted like a total psycho.

"Aha!" Miss Powell said. "Found them." She popped the tea bags into mugs and poured in the hot water. "Milk?" she called over to Harry. "Sugar?"

"Whatever." He hated tea. It tasted like boiled metal.

Miss Powell added two heaped spoonfuls of sugar to each

mug and set one down in front of him. "It was Emma's favorite book, wasn't it?"

Harry nodded, avoiding her eyes. "She read it to me when I was little, before I knew how to read."

He'd been trying not to think about his sister since his last visit to the graveyard. But while hunting for a clean pair of socks this evening (he and his mates were going to try to sneak into the George), he'd found the book he'd been sent, on the floor, buried under a pile of dirty clothes. He thought he'd thrown it out, but his mum or dad must have found it and chucked it in his bedroom.

The party invitation had fallen out of the book and the anger he'd felt when he received the parcel flared up again, fueled by the fact that it was Christmas Eve. Emma should have been curled up in front of the Christmas tree in one of her sparkly sweaters. But she wasn't. Just like she wouldn't be there tomorrow morning to put on the earrings shaped like Christmas puddings he'd got her, even though he knew she would never open them.

How dare these people have a party, when Emma was dead.

Something inside him had snapped. He was going to give them a piece of his mind. He'd found himself running down the high street through the snow, his fury building with every step. And when he got to the shop, he'd exploded. He'd made a complete idiot of himself, and now he was stuck up here with old Miss Powell.

Actually, that wasn't so bad. Miss Powell had been one of his favorite teachers. Emma's, too. She was strict, but she didn't have favorites. *Well*, thought Harry, *she probably did—but she was good at hiding it.*

Unlike his parents.

"Emma always had her nose in a book," Miss Powell said fondly. "She worked her way through the school library."

"She got the top score in the whole school on her English GCSE," Harry said. The head teacher had given Emma's certificates to Harry at school a few weeks back. When he brought them home, his mum had cried for hours.

"That doesn't surprise me a bit." Miss Powell sipped her tea. "And how are *you* doing in school?"

Harry shrugged. "I hate it. They forced me to see a stupid counselor to try and make me talk about stuff."

"You don't want to talk about Emma?"

Harry shook his head. "And I keep getting into fights because I feel pissed off all the time."

"I think you have every right to feel angry. Life's a bitch, Harry."

Harry laughed. "I didn't think teachers were allowed to swear."

"I'm not a teacher anymore." Miss Powell winked at him. "But between you and me, you hear some pretty ripe language in the school staff room."

"Probably when teachers are talking about bad kids like me."

"You're not a bad kid, Harry. You're just going through a very tough time."

He took a sip of his tea, burning his tongue. It didn't actually taste that bad. Maybe the trick was to add lots of sugar.

"If you don't want to talk about it, maybe you could write about it," Miss Powell suggested. "I remember your stories from when you were in my class—you're a talented writer, Harry."

He shrugged. "Maybe."

"It's not good to keep things bottled up. The anger always comes out eventually—"

Harry gripped his hair in anguish, making it even messier. "I know I shouldn't have gone off on one. It just freaked me out. I actually thought the book might be from Emma." He shook his head. "Stupid, I know."

Miss Powell gazed at him sympathetically. "I don't think that's stupid at all, Harry. It just shows how much you miss your sister. How much you loved her."

"But I was always such a jerk to her. She didn't even know I loved her."

"I promise you she knew, deep down."

There was a long pause as they both sipped their tea. Harry found himself saying something he'd been thinking for months, but could never bring himself to say out loud. Not to his parents. Not to his friends. Definitely not to the annoying counselor at school. "It's my fault Emma's dead."

"What do you mean?"

"The only reason she was walking home was because we'd had a huge fight over something stupid," Harry confessed. "When she called to ask my mum for a lift home from the Copper Kettle, I could see it was Emma and I didn't tell Mum her phone was ringing. So, I killed her."

"Oh, Harry, that's not true."

"Yeah, it is," Harry said miserably. "If my mum had picked her up, she wouldn't have been hit by a car. She died because of me."

"You weren't the one driving recklessly," Miss Powell replied. "It was a tragic accident."

Harry shook his head. "I was pissed off because she borrowed my new headphones and broke them. The last thing I said to Emma was that I hated her. And now she's dead."

Miss Powell sipped her tea quietly, not saying anything for a long time. When she did finally speak, her question surprised him. "Who was Emma's favorite character in *The Lion, the Witch and the Wardrobe?*"

He thought for a moment. "Um, Edmund, I guess."

"Tell me about Edmund, Harry."

What is this, an English lesson?

But the teacher was staring at him intently through her glasses, and Harry felt like he had to answer. "Well, at the beginning he's greedy and kind of a jerk to his brother and sisters. But he changes. By the end he's really, like, brave. He helps defeat the White Witch."

Miss Powell nodded thoughtfully. "Exactly. It's a story about redemption." She paused for a moment. "None of us is perfect, Harry. Siblings can be awful to each other—god knows, my sister and I used to fight like cats and dogs—but they forgive each other." She patted Harry's knee. "You need to forgive yourself. Emma wouldn't want you beating yourself up."

Harry picked at a small rip in the knee of his jeans. There was a lump stuck in his throat that made it hard for him to speak. "I . . . I miss her so much."

A drop of water landed with a plop on his thigh. And then another. He hadn't shed a tear since hearing that Emma was dead. Not even at the funeral. But now, months of unshed tears flooded out, as if a dam had burst.

"There, there," Miss Powell murmured. "Let it all out."

He rested his head on her shoulder and sobbed until the sound of creaking boards alerted him to the fact that someone was coming up the stairs. Embarrassed, Harry quickly pulled away from Miss Powell and used his sleeve to wipe his snot-stained face.

The bookshop lady—he supposed she must be Charlotte's mum—came into the flat. "How's it going up here?"

"Fine," Mrs. Powell said. "Thanks for letting us use your flat. We were just catching up. Harry, this is Nora. She and her husband run the bookshop downstairs."

"I've just remembered where I recognize you from," Nora said, sitting down on the other side of Harry. "I saw you in the cemetery a while back."

Harry nodded. "My sister died. It's stupid, but I sometimes go there and talk to her." He could feel his cheeks flushing with embarrassment.

But Nora didn't seem to think it was weird. "Then I'll probably see you there again. My mum died years ago, but I still go and visit her for a chat every so often."

"I'm . . . uh . . . sorry I freaked out. It's just . . . that book was Emma's favorite."

"I can see how that must have been really upsetting," Nora said. "Can I make it up to you? There's another book you might find helpful. Funnily enough, it's also by C. S. Lewis. If you come downstairs with me, I'll find it for you."

"I don't know . . ." Harry wasn't sure he could face those people again.

"Don't worry—everyone's had a few glasses of wine by now, they'll have forgotten all about it. Besides, what's a good party without some drama?"

"Can I use your loo first?" Harry asked.

In the bathroom, he splashed water on his face and looked in the mirror. Weirdly, even though he looked like shit, his eyes swollen and his face blotchy, he felt better than he had in a long time. Lighter. As if the tears he'd been storing up had weighed him down. Which was stupid, really, since tears weren't even that heavy.

They went downstairs, where the party was in full swing. Miss Powell went over to the refreshments table to get a snack, while Nora led him down a row of bookshelves.

"Here it is," Nora said, handing him a copy of a book called *A Grief Observed*. "When my mum died, this really helped me. It's not going to stop you from missing your sister, but it helps to know that all the mixed-up emotions you're feeling—the guilt . . . the anger . . . the fear—are completely normal."

"Thanks," Harry said, tucking it under his arm self-consciously.

"Now, I've got a teenager myself, so I know you're probably starving," Nora said, leading him over to the food table.

She was being really nice, but Harry wanted to get out of there. "I should probably get going . . . My parents are probably wondering where I am."

Yeah, right.

"How are they doing?"

"Um . . . OK, I guess."

His mum had taken a sleeping pill and gone to bed straight after dinner, and his dad was probably watching some crap on TV and working his way through a bottle of vodka.

Happy fucking Christmas.

"Talk to them," Nora said. "Even though it's hard. Even if you think they don't want to. Because, trust me, everything that you're feeling, they're feeling, too."

"Yeah, maybe . . ."

What could he say? *Hey Mum and Dad, by the way, I killed Emma. Oh, and also, I kind of feel like you've forgotten I exist.*

"Talk to them," Nora insisted. "And don't leave until you've tried one of my mince pies." She patted him on the shoulder, then went over to talk to someone else.

Harry's stomach rumbled. *The mince pies did look pretty good . . .*

As he helped himself to a pie, two little kids with blond hair marched up to him. "You said a bad word," the girl said, grinning.

Harry nodded sheepishly. "Yeah, sorry about that."

"It's OK. I already knew it," she boasted. "Daddy said it when the toilet got all clogged up. Adam's older than me, but I know way more rude words than him."

"That's not true, Julia," the boy said. "I know more bad words than you, you poo head!"

"Liar, liar, pants on fire!" Julia shouted, prompting her brother to give her plait a yank.

Watching Julia retaliate with a pinch, Harry felt weirdly comforted by their squabble. *Miss Powell was right*, Harry realized. All brothers and sisters argued, but then they made up. If Emma hadn't been hit by a car, he would have eventually forgiven her for breaking his headphones. And she would have forgiven him for saying he hated her. That stupid fucking driver had robbed them of the chance to argue—and make up—hundreds more times.

"Hey!" Harry waved the book like a white flag, interrupting their argument. "Don't fight, you guys."

"Is that a rude book?" Julia asked hopefully.

"Nope."

"Will you read it to us?" Adam said.

"Nope."

The kids looked disappointed. Julia frowned. "We're bored. There's only stupid grown-ups at this party."

Harry shrugged. "I guess I could read you something else . . ." It wasn't like he had any other plans. There was no way the scary landlady at the pub was going to serve him and his friends, anyway.

He took the two kids into the children's section and let them pick out a book. After another squabble, the twins finally agreed on Raymond Briggs's *Father Christmas*. Emma had loved that book, too. Then they all sat down in front of the fire and Harry read to the twins, the way that Emma had read to him when he was little.

21

DAVID

David Langdon steered his Mercedes S-Class down Stowford's high street at a snail's pace. The car was capable of doing up to 150 miles per hour (not that David had ever tested it to its limits), but snow was falling so heavily he'd had to crawl the whole way from Yew Tree Manor. The windscreen wipers could barely keep up with the steadily falling flakes.

"There's a space right outside," Kath said, pointing.

David parked in front of the bookshop and got out of the car, pulling his overcoat collar up to ward off the cold. The bookshop's windows were fogged up and the sounds of music, laughter and chatter spilled onto the street. He let out a deep breath, releasing a cloud into the cold night air.

"Are you sure you're feeling up to this, Dad?" Kath asked, linking her arm through his.

He nodded, even though a part of him wanted to climb back in the car and go home.

Don't be ridiculous. This was a Christmas do in a rural bookshop, for God's sake, not the annual party conference. In political circles, he was a popular party guest—a charming raconteur, a famous bon viveur and a free-flowing source of juicy Whitehall gossip. He'd been the last man standing at countless Westminster bashes, but he could barely recognize himself as that person anymore. Depression made even simple conversations exhausting.

"It does me good to get out and about." At least, that's what Dr. Dhar had told him. He'd forced himself to attend the village carol concert—an event he'd always avoided like the plague—and he'd actually found it rather moving. Maybe this party wouldn't be too much of an ordeal, either.

"Let's go in," Kath said. "My feet are going numb."

They pushed through the front door and there was the familiar dip in volume levels as the guests noticed him and began whispering among themselves. He could guess what they were saying:

Oh, look, it's the MP who lost the leadership contest.

Isn't he that one who had the affair?

God, David Langdon is looking rough.

Ignoring the whispers, Kath helped him navigate through the clusters of partygoers. They found their host by the fireplace, her cheeks flushed, though David couldn't be sure if it was from the fire's heat or the glass of mulled wine in her hand.

"I'm so sorry we're late, Nora," David said. "I was finishing off my newspaper column and I lost track of time." He'd spent the past few days drafting and redrafting his article, deliberating about whether to send it to his editor. It was probably the best piece he'd ever written. It was also the most honest . . .

"I'm so glad you could make it!" Nora beckoned to a tall man, who came over and put his arm around her waist. "This is my husband, Simon."

David stared at him in disbelief. It was the man from the train station; the one who had come and stood next to him. The man who had, unwittingly, saved his life. This couple really were his guardian angels.

"Can I get you a glass of wine?" Simon asked, holding up a bottle with his free hand.

"Red, please," Kath said.

"A soft drink, if you have one." David eyed the bottle of wine longingly—it was a great vintage—but he wasn't supposed to mix alcohol with his antidepressants.

"Coming right up."

"How are you doing?" Nora asked, as her husband went off to fetch the drinks.

"I have good days and bad days," David said. "I'm waiting for the medication to kick in."

"The doctor said recovery is slow," Kath reminded him.

Frustratingly slow, especially for a man who prided himself on getting things done.

"You're looking better," Nora remarked. "There's some color in your cheeks."

"I've been trying to get out and walk most days." Dr. Dhar had also said to take exercise, so Kath had been accompanying him on long countryside walks, despite the freezing temperatures. Even though he never wanted to go out, he had to admit that he always felt a bit better afterward. David glanced over at this daughter, who was crouched down, chatting to some kids reading by the fire.

"What are you reading?" she asked them.

The little girl held up a copy of *Father Christmas*.

"Oh, that's one of my favorites," Kath exclaimed.

"I know you," the younger boy said, pointing at David. "You were at the carol concert."

"That's right. I read a poem." David didn't really know how to speak to children, probably because he'd missed so much of Kath's childhood. He'd had to do his fair share of baby-dandling on the campaign trail, but it had never come naturally.

"It was boring."

The teenage boy reading to the kids said, "That's kind of rude, little dude."

"That's OK," David said, smiling. "I used to think poems were boring, too."

A man hurried over to them. "I hope my kids aren't bothering you, sir."

"Not at all," David said. "They were just giving me some honest feedback on my appearance at the carol concert."

"Daddy was the donkey," the little girl said proudly.

Kath stood up, smoothing down her dress, and laughed. "You were brilliant." She held out her hand. "Kath Langdon."

"Will Fitzpatrick," he said ruefully. "Too bad that wasn't a viable career option."

Kath's brow creased in concern. "Are you looking for a job?"

Will nodded. "I got made redundant a few months ago. The food processing plant I worked at shut down some of its production lines. It's been tough."

Let's go, David thought impatiently. He wasn't sure he could deal with disgruntled constituents tonight.

But Kath showed no sign of wanting to get away. "I'm very sorry to hear that," she told the unemployed man.

"I've been looking for a new job, but there's not much work around here," Will said. "Is it true there's going to be a big new retail park outside of Stowford?"

"There's an advisory committee looking into the plans," Kath told him. "But we want to ensure the development doesn't drive independent shops out of business."

Kath caught her father's eye, and he knew she was thinking about what Nora had told them about the bookshop closing down. A retail park would be the death knell for several other shops on Stowford's high street—and in the surrounding villages.

"There are also concerns about the environmental impact

on local wildlife," Kath added. "A rare type of wildflower—pennycress—grows on the proposed site."

"Too bad I can't eat pennycress," Will muttered, before sloping off to the refreshments table.

David felt sorry for the guy. There wasn't much new business development in the Cotswolds, even though he'd established grants for just that purpose. Rural areas lacked the transport links people needed to get to work. And workers needed affordable housing, which was in desperately short supply locally. Every solution seemed to beget ten more problems, and David just didn't have the energy for it anymore.

A short, white-haired lady wearing a reindeer brooch bustled over to them.

Oh god, David thought, expecting a diatribe about some local matter or other.

"Mr. Langdon, Kath, so nice to see you again."

David blinked, trying to place her, but Kath greeted the woman warmly. "Hello, Miss Powell. We were just talking about how much we enjoyed the carol concert."

Ah yes, Olwyn Powell, David remembered. They'd spoken briefly just before the carol concert, when she'd been corralling her flock of shepherds, angels and wise men.

"I was hoping to have a word with you after the concert, but you hurried off as soon as it was over. St. Stephen's, our local primary school, is under threat of closure. It would be a real blow to the village if it shuts."

"But its last Ofsted report was outstanding, wasn't it?" Kath said.

"Oh yes," Olwyn replied. "The results are excellent—that's not the problem. But pupil numbers are falling because families can't afford to live in the village. A lot of the staff are nearing retirement age, and it's hard to recruit new teachers, because they can't afford to live here on a teacher's salary. The school's got a serious budget shortfall, as well. Teachers are having to buy their own classroom supplies, and the head is having to empty bins and mow the playing fields because they can't afford a caretaker."

David frowned. "How's that possible? The prime minister just pledged millions for schools in the last budget." The education secretary was one of his former allies—someone who had promised him his backing for party leadership, only to withdraw it in exchange for a Cabinet position. Ever since, David couldn't face reading the Department of Education briefings. He had obviously taken his eye off the ball.

"It's to do with pupil premiums," Kath explained. "Schools like St. Stephen's have fewer pupils than schools in urban areas, so they get less funding."

"That's right," Olwyn said, nodding. "A lot of our local families are struggling, but just about getting by. They fall slightly under the threshold for pupil premiums, so we also get less money per head."

David glanced over at Will and his kids. They were probably scraping together barely enough to manage. So as far as the government's pencil pushers were concerned, they didn't qualify for help. He sighed wearily. Rural poverty was the Cotswolds' dirty little secret. Underneath the area's picturesque golden glow, the touristy tea shops and the B&Bs, there was severe deprivation. It was something he'd tried to address, but there was still so much to be done. He felt exhausted just thinking about it.

As Olwyn continued to describe the problems the local school faced, Kath listened carefully, nodding her head and asking questions.

"We should put together a task force," Kath said. "I'm sure we could find some solutions."

Kath is good at this, David realized. *She genuinely cares about the people who live here.*

"Sorry this took so long." Simon returned, handing David a glass of orange juice. "The newspapers say there will be an election in the new year. Are you going to stand again?"

David smiled mysteriously. "You'll just have to wait and see."

Only days ago, he had been feeling suicidal, unable to see any point in carrying on. Now, he *wanted* to get better and was finally doing everything he could to make that happen—from medication to meditation. But recovery was hard work. And the therapist he'd begun seeing had warned him that the chance of a relapse was high, unless he made some permanent changes to his lifestyle.

Unless he prioritized his mental health over his political ambitions.

Maybe it was time to step aside. To let someone else take the reins and continue the work he had started. Someone with energy and enthusiasm, compassion and conviction.

Someone like Kath . . .

MATEO

It was nearly ten o'clock when Mateo pushed his way inside the George, brushing snow off his tight curls. On the walk from the station to the pub, so much snow had fallen on him that he looked like a walking snowman. He didn't mind, though—as a Californian, snow was still a novelty to him. This was what Christmas looked like in movies.

He'd never seen the pub so busy before. It was standing room only as Stowford's residents got increasingly merry. Someone had rigged up a karaoke machine and Howie was crooning The Pogues' "Fairytale of New York" into the microphone.

Squeezing past the revelers, Mateo made his way to the bar.

"All right, kid? How did the audition go?" Sue shouted over the din.

He gave her a thumbs-up. "Pretty well, I think. But the trains were screwed up because of the snow—it took me ages to get back. Do you need me to help behind the bar?"

"No, you're OK, kiddo," the pub landlady said. "You must be exhausted."

It had been a long day, but Mateo felt wired, the way he always did after an audition. And cold. The snow had soaked through his shoes, right through to his socks. He could hear his mother's voice in his head saying, *You'll catch pneumonia!* So he went upstairs to his room, peeled off his damp socks and rolled them in a ball.

"LeBron James shoots and he scores . . ." He took aim, but the socks missed the laundry hamper, knocking *Twelfth Night* off the dresser. (There was a reason he'd run long-distance in high school instead of playing on the basketball team.)

Crossing his room in two paces, Mateo picked up the play, and the card he'd been using as a bookmark fell out. It was an invitation to a party tonight at the bookshop. In his excitement over the audition, he'd completely spaced about it.

If it wasn't for the copy of *Twelfth Night*, he probably wouldn't even have bothered going to the audition. His acting teacher at LAMDA had loved to quote the gloomy statistic that ninety-two percent of actors are "resting" at any given time. Those weren't great odds. Mateo knew he'd probably have been better off spending the train fare on twenty lottery tickets. Or treating himself to a takeaway.

But reading *Twelfth Night* had reminded him of why he wanted to be an actor. Not to get rich or famous, but because he loved Shakespeare. Mateo still had no idea why he'd been sent the book. Maybe it had been some sort of sign not to give up. He glanced at the poster on his wall. *Macbeth* was full of omens—owls and storms and bad dreams. Who was he to ignore a Shakespearean-style portent when it arrived in an envelope addressed to him? So when his agent had called this morning, offering him a last-minute audition for a production of *Romeo and Juliet* at the Globe (the actor originally chosen to play Romeo had dropped out when he'd bagged a part in a Steven Spielberg movie), Mateo had legged it to the station.

The audition had gone pretty well; the casting director had seemed to like him. After the balcony monologue—which luckily he'd mostly remembered from high school, and he'd spent the whole train journey muttering under his breath—she'd asked him to read a few scenes with the actress playing Juliet. You never could tell, though, so Mateo was trying to manage his expectations. He wouldn't hear back until after Christmas, so he just had to try not to obsess over it.

Easier said than done.

He'd just have to stay busy. Going over to the window, he peered across the street at the bookshop. The party looked like it was still going on. So, a few minutes later, wearing clean socks and his running shoes, Mateo pushed the bookshop door open and—

"Ouch!" A petite, smartly dressed woman with her dark hair in a bun held her forehead, wincing in pain.

"I am so sorry!" The door's glass had been completely fogged up and Mateo hadn't realized anyone was standing on the other side when he'd pushed it open. *Way to make an entrance.*

"It's OK," she said, waving away his concerns. "I'm fine. I was just about to leave."

"No! Hang on a sec," Mateo said. He dashed out of the shop, quickly formed a snowball and came back inside, handing it to the woman.

She looked down at it, confused. "What am I supposed to do with this?"

"Put it on your forehead."

"Look, I was about to go . . ."

"Humor me, please," Mateo said. "I'd feel terrible if you had a concussion or something and froze to death because you collapsed on your way home."

"Well, that's a bit dramatic, isn't it?" She raised an eyebrow, amused, and Mateo suddenly noticed how pretty her long-lashed brown eyes were behind her glasses.

He grinned. "I'm an actor. Being dramatic is kind of my specialty."

"Oh, yeah? What's your name?" she asked. "Maybe I've seen you in something."

"It's Mateo. And the only place you're likely to have seen me is in the George, where I work."

"I'm Sam," the woman said. She pressed the snowball against her forehead. "You're American."

Mateo nodded in confirmation. "I'm from California." He waited to see how Sam would react. Americans didn't always receive the warmest welcome around here. The coachloads of loud tourists who shuffled through the Cotswold villages in their white sneakers, demanding ice in their drinks and hogging up the sidewalks as they took photos of the "quaint" buildings, gave his compatriots a bad rap. But she didn't seem to hold his nationality against him.

"Must be tough being so far from home over Christmas."

"Yeah. Christmas is a big deal in my family. Right now my nonna is probably cooking her lasagna for tomorrow. And my dad's making jollof rice. I know that sounds strange, but my family's half Italian, half Nigerian."

"Trust me, it's no weirder than my family's Christmas dinner. My mum serves pistachio ice cream with our Christmas pudding."

Mateo grimaced. "That stuff is nasty, with or without pistachio ice cream."

Talking about food, Mateo realized that he hadn't eaten any-thing since grabbing a sandwich in London. "Do you know if there's anything to eat? I'm starving."

"Sure—I'll show you where the food is." She led him over to a table with some empty bowls and plates. "Or rather, was."

Mateo fished out some crumbs from a bowl of crisps.

"So how are you going to spend tomorrow, then?" Sam asked.

Mateo brushed crisp crumbs off his hands. He thought about pretending he had plans, so Sam didn't think he was a total loser. But there was a shrewd intelligence about her that made him think she'd see right through him. "The pub's shut, so I'll prob-ably go out for a run. Anything to distract myself from thinking about the audition I had today."

"Sounds good—well, the running part, anyway. I'd rather be running than fending off questions from my extended family about why I'm nearly thirty and still not married yet."

She's single. Mateo felt a little surge of excitement at the realiza-tion. "Where do you usually run?"

"I usually do a 10k loop around the village, out past Blackberry Hill and back along the river."

"I like that route, too. I'm surprised I haven't seen you before." *Because I definitely would have noticed you,* he added silently.

Sam shrugged. "I work long hours so I run at strange times. I'm only living at home until I can find another place in London."

Of course. He should have guessed from her clothes that she did something in the City.

Simon, the guy who ran the quiz at the George, came over to replenish the crisp bowl and noticed the melting snowball pressed against Sam's forehead. "Oh, dear. What happened here?"

"I accidentally bashed Sam in the head when I came in," Ma-teo admitted.

"That reminds me of when I first met my wife," Simon said.

"I came into the shop and smacked my bonce on one of those bloody beams. Nearly gave myself a concussion."

"Sounds like something out of a rom-com," Sam quipped.

Simon chuckled. "I've always thought Hugh Grant could play me in a film."

"By the way," Mateo said. "I wanted to say thank you for sending me that book. I mean, if it was you."

"You're welcome," Simon said. "Which one did you get?"

"*Twelfth Night.*"

"'If music be the food of love, play on,'" Simon quoted, brandishing his glass of red wine in a theatrical fashion.

"That's right," Mateo said, helping himself to a big handful of crisps. Right now, *any* food sounded good to him.

Sam dropped the remains of the snowball into an empty wineglass and wiped her hands on her skirt.

"Did you send it to me because I'm an actor?" Mateo asked Simon.

"Actually, that was pure coincidence. People nominated friends or family they thought could use cheering up, and we sent the books out randomly."

Sue, Mateo guessed. His boss knew he'd been feeling homesick and down about his acting. It had to be her who had nominated him. He didn't know many other people in Stowford.

Unless you counted Howie, who—speak of the devil— had just walked into the bookshop and was talking to Simon's wife.

"We're just so glad all six of you came to the party tonight," Simon said, gesturing to Mateo and then at Sam. "Now if you'll excuse me, I need to rescue Nora."

"How's your forehead?" Mateo asked Sam. He stepped closer to peer at it, catching a faint whiff of coconut from her hair. There was a small red bump where the door had bashed her.

Sam prodded the bump gingerly. "I'll survive. I'm tougher than I look."

I bet you are. But, unless he was mistaken, Simon had implied that he'd sent *both* of them a book.

"They sent you a book, too?"

She nodded. "Yeah. It was probably my mum who thought I needed cheering up. My boyfriend dumped me a few months ago."

"He's an idiot," Mateo said.

Sam laughed. "You've never even met him."

He looked at her intently. "I don't need to meet him to know he's an idiot."

He dumped you, for starters.

Sam blushed. "Yeah, well, I wasn't exactly a perfect girlfriend."

Mateo studied Sam, raising his eyebrow. "So, we both turned up at a Christmas party on our own after receiving mystery books . . . This is sounding more like a rom-com by the minute."

Sam pulled a face.

"What? Don't you like rom-coms?"

"No, I hate them."

"What do you have against them?"

"Ugh," Sam said, wrinkling her nose. "Where to begin? The heroine is always some dorky girl, who when she takes her glasses off is actually totally gorgeous. She always meets the hero in an adorably clumsy sort of way—like spilling coffee over him, or a mix-up over hotel bookings. She always has a sassy gay best friend. And she always, *always* has a ridiculously whimsical job. She's either a magazine editor or a dog walker or runs a cupcake bakery . . ." Sam was growing adorably animated as she ranted. "Rom-com heroines are *never* management consultants!"

Ahh . . . so that's what she does for a job.

"And the plots are always so contrived," Sam continued. "Like . . . she falls in love with a handsome stranger, only to discover he's a prince. Or they'll be enemies who have to work to-gether on a project and fall in love. The last one I saw, the heroine had to pretend she was married to someone to appease her family, and then she actually fell in love with him. I mean, *puh-lease*."

"For someone who doesn't like rom-coms, you sure seem to know a lot about them," Mateo teased.

"My sister likes them. She's forced me to watch loads of them. Especially at Christmastime. Don't tell me you actually like rom-coms?"

Mateo shrugged. "Most of Shakespeare's comedies are as far-fetched as any Netflix Christmas movie."

Sam's eyes suddenly widened and her mouth formed an *O*.

"What?" Mateo said. "You don't think the Bard would have loved *The Princess Switch*? Not that I've watched that," he added hastily.

Sam shook her head. "No, it's not that—I've just had the *best* idea. You can come to Christmas dinner with my family. You can pretend to be my boyfriend!"

Mateo stared at her, unsure if she was joking.

"Oh, god," Sam said, suddenly blushing. "You probably have a girlfriend back home or something . . ."

Mateo laughed. "No, it's not that. But won't your folks wonder why you've never mentioned me before?"

"I'll tell them I didn't want to introduce them to you until I was sure it was serious."

"I doubt they'll be impressed—a penniless resting actor isn't your typical rom-com hero."

"You can say that you're an architect . . ." She clapped her hands excitedly and squealed. "No—a vet! That's even better." She peered at him through her glasses. "You're not allergic to cats, are you? My parents have one."

"I like cats, but I'm not really comfortable deceiving your

family like that. Besides, if they live here, they'll probably recognize me—there aren't exactly a lot of black guys in Stowford."

"OK, forget the bit about being a vet. Just treat it like any other acting job. Don't you pretend to be in love with people onstage?"

Mateo looked at Sam. During her diatribe against romantic comedies, her hair had come loose from its bun and was falling around her face in silky black tendrils. He wouldn't have to pretend to be attracted to her. She was pretty.

Very pretty.

Smart and funny, too.

"I know you don't like Christmas pudding—but my mother's vegetable biryani is ah-may-zing."

Mateo considered it. It was a totally bonkers plan, but he was definitely tempted. Home cooking sounded better than spending the day in the empty pub, or alone in his cold, damp room . . .

There was a glint in Sam's eyes as she offered her final gambit, clearly confident that she was going to seal the deal. "Besides, didn't you say you needed to be distracted?"

He had to hand it to her—she was *very* persuasive.

I bet she's really good at her job.

Playing someone's pretend boyfriend wasn't the part he'd been hoping to land today. But actors had to be prepared to take risks. That was another thing they were always telling the students at drama school.

Mateo kept her on tenterhooks for a beat longer.

"OK. But I've got to warn you—I'm a method actor."

"What does that mean?"

Mateo stepped closer to Sam, gently tucked a lock of hair behind her ear and, gazing deep into her brown eyes, delivered his line huskily. "It means I'm going to be the best fake boyfriend you've ever had . . ."

22

NORA

Nora checked her phone, hoping to see a message from Charlotte about what time they could chat tomorrow. Nothing. *She's probably out diving,* Nora thought. Checking her e-mails, she saw that there was a message from Seb Fox. Nora clicked on it and grimaced.

> Let me know if you are happy with these pics. Santa's
> gonna bring me a big fat commission LOL!

The photos the estate agent had attached were good—but they didn't do justice to the real thing. Nora gazed around the bookshop now, taking a mental snapshot to preserve the moment forever. Through the fogged-up windows she could see that it was still snowing heavily outside, but the bookshop felt almost too warm, thanks to the fire and the sheer number of people crowded inside, chatting happily in small clusters. This was their best turnout ever, she realized. So many of their friends—old and new—had come. Mateo from the pub was deep in conversation with the Patels' daughter Sam. Maeve, who had brought Nora a gorgeous poinsettia from her flower shop, was chatting with Alice. Doug Jenkins, the farmer, and his eldest daughter were having an animated conversation with Olwyn. Lucy, wearing a skin-tight green dress from her boutique, was dancing to Wham's "Last Christmas" with Nigel from the butcher's shop.

The only thing stopping it from being the perfect Christmas Eve was that Charlotte wasn't there, but if life had taught Nora anything, it was that *almost perfect* was good enough.

Nora grabbed the last bottle of Simon's parents' wine. She never did this sort of thing, but tonight was no ordinary night. She tapped a knife against the bottle, but nobody heard it over the noise. Eventually, Nora put her fingers in her mouth and whistled, and *that* got people to quiet down.

Nora cleared her throat nervously. "Um, thanks so much to all of you for coming tonight," she said to the guests, feeling her cheeks reddening as everyone looked at her. "You have all been such good friends to us—and the shop—over the years." Her voice cracked with emotion as she spoke, but she forced herself to continue. "I just wanted to say . . . thank you . . . we love you . . . and, well, Happy Christmas!"

"Happy Christmas!" everyone cried, raising their glasses.

Relieved her impromptu speech was over, Nora opened the bottle and went over to Liz and Will, who were chatting about their kids.

"Anyone need a top-up?"

Liz covered the top of her glass with her hand. "No, thanks. I'm going to head home. I don't want to be too hungover to cook tomorrow. I'm going to get as much of it done in advance as I can."

"Let me know how your trifle turns out," Nora said. She thought of the enormous goose upstairs. She'd have to get it in the oven early to stand any chance of eating it for lunch.

Will checked his watch. "It's nearly midnight. I should probably get the kids home."

Nora glanced over at the twins, who were squealing in delight as they played with Harry. Julia was on his back, while Adam was attempting to arm-wrestle the teenager. "They don't seem very tired," she said, laughing.

"They'll probably still wake up at the crack of dawn," Will said. "I just hope they won't be too disappointed with what they find under the tree."

An idea suddenly occurred to Nora. "Can you hang on a few minutes? There's something I want to get for you . . ."

Squeezing her way through the guests, she found Simon, who was chatting to David Langdon and Kath. They were in the midst of a lively debate about the greatest prime ministers of the twentieth century. A cluster of ladies Nora recognized from the book club had gathered around them and were hanging on the MP's every word.

"Churchill was an inspirational and charismatic leader," David said. "His achievement of unifying the country during the war can't be overstated."

"True," Simon replied, "but Attlee was a progressive force—he shaped modern Britain and—"

"Simon," Nora cut in. "Sorry to interrupt, but can you help me get something out of the shed?"

"Now? Can't it wait until morning?"

"Not really."

The MP and his daughter exchanged glances. "We should probably make a move," Kath said. "Before we have to dig the car out of the snow."

Once they realized that David Langdon was leaving, his fans from the book club decided to go home, too. After saying goodbye to their departing guests, Nora and Simon made their way through the back room and out into the alleyway.

"Nice speech, honey," Simon said, putting his arm around her.

The icy air outside cooled Nora's still-flushed face, and felt wonderful after the heat of the shop.

"I don't know how you do the quiz every week," Nora said. "I get so embarrassed when I have to talk in front of a crowd."

"What was so urgent?" Simon asked, as they trudged through the snow to the shed at the bottom of the passageway.

"I need you to get the old wooden sledge down."

"Why?" Simon chuckled. "Did you fancy sledging down Blackberry Hill by moonlight?"

"I thought we could give it to Will's kids for Christmas."

Simon unlocked the padlock and opened the shed door. Inside, there were boxes piled from floor to ceiling, a rusty old bike, a beach parasol, various tools, a broken microwave that they'd never got around to taking to the dump, and assorted stuff that they'd shoved in the shed, on the off chance they might need it again. What were they going to do with all of it when they moved?

Don't think about that tonight, Nora scolded herself.

Pushing boxes out of the way, Simon cleared a path to the back of the shed, where the sledge was hanging by its rope handle from a nail on the wall. He reached up and lifted it down. Using his sleeve, he wiped dust off the seat's wooden slats. The red metal runners gleamed in a shaft of moonlight coming through the small window. It was over forty years old, but still in mint condition.

"I remember the Christmas I got this," Simon said. "Daniel and I spent hours sledging down Primrose Hill."

"Are you OK with giving it away?" Nora checked.

"Of course. It's only gathering dust in here."

They carried the sledge inside and Nora quickly made a label for it. TO JULIA AND ADAM, she wrote on a piece of paper, FROM

SANTA. She taped it onto the sledge, and they carried it over to Will, who was wrestling the twins into their coats, hats and gloves.

"Look what we found outside," Nora said, winking at Will. "Santa must have already started on his rounds."

"Oh, wow!" Julia exclaimed, her eyes widening.

"Is it for us?" Adam asked.

Simon pretended to check the label. "Well, as long as you're Adam and Julia."

"Yay!" Julia cried, jumping up and down.

"I want to try it now!" Adam said.

"I'll pull you home on it," their dad said. Then he turned to Nora and mouthed, *Thank you.*

The excited expressions on the twins' faces was more than enough thanks for her.

Nora held the door open for Will, so he and the twins could carry the sledge out. She paused in the doorway for a moment, leaving the door ajar to let cool air into the shop. Julia sat down on the sledge and wrapped her arms around her brother's waist. As Will began to pull the twins home through the snow, the church bells rang out from St. Stephen's.

Ring, happy bells, across the snow . . . The words of Tennyson's poem echoed in her head.

Shutting the door, Nora returned to the party. The crowd was beginning to thin out, as guests took their leave.

Olwyn came up to Nora, pulling on her coat. "Thank you for a lovely party, Nora, dear," she said, giving her a hug. "I'd better get going or I won't get a seat at midnight mass."

Nora suddenly wondered how the retired schoolteacher would be spending Christmas Day and chided herself for not asking her earlier. "What are you doing tomorrow, Olwyn? Would you like to join me and Simon for lunch? We did something rather silly and ordered an enormous goose, and there's no way the two of us will be able to eat it all . . ."

Olwyn beamed. "That's very kind of you, Nora. If you're sure you don't mind having company."

"You'd be doing us a favor. Why don't you come around two o'clock?"

Harry Swann approached them and stood there shuffling his feet, the book Nora had given him shoved into the back pocket of his jeans.

"Thanks for coming, Harry," Nora said, "and for keeping Adam and Julia entertained."

The teenager nodded, his cheeks flushing. "Sorry again for . . . you know."

"No worries. I hope you find the book helpful."

He continued to stand there awkwardly, shuffling his feet.

"What is it, Harry?" Olwyn prompted him.

"Um, Miss Powell, would it be OK if I go to church with you?"

Olwyn smiled and nodded.

"I'd like that very much, Harry."

"On Christmas Eve, my family used to go out for a curry and then go to midnight mass. Emma would always wear one of her glittery sweaters."

Olwyn pressed her reindeer brooch, making it flash. "Emma will be with us in spirit." She linked her arm through Harry's, and the two of them headed off to the church.

By now, there were only a few guests remaining. Mateo and Sam had claimed the sofa and seemed oblivious to the fact that the party was winding down. Sam had slipped off her heels and curled her feet underneath her, and Mateo was sitting so close that their knees were touching. The sparks coming off them were brighter than the ones in the fireplace, where a log was smoldering into embers.

They certainly made an attractive couple. Mateo was movie-star handsome, with his wild curls and startlingly green eyes. Sam's brown eyes sparkled as she laughed at something Mateo was saying. She looked a lot more relaxed than she had earlier in the evening.

"They look cozy," Simon murmured.

"That's just what I was thinking."

"And to think—our books brought them together . . ."

The two young people must have felt their eyes upon them, because they both turned around at the same time and realized there was hardly anyone left at the party.

"I'm so sorry," Sam said, quickly standing up. "We've overstayed our welcome."

"Not at all," Nora assured her. "It's been a wonderful evening."

"Are you working tomorrow?" Simon asked Mateo.

He shook his head. "The pub's shut."

"Why don't you pop over for dinner?" Nora asked. "I'm cooking a goose the size of Gloucestershire."

Mateo looked bashful. "Actually, I'm going to Sam's house."

Well, well, well.

Nora and Simon exchanged knowing looks.

"Just as friends," Sam clarified, tucking her hair behind her ear self-consciously and sliding back into her shoes.

Just friends, my foot, thought Nora.

Sam gathered up the huge bag of books she'd bought earlier that evening. "Well, I'm going to make a move. My niece and nephew will be arriving early, and Auntie Sampriti is going to be *very* hungover."

"It's late," Mateo said. "I'll walk you home."

"But you're just across the road. My parents' house is on the other side of the village."

"I insist," he said, gallantly taking the heavy bag of books from her. "That way I'll know where to come tomorrow."

Now the only guest left in the bookshop was Howie, who had fallen asleep in one of the armchairs near the fire and was snoring loudly.

Simon groaned. "Please don't tell me he's sleeping here tonight."

Nora crouched down and gently shook Howie's shoulder.

"Any more wine, Nor?" Howie asked sleepily, fumbling for his empty glass. "That posh plonk weren't half bad."

Nora would have loved to see the look on her father-in-law's face if he'd heard Howie's assessment of his prize vintage.

Empty bottles littered the tables and bookshelves. Somehow, they'd managed to work through both cases of wine. "'Fraid not."

"Ah, well, then I'd best be on my way." Howie heaved himself out of the armchair and stood unsteadily.

Nora knew Simon wouldn't be thrilled at the thought of sharing Christmas dinner with Howie, but she had to ask. "What are you doing tomorrow, How?"

Howie burped loudly and swayed slightly. He chuckled as Nora reached out a hand to steady him. "You're all right, Nor," he said. "Me cousin's invited me over for Christmas dinner over Chipping Campden way."

Phew!

"See you soon," she said, giving him a peck on his florid cheek.

"Happy Christmas, Bookworm," Howie called, saluting Simon on his way out.

"And then there were two," Nora said. She started gathering up empty crisp bowls.

"Leave all that." Simon took the bowls out of her hands and set them back down. "There's something I've been meaning to do all night." He wrapped his arms around Nora and gave her a kiss.

Just then, the bell above the shop door jangled.

"That had better not be bloody Howie," Simon muttered in her ear.

Merry, who was dozing by the fire, raised her head. Giving a sharp bark, she ran to the door, wagging her tail. Nora turned around, and saw a figure covered in snow, holding an enormous backpack.

"Did I miss the party?" she said, dropping her backpack onto the floor.

Could it really be . . .

"Charlotte!" Nora cried, running over to wrap her daughter in a snowy hug. She clung to her for dear life as Merry yapped and pranced around them.

"I can't breathe, Mum." Charlotte laughed.

Nora reluctantly released her daughter. Charlotte bent down and Merry jumped straight into her arms.

"Did you miss me, girl?" Charlotte asked, as she nuzzled noses with her dog.

Oh yes, Nora thought, drinking in her daughter like a parched traveler lost in the desert, happening upon an oasis. After months in the sunshine, Charlotte's cheeks, which Merry was joyfully licking, were more freckled than ever. Her hands, as they tousled the terrier's white ears, still bore faint traces of henna designs.

"Why didn't you tell us you were coming?" Simon asked, rushing over to give Charlotte a kiss.

"I wanted it to be a surprise. But I hadn't counted on the snow. The last train to Stowford was canceled, so I ended up having to get a coach. I'm so sorry I missed the party."

"That doesn't matter," Nora said. "You're here now."

Her daughter was home. Now it truly *was* a perfect evening.

23

SIMON

"Happy Christmas," Charlotte sang out, bringing two cups of tea into her parents' bedroom. She sat cross-legged on their bed in an old T-shirt and a frayed pair of jogging bottoms.

"No," Nora groaned, burrowing under the duvet. "It's too early."

"I let you lie in until eight," said Charlotte, who had collapsed in bed almost as soon as she'd arrived. "I've been up since six. Jet lag . . ."

"This brings back memories," Simon said, yawning as he sat up in bed. When she was little, Charlotte had always brought her Christmas stocking into their bedroom and opened her presents on their bed.

Nora's head suddenly emerged, her auburn hair wild. "Oh no! I didn't do you a stocking this year, Charlotte!"

Charlotte laughed. "It's OK, Mum, really. I'm eighteen. I haven't believed in Father Christmas for a while now."

Even so, Charlotte's arrival last night had felt like a bit of Christmas magic. The look of joy on Nora's face when their daughter had walked through the shop door had been priceless.

"The goose!" Nora cried, pushing off the duvet and jumping out of bed. "I've got to get it in the oven!"

Charlotte had already taken Merry out for a little tramp through the snow, so there was no need for Simon to get out of his pajamas. He put on his tartan dressing gown and followed his wife and daughter into the kitchen.

"Please don't tell me you've gone vegan," Nora said, taking the goose out of the fridge.

Charlotte laughed. "I've eaten enough dal to last me a lifetime. Goose sounds great."

Nora peered inside the goose and wrinkled her nose. "Ugh. I hate this bit."

"Step aside, ladies." Simon rolled up his sleeves and delved into the enormous bird, removing the giblets.

Merry eyed them with a hopeful whine.

"Be patient, Fuzzy Face," Simon said. "These will be your dinner later on."

While Nora and Charlotte made an apple and herb stuffing, Simon peeled potatoes, thinking of all the luxurious goose fat they'd soon have to roast them in.

"I hope you don't mind, sweetie," Nora told Charlotte, "but we've invited Olwyn Powell to join us for Christmas dinner."

"Cool," Charlotte said, munching a slice of apple. "I haven't seen Miss Powell for ages."

Once the goose was stuffed and cooking in the oven, they moved into the living room. Nora settled on the sofa, while Charlotte stretched out on the floor next to Merry.

"We didn't get a big tree this year," Simon said apologetically, switching on the fairy lights before sitting down next to Nora. It wasn't just because they weren't expecting Charlotte; real Christmas trees were expensive.

"It's fine, Dad. I'm just so happy to be here."

"I know it sounds soppy, but I've missed you so much," Nora said. "Especially hearing your voice. I know you were probably having so much fun on your travels that you barely had time to think of us."

"Not at all. I didn't call very often because talking to you made me homesick. Every time we spoke, I wanted to get straight on the first plane back home."

"Oh, honey," Nora said, leaning down to plant a kiss on Charlotte's head.

"Don't get me wrong," Charlotte continued. "I loved India. Oh! That reminds me—I brought you guys back some presents . . ." She disappeared into her bedroom and returned holding a few parcels wrapped in hot-pink paper. "Sorry—I couldn't find any Christmas wrapping paper."

"You didn't have to do all this, sweetie," Simon said.

"I *wanted* to," Charlotte insisted, handing her father a package.

Simon opened his gift and found a wooden chessboard inside. Opening it, he discovered a set of playing pieces, intricately carved from sandalwood. The kings were elaborately turbaned maharajas, the bishops were elephants and the knights were saber-wielding warriors in long tunics. "Thank you so much. It's stunning."

Charlotte grinned up at him from the floor. "As I keep beating you in online Scrabble, I thought you might stand more chance of winning with chess."

"Cheeky," Simon said, nudging her playfully with his foot.

"Did you know chess was invented in India?" Charlotte said. "In the sixth century AD."

"You can use that in one of your quizzes," Nora said, winking at Simon.

Simon turned a pawn over in his hands, remembering how his father had taught him to play chess over the Christmas holidays when he was about ten. They didn't have much in common—but they did both enjoy a good game of chess.

"You should invite your dad over and challenge him to a game," suggested Nora, reading his mind.

"Mmmm," Simon replied.

Not going to happen. He wasn't ready to forgive his father, even though it would be satisfying to give him a good drubbing on his new chessboard.

"Oh, yeah," Charlotte said, handing her mother two parcels. "It would be good to see Nana and Grampy."

Nora opened the larger one first and took out a shawl with a traditional swirling pattern, shot through with gold embroidery. "Oh, it's gorgeous," she said, wrapping it around her neck and stroking the fabric. "And so soft."

"I got it at a market in Kashmir," Charlotte said. "I thought it would look nice with your coloring."

"It does," Simon agreed. Nora was still in her pajamas, her hair was uncombed and there were smudges of last night's mascara under her eyes. But to Simon she looked radiantly beautiful because she was so happy.

"I love it," Nora said, beaming. She sniffed her second parcel. "I think I can guess what this is . . ." Her eyes lit up as she opened it to reveal several pouches of spices. She opened one and inhaled deeply. "*Mmm.* I might use this garam masala later on."

"I've got gifts for both of you, too," Simon said. He went into their bedroom and, from the depths of his sock drawer, retrieved the silver jewelry he'd purchased at the market a few weeks back.

"I didn't think you were coming home, but I got you something anyway," he said, handing Charlotte her bangle.

"It's perfect, Dad," she said, giving him a kiss on the cheek. She slipped it onto her wrist, along with her other bracelets. She seemed to have accumulated even more on her travels.

"Open yours, Mum," Charlotte said, nudging Nora.

"Oh, Simon," Nora exclaimed, holding the earrings up to the light. "They're beautiful . . . but I thought we weren't doing presents this year." Despite her protests, she looked pleased and put the delicate silver teardrops on. Then she grinned and confessed, "Actually, I broke the rules, too."

Nora pulled a squishy parcel out from behind the sofa and handed it to Simon.

"What could it be?" Simon said, giving the parcel a squeeze. He ripped his present open and wasn't a bit surprised to find a hand-knit sweater inside.

"Just what I wanted." Shrugging off his dressing gown, Simon pulled the chunky, fisherman-style sweater over his head. "Fits perfectly."

"Yours isn't wrapped," Nora said, handing Charlotte a pale blue sweater. "Because I didn't think you were coming home."

Charlotte slipped her sweater on and modeled it with a mock-catwalk stride across the living room. She struck a pose, making her parents laugh. "Thanks, Mum. It's gorgeous."

"I know you're probably not going to need it on your travels, but it will come in handy next autumn. University digs are always freezing."

Charlotte chewed on her bottom lip. "Actually . . . I haven't decided what I'm going to do after Christmas. I don't want to waste my round-the-world ticket. But being back in Stowford has reminded me how much I love it here. There really is no place like home."

Simon and Nora exchanged glances. Should they tell Charlotte about what was going on now? Simon didn't want to spoil Christmas, but they had to break the news to her at some point . . .

"There's, er, something we need to tell you, sweetie," Nora said falteringly. Simon took her hand and gave it a squeeze for encouragement.

Charlotte's eyes darted from one parent to the other, instantly alarmed. "What is it? Is it Dad's heart again?"

"No, nothing like that," Simon quickly assured her. "Dr. Dhar says I'm doing great."

Nora cleared her throat and took a deep breath. "Dad and I have decided . . . well, to be honest, we didn't have much of a choice in the matter . . . that we're selling the shop."

"What?" Charlotte stared at them, aghast. "No! You can't do that—you love this place!"

Simon saw a look of pain flicker across his wife's face.

"We all love the shop, Charlotte," he explained. "But we're in serious debt. We can't afford to keep running it at a loss."

"What about my uni savings?" Charlotte said. "Use that. I'll take out loans. That's what most people have to do."

"No," Nora said firmly. "That money is for your education."

"What about Nana and Gra—"

Simon held up his hand, cutting her off. "I know this is hard to take in, honey, but we've exhausted all the other options. We really have tried everything. We didn't want it to come to this, but we're putting the shop on the market in the new year."

Charlotte wrapped her arms around her knees, letting the news sink in.

"I'm so sorry, sweetheart," Nora said.

"I'm the one who's sorry," Charlotte replied, shaking her head mournfully. "I can't believe you two were going through all this and I didn't even know about it."

"There was nothing you could have done," Nora assured her.

"I still feel terrible. I've been living it up thousands of miles away, completely oblivious to what was going on here."

"Look," Simon said, getting to his feet. "This is going to be our last Christmas here. Let's not worry about the future, and just enjoy the day."

Nora nodded and smiled bravely. "Dad's right. We're thrilled that you're home and we aren't going to let anything spoil that."

By now, the delicious scent of roasting goose was wafting out of the kitchen. Simon checked his watch. He'd had it appraised in London, but it hadn't been worth nearly as much as he'd thought. Its only real value was sentimental. "We'd better get on with the rest of the cooking before Olwyn gets here."

Nora leaped up. "And we'd better get dressed, too!"

Once they had changed, it was all hands on deck in the kitchen. While Simon basted the goose, draining off the fat for the roast potatoes, Nora and Charlotte prepared the rest of the veg. Nora made a honey and ginger glaze for the carrots, and Charlotte whipped up a vegetable curry.

"I learned how to make this in Kerala," she said, adding some of the garam masala.

"I hope it's not *too* spicy," Simon said, tossing chunks of potato into piping-hot goose fat.

"You're such a lightweight, Dad," Charlotte teased.

As they cooked together in the warm, spicy kitchen, they chatted about everything except the fact that this was the last Christmas dinner they would prepare here. Charlotte set the table, using a cotton wall hanging she'd brought home from India for a tablecloth and putting a cracker at each place setting.

"Looks wonderful," Nora said, lighting candles in the middle for a centerpiece.

Just after two, the doorbell rang. "That'll be Olwyn," Simon said. "She doesn't know about the shop yet, so please don't mention it," he told Charlotte, then hurried downstairs to let their guest in.

"Happy Christmas." Olwyn handed him a bottle of wine and a tub of chocolates. "Something smells delicious."

It *did* smell good. Simon's stomach rumbled in anticipation as he helped Olwyn up the stairs to the flat.

"Charlotte!" Olwyn exclaimed. "What a lovely surprise!"

Charlotte gave her old teacher a hug. "It *was* a surprise—they had no idea I was coming."

"I do hope I'm not intruding," Olwyn asked anxiously.

"Don't be silly," Nora said, taking her coat and giving her a kiss on the cheek. "We're delighted to have you."

"Can I help with anything?"

"Absolutely not," Simon said, escorting their guest to the sofa. While Olwyn stroked Merry and sipped a glass of sherry, the rest of them carried the food to the table. Soon, it was groaning under the weight of crisp, golden roast potatoes, gleaming glazed carrots, a fragrant bowl of stuffing, Charlotte's curry and a revolting-looking Brussels sprout and pecan stir-fry Nora had concocted in tribute to her mother.

"Dinner is served," Simon announced grandly, carrying out the goose and setting it on the table. He carved thick slices of meat, so tender it practically fell off the bone, and served their guest first.

"Everything looks delicious," Olwyn said, helping herself to roast potatoes.

Before tucking in, Olwyn said grace and then they all pulled their crackers, in a cacophony of bangs that sent Merry scurrying under the table.

"Ooh, very appropriate," Nora said, chuckling as she read her joke. "'What type of books does Santa like best?'"

"Children's books?" Charlotte guessed.

"Nope—*elf*-help books," Nora said.

Everyone groaned cheerfully.

"This will come in handy," Simon said, holding up a key ring with a miniature corkscrew on it. He used it to open the bottle of red Olwyn had brought and poured everyone a glass.

"I remember when I was a girl, we couldn't afford shop-bought crackers," Olwyn recalled, donning a purple paper crown at a rakish angle. "My mother used to make them herself."

Over dinner, Charlotte filled them in on her travels. She'd visited temples, palaces and forts, studied yoga in Goa, toured a tea plantation in Darjeeling, and even gone on a camel safari in the Thar Desert.

"But what was the *best* thing you did?" Simon asked.

Charlotte scrunched up her nose as she considered the question. "Probably volunteering in a school in Kerala," she said. "It was so rewarding. And it made me realize how lucky I was to grow up with so many wonderful books—they barely had any."

"Teaching is the best job in the world," Olwyn agreed.

"What about you, Miss Powell?" Charlotte asked. "Are you still at St. Stephen's?"

"Oh no, I retired at the end of last summer term. I still volunteer there one day a week, though, and I've just agreed to help two boys with their reading."

"Olwyn's writing her own book," Nora told Charlotte.

"Oooh, that's exciting," Charlotte said. "What's it about?"

Olwyn filled them in on her detective story in enthusiastic detail, sawing away at a slice of roast goose while she described the murder victim's dismemberment. "But I've only just started it," she told them.

"I can't wait to read it," Nora said.

"Sounds like the sort of thing our book club would love." No sooner were the words out of his mouth than Simon remembered that soon, there would be no book club—because there would be no bookshop. He took a swig of wine, willing himself to remain cheerful.

"I'm not sure if it's any good, but I'm certainly enjoying writing it."

"I propose a toast," Nora said. "To good books!"

"To good food," Simon countered.

"To good friends," Olwyn said, raising her glass.

"And to home," Charlotte said, smiling at her parents. "Which is wherever your friends and family are."

24

SIMON

On Boxing Day, the sound of Charlotte's voice woke Simon up from a dream in which he was playing a life-size game of chess, but where all the pawns were geese wearing knitted sweaters. *That will be the cheese*, thought Simon, blaming his weird dream on the Stilton he'd tucked into late last night. Dr. Dhar definitely wouldn't approve.

It had been a brilliant Christmas. They'd all eaten too much and stayed up far too late playing games and cards. She looked like a sweet old lady, but Olwyn Powell was quite the card shark. It was a good thing they'd only been playing for matchsticks, or they would have found themselves in even more debt.

Simon shuffled into the living room and found Charlotte lolling on the sofa in her pajamas, chatting on her phone as she ate a bowl of leftover Christmas pudding for breakfast.

Who's that? he mouthed.

"Dad's just got up, Grampy," Charlotte said. "I'll let you say hi." She held out the phone.

Simon shook his head, but Charlotte just smiled and batted her eyelids with faux innocence.

Sighing resignedly, Simon took the phone from his daughter. "Hello, Dad."

"Only just getting up?"

Simon bristled. Why did everything his father say to him sound like a criticism? "Happy Christmas to you, too. Did you and Mum have a nice time with Daniel and his boys?" He'd got a text from his brother yesterday, and knew that they'd all gone for dinner in a posh hotel.

"The service was terrible and the turkey was dry," his father complained.

It wasn't just Simon that his father could find fault with. Even Michelin-starred chefs fell short of Charles Walden's exacting standards.

"We had goose," Simon said stiffly. "It was delicious. And Charlotte came—"

"Have you seen *The Times* this morning?" his father interrupted.

"Not yet."

"Well, make sure you do—there's an article you'll be interested in. Page twelve."

"OK, Dad," Simon said. Walden Creative was probably in the news, announcing record-breaking profits, and his dad wanted to rub his nose in it. Or Casa di Carlotta had got a good write-up by *The Times'* wine critic. "Thanks for the booze, by the way."

"It should last you awhile."

Or not. Empty bottles from both cases were in the overflowing recycling bin outside. And judging from the way Merry was dancing around the door, she needed to go outside, too.

"Listen, Dad, I've got to go. The dog needs walking. Wish Mum a Happy Christmas for me."

Nora emerged, yawning, from their bedroom, as Simon handed the phone back to Charlotte.

"Who was that?"

Simon grimaced. "Dad."

"I don't know why you're so rude about Grampy," Charlotte said. "He's lovely."

"To you."

Nora squeezed his arm sympathetically as she gave him a good-morning peck on the cheek.

"I'm going to take Merry out for a walk," Simon said. "Anyone want to join me?"

"A Boxing Day walk sounds perfect," Nora replied, rubbing her belly. "I dread to think how many calories I consumed yesterday."

"I'll come, too." Charlotte grinned. "But you need to help me up." She held out her arm and Simon hoisted her off the sofa.

They all got dressed and headed out into a cold, crisp morning with a cloudless blue sky. The temperature hadn't risen, so the heavy snow that had fallen over Christmas still swaddled the countryside in a pristine white blanket. They walked down the high street, and Merry rubbed noses with every dog they passed along the way. Everyone was craving fresh air and exercise after a day of overindulgence.

Turning off the high street at St. Stephen's, they passed the churchyard and Simon saw a familiar flash of red hair.

"Isn't that Harry?" he asked Nora.

The teenager was with a man and a woman—his parents, Simon assumed—and he was holding a miniature Christmas tree, decked out with flashing lights, glittery tinsel and garish baubles.

"They must be taking that to Emma's grave," Nora said.

"You mean the girl who died last summer?" Charlotte asked.

Simon nodded. As he watched the Swann family make their way through the graveyard, he gave a sidelong glance at Charlotte. His daughter's cheeks were ruddy from the cold, her eyes sparkled with vitality. Simon felt overwhelmed with gratitude that she was here with them now.

"It's good to see them out and about," Nora said, noticing Harry's father put his arm around his son.

"Are you going to say hi to your mum?" Simon asked her.

Nora shook her head. "I think we should give Harry and his family their privacy."

They carried on walking past the school. As they neared Olwyn's cottage, Charlotte asked, "Should we see if Miss Powell wants to join us?"

"Good idea," Simon said.

They went up the path and knocked on Olwyn's door. There was no answer so Simon knocked again, louder this time.

"Maybe she's out," Nora said.

But just as they were turning to leave, the door opened. Olwyn, wearing a pink fleece dressing gown, blinked at them. A cat slunk out from behind her. It yowled and swiped a paw at Merry, who cowered behind Charlotte's legs.

"Be nice, Tuppence," Olwyn scolded, shooing the cat back inside the house.

"Happy Boxing Day," Simon said. "We were wondering if you'd like to join us for a walk."

"Oh, that's very kind of you, but I'm not even dressed. I've been writing all morning. I'm right in the middle of a particularly juicy scene. My detective, Clay Thorne, is questioning a suspect who threatens him with a pair of pruning shears . . ."

"No worries," Nora replied. "Sorry to have disturbed you."

"As you're here—what do you think is a better name for an adulterous gardener with a jealous streak? Jasmine von Teasle or Rosalind Moss-Oakley?"

"Jasmine von Teasle!" they all said at the same time.

"Jasmine it is, then!" Olwyn said happily. Waving them good-bye, she shut the cottage door.

"'Adulterous gardener,' eh?" Simon chuckled. "Olwyn Powell is a dark horse."

"If the novel doesn't work out, she can always go to Las Vegas and become a professional poker player," Charlotte joked.

Climbing over a stile, they followed a footpath across a snowy field to Blackberry Hill. Shouts of glee rang out as children whooshed down the slope—some on shiny new sledges, others improvising makeshift toboggans out of swimming rings and tea trays. One child was even using a plastic kayak as a sledge!

"Hang on," Charlotte said, squinting at the hill. "Isn't that my old sledge?"

Looking at where she was pointing, Simon spotted Will and the twins.

"Not anymore," Simon said. "We gave it to some new friends."

They traipsed across the snowy field, arriving at the bottom of the hill just as Adam and Julia sped down it on the wooden sledge.

"Merry!" Julia shouted, hopping off the sledge.

"How was your Christmas?" Nora asked the children, as they stroked Merry. The children's cheeks were flushed from the cold, and their hair was sweaty from the exertion of trudging up the snowy hill.

"Brilliant!" Julia said. "Santa brought us a new puzzle and we did the whole thing with Daddy yesterday."

"But the sledge is our best present!" Adam said.

As the twins put Merry on the sledge and proceeded to pull her around the field, their father came over to say hello.

"Will, this is our daughter, Charlotte," Nora said.

"I hope you don't mind that your parents gave Adam and Julia your sledge," he said.

"I'm glad they're having so much fun with it," Charlotte assured him.

Merry jumped off the sledge and ran back to them, barking.

"Bye!" Adam and Julia cried, dragging the sledge behind them as they raced up the hill.

Simon, Nora and Charlotte headed back toward the village along the country lane. Clumps of snow fell from tree branches that curved over the road like a white canopy, startling Merry every time.

"Don't be such a wimp, Merry." Simon laughed. Then a clump of snow landed on his head, making him yelp.

Nora and Charlotte clung to each other, giggling, as Simon shook the snow out of his hair.

"Glad you're both finding this so amusing," he said, as icy-cold melted snow trickled down his neck.

As he looked up, two runners were approaching them at speed from the opposite direction—one tall, one short, but both with dark hair.

"Wow," Charlotte said. "They're going fast."

As the runners came closer, Simon saw that it was Mateo and Sam. Although Mateo's legs were longer than Sam's, their strides were perfectly in sync as they ran side by side. Noticing them, the runners slowed to a halt.

"Happy Boxing Day," Sam said, barely out of breath.

"I still don't really get Boxing Day," Mateo remarked. "I mean, what's the point of it? We just had Christmas."

"Americans," Sam said, rolling her eyes.

"Traditionally, it was the day servants could go home to celebrate Christmas with their families," Simon explained. "And since the Middle Ages, it's been a day of almsgiving to the poor—"

"We don't need a history lesson," Nora interrupted. "How was your Christmas?"

"I was a big hit with the Patel family," Mateo said, grinning down at Sam, who blushed as she jogged on the spot.

It looked as if it wasn't just Sam's family he'd made a good impression on.

"Don't stop on our account," Nora said, and the runners set off again.

"He's a hottie," Charlotte murmured, watching Mateo and Sam vanish down the lane. "Where did he come from?"

"California," Simon said. "But he works at the George."

"I think you're too late to get in there," Nora teased. "He and Sam seem to have hit it off, thanks to us." She beamed at Simon. "Maybe that should be our new career—matchmakers!"

They made it back to the village without any more snow landing on Simon's head. As they passed the corner shop, Simon remembered what his father had said about *The Times*. "I'm going to pop in and get a newspaper."

"We need milk, too," Charlotte called after him.

When they got back home, Nora put the kettle on. Simon sat down at the kitchen table and opened up the newspaper, scanning the headlines as he flicked through the pages.

When he came to page twelve, he froze. "Bloody hell!" A picture of him and Nora, taken from the bookshop's website, stared out at him from the newsprint. Next to it was David Langdon's column.

"What's wrong?" Nora asked.

He held the page up. "We're in *The Times*."

Grabbing the paper out of her father's hands, Charlotte proceeded to read the whole article aloud:

I shouldn't be here to write this column. You see, just a few weeks ago, I was planning to kill myself. It wasn't so much that I wanted to die. More that I didn't want to suffer any longer, my severe depression dragging me down like a sodden overcoat.

It is no exaggeration to say that I owe my life to two unlikely guardian angels—Nora and Simon Walden. The Waldens are a married couple who run the Stowford Bookshop, a charming literary haven in a small village in my constituency. Realizing that many people find this a tough time of year, Nora and Simon launched an appeal to send uplifting Christmas books to strangers in need of a boost. I was one of the recipients of their random acts of literary kindness. You may not have heard of the book they sent me—*The Greatest Gift*—but you are likely to know of the film it inspired—*It's a Wonderful Life*.

Reading this book when I was at my lowest ebb helped me to see that, for all my faults, the world is a better place with me in it. Above all, it showed me that I am not alone.

The Waldens' kindness and my daughter Kath's tireless support have given me the courage to seek help and speak openly about my ongoing battle with depression. And if this column helps even one person reading it today, my speaking out will have been worthwhile.

As I approach the end of what has been a difficult year, I look forward to happier times in the months ahead. But to recover fully, I will need to make some changes in my life. To that end, I have made some resolutions that I'd like to share with you, my faithful readers.

Firstly, I will be resigning from my seat in Parliament at the next election. It has been an honor to represent my constituency for so many years, and I am immensely proud of what I have accomplished while serving in this government, in particular the Marriage Act and recent initiatives to preserve our environment for future generations. But it is time for fresh voices to be heard, and for new talent to lead. Going forward, I will focus my energies on raising mental health awareness and improving access to treatment. While we have made great strides toward eradicating the stigma of mental illness, there is still much work to be done. Over four thousand people in the UK take their lives every year. No one should suffer in silence, and I intend to work to ensure that help is available for everyone who needs it.

Secondly, while I remain in Parliament, I will lobby the Chancellor of the Exchequer to abolish business taxes for smaller businesses earning under a certain threshold. This will ensure that our nation of shopkeepers can continue operating the independent shops that so enrich our high streets.

My third resolution concerns the Stowford Bookshop. Sadly, it has fallen on difficult times. A combination of rising business taxes and fierce online competition has meant that their wonderful shop is unable to continue trading. So I am hereby launching a fundraising campaign to save the Stowford Bookshop. I have seen first-hand how important this shop is to its local community. From its popular book club to its weekly toddler story time, Nora and Simon's brilliant bookshop provides a much-needed space for supporting culture and fostering friendship and connectedness.

Please donate to keep Nora and Simon's bookshop afloat. Better yet, buy a book from them to share with someone you care about.

You never know, it might just save their life.

"Oh, my goodness," Nora said, sinking into a chair. "That was so brave of David."

"Did you know about this?" Simon asked.

"I knew he was unwell," Nora replied. "He told me when he and Kath came into the shop to thank us for sending him the book. I didn't tell you about his depression because he told me in confidence and I didn't want to betray his trust."

Charlotte took out her phone and typed in a link to the fund-raising site.

"OMG," she exclaimed. She held out the screen, showing her parents the amount that had been raised.

"Nine thousand pounds?" Nora gasped.

"All of that's for us?" Simon asked, staring at the figure in disbelief. Then right in front of his eyes, the total changed, going up by another twenty pounds.

"That's almost enough to pay off our debts," Nora said.

"And that's just since this morning—I bet it will raise even more," Charlotte said.

"I can't believe this." Nora's eyes filled with tears. "All of these strangers giving us money . . ."

"It's like you sending books out to people, Mum," Charlotte replied, giving her a hug. "People *want* to help."

"What did I tell you?" Simon said, grinning. "Giving alms is a Boxing Day tradition."

They sat around the table in silence, each trying to process this unexpected turn of events.

"What should we do now?" Nora asked.

"What we always do on Boxing Day," Simon said. "Watch a movie."

"*Elf*?" Charlotte suggested.

"I was thinking *Die Hard*."

"No," Nora said, shaking her head. "There's only one thing

we should be watching today." She held up the newspaper article. "*It's a Wonderful Life.*"

It most certainly is, thought Simon, as he snuggled up on the sofa with his wife and daughter and they watched Frank Capra's classic film. And despite it being almost eighty years old, it had never felt more relevant.

25

NORA

Nora pulled a face as she stuck a copy of *The Oculist of Leipzig* into a padded envelope in the back room of the bookshop. "I feel like I should include a warning note," she joked. "Telling them not to waste their time."

"You never know—they might love it," Simon said. "I'm just glad we didn't have to burn all our copies to stay warm."

"Amen to that," Nora replied, sticking a label on the envelope and adding it to a tall stack of parcels.

Since reopening on December 27, the shop had been inundated with customers and online orders, thanks to David Langdon's newspaper column. Nora and Simon had been working round the clock to fulfill all the orders, but she wasn't complaining. Because of the fundraising campaign, they'd raised enough money to pay off their debts, and there was even some left over to replace the roof.

Nora stuck a copy of *David Copperfield* in an envelope and shook her head, thinking back to that fateful, wine-fueled night she and Simon had sent out another Dickens classic. "I still can't believe all of this happened because we sent out a few books."

"It feels like a fairy tale," Simon agreed, adding another envelope to the pile. "With David Langdon as our very unlikely fairy godmother."

A few days earlier, Nora had walked over to Yew Tree Manor with a batch of homemade ginger biscuits to thank David for his role in saving the bookshop. "It was so brave of you to go public about your illness," she'd told him.

"It was the least I could do," the MP had said, munching on a biscuit. Nora was happy to see that he had put on a bit of weight. Perhaps the antidepressants were beginning to work, or maybe it was just the relief of sharing the story of his depression. "And the response has been overwhelmingly supportive."

"Well, Simon and I will be forever in your debt. Please let me know if there's ever anything we can do to help."

"There is one thing . . . You can help me persuade Kath to run for Parliament."

"Dad, I've told you I'm not sure I'm cut out for public office. Do you seriously think your constituents will elect a gay MP?"

Nora had seen how good Kath was with people. The young woman was kind, empathetic and intelligent—everything you could hope for in a leader. "Your dad is right. You'd be great."

Nora filled out a label and stuck it on the envelope, then crossed off an order on her list. "David is trying to convince his daughter to run for Parliament," she told Simon. "I wonder what he'll do next . . ."

"Maybe he should follow Olwyn's example and write a book."

Nora thought about all the affairs the politician was alleged to have had. It was bound to be a juicy read. She chuckled. "I'll definitely read it if he does."

Simon finished packing up another book, then he stood up and stretched. "Come on, honey. Let's head over to the George."

"But we still haven't finished packing everything up," Nora said, glancing down at the long printout of online orders.

Simon gently tugged the list out of her hand. "It's New Year's Eve. There's no post tomorrow—these can wait till next year."

Nora smiled. They *could* wait. Because thanks to David, and the kindness of thousands of book-loving strangers, the shop would still be there in January. "Go on then, twist my arm."

Upstairs, Nora put on some lipstick and ran a brush through her hair, then she and Simon headed over the road to the George.

The pub was full of revelers. Sue had hung up a banner reading HAPPY NEW YEAR above the bar, and bunches of balloons decorated each table. Nora waved to Charlotte, who was sitting at a table in the corner, surrounded by a group of her school friends, all back from uni for the holidays. Having Charlotte at home had been a godsend. She'd helped out in the shop tirelessly, but Nora had insisted that she take the evening off to catch up with her mates.

Simon took Nora's hand and guided her to the bar.

"What can I get you folks?" Mateo asked, flashing them his perfect smile. "The usual, Simon?"

Simon nodded, and Mateo began to pour him a pint of bitter.

"And a glass of red wine," Nora supplied.

"Fancy seeing you in here, Nora," Howie teased, sidling up to them. "Now that you're famous."

"I'm hardly famous, Howie." It was true that there had been a lot of media interest in the bookshop since the article had appeared. Several newspapers had interviewed Nora and Simon and asked them to do roundups of the most uplifting books coming out in the year ahead. A women's magazine had offered Nora a monthly book column. Nora was still struggling to get her head round everything that had happened over the past few days, and didn't want to rush into anything. The only decision she hadn't had to consider—even for a second—was informing Seb Fox that the Stowford Bookshop was no longer for sale.

The estate agent staggered over to them now, holding a bottle of imported lager. From the state of him, Nora guessed he'd been in the pub for a while. "I'm happy for you guys," he slurred (sounding anything but). He took a swig from his bottle. "Let me know if you change your mind."

"I don't think we will," Nora told him.

"Piss off, Foxy," Howie said. As the drunk estate agent lurched back to his braying friends, Howie shook his head. "Some people just can't hold their drink." Then he jabbed Simon in the chest with his finger. "Oi, Bookworm, how 'bout you buy me a drink now that you're in the money."

"We're hardly millionaires," Simon said drily. But he ordered a pint for Howie.

Nora looked around for somewhere to sit. Alice, Maeve and Lucy were sharing a bottle of wine with Nigel and some of the other local shopkeepers. Sam and her parents were sitting with Dr. Dhar and her husband, but there was no room at their table.

"Nora! Simon!" Will waved at them from a table he was sharing with Liz.

They plunged through the crowds of people, and Nora slipped gratefully onto a velour-covered barstool at their table.

"No kids tonight?" Simon asked them.

"I got Harry Swann to babysit mine—he was a big hit with them at your party," Will said.

"Mine are with my ex," Liz added.

For a moment, Nora wondered if she and Simon were gate-crashing a date. Were Will and Liz another example of their matchmaking? Or were the two single parents just friends?

"So how did your Boxing Day feast turn out?" she asked Liz.

"The boys wouldn't touch the Brussels sprouts, and I over-cooked the potatoes, but the gammon was delicious and the trifle was a big hit."

"Any plans for tomorrow?" Simon asked.

"We're going sledging again," Will said. "With Liz's boys. But first we'll pop in to visit my mum. She's in a care home here in the village."

They chatted for a while. Nora convinced Liz to attend the next book club meeting, and Simon invited Will to come along to his five-a-side soccer team's next kickabout.

Suddenly, a loud whoop came from across the pub. Nora turned round just in time to see Mateo hurdle over the bar, phone in hand. He ran over to Sam shouting, "I got it! I got it! My agent just rang—I got the part!"

Sam squealed with delight, then jumped into his arms and gave him a passionate kiss.

The whole pub burst into applause. Sue, the landlady, rang the bell above the bar in celebration, while Howie gave a loud catcall.

Nora stood up. "This calls for a celebration. Anyone for another drink?"

Nora made her way over to the bar and ordered a round of drinks—and a bottle of champagne.

"I'm pleased for Mateo," Sue said, as she poured out Nora's order. "But I'm going to be a bit shorthanded behind the bar."

"Make sure to get a signed photograph of him to hang up when he's a famous star," Nora joked.

She brought the champagne over to the Patels' table, where Sam was sitting on Mateo's lap.

"Congratulations from me and Simon," she said, handing Mateo the bottle.

"Isn't it just wonderful news," Mrs. Patel said, beaming at the loved-up couple.

"What's the part?"

"I'm playing Romeo at the Globe," Mateo said, grinning. "It's a dream come true."

"Dinesh and I will book front-row seats," Mrs. Patel said proudly.

"Simon and I will have to come and see you, too," Nora said.

"Thanks," Mateo replied. "I start rehearsals in two days' time."

"In London?"

He nodded.

"That doesn't give you much time to find somewhere to stay."

"Actually, I found a flat in London a few days ago," Sam said. "I'm moving out of my parents' house—and Mat's going to stay with me."

"I don't see why you can't stay in Stowford," Mr. Patel said. "We have plenty of room. There's no need to rush these things . . ."

"Well, Romeo and Juliet fell in love at first sight, too," Nora pointed out with a smile.

"Nora's right," Dr. Dhar said, looking tenderly at her husband, Vikram. "Sometimes, you just know." Then she looked up at Nora. "By the way, we both loved *The Oculist of Leipzig*."

Nora smiled. It proved that there truly was a book for everyone.

Leaving Mateo to celebrate his success with Sam and her family, she went back to the others. While she'd been gone, Charlotte had come over and stolen her stool.

"You can share with me, Mum," she said, shuffling over.

"I'm not sure about that," Nora said. "I think my bum has doubled in size thanks to that huge box of chocolates Olwyn gave us." She squeezed onto the stool next to her daughter.

"Mateo's moving to London, so Sue will probably be looking for someone to replace him," Nora told Will. "If you're still looking for a job."

"Oh, I forgot to tell you!" he said. "I got the position up at

St. Stephen's, filling in for the soccer coach! Miss Powell put in a good word, I had an interview a few days ago and the head offered it to me on the spot."

"That's wonderful!" Nora exclaimed.

"Even more cause for celebration," Simon said. "Well done."

"Cheers." Will sipped the froth off his pint. "I'm really chuffed. The head said that if I do some training classes, they'll take me on as a teaching assistant after the coach comes back to work."

"You might not be so happy after a few days with my little monsters," Liz said, laughing.

"I might be interested," Charlotte said.

"In working here?" Simon asked.

Charlotte nodded. "I was thinking of sticking around for a bit. I want to save some money up before I head off traveling again."

"You *are* still planning to start uni in the autumn?" Nora asked anxiously. Much as she was happy to have her daughter back home, she didn't want her to miss out on her studies.

"Actually, there's something I've been meaning to speak to you about . . ."

Oh no, Nora thought, panicking. Had Charlotte decided to give up her university place? Did she want to move back to India permanently?

". . . I'm thinking I might change my course."

"What to?" Simon asked.

"Education."

Nora let out a breath of relief.

"Part of the reason I wanted to take a gap year was because I wasn't sure I'd made the right choice with anthropology," Charlotte explained. "Teaching those kids in Kerala was amazing. It got me thinking that I'd like to teach when I graduate. What do you guys think?"

"You'd be a wonderful teacher," Nora said, her heart swelling with pride.

"You don't mind that I don't want to take over the bookshop?"

"Of course not," Simon said. "I didn't follow my parents into the family business."

"But that's what I'm afraid of," Charlotte said. "You aren't close to your parents, and I don't want that to happen to us."

"That's completely different," Simon assured her.

Nora nodded. If the events of the past week had taught them anything, it was that the bookshop didn't just belong to her and Simon—it belonged to everyone who loved books. That's why complete strangers had donated money to keep it afloat. She and Simon were just the shop's caretakers.

"You'll be teaching a whole new generation of children to become readers," Nora said, beaming. "What could be more important than that?"

"Yes," Simon agreed. "Those are our future customers."

A countdown began and everyone around the table stood up and scrabbled around to pick up their drinks.

"I can't believe it's already midnight," Nora said, raising her glass of wine.

Three . . . Two . . . One!

"Happy New Year, Mum!" Charlotte cried, giving Nora a hug.

Everyone around the table clinked glasses, blew on noisemakers, pulled party poppers and wished each other a happy new year as, over by the bar, Howie kicked off a noisy chorus of "Auld Lang Syne." Above the din, Nora could hear bangs from fireworks exploding around the village. She glanced across the pub and saw fireworks of a different sort going off, as Mateo and Sam kissed.

Ah, young love, Nora thought.

She turned and saw her husband looking tenderly at her, with love that had only grown deeper and stronger over the decades.

"Happy New Year, Nora," Simon said.

Nora threw her arms around him and kissed him.

The weight of worry she'd been carrying for weeks had lifted and Nora felt almost dizzy with relief. She clung to her husband, afraid that if she let go she'd float into the air like one of the balloons that had broken free from a table and floated up to the ceiling.

The shop was saved. She and Simon were going to stay in their home, doing the job they both loved. The future shone as bright as the sparklers lighting up the night outside the pub window. Nora squeezed her eyes shut and made one resolution for the year ahead: to be grateful for her good fortune and all the love in her life.

"Happy New Year, Simon," Nora said.

And she meant it with all her heart.

26

THE FOLLOWING DECEMBER . . .

Nora emptied the crate of wineglasses they'd borrowed from the George as Simon poured crisps into bowls.

"Ooh," Nora said, glancing at the label. "Sea salt and balsamic vinegar—very posh."

"Well, it's not often that we host a launch party for such a high-profile book," Simon said, popping a crisp in his mouth.

"Do you think we ordered too many copies?" Nora asked Simon, glancing over at the piles of the hardbacks on the table, ready to be signed by the author. David Langdon's handsome face stared out from the dust jacket, his blue tie hinting at his political allegiance. The former MP had asked Nora and Simon to host the launch event for his tell-all memoir, *Feeling Blue.* Tickets for the launch had sold out, with all proceeds going to the mental health charity David had set up over the past year.

"If we don't shift all of these today, I'm sure we will in the run-up to Christmas," Simon said. Although business had slowed down a bit after the initial interest David's newspaper article had generated, the shop had continued to benefit from its raised profile. They were on track to make a healthy profit for the first time in years, mainly driven by the success of their online business. The freeze on taxes for small businesses had helped, too. David had been integral in getting the legislation passed before he stepped down.

"It was nice of your parents to donate the wine," Nora said, as Simon carried a case of Casa di Carlotta out from the back room. They'd cleared as much furniture out of the way as they could to make room for the crowd they were expecting.

"Oh, they're probably just hoping that David will give it a glowing endorsement," Simon said.

"Did you tell them he's teetotal now?" Nora asked.

Simon grinned. "I may have forgotten to mention that."

The bell above the shop door rang and David came in, followed by Kath and a publicity executive from the publishing company.

"Ah, it's the man of the hour!" Simon said, going over to greet them.

"I hope we're not too early?" David asked.

"Of course not," Nora replied, giving them both a hug.

Kath Langdon had won her father's seat by a landslide, becoming one of the youngest MPs in Parliament. She'd quickly made a name for herself, giving an impassioned speech in the House of Commons about the need to increase education spending in areas of rural poverty. Closer to home, she'd also succeeded in stopping the development of the retail park outside of Stowford.

"How are you feeling, Dad?" Kath asked. David Langdon looked well and radiated confidence, but his daughter clearly still worried about him.

She probably always will, Nora thought. That's how it was when you came close to losing someone you loved.

"Excited—but a bit nervous."

"You have nothing to worry about," Nora said. "Everyone loves the book."

Feeling Blue had garnered rave reviews, with readers praising the author's honesty about his battle with mental illness, and his entertaining anecdotes about the cutthroat world of Westminster politics. Nora herself had given it a glowing write-up in her monthly book column. She'd taken pains to point out that she wasn't exactly unbiased, as David had devoted a whole chapter to the bookshop's role in his recovery from depression.

"So how does this work?" David asked the PR executive, a young woman with long hair and trendy glasses.

"We thought you might like to read an extract?" she said, her upward inflection making everything she said sound like a question. "Then we'll do a short Q&A, followed by a signing?"

Simon invited them upstairs to the flat for a cup of tea, while Nora collected tickets as people arrived for the launch party. Alice, Lucy and Maeve were among the first to turn up.

"He *is* quite dishy," said Lucy, who was clutching a copy of David's book, as giddy as a teenage girl at a pop concert. "Maybe I'll slip him my phone number."

"I could never be in a relationship with a Tory," Alice said.

"Who said anything about a relationship?" Lucy giggled, sparking off a torrent of hysterical laughter from the others.

"Help yourself to a glass of wine," Nora said. If her friends were this excited now, what would they be like after a glass of prosecco?

Margaret and Charles arrived soon afterward.

"How was your journey?" Nora asked her in-laws.

"Long," Charles said, giving her a dry peck on the cheek. "You get all sorts of riffraff in the first-class carriage these days."

"Is David Langdon here yet?" Margaret asked, looking around

eagerly and patting her white chignon. "He's so witty." Her mother-in-law was clearly another fully paid-up member of the David Langdon fan club.

"He's upstairs with Simon." Spotting a familiar face coming into the shop, Nora said, "Now if you'll excuse me, duty calls." She went over to greet Sam. "I didn't expect to see you here."

"Kath invited me," she said, handing Nora her ticket. "I did a bit of consultancy work on her campaign strategy."

A few months back, Sam had resigned from her job and set up her own boutique consultancy firm. One of her first clients had been the bookshop. Nora and Simon had hired Sam to suggest ways they could run their business more efficiently, as they didn't want to ever find themselves in debt again. Sam had suggested lots of brilliant cost-cutting ideas and helped them build their online business. They'd also launched a monthly book subscription business that was going from strength to strength.

"I've been meaning to ask you, Nora," said Sam, shrugging off her coat. "Could you recommend a good pregnancy book?"

"Absolutely," Nora said. "Is your sister expecting another baby?"

She hadn't seen Dr. Dhar since Simon's last checkup, in which he'd been given a clean bill of health.

Sam smiled and rested her hand on her belly. "No. I am."

Nora looked down and saw that under Sam's chic cashmere sweater, a neat baby bump was burgeoning. "Congratulations!" she squealed, giving her a hug. "That's fantastic news."

"My parents are a bit freaked out, because Mat and I aren't married," Sam said. "But we're both over the moon."

"They'll come round," Nora assured her.

"I hope so," Sam said, grinning. "Because I don't know the first thing about babies."

"I saw Mateo in that crime drama on telly a few weeks back," Nora said. "He was really good. What's he working on now?"

"He's just shot a film in LA," Sam said, with obvious pride. "I went over to California to visit him on set and met his family while I was out there."

"How exciting," Nora exclaimed. She shook her head. "Can you believe last Christmas he was running around Blackberry Hill—now he's hanging out in the Hollywood Hills!"

"Not for much longer. He's been asked to join the Royal Shakespeare Company. It's literally his dream job."

"That's wonderful. We'll have to go and see him when he's in Stratford," Nora said. She and Simon had traveled up to London to see Mateo in *Romeo and Juliet* at the Globe and had been blown away by his performance. He'd even invited them backstage for a tour afterward.

"We might move back to the Cotswolds," Sam said, stroking her bump.

"Well, Stowford is a wonderful place to raise a family."

Checking the time, Nora headed upstairs to fetch the guest of honor. In the living room, David was thumbing through a copy of his book, while Kath was giving Merry a tummy rub.

"Ready?" she asked them.

David nodded and bounced on the balls of his feet like a boxer.

"I hoped Kath could do the introduction?" the PR woman said.

Phew! Nora thought, relieved she wasn't expected to do any public speaking.

A hush fell across the shop as they all walked downstairs. Kath stood in front of a lectern they'd set up, her father at her side.

"Welcome, everyone," Kath said, smiling at the audience, which had gathered in a semicircle around them. "I'm Kath Langdon, MP for the Cotswolds. Firstly, I'd like to thank Nora and Simon Walden for hosting us tonight. As you know, we're here to celebrate the publication of *Feeling Blue*, a book that *The Times* has called 'a poignant and powerful memoir, told with the flair and intimacy of a consummate raconteur.' Without further ado, I present its author—my inspirational father, David Langdon!"

David read a few extracts from his book. The first was an account of getting lost on his first day in Parliament and accidentally barging in on two Cabinet ministers in flagrante delicto.

"That taught me a valuable lesson," David concluded, to appreciative laughter, "always knock first." He then launched into a hilarious anecdote about a late-night karaoke battle with a former Chancellor of the Exchequer at a party conference in Blackpool. The chancellor had sung ABBA's "Money, Money, Money," fittingly enough.

David's tone grew more serious as he read the final excerpt, about his depression. Nora welled up as he described the despair that had almost driven him to take his own life, just over a year ago.

Simon wrapped his arms around Nora and she leaned back against him, as David described how receiving a copy of *The Greatest Gift* had changed his life and started him on his journey to recovery.

The author shut his copy of the book. "The message I hope people will take away from my book," he said, "is that in times of trouble, help comes in many different forms: from family, from friends, from strangers"—here, he caught Nora's eye and nodded—"and from between the covers of books. Never lose hope, because happy endings are possible and the next chapter of your life might turn out to be the best."

The audience broke into rapturous applause.

After the question-and-answer session—one of which was a marriage proposal from one of the book club members, which David politely declined—he signed books. Nora and Simon stationed themselves behind a table, selling the memoir to anyone who didn't already own a copy.

"Oh, hello, Olwyn," Nora said, looking up and recognizing the next customer in line. "How's your book going?"

Olwyn had self-published her first mystery and was already hard at work on the sequel. In this one, Olwyn's hard-boiled detective, Clay Thorne, was investigating the case of an onstage murder committed during the village's Christmas pantomime.

"Very well," Olwyn said, touching her card on the card reader. "My writing group has been so supportive. I was struggling with the ending, but they've helped me work out a very clever plot twist."

Olwyn had set up a local writers' group, which met at the bookshop once a week. Nora knew, from eavesdropping on their sessions, that (spoiler alert!) the whole cast was in on the murder.

"I noticed that Harry Swann has been attending the group."

"Oh yes," Olwyn said. "Young Harry is very talented—he's going to do English Literature A-level. He writes wonderful fantasy stories, but I've also been encouraging him to write about his grief."

Nora had bumped into Harry and his parents a few times in the churchyard, while visiting her mother's grave. They'd set up a scholarship fund in Emma's memory, and had planted an apple tree outside St. Stephen's. There was a gold commemorative plaque with her name on it.

"It's a Tree of Protection," Harry had explained to Nora.

"From *The Magician's Nephew*," Nora had said, picking up on the Narnia reference. In the story, the tree's apples had had healing powers. These apples weren't magical, but Nora suspected that in celebrating Emma's memory, the tree had helped Harry and his parents to heal as much as any fictional fruit could have.

"Is Charlotte here tonight?" Olwyn asked, looking around.

Simon shook his head. "She doesn't finish for another few weeks. But she'll be home for Christmas."

After working at the George for a few months, Charlotte had set off on the South American leg of her travels. She'd watched sea turtles being born on the Galápagos Islands, hiked the Inca Trail to Machu Picchu and taught English at a school in Ecuador. Of course, Nora had worried about her—that would never change—but, as promised, she'd come home, bearing alpaca-wool hats with earflaps for both of her parents (one of which Simon insisted on wearing while walking Merry), in time to start uni.

"She's really enjoying her education course," Nora said.

"We thought we'd see more of her," Simon said, "as Warwick isn't very far away."

"She only comes home when she wants to raid the fridge or use the washing machine." Nora laughed. But she wasn't complaining—she was happy that Charlotte was working hard and having fun.

"She'll be a great teacher," Olwyn said. "Oh, that reminds me—Will sends his regards. I saw him the other day when I was volunteering at St. Stephen's. He's a teaching assistant now. He's ever so good with the little ones." She lowered her voice to a whisper. "I don't know if it's true, but I heard a rumor that he and Liz are dating . . ."

Someone in the queue to pay for their copy of *Feeling Blue* coughed loudly.

"Oh dear," Olwyn said, glancing behind her. "I'm holding up the line. See you at the carol concert." She waved goodbye cheerfully, before getting her book signed by David.

After they'd sold the last few copies, Nora and Simon went over to see Simon's parents.

"Look, Nora," Margaret said, showing her David's signature on the title page. "He wrote: 'With all my love, David Langdon.'"

Simon's father rolled his eyes. "It's ridiculous. She's like a schoolgirl with a crush."

"Jealous, Dad?" Simon teased.

"I'm afraid you've got a bit of competition," Nora told her mother-in-law. Lucy, Maeve and Alice, emboldened by the free wine, had surrounded the author and were ignoring the publicity executive's attempts to extricate him from their clutches.

Simon's father looked around the shop, full of customers chatting, browsing and sipping wine. "Business looks good. Are you still looking for investment?"

So now he's interested. Nora had to bite her tongue to stop herself from telling her father-in-law where he could stick his money.

"No, thank you," Simon said evenly. "We're fine. Better than fine, actually."

"I'm proud of you, son," his dad said, clapping him on the shoulder.

Nora goggled at her father-in-law, astonished. For Charles Walden, that was tantamount to gushing.

"We'd better be on our way," Margaret said. "Don't want to miss the last train. Tell that gorgeous granddaughter of ours to come down to London and visit us over Christmas."

"We will," Nora promised.

Once his parents had gone, Simon turned to Nora, an incredulous look on his face. "Am I imagining things, or did my father just say he's proud of me?"

"You didn't imagine it," Nora said. "And I'm proud of you, too." For different reasons, she suspected. Of course, she was thrilled with how they'd turned the business around. But not as proud as she was of Simon for forgiving his father.

For always putting family first.

She felt a hand on her arm and turned round.

"Hello, Nora," said an elderly gentleman with white hair, leaning on a walking stick. Next to him was a boy with sandy brown hair and a backpack slung over his shoulder. "Do you remember me?"

"Arnold!" Turning to her husband, Nora said, "Simon, this is Arnold, who bought the Christmas-truce book!"

"Nice to finally meet you, Arnold," Simon said, shaking his hand. "I've heard a lot about you."

"I moved away to be closer to my son's family," Arnold said, "which is why I haven't been back in here. But when I read in the newspaper that you were hosting an event tonight, I decided to come along."

"It's so good to see you again," Nora said, beaming at him.

"This little nipper is my grandson, Noah," Arnold said, tousling the boy's hair. "His leukemia is in remission. He's been cancer-free for nearly six months."

"I'm so happy to hear that!" Nora had thought about Arnold—and Noah—often over the past year, and had wondered how they were getting on.

Arnold nudged his grandson. "There's something you want to show Nora, isn't there?"

Noah took a folder out of his backpack. "I got an A for my First World War project."

"This is so good," she said, reading through the project, which had a whole section about the famous Christmas Day soccer game.

Simon read it over her shoulder. "I can see that you love history," he said to Noah. "Do you play soccer, too?"

The boy grinned. "I'm the top scorer on my team."

"I've got something for you, too, Nora," Arnold said. He handed her *The True Story of the Christmas Truce*. "It belongs here, with the two of you."

"Are you sure?" Nora asked him.

"I'm positive," Arnold said, winking. "I told you it would bring me luck—and it did."

It brought us luck, too, Nora thought, as she went over to the fireplace and propped the book up on the mantel. That was where it would live from now on—as a talisman for the shop. The gold lettering on the cover twinkled in the firelight, and Nora could almost believe that there *was* something magical about the book.

If she and Simon had been David Langdon's guardian angels, Arnold had been theirs. His visit had inspired them to send out books as beacons of hope to people who needed a boost. Who needed a friend. That decision had changed all of their lives, in ways she'd never imagined possible. The six strangers they'd sent books to were all her friends now and—inextricably bound by their shared story—would be for life.

That was the *real* magic of books. They brought people together.

Gazing around the bookshop, from the ancient oak beams to the scuffed floorboards, Nora wished her mother could be there to see the bookshop today. It had changed much over the years, but in the most important ways, it was still exactly as it had been in Penelope's day. The books lining the shelves still held worlds of possibility, and the power to transform lives within their pages.

Here's to happy endings, Mum, she thought. *And to the new chapters ahead of us!*

ACKNOWLEDGMENTS

As someone who normally pens children's books, writing my first book for adults felt like embarking on a marathon, when I'm used to running sprints. I want to thank everyone who cheered me on along the way—my friends, my colleagues, my mom, Helene Ryan, my sister, Erin Ryan, and Dermot Martin, who helped me find my voice. I wouldn't have reached the finishing line without the support of my daughters, Eve and Rose, and my husband, Robert, for whom the festive period stretched *waaaaaay* beyond the month of December as I wrote *Christmas by the Book*.

I am overjoyed that my book is finding its way into American readers' hands. I couldn't be prouder to be published by Putnam. It's no surprise to me (being an editor myself), but . . . editors are awesome! Thanks to the amazing editorial and production superstars at Putnam—Patricja Okuniewska, Sally Kim, Claire Winecoff, Nancy Resnick, Meredith Dros and Maija Baldauf. Thanks, as well, to Tal Goretsky for creating such a gloriously inviting jacket. I am also hugely grateful for Putnam's marketing and publicity team—Kristen Bianco, Emily Mlynek, Cassie Sublette, Ashley McClay and Alexis Welby—for all their work promoting this book.

Finally, thanks to all the devoted booksellers helping readers find great books, but especially Fiona Kennedy at the wonderful Pitshanger Bookshop in Ealing, London, for giving me insight into running an independent bookshop. I feel so lucky to have such a fantastic bookshop in my community. I hope that readers who have enjoyed Nora and Simon's story will feel inspired to visit their own local indie and buy a book (or two). You never know—it might change someone's life!

DISCUSSION QUESTIONS

1. *Christmas by the Book* opens at the Stowford Bookshop. What were your first impressions? Did it remind you of any bookstores you have visited?

2. Nora and Simon are struggling financially at the start of the story, but when a man comes in and buys a book they've never been able to sell, it gives Simon an idea. Why does the couple decide to start the anonymous book deliveries? What six books would you choose to give away?

3. There are a number of great characters in this story, including Sam, Olwyn, Will and Mateo. Discuss some of their backstories, and whether you connected with any in particular.

4. David Langdon is a complicated character in the book. How does he change, and how does the village's perception of him shift?

5. The magical spirit of the holidays is an important theme in *Christmas by the Book*. What part does Christmas play in the story, and why is it an important time of year for Nora and Simon?

6. What did you think of the fictional village of Stowford? In what ways do you think the story would have been different if it took place in a metropolitan city like London?

7. Discuss the role of community in this story. In what ways are Nora and Simon able to use social media to bring people together? How does it change the dynamic of Stowford?

8. Discuss how the residents of the village come together at the Stowford Bookshop Christmas party. What comes to light that evening, and how does it end up impacting the fate of the business?

9. At its heart, *Christmas by the Book* is a story about how books can bring us hope. How do the book deliveries connect with the recipients? What books have brought you comfort?

10. What were your thoughts about the ending, and what do you think is in store for Nora, Simon and the bookshop?

ABOUT THE AUTHOR

© Carla Marker

Anne Marie Ryan works as a book editor in the UK and has written several successful children's fiction series under a variety of pseudonyms. *Christmas by the Book* is her first novel for adults. Born and raised in Massachusetts, Anne Marie now lives in London with her husband and two teenage daughters. When she's not reading or writing, Anne Marie plays tennis and does improv (much to her family's embarrassment).

VISIT ANNE MARIE RYAN ONLINE

🐦 AMRyanAuthor